I0545101

Cyber League Crimes:
Book 1: The Popularity Contest
Book 2: The Hero Contest
Book 3: The Criminal Contest

By Julie C. Gilbert

Aletheia Pyralis Publishers

http://www.juliecgilbert.com/
https://sites.google.com/view/juliecgilbert-writer/

Love Science Fiction, Fantasy, or Mystery?

Choose your adventure!

Visit: **http://www.juliecgilbert.com/**

For details on getting free ebooks.

Cyber League Crimes Book 1: The Popularity Contest

By Julie C. Gilbert

Dedications:

The Popularity Contest:
To Ben Zito and Liz Brand, the fantastic team behind the audio productions of the Shadow Council and Eagle Eyes series.

The Hero Contest:
To my parents. Thanks for teaching me to love stories.

The Criminal Contest:
To my siblings and friends. These two types of love are at the heart of this story.

Note: This is a standalone series of novellas featuring FBI Special Agent Megan Luchek. Her previous adventures are the Shadow Council and Eagle Eyes series. You don't have to have read them to understand this series, but it may be more fun for you to already know some of the characters you'll meet.

Table of Contents:

Prologue:
Exciting Investment Opportunity

"Your turn, Turner," said Officer Pete Rathberger cheerfully.

Silently mouthing the words along with the corrections officer, James Turner ground his teeth together and forced his hands to remain unclenched. Reminding himself that Rathberger was one of the less annoying prison guards, he calmly rose and walked to the bars to receive the handcuffs. At least his roommate had already been summoned to the kitchen. He wouldn't have to deal with Akamu's stupidity on top of the humiliation of toilet cleaning duty.

One year, sixty-seven days, he thought, automatically following the officer along the path that would lead to the restrooms and showers.

Maybe he'd fire his lawyer and go for an appeal with somebody else. The FBI had a lot of evidence against him, but there had to be loopholes somewhere in their case. If the man couldn't even destroy a simple embezzlement case, what good was he? Then again, he had gotten Turner sentenced to the Kulani Correctional Facility, arguably the cushiest option among the available prisons. The prosecutor had been angling to have him sent to a contract prison in Arizona. That would have been horrible.

"Make a left here," said Officer Rathberger. He stopped in front of the doorway to the restroom, blocking the entrance with his body. "There's a supply closet about halfway down the hallway on your right. Go to it."

The impulse to demand why slammed into a surge of excitement, making James cough. Maybe his lousy lawyer had done something right. He'd waited for something like this to happen for two weeks. Throwing one more glance at Rathberger, he stepped quickly to the indicated door.

As he approached, the door swung open. An arm reached out, clamped around James's right forearm, and hauled him inside. He didn't even have time to shout a protest. His back slammed up against a supply rack, causing dust to rise from some rolls of paper towels.

"You have five minutes. Make them count," said Officer Glenn Burke's voice.

James barely caught sight of the man's back as he exited the tiny closet.

The buzz of a vibrating cell phone made James flinch. Whirling, he scooped up the phone. In his haste, he nearly dropped the thing. After two awkward juggles, he caught it and settled it on the nearest shelf before accepting the call. Silently cursing the handcuffs, he poked the speaker button.

A cool, efficient female voice spoke.

"Good evening, Mr. Turner. I understand you have some surplus income you'd like legitimized. I represent an organization that can help you with that. This line is secure, but we haven't much time. If you tell me the volume you're talking about, I can lay out your investment options."

Silence lingered while Turner absorbed the woman's voice. His stay in Kulani had only started a few months ago, and the prison certainly had female employees, but this was different. Until now, he hadn't realized how much he missed making business deals. Normally, he played the part of seller, but this buyer experience sounded emotionally satisfying too.

"Yes. Yes, I did," said James, scrambling to get the conversation moving. "Are you sure this call is confidential?"

"As sure as I can be," said the woman. "Nothing is guaranteed, but we pay premium to get quality service and discretion where needed. The organization has over a decade of experience in many fields, but I think you may be most interested in the high-risk, high-rewards options."

"You are correct," James confirmed. "May I know your name?"

"You can call me L," said the woman. "The line is secure, but people talk and testify. It's safer for you to maintain as much deniability as possible."

James didn't like being at a disadvantage, but he admitted that he would likely say the same if the situations were reversed.

"What volume of funds are we talking about?" prompted L.

"Time is short, and there are many options to explain."

James hesitated. This could be an elaborate government plot to get their grubby hands on his money. They had only pinned the embezzlement of $550,000 on him, but he knew they suspected he had stolen more. Which was true. He had another $3.2 million squirreled away in secret accounts. Unfortunately, accessing those accounts without bringing the government down on his head would be very tricky.

"A quarter-million," said James.

"You have at least that much in your real savings accounts, Mr. Turner," said L. Her tone hardened with irritation. "If you're done wasting my time, I suggest you use your remaining four minutes to contact a stockbroker."

"Wait! Don't hang up!" James's mind raced. How much did he trust this woman? If she walked off with his account numbers, he would have zero recourse. "One million."

"You have my attention, but clearly, you still don't trust me," said L. "I can hear it in your voice. Without trust, this is going to be a very short, troublesome relationship. Try one last time. What are you offering?"

"Just over three million." The admission felt surprisingly good.

"I can work with that," said L. "It would make you a low-end, high roller investor. What is your risk factor? Low risk would mean slow and safe returns over the next thirty years. You'd get your money, minus our twenty percent commission. High risk means your money starts earning immediately."

"What sort of risks are we talking about?" asked James.

"There's always the chance our venture fails," said L. "If the organization collapses, everybody loses. That's why we have some strict guidelines. I'll also need to know your limitations in terms of violence."

"Just say what you mean," said James. He didn't have the mental capacity to deal with euphemisms and runarounds right now.

"I'm going to send you a list of possible activities. Investors at your level get several high roller advantages and perks, including the ability to vote on which games are played," L explained.

"What exactly am I investing in?" James wondered.

"Over the past twenty years, online gambling has turned into a booming industry," said L. "It's only become legal in the last few years, but rather than harm existing systems, it's brought about a fresh wave of clients. As such, we run both aboveboard and illicit gambling systems. All high-risk options are on the illegal side of that fence. Hence my need to know your tolerance level for violence."

The question didn't bode well, but it piqued James's curiosity.

"Show me the list," he said.

"Done," replied the woman. "Text me account numbers and your top three picks and you're in. Leave the phone. One of the officers will deal with it. Somebody from the organization will be in touch within the week to let you know what's happening with your investment."

A long text message, complete with hyperlinks, appeared on the phone. James skimmed the titles eagerly.

Possible World Series Events:

Mild Incidents: Baby's Grand City Tour, Street Sweeper, Petty Cash

Medium Incidents: Beauty Contest, Popularity Contest, Hero Contest, Sweet Fond Farewells, Far and Away

Messy Incidents: To the Point, Fandom, Hands On, Personal Space, Batter Up, Cry Crow, Panic Room

Games of Chance: Roulette, Lucky Number Nine, Survival of the Fittest, Card Shark

Curious, James tapped on Cry Crow to read the description. Upon reading that players were to leave a body out in a place accessible to scavengers, he promptly closed out of the description and avoided all other things labeled *Messy Incidents*.

Deciding to try one other, James followed the hyperlink for Popularity Contest. The description depicted a game wherein players kidnapped people from various professions to serve as their proxies in a competition. The victims would play games for perks and advantages. The gamblers got to bet on outcomes and spend money to help their favorites win.

A knock startled James enough to make him drop the phone. When he picked it up again, he saw that the phone had chosen for him. A new box prompted him to input the relevant account numbers.

Guess my vote's going to Popularity Contest.

James would have liked to know more about the others, but the game that got his vote did interest him.

"Time's up," called Rathberger, entering the room.

"One second," said James. He wondered if he'd be able to place some bets. He needed something to help him pass the time between therapy sessions and work programs. As quickly as his fingers would let him, James entered the account numbers, placing his hidden millions in the hands of L and the mysterious organization that promised to cleanse and multiply it.

***

Lillian Marquez stared at the computer screen and watched James Edson Turner's account numbers appear one by one. While she waited, Lillian explored her mixed feelings about the job. It might be better as a true scam. Rock-bottom desperation was the only reason these people turned to the Club or organizations like it to launder their ill-gotten gains. She had nothing against illegal activities, but something about the elaborate nature of the scheme made her nervous.

There are too many moving pieces.

In theory, the guidelines should prevent law enforcement officials from catching on, but the sheer amount of people involved guaranteed at least a few unpredictable events. Lillian had been ready to leave the Club behind and move on to the Shadow Council when this *promotion* came her way. She half-suspected she'd been duped into another menial customer service position, but reality stretched her responsibilities to predicting possible flaws and troubleshooting as necessary.

After forwarding the account numbers to the tech department, Lillian read over the list of proposed events again. She didn't need to read the descriptions as the details had been burned into her brain by the other hundred read-throughs. Most schemes she had no problem with because mistakes would never be connected to the Club.

Beauty Contest involved posing a body in a creative way. The rules let the contestant decide whether to kill the victim or not. The media might get two days of stories out of it before something more intriguing popped up. Same for Fandom, which asked players to emulate their favorite serial killer. The modular nature of the crimes would make them extremely difficult to link together. That would be the saving grace of most murder scenarios like To the Point, Far and Away, Hands On, and Batter Up.

A contestant who got arrested would be disqualified.

The two that stood out to Lillian as the most dangerous were Popularity Contest and Sweet Fond Farewells. Both involved contact between the victim and their families or members of the public, which would increase the chances of kicking law enforcement into action. If possible, they should be avoided. Unfortunately, a quick peek at the polls revealed strong support for both ideas. Her recommendation would be weighed, but if the paying clientele wanted something badly enough, the Club would strive to give it to them.

Chapter 1:
Cybercrimes Task Force

Checking her reflection in the mirror one last time, Megan Luchek smiled, unable to suppress a thrill of anticipation. She had opted for two twists in honor of returning to work today. After the eventful vacation in Vegas, Reno, and Dallas, anything normal sounded fabulous. Her meeting this morning with Special Agent in Charge Bryan Maddox would determine the course of the next few weeks. He likely had something new for her, but she wouldn't mind reviewing cold cases or even polishing a testimony for court.

Never thought I'd see the day court prep looked appealing.

Grabbing her keys, Megan blew a kiss to her betta fish. Handsome turned away from her and swam to the far side of the tiny tank. She partly deserved the cold treatment for abandoning him so long with her friend Kai.

"You'll get over it, buddy," Megan called. "If I can make it to the pet store, I'll have some brine shrimp or bloodworms for you later. Be good and stay in the bowl."

As she gave Handsome his marching orders, Megan plucked her gun off the kitchen table and slipped it into her shoulder holster. The move made her grateful Dan and his wife weren't present. They would scold her for not keeping the gun in a safe.

No kids. No worries.

Aware of the many holes in that logic, Megan slung her purse over her shoulder and charged to the door. She nearly took the thirteen stairs all at once when her right foot collided with a plain bubble wrapped envelope. Instinctively flinging her arms wide, Megan yelped and caught her balance at the cost of wrenching her right arm and dropping her keys.

Straightening with as much dignity as she could muster, Megan retrieved her keys, locked her apartment, and gave the offending package a good three-second stare down to give it time to burst into flames or explode. When it did nothing, she slowly descended and studied it up close. The side that landed faceup bore no markings. The smart decision would be to call in the suspicious envelope, but that would make her feel like an idiot when it turned out to be nothing.

Embarrassed is better than dead.

Despite the thought, Megan cautiously turned the envelope over and saw that the other side also lacked marks. She tried to keep her fingerprints to a minimum in case something nasty crawled out after she opened the package. Oddly, knowing that somebody had to hand-deliver the envelope made her feel slightly better. To her knowledge, only one person would bother commissioning personal delivery.

Coming to a decision, Megan sat down on the steps and turned the envelope over a few times, searching for a seam. Her heart pounded in her ears. Finding no convenient tab to pull, she adjusted her grip and shoved a key through the top to create an opening. Inside, she found a folded note, a black card, and a cell phone.

The note read: **Changed my mind. Be safe.**

A quick check confirmed that the cell phone had the number from the black card programmed into the contacts.

Relief made Megan want to curl up and take a nap, but she didn't have the luxury. The envelope diversion would make her five minutes late even if she hit every light right. Shoving everything back into the envelope, Megan sprang to her feet and ran to her car. She'd move the phone to her purse when she found a parking spot.

Assassin, I hope you're taking your own advice.

Megan had used the long flights from Dallas to Vegas to Honolulu to catch up on sleep and wrestle with Cassandra Mirren's announcement of fading into the background to keep her safe. She couldn't decide whether the quick turnabout meant good things or bad things. She idly wondered how long the number would be valid. Cassandra went through phones like cheap napkins.

***

Despite being distracted, Megan made it to work safely. Parking and security checks added another ten minutes, but she reached her cubicle with two minutes to spare before she was expected in Maddox's office.

The sight of a large coffee next to her keyboard made her smile.

"Thanks!" she called in the direction of Daniel Cooper's cubicle.

"You're welcome," he replied, appearing in the doorway. "Figured your first day back deserved the royal treatment. Besides, I owe ya."

"You don't owe me anything," Megan assured her partner. Impulsively, she gave him a quick hug. They didn't work every case together and she had worked with other agents before, but the tall Texas native would always be her partner. "I didn't think you'd be back so soon. Why aren't you staying with your family this week?"

"Couldn't delay my testimony for the Clemson case any longer," Dan answered. "It's going to happen with or without me tomorrow morning. Beth and the girls are returning tomorrow. Charlotte and her boys will fly back to New Hampshire on Friday. Her husband, Tom, had work obligations too, so we both left yesterday. David's contemplating moving back home to help with the farm." Dan's grim expression made his opinion of the idea crystal clear.

"Why don't you approve of David's plan?" Megan wondered.

"My brother and the words 'hard work' have never occupied the same sentence," Dan explained. "I'm afraid if he moves in, it'll just mean more work for my mother."

Megan nodded. She had only met Dan's siblings briefly at his great-aunt's funeral over the weekend, but David Cooper had struck her as the carefree type. Her sister, Tara, fell into the opposite category of overachiever, but Megan knew the freeloader type of person well enough too. One of her college roommates could have been the poster child for the phrase *chronic slacker*.

"Gotta go meet Maddox now," said Megan, "but maybe we can catch lunch later. You can refresh me on the Clemson case details."

"Kid got busted moving drugs for the Wang family," said Dan. "Won't flip on his masters, so the prosecutor's going at him with everything they've got."

"Same kid who ended up in the hospital because a drug bag opened in his stomach?" Megan asked. She struggled to recall much more than that since the case never fell to her. Cooper had handled the case with Gianna Krantz.

"That's the one," Dan confirmed. "Have fun meeting the boss man."

The excited feeling returned as Megan slid past Dan and made her way to Maddox's office.

"They're ready for you now, Agent Luchek," said Ms. Walker. The administrative assistant waved for her to go into the office.

Nodding thanks, Megan drew a bracing breath and entered her boss's lair. Ms. Walker's words didn't sink in until she had crossed the threshold and stood face-to-face with Jeffrey Gatton.

Shock made her stiffen. Her gaze darted between the young billionaire and her boss. Part of her wanted to hug Gatton. The other half wanted to punch him. His Eagle Eyes program had saved her life more than once last week, but it—and the boy wonder—had also put her in danger several times.

"I can explain," said Gatton, holding a hand up in a disarming gesture.

"Have a seat, Agent Luchek," said Maddox. "Mr. Gatton is here with a unique proposal for you."

Megan doubted Gatton was capable of a normal proposal. She tried to gain a clue from her boss's reaction, but he kept his tone businesslike. In a daze, she crossed to one of the guest chairs and sank onto the hard leather.

"Let's have it," said Megan. Belatedly, she remembered she should attempt cordiality for her boss's sake, but she didn't have the energy to spare.

"I'd like you to join the Cybercrimes Task Force," said Gatton. "My company recently won a bid to help the FBI update their efforts to crack down on internet-based crimes."

"Since when do you make personal pitches?" asked Megan.

"Since I concluded you'd turn down any of my people," Gatton replied.

Megan silently conceded the point.

"It's a multi-agency task force since jurisdiction of web-based crime is anybody's guess," Maddox explained. "Mr. Gatton requested you by name, but given the unique nature of the case, I'm leaving the decision up to you. I have three other cases you could claim."

"What would I be doing?" Megan asked.

"We don't know yet," Gatton admitted, drawing sharp looks from Megan and Maddox. "Rumors on the Dark Web indicate something big is in the works, but for now, it might be a lot of data and report analysis. I'll have to introduce you to ADAM and IRA sometime. ADAM's the program that warned me you'd have trouble in Texas. IRA's basically the same type of program, but she's more interested in analyzing police incident reports."

"What's your timeframe for the case?" Maddox demanded. "This isn't a permanent arrangement."

The defensive and possessive notes in her boss's tone intrigued Megan.

"My contract is for two years." Gatton directed the statement to Maddox before turning to Megan. "You can join for as long as you like. Besides the general updates in every field office and resident agency—which my people can handle—the major push will be to identify and shut down everybody related to the Cyber Council. That's the governing body behind the Cyber League."

Another council. Wonderful. Probably overflowing with psychopaths.

"If you're in, there's a file to get you up to speed," said Maddox.

"I don't have evidence yet, but I think they're connected to our old Club friends," said Gatton.

Megan narrowed her eyes at him. He could have saved her some decision-making angst by starting with that little gem of information.

"I'm in," she declared, reaching for the file.

Chapter 2:
Special Guest Substitute

The first batch of reports took Megan three hours to digest. Gatton had assured her future samples would be further culled and tiered to reflect only the most relevant pieces, but he didn't stick around long. As soon as he escorted her back to her cubicle and walked her through the nondisclosure papers, he gave her a lightning-quick tutorial on accessing the case files. Then, he rushed back to his private plane to chase down his next task force sucker somewhere on the mainland.

Only a short lunch with Dan Cooper interrupted the monotony. Sometime during the afternoon reading marathon, Megan's brain finally flipped the switch to allow her to effectively skim, speeding up progress tremendously.

Eagle Eyes would make this work much easier.

Pride told her to dig deep and get it done, but her aching head said there must be a better way. After a half-hour debate against herself, Megan finally emailed Gatton the request.

He promised to have a prototype delivered to her by Wednesday.

To celebrate, Megan dragged Dan to a pet store to pick up freeze-dried bloodworms for Handsome. Then, they went to a luau so he wouldn't spend the night moping about being away from his family or studying his Clemson case testimony until dawn.

By lunchtime the next day, Megan had read more reports for the Cybercrimes Task Force than she had in the previous six months. Both ADAM and IRA provided thorough summary paragraphs, but Gatton's minions hadn't taught the programs how to write like normal people talk or think. Megan felt like she was watching a weatherman gush about hurricane spiral patterns. One could witness but not fully comprehend the fascination. The abundance of facts within each report pleased her, but the sheer number of incidents would overwhelm anybody.

I take it back. Paperwork still stinks. I need action.

Her phone buzzed and danced on the desk to announce a text message.

Seizing the excuse for a break, Megan picked it up and checked the message.

Dan: **Head's up. Maddox calling soon. Nothing bad. Promise.**

She sent back a monocle face and the word *cryptic*.

Before he could respond, Megan's desk phone rang. She stared at the phone dubiously and considered what would happen if she ignored it. Unfortunately, that would only serve to needlessly anger her boss. He had her cell number and several dozen agents available to track her down anywhere in the building. Returning to her senses, Megan answered on the third ring.

"Agent Luchek speaking," she said.

"Cooper's stuck in court," Maddox announced. "He said to consider you to take his place at the assembly this afternoon. Ms. Walker has a memo with the address. Don't be late. It starts at 3:30 but aim to be fifteen minutes early." His tone added: *And try not to say something stupid.*

He disconnected before she could formally accept or protest the assignment.

"Yes, sir," Megan murmured to the empty air. "I'll be there."

The optimistic side of her said at least she wouldn't have to read reports the whole afternoon. The pessimistic side said an assembly meant lots of kids. While her kid-wrangling skills could be described as fair to good, public speaking bothered her.

She sent Dan a cry emoji and a message saying he'd better knock that testimony out of the park.

Resigned to her fate, Megan went to Maddox's office to speak with Ms. Walker. If anybody could give her the pertinent details, it was Shauna Walker. The administrative assistants always knew the best gossip and the most details on anything.

"Maddox said you had an address for me," said Megan after the customary pleasantries were exchanged.

"I do," said Ms. Walker, handing Megan a thick file. "Everything you need is in there. Who to meet, what the slide show will say, things to cover, things to avoid, and common questions the kids like to ask."

"You're a lifesaver." Megan accepted the file gratefully.

"You're not the first special guest substitute, and I'm sure you won't be the last," said Ms. Walker with a one-shoulder shrug. "Please return the file when you're done."

"Yes, ma'am," Megan said, understanding the request to be an order. "I won't let it out of my sight."

"Better get studying," Ms. Walker advised with a sympathetic smile. "We try to give the agents at least a week with the file before showtime. You have a few hours. Good luck."

Thus dismissed, Megan retreated to her cubicle and settled down to familiarize herself with the Special Agent Interest Community Outreach Program. It usually ran in schools over several weeks, but sometimes a modified version ran in youth centers like the Big Brothers Big Sisters she was set to speak at this afternoon.

At least it's close, Megan thought, noting that the location was a five-minute drive away.

Though she dutifully skimmed the slides, she could already predict most of the lesson, which consisted of standard we're-the-good-guys messages. In theory, the host location would have the slideshow cued up and ready to go. Her job would be to show up, walk through the predetermined talking points, and hand out plastic badges.

Where are the badges?

A short call to Ms. Walker yielded nothing.

Can't go without the badges.

After wallowing in despair for a few seconds, a flash of inspiration struck Megan. Only one agent had never let her down when she asked for something obscure.

Soon, she had Special Agent Ophelia Pitman on the line and explained the situation.

"Lady O, you're my last and best hope," said Megan. "Do you know where I can get a box of the plastic Special Agent badges?"

"You're in luck, Maggie dear." Ophelia's deep voice never sounded so good. The Georgian accent lent it a rolling cadence. "There are two places you can check. Agent Krantz has a box, but she won't need 'em until Thursday. And the mailroom keeps a box of seconds. They're the ones with little imperfections. When we get enough, they get shipped back, but I think there's a stack of 'em there now."

Thanking Lady O for the leads, Megan searched for Gianna Krantz. Finding the agent's cubicle empty, she peeked in nearby sections to ask about her whereabouts. Only Agent Zeller was present, but given his head-bobbing, earbud wearing state, Megan doubted he'd have any answers for her.

Deciding to check the mailroom, Megan grabbed her purse and headed for the elevator that would take her to the destination, which was located down a few floors. She really wanted to leave the building to catch lunch elsewhere, but she still had a list of possible kid questions to go through. Picking up the badges from the mailroom proved surprisingly easy. Haley even loaned her a mail carrier box because the original box holding the seconds would have taken three people to haul to her car. Megan felt guilty for using the box when it clearly said not for personal use.

"It's fine," Haley assured her. "Pay no attention to the threat of fine and imprisonment. It's for a good cause, and I'm fairly certain I'll get this one back since you're not likely to steal any surplus badges."

"Why would people steal mail carrier boxes?" Megan asked.

"I've stopped asking why people do most of what they do," said Haley. "And they are nice boxes if you can ignore the threats on the outside."

Upon leaving the mailroom, Megan paused to think through her options. She could return to her office and use her go bag to transport the badges or look ridiculous hauling this mail carrier box down Ala Moana Boulevard to her car. Her aching arms decided the matter, so she lugged the box over to the elevator and returned to her tiny slice of office paradise.

Transferring the badges to her go bag involved displacing the suit and shoes she kept there, but she didn't have many other options. She left the T-shirt and gym shorts inside to cushion the badges, hoping they wouldn't clatter too much.

Lunch consisted of bottled water and the last two granola bars from her desk stash since she didn't feel like leaving again. She didn't even have cold coffee since Dan went straight to the courthouse this morning. The tour through questions to anticipate took her way past lunch.

Only a call from Ms. Walker sent Megan out the door in a timely fashion. Her shoulders hurt by the time she reached the car, but the drive proceeded smoothly. She made it to Big Brothers Big Sisters in good time and met the Program Coordinator, Rita Carlson.

"Have you done one of these programs before?" asked Rita.

"Not in this capacity," Megan admitted. The most she'd done with these programs was hand out badges at the end of Dan's stint at the local middle school.

"You'll be fine," said Rita with a forced smile. "I have everything set up in the gym."

Nerves didn't kick in until Megan accepted the microphone and stood in front of sixty-three elementary students. Then, it felt like a hundred bees had been set loose in her stomach. After stumbling through the first few slides, she found her rhythm by reminding herself that facing school children ought to be way less scary than facing the wrong end of a gun, which she'd done several times recently.

It's just like talking to Jaden.

That thought also helped. Jaden Melkin, her friend's ten-year-old son, had run a thorough interrogation upon their first meeting, including the most common question about seeing her gun. This time she had her gun with her, but she had no intention of displaying it for the kids. That would be the fastest way to skyrocket Maddox's blood pressure.

Megan ran the Q&A session while the volunteers distributed the badges so the children wouldn't get too restless. The unknown agent who'd prepared the questions successfully anticipated more than half the questions the kids raised, including why she joined the FBI and what agents make. She told a version of the truth to answer the first question and dodged the second one, choosing to emphasize the many other job benefits.

As the session wound down, Megan's attention fixed on a young boy with his hand raised.

She knew that face because she had seen it in a different setting.

The boy looked exactly like his brother, Donean Gavriel.

Her breath caught and her stomach lurched.

"Last question. Go ahead, Diaz," said Rita Carlson, oblivious to Megan's reaction.

"Why'd you arrest my brother?" The boy's voice held more plea than accusation, which made the question especially devastating. "Things were fine until then. You got him killed."

"Maybe he deserved it," said a girl a few seats down from Diaz.

He whirled to face her.

"Take it back!" he barked, jumping to his feet.

Rita and several volunteers rushed to stop a fight, but they wouldn't reach the kids in time.

Only the boiling crisis let Megan maintain her composure.

"Arresting people is a tough part of the job," Megan said, purposefully speaking calmly into the microphone. Internally, she admitted that Donean Gavriel and so many others made it much easier by deserving to be arrested. The part about getting him killed came way closer to the truth than she liked. While her words held everybody's attention, Megan moved to stand in front of Diaz. "I'm sorry you lost your brother."

"Will you find out who killed him?" asked the boy. His shoulders dipped and tears made his eyes shiny.

I already did.

Megan didn't know who had killed Donean, but the man responsible for ordering it had been dealt with. Unfortunately, the sensitive nature of the active investigation meant the case details would be sealed for many years. She was surprised the Honolulu Police Department hadn't let the family know they'd closed that portion of the investigation. Maybe they had and the family never told the boy.

"I'll do my best," Megan promised.

A bunch of children and volunteers asked more questions, but Megan couldn't muster the energy to answer.

Thankfully, Rita picked up on this and sent everybody else off to play. She ushered Diaz and his friend—the girl who'd challenged him—to her office to chat with the psychologist, Dr. Aspree.

Megan took advantage of the lull to gather the leftover badges and escape. Her heart hurt for these kids. If she had a normal life, she'd volunteer to work with them, but the FBI life was essentially the complete opposite of normal.

On a whim, Megan did the time zone math to make sure it was still a decent hour to call her sister. She had missed three calls from her sister's husband, Jason. He occasionally called if they were fighting since Tara tended to confide his misdeeds to her. Together, they'd solved more than one mystery of Tara's strange moods. If Megan needed to get two halves of a story, she might as well start with her sister. After a few rings, Tara's voicemail greeted her.

"Congratulations, you've reached my personal cell phone. If you don't know who I am, hang up. Otherwise, leave your message, and I'll get back to you."

What could she possibly be doing this early on a Monday night?

Tara sometimes kept late hours, but rarely on Mondays. A tiny chance existed that she was ignoring Megan's call on purpose, but that wasn't Tara's style.

Megan left a brief message saying hi and ended the call. Once tucked into the driver's seat, she felt another tug to connect with family, so she tapped over to contacts and called her mother. It had been a while, and this way, there was a deadline that would keep the conversation relatively short.

Chapter 3:
Family Ties

Tara Sidell pressed the button to unlock her Nissan Altima. It flashed an acknowledgement. A full day of work followed by two hours of serving soup had worn her out. She couldn't wait to drive home and curl up on the couch with Jason and Charles. Her husband might be warmer, but their Maltese was fluffier. She loved cradling the dog while her husband held her. She also had big news for them.

How should I tell them?

Taking out her phone, Tara contemplated calling her husband. She didn't want to blurt the news over a phone but needed to hear Jason's voice.

Something knocked into her arm. The phone tumbled from her hand and hit the sidewalk with a sickening crunch. Instinctively, she halted even though her brain ordered her to forget the phone and run.

An arm wrapped around her neck, pulling her backwards off balance. Dropping her right shoulder, Tara pivoted toward her attacker, throwing out both hands to break free. Something else smashed into her back right between the shoulder blades, dropping her to the ground. Before she could recover, a gun appeared in her face.

"Stop moving, or I shoot you," said a male voice.

A hood slipped over her head. Hands pulled her upright and used zip ties to secure her wrists behind her back.

"Please—"

The rest of her protest died in the chokehold that knocked her out.

***

"Oh, man, this is bad," said one of the young tech guys.

"What's wrong?" asked Lillian Marquez, pausing in the doorway to their cave. She'd been on her way to the kitchen to get a drink when she heard the kid's complaint.

The screen in front of him showed the image of a smiling woman with striking blue eyes and wavy blond hair that fell past her shoulders. She looked familiar, but that could mean nothing beyond the fact that she gave off a girl-next-door vibe.

"C-Team got an early start tonight," said the young man. He nervously ran hands through his greasy brown hair and gripped his head.

Lillian couldn't remember his name. She'd just arrived at this safehouse tonight to begin monitoring the competition. This kid was one of four tech boys kept on staff. Thus, his problems were inherently hers.

"It's early, but they're allowed to begin," said Lillian. She carefully modulated her tone so they wouldn't pick up on her misgivings about the whole deal. Apparently, her recommendations meant little to the higher-ups. "Did they document the kidnapping properly?"

"They did, but G-Team messed with their info." The kid looked genuinely scared, but at least he stopped gripping his head like it would fall off.

"How?" demanded one of the other tech guys. He shoved the first young man out of the way and tapped a few commands into the computer. Soon, the woman's picture disappeared, replaced by a wall of green and blue code. His head started bobbing as he read the code. "Crude but effective." The way he rendered the conclusion emphasized his New York accent.

"What happened?" Lillian enunciated carefully so the tech guys would get the message that she needed answers immediately.

"You discovered it, V," said the second tech guy, sliding his rolling chair to the left. "Sharing honors belong to you."

The letter designation let Lillian attach a name to the first tech guy, Vinny Carbonelli.

Taking his place in front of the computer again, Vinny brought back the woman's picture. Then, he opened a new screen.

"G-team hacked C-Team's guidelines, flipping the Primary Target List with the Protected List," Vinny explained.

"It's ingenious if you think about it," said the other tech guy.

"Shut up," snapped Vinny. His eyes darted back to the screen. "We made that list for a reason. We're in big trouble."

"Who is she?" Lillian wondered, trying to stave off a sinking feeling.

"My cousin," said Vinny.

The announcement sobered the second tech boy. He sat up straighter and cursed.

"No way! They caught the fed?" he said, grinning stupidly. "They're my new heroes."

"No," Vinny said with strained patience. "They caught her sister, you moron. The family court judge."

"Why does that matter?" asked the second tech guy. "Judge is one of the target professions."

"It matters 'cause she's family," said Vinny. "My family. And she's not a backwoods, small town judge. The police are gonna have media and politicians camping in their parking lots until she's found."

"So, we have them kill her and start over," said the callous one.

"Gary! She's my cousin!"

The tech guys continued to yap at each other like puppies, so Lillian kicked them out of the room. She needed to think. The Club had several FBI agents under their thumb or on the payroll. In recent dealings, she had come across exactly one who would be a thorn in the side no matter what they did.

What are the odds?

Lillian firmly believed that the power running the universe had a mean streak and a nasty sense of humor, but she needed confirmation. Noting the woman's name, she accessed the internet and ran the name across a few social media sites.

Neither the agent nor the judge kept much of a social media profile that wasn't under cyber lock and key, but old high school pictures showed Lillian that Sidell was the married name of Tara Olivia Luchek.

Eventually, she came across an old picture with a clear caption: **Congratulations to my baby sister for graduating from the FBI Academy! We love you, Maggie.**

Picking up her phone, Lillian called the one person she could trust. She needed to update O about the situation, but she wanted to hash through the possible recommendations with Steel first. Even if O disregarded nearly everything she said, she intended to do her job well.

Lou Sands—Steel—answered her call promptly.

After locking the door to keep the conversation as private as possible, Lillian sketched the situation for him.

"I've got two teams in trouble, and we've barely begun," Lillian said, attempting to keep a level tone. "One hacked another and got that team to snatch somebody on the Protected List. It's going to kick up unnecessary heat and make the entire competition much harder to run."

"It's also going to make the competition more lucrative," Steel noted.

Lillian made a face, even though Steel couldn't see her.

"I know O's going to make that argument, but I strongly feel we should release the woman and lay low for a few months," said Lillian. "Maybe start with a low-risk venture like Street Sweeper."

"Release?" Steel echoed, incredulous. "Any delay is gonna cost us big time. Who got bagged?"

"Megan Luchek's sister. I'm told she's a family court judge," said Lillian. "That's two reasons to worry."

An uncomfortable silence fell.

"You know how to fix the problem," Steel said eventually. "End the agent. That's what O's gonna say." He sounded nervous.

How does he always know what O's going to say?

"I know," said Lillian, "but what do *you* say?"

"If you make it hunting season on feds, the investigation is gonna be intense because it raises the stakes," Steel reasoned. "But it might make it easier to muck with if we plant people in the right places. I'll check in with Little G-man and see what he thinks. We might not have the manpower for that approach. Do you want me to have BB send you some boys as backup?"

"I should be fine," said Lillian. "O has a security detail in place to control the contestants and their victims as necessary."

She considered bringing up the issue of the tech guy and his connection to Megan and Tara, but she dismissed the idea. She didn't want to hear Steel say she should kill the kid. Involvement with Club business always involved dark deeds, and she accepted that. Still, killing a kid because he might be trouble in the future seemed exceedingly cold.

"Be careful. And control the situation," said Steel.

"I will," Lillian promised. "Thanks for listening. I'll make my call to O now."

"I can tell you what he will say, and for once, I agree," said Steel. "Let the team that caught the judge keep her if she has decent pull with the gamblers."

"And Agent Luchek? What do you think he'll say about her?" asked Lillian.

"You can try to control the agent through the sister if you like," Steel reminded her, "but it's safest to remove her altogether through one of the other events. If your tech people are good enough, have them run several events simultaneously to overwhelm law enforcement and keep betting interests high."

An odd feeling stole over Lillian as she ended her call with Steel. Something about his last piece of advice didn't sit well with her. His plan—like O's—was pointlessly reckless. It's like he wanted the venture to fail.

Paranoia doesn't suit you.

She agreed with the sentiment but couldn't snap out of the odd mood. The exchange played through her head several times. Deciding she needed that drink before dealing with O, Lillian unlocked the door and headed for the kitchen.

***

Steel watched Lillian pace the technology room in the safehouse. Her troubled expression spoke volumes.

"She's too soft," declared O. His harsh whisper made the words more sinister. *"Get rid of her. She'll destroy everything."*

"No!" cried Steel, shaking his head vigorously. Rushing to the mirror, he glared at his reflection. "She's Carlos's kid!"

"Carlos is gone," O hissed. *"What's left is an empty shell. Think of his legacy. Protect it. Like he protected us."*

"I won't have her killed," Steel said stubbornly. He set his shoulders in defiance.

Slowly, the stiffness faded, and his lips curled into a lazy smile.

"I will," O said. *"You made me the boss. One word and she dies."*

"Give her time!" Steel begged, taking a different tact. A desperate expression crossed his face. "She's good at what she does. She can do the job. I swear it."

The tension eased from his muscles.

"I hope so," said O absently. *"I know you're fond of her."*

A dull throbbing in Steel's head announced the end of the episode. Usually, a firm hand could control O, but lately, he'd grown bolder. For years, as the mysterious boss nobody but the truly privileged got to meet, he had been a convenient way of controlling others. But his taste for violence was getting stronger.

Pushing his concern aside, Steel sat down at his desk and toggled through the hidden camera feeds from the safehouse. Once the prisoners and competing teams arrived, he could have them ramp up the betting.

Chapter 4:
Troublesome Breakthroughs

Please be wrong.

Jeffrey Gatton read IRA's report and ADAM's summary statement several times. Using the programs in concert with each other hadn't occurred to him until fifteen minutes ago. Since it was too early for bed and he had the latest prototype of Eagle Eyes with him, he decided to get some work done. IRA needed some exercise anyway.

The Incident Report Analysis program was far younger than the Automated Danger Analysis Machine developed on behalf of the United States Government. Jeff had kept the sibling programs far away from each other during their developmental stages because he didn't want to risk code corruption or cross-contamination. However, the fact that ADAM's self-correcting subroutines sailed through three intense batteries of tests within the past week made him bold.

The programs complemented each other beautifully. IRA targeted police reports while ADAM focused on media articles. Although he had no firm data yet, Jeff estimated that combining IRA and ADAM could make each program 20% more efficient. The elation at discovering how to make his babies work better was tempered by the tale being told.

Following Megan Luchek's Dallas adventure, Jeff had added her entire family to ADAM's watchlist. The program had automatically transferred every watchlist he'd ever created over to IRA.

A missing person report for Megan's sister, Tara, had hit the system three minutes ago.

Jeff wanted to believe IRA was lying to him about the victim's identity, but he had personally coded several checkpoints into place to avoid cases of mistaken identity. A few basic searches confirmed the family connection between Megan and Tara. A deeper probe into the Fairfax County Police Department's database verified the report's legitimacy.

Curious, Jeff read the original report filed by Officer Elias Barton.

Name: Tara Olivia Sidell
Race: White
Gender: Female
Age: 36
Height: 5' 7" (67 inches)
Weight: 148 pounds
Hair Color: Blond
Eye Color: Blue-Gray

As the report started listing time, date, and location details, Jeff stopped reading and started plugging the information into Eagle Eyes, bidding the program to pull up every camera within a four-block radius of the soup kitchen mentioned. Soon, he watched the kidnapping take place. Start to finish, it took twenty-two seconds for a two-man team to subdue and bundle Megan's sister into a van.

Three.

At least three people needed to be in on the kidnapping since the van pulled away while both assailants disappeared into the back. The team effort shot very large holes through any theories banking on Tara's troubles being random bad luck. A small leap of logic brought Jeff to the idea that the kidnapping had to do with Megan or the Cyber League case. Snatching a respected judge off the street could qualify as the "something big" they were looking for, but his gut said he didn't have the whole story.

Once again, Jeff had blundered straight into unexplored and highly illegal territory, resulting in him having forbidden knowledge.

Should I tell Megan?

While the question sat on his brain, Jeff set some bots loose on the Dark Web to sweep for news of a woman matching Tara's description. Finishing that task brought him back to the question of telling Megan or saying nothing. The obvious answer was *tell her*, but he needed a second opinion. None of his people would do. Very few of them even had the clearance for the information he needed to discuss.

Trembling slightly, Jeff activated the two programs that would help secure the call he needed to make.

The woman answered at the end of the first ring.

"What can I do for you, Gatton?" asked Cassandra Mirren. "You usually don't do social calls at this hour."

"Megan's sister was kidnapped," Jeff blurted without preamble.

"How certain are you it was Megan's sister and a real event?" Cassandra inquired.

"Positive on both accounts," said Jeff. "IRA found it. ADAM confirmed it, and I hacked into the camera feeds to witness the kidnapping. It's her, and it's real."

"Why are you calling me and not the agent?"

The scary woman's tone held only mild curiosity, but Jeff felt like a verbal trap waited to slam down on his head any second.

"Because I didn't know if I should!" Jeff cried, disturbed by how high his voice sailed. "That's what I'm calling to ask!"

"Tell her," Cassandra ordered.

"Are you sure?" Jeff pressed. "She's going to do something dangerous and stupid and—"

"She deserves to know," Cassandra interrupted. She drew a breath and released it slowly, so that it came across like a sigh. "But I amend my earlier statement. I'll tell her."

"You will?" The reflex question contained fear and relief.

Cassandra never did anything idly. Calling to tell Megan the news would only be a precursor to some other action.

"I will," Cassandra promised. "And then you're going to tell me where they took Tara, and I'm going to get her back."

The measured way Cassandra delivered the follow-up statement reminded Jeff why he found the former assassin very scary. He hadn't even mentioned Tara's name.

"If I knew where she was, I would send the cops myself," said Jeff.

"You can't do that without alerting your handlers, which is why you called me," Cassandra reminded him.

"I could send an anonymous tip," Jeff said defensively.

"You wouldn't because you know these people are dangerous," Cassandra explained. "Same reason you're not mustering your security teams. Get on that search, Gatton. Time's always short with kidnappings."

"Why do you care?" Gatton hadn't meant to ask the question, but once it hit the air, he wanted to hear her answer. "About Megan, I mean. This isn't the first time you're stepping into danger for her."

A short silence nearly destroyed Jeff's nerves.

"There are very few pure things in this world," Cassandra noted. "They're worth defending."

The sentimentality caught Jeff short. He didn't know how to respond.

"I also need to keep my skill set sharp to be prepared when you and I are ready to exorcise our demons," Cassandra added. "Megan has a knack for getting her neck caught in nooses that require that skill set."

"Agreed, but you need to live through this crisis to reach the demon-slaying moment," said Jeff. He regretted that the opportunity had not yet arisen, but right now, the CIA had too many claws in him to gracefully break free. Working with the semi-retired assassin in Texas had convinced him that he never wanted to get on her bad side.

"Then you're going to have to earn your keep," said Cassandra. "If you'll excuse me, I have a phone call to make. Let me know when you have a location or relevant information."

Jeff listened briefly to the dead air and battled the irrational thought that he'd never hear from her again.

***

"Fight! Fight!" cried Ashton.

A loud crash punctuated his excitement.

Lillian Marquez raced into the tech cave and took in the scene.

A monitor and rolling chair lay side by side on the floor. Gary Sheffield lay flat on his back trying to cover his face. Vinny Carbonelli had an arm cocked back to deliver a punch.

Catching Vinny's arm, Lillian yanked back and spoke at the same time.

"Stop it!" She left it at that until certain she had their attention.

Vinny twisted his head around and glared up at her.

"He did it!" Vinny declared, wrenching his arm free.

"Did what?" Lillian asked, purposefully slowing her question to give Vinny an extra second to cool down.

"He switched the lists," Vinny explained.

Dropping his hand, Lillian took a half-step back to give the young man room to rise.

"Get up and explain from the beginning," Lillian instructed.

"Aw. I wanted a real fight," complained Ashton.

"Get out," Lillian ordered, certain she'd have enough trouble with Vinny and Gary. "And close the door behind you."

The wait for Ashton to vacate the room gave Vinny and Gary time to right the chair, pick up the monitor, and sit down.

Crossing her arms, Lillian gave each tech guy a once over. Vinny still looked angry. Gary appeared defiant.

"You. Explain. Now," said Lillian, pointing to Vinny.

"I can show you," said Vinny. Spinning the chair to face the nearest computer, he entered a few commands.

Several parts of the screen were highlighted in yellow.

"This shows the alterations made to the Protected List given to C-Team," Vinny explained. "I wanted to know how it happened, so I unraveled a bit of the code. He tried to hide it by being sloppy, but I know Gary's work."

Lillian let her arms drop to her sides and leaned in to look. She could tell changes had been made, but she wouldn't be able to tell who had made them.

"Did you alter the document?" she asked, fixing Gary with a hard gaze.

The accused man nodded once.

Vinny shifted, but Lillian stilled him with a look.

"Do you understand that you put everyone at risk by doing so?" Lillian hardened her tone to lend gravity to the question.

"I had orders to do it." Gary raised his arms in a gesture of innocence. "What was I supposed to do?"

"Who gave you the order?" Lillian demanded.

"O did," Gary said. Smug satisfaction crept into his expression.

"Liar," Vinny muttered.

"Why would I lie about—"

"From now on, you run any sudden or strange orders by me," Lillian said, interrupting Gary's protest. "I don't care who they come from."

"He said it would raise the stakes," said Gary.

"It can also land us in prison." Lillian spoke the reminder absently. Something about Gary's last statement stuck with her, but the nagging feeling refused to resolve for her.

It could also get us killed.

She managed to keep that thought to herself.

"And it worked," Gary argued, oblivious to the hints he should take the warning to heart and shut up. Turning to his computer, Gary pulled up a summary of the latest poll.

88.25% of the votes said taking a judge was worth the added risk.

They're not facing prison time if something goes wrong.

The poll had 4,674 votes. Since not everybody who visited the website bothered with polls, the numbers indicated that the first event had resulted in a solid uptick in activity.

"Show me the betting fields," Lillian ordered.

She didn't understand everything, but the numbers looked strong. The success felt good, but she feared it might drive O to make increasingly risky decisions.

Chapter 5:
Find Her!

Megan's call to her mother went through instantly, surprising her.

"Maggie! What's going on?"

The terror in her mother's voice instantly snapped Megan to full attention. She almost drove into oncoming traffic.

"Hang on, Mom. I need to get off the road." Finding herself near Aala park, Megan found the nearest open spot and pulled in.

Somebody honked at her, but she ignored them.

"Is she there? Did you find her? Please! Tell me you found her!"

The desperation in her mother's tone shot adrenaline through Megan. Instinctively, she gripped her phone harder and fell into work-mode.

"I need you to back up and tell me what happened," Megan said, speaking slowly and clearly.

"It's Tara!" Her mother's voice caught on her sister's name. When she spoke again, her voice was a ragged whisper. "She's gone."

"Why do you think that?" Megan thought about the phone call that went unanswered. With effort, she refrained from firing another dozen questions at her mother.

"I know it!" declared her mother. She sniffled and breathed hard into the phone.

Megan didn't want to further upset her mother, but she needed answers.

"Who told you Tara is gone?" asked Megan.

"Jason." The one-word answer seemed to calm her mother.

"What did he say?" Megan made a mental note to call her

brother-in-law immediately after finishing with her mother.

"Why does it matter?" cried her mother.

"The details will help us find her," said Megan. Thoughts of her sister tried to intrude, but she shoved them behind a mental wall. She couldn't afford a breakdown now. Her list of people to call ticked up by three: Dan, Cassandra, and Gatton. Maddox probably needed to be on the list as he would have to clear any time off, but he could wait.

"Tara worked late tonight then went to the soup kitchen. She was supposed to be home by 8:00, but she never showed." The story started strong but stopped suddenly. Three rapid breaths spoke of her mother's efforts to keep from sobbing. The rest came out in hoarse whispers. "Around 9:00, Jason started looking for her. Their apartment is a few blocks from the soup kitchen, so he backtracked her route home. He found her car and cell phone right by the back door!"

"Did he call the police?" Megan asked. "The hospitals? The FBI?"

"I'm calling you! You're FBI!"

Technically, Megan had called her, but she had no doubt that if she had delayed half a second, her mother would have called.

"Mom, I'm in Hawaii," Megan said quietly. "I will be there as soon as I can, but you need to contact the Washington Field Office. They'll have jurisdiction over Fairfax."

"Oh, Maggie! What do we do? Do we go there? Do we stay here? Will there be a ransom demand?"

The heartbreaking sense of helplessness that characterized the questions nearly undid Megan's resolve to be strong. Susanne Falco Luchek was not the sort of woman to lack direction. Forming plans and charging forward amid uncertainty were usually things she excelled at.

Only the experience of working many kidnapping cases let Megan answer her mother coherently.

"Make a missing persons flyer," Megan instructed. She couldn't begin to speculate about the ransom question this early.

"Do those really work?" asked her mother.

"Every case is different," said Megan. "Call the media and get them to spread the word. Use social media contacts too. Somebody had to have seen something. Call the police and ask for an update. It's probably too early but let them know you want to be kept in the loop."

"Find her!" demanded her mother.

"I will," Megan promised. "Let me call some other people and make some arrangements. I'll meet you at Tara's place tomorrow."

"Is she alive?"

Her mother's question stabbed Megan in the gut.

I don't know.

"Yes," Megan answered, unable to entertain any other possibility.

"Make your phone calls, and call me in an hour," her mother ordered.

"I'll try," said Megan.

"Not good enough, Maggie. I *need* to hear your voice."

Megan had only heard that cold, carefully controlled tone a few times in her life, and she never argued with it.

"I'll call," she promised.

After a few more assurances that she would stay in touch, Megan finally convinced her mother to get started on the flyer. That would mean calling Aunt Silvia or Cousin Vinny since Mom's computer skills left a lot to be desired, and Dad's tech abilities weren't much better.

When the conversation ended, Megan slumped in her seat. The tension had given her a headache, and her muscles felt sore from the fading adrenaline rush. A glance outside the windshield showed many people enjoying the late afternoon sunshine. The location near downtown Honolulu guaranteed a steady stream of tourists commingled with locals. Everybody looked content and carefree.

Finding Jason's number in her contacts, Megan sent the call through. The first three attempts ended at his voicemail box. Finally, she left a message and dropped her phone onto her lap.

Before Megan could gather the energy to make another call, the point became moot.

Her phone lit up with a blocked number. It didn't vibrate because she'd temporarily turned off that feature for the assembly a lifetime ago.

A firm swipe activated the call.

"Tell me everything." Megan didn't bother with a greeting and assumed the caller to be Cassandra or one of the kidnappers if she was part of their agenda. At this point, she'd take either.

"Your sister was kidnapped a few hours ago," Cassandra reported. "But Gatton or my people will find her, and I will get her back."

"I can't ask you to do that," Megan protested.

"You don't have to, Megan," Cassandra replied. "I'm going to do it anyway."

This wasn't the only time the former assassin had used her first name, but for some reason, it brought Megan to the brink of tears. Their relationship was complicated. They had met on opposite sides of a case, found common ground protecting a young girl's life, foiled a terrorist plot, and survived several attempts to kill them. Somewhere along the way respect had grown between them and forged an unconventional friendship.

"Thank you, but you're not working on this alone," said Megan. No matter what motives Cassandra had, Megan needed every scrap of help she could get. Clearing her throat, she continued, "She's my sister, and I'm helping with the investigation whether you like it or not."

Two seconds of silence threatened to stretch into forever.

"Fine. We have a lot of work to do," said Cassandra. "Meet me in Lincoln, Nebraska tomorrow. I'll send you a text with the instructions when you arrive."

"Why Lincoln?" Megan asked.

"It's roughly in the center of the country," Cassandra answered. "I'm hoping Gatton will have a more specific location for us by then. If he fails to give us answers, we can continue to the source in Virginia and start our investigation there."

"All right. I'll be there." It occurred to Megan that keeping this new meeting would mean breaking the previous plan to see her parents, but if she went home, she would be relegated to waiting for others to find her sister.

I need to help. Sorry, Mom.

"One more thing," said Cassandra, regaining Megan's attention. "Don't go home or to your office."

"What? Why?" The two questions almost merged as they burst out of Megan. "You think I'm the target?"

"It's a possibility." Cassandra sounded thoughtful. "Go to the same safehouse you saw before our second meeting at Tantalus Lookout. Grab some clothes, cash, and an ID set, and then get to the airport. There should be something you can pass for. Have Cooper cover for you at work, but do not go to the federal building."

"Am I telling Dan the truth?" Megan asked.

"If you like," said Cassandra. "What you tell Cooper doesn't matter. The important part is getting you onto a plane before your boss makes the connection to your sister's disappearance. If he thinks you're in danger, he'll either help, bury you in agents, or both."

"Was Tara taken because of me?" Megan wasn't certain she

wanted to know the truth.

"I can't answer that yet," said Cassandra. "Concentrate on getting to the mainland so we can form a plan when Gatton tells us where to find her."

"Can you have him call me? Please. I don't have his number with me," said Megan. "It was programmed into Eagle Eyes, and most of the paperwork for the case he initiated is in my office."

"I'll pass the message along and see if we can get you another Eagle Eyes prototype," Cassandra promised. "Be safe, agent."

"You too … assassin." Megan smiled faintly as she said it. She could do far worse than the former assassin for people to stand by her in a crisis, but just once, she wanted to meet the woman for coffee and a meaningless conversation.

Maybe someday, she thought as she pulled up Dan's number and placed the call. With emotional reserves hovering near empty, Megan hoped to reach a machine, but the connection went through on the fourth ring.

"Hi, Megan. Dan's just washing up. He'll be back in a few minutes." The light, cheerful voice of Bethany Cooper reached out and shook Megan. "How was your day?"

A banging noise and incoherent, high-pitched squeals also floated through the phone, telling Megan that the girls must be present. She honestly couldn't dig up words to say for a few painful seconds.

"Have him call me back," she said at last. Megan wanted to soften the words, but pleasantries seemed pointlessly stupid right now.

"Something's wrong," Beth commented. "Ya don't have to tell me about it but stay on the line. I'll get ya to Dan as quick as I can."

"It's my sister," Megan blurted. The helplessness crystalized into anger, causing her next statements to release in short bursts. "She's missing. Probably kidnapped. I'm going to find her."

The news would hit official channels soon anyway.

"Oh, honey. That's terrible!" Beth's voice flipped from surprise to a more business-like tone. "Where are you? What can we do?"

"Don't tell Maddox," said Megan.

"But don't you want him to help?" asked Beth.

"He's more likely to throw me into protective custody than let me help with the search," Megan explained. "I can't let that happen." Part of her admitted the thought might be unfair to her boss, but she couldn't risk being wrong.

"That might be a good idea, if that's the true motive for taking her," said Beth gently. "But here's Dan. Talk it over with him. And keep in touch, ya hear?"

"I'll do my best. Thanks, Beth."

A short time later, Dan's voice washed over her.

"Beth says it's urgent. Tell me whatcha need."

Megan explained everything she knew in one long speech, barely pausing to breathe.

"I know I'm asking a lot," said Megan. "I'll understand if you have to notify Maddox but give me four hours to get on a plane."

"Megan, there are protocols for these situations for a reason," Dan reminded her. "This could be about a case or something entirely different, but we don't know. Come on in and let's wake the beast together. You could have a hundred agents at your disposal in an hour."

The possibility lit Megan's entire being up with hope before fear doused it.

"Will you rally the troops for me after I'm safely away?" Maybe Megan could have the best of both worlds. "I need to go to the mainland, but there's a lot of ground you can cover from here. I just can't risk Maddox chucking me into a safehouse and losing the key."

A long silence passed before Dan sighed.

"Of course, I'll help," he said wearily. "It's clear you're gonna do this with or without help. I might as well do my level-best to make sure you live long enough for Maddox to yell at."

"I intend to," Megan said solemnly.

"Before I let ya go, here are some ground rules," said Dan. "You check in as often as possible. You wait for backup before checking any leads, and you carry a gun everywhere."

"Yes, sir," Megan responded, though she wasn't sure she could obey the carry-a-gun-everywhere thing.

The plane would be no problem. The FBI and certain other agencies had an understanding with airlines that boiled down to "our agents will carry their weapons everywhere, end of story." Her badge would be enough in most places, but certain states were stuffier about letting armed people roam freely. She couldn't worry about the "what ifs" now. She had a plane to catch.

Chapter 6:
Buddy System

Megan Luchek tried four keys before she found the correct one for Cassandra's Honolulu safehouse. As the door swung open, she drew her gun and entered. A minute later when she cleared the last room, she felt foolish, but being needlessly paranoid beat dying any day. The apartment hadn't changed much since her last visit a few months ago. A lack of dust told her somebody came in and cleaned from time to time. Cassandra didn't strike her as the housekeeping sort, but she also didn't seem likely to trust a stranger to do the cleaning.

How many safehouses does she have? How does she afford it? Who does the cleaning?

As the third question formed, Megan pushed them out of her head, deciding to remain blissfully ignorant. Curious as she was about Cassandra, she suspected too much knowledge would put her in the morally awkward position of being obligated to arrest her friend.

All right, assassin. What goodies did you squirrel away in this place?

Megan's stomach announced that lunch had been several hours ago, but she figured she'd have time to kill at the airport. Right now, she needed paperwork, money, and clothes.

Feeling like a burglar, she found the plastic crate of cash and identifications in the guest bedroom. Flipping through the IDs, she systematically rejected each one. They'd been made for Cassandra. It would take Megan the whole night to successfully transform into one of the fake identities.

If she bought the ticket with cash, she might get away with using a nickname. The TSA agents might yell at her, but she doubted they'd care enough to prevent her from boarding. Cassandra had left almost $3000 in this stash. Megan borrowed $1500. A large chunk of that would go towards the plane ticket. The rest would get her food and the clothing items not stockpiled in the safehouse. If she was careful, it might even stretch to cover a hotel room. She could worry about money problems later.

After retrieving her go-bag from near the front door, Megan brought it into the bedroom and dumped out the plastic special agent badges. Lacking the time to properly try things on, Megan stuffed two pairs of pants, one of Cassandra's special shirts, and a navy suit jacket into the black duffle bag. She would need to grab toiletries and other necessities at a tourist trap in the airport.

As she moved to zip the bag shut, a gut feeling made Megan pause and take out the special shirt again. It had the huge advantage of being impact resistant. She wasn't eager to test the tech against a bullet, but it would be safer. Stripping off her jacket, shoulder holster, and shirt, Megan slipped into the new shirt, rearmed, and stuffed the old shirt into the bag. She wanted to carry her suit jacket since the nanoweave technology made the fancy shirt several times heavier than a normal blouse, but she also wanted to conceal her weapon for as long as possible.

Once packed, Megan caught a taxi to the airport. A travel app would have let her save money, but anonymity interested her more. The driver played weird music the whole way, which suited Megan fine as she didn't feel up to twenty minutes of small talk. Upon reaching the Daniel K. Inouye International Airport, formerly Honolulu International Airport, Megan thanked her driver, paid the man in cash, and climbed out.

The ticket buying process proved relatively painless but still took a half-hour. Soon thereafter, she stood in line at Checkpoint 5 in Terminal 2 silently rehearsing her speech. Dealing with TSA was her next headache.

Her phone buzzed with a call from Maddox. She tapped ignore and waited. Two seconds later, the phone buzzed again. Cringing, she hit ignore again, aware that she would pay for the move later.

A text message appeared on her screen.

PICK UP NOW.

Her phone came to life again. The vibration made her hand tingle.

"That's one persistent person," commented the man standing

behind her.

"You have no idea," said Megan, glancing up at the man. He seemed harmless enough, but she inched forward in the line to gain a bit more personal space.

The phone reached its fourth buzz. After one more, it would kick over to voicemail.

Knowing she couldn't dodge her boss forever, Megan finally accepted the call.

"I'm here, sir."

"Where is *here*, Luchek?"

Maddox's rock-hard tone told her that the Special Agent in Charge knew the truth and wanted to see how straight she would be with him.

"Airport," she answered.

"I heard what happened." Maddox's tone softened with concern. "I'm sorry."

Manners kicked in enough for Megan to thank him for the sentiment, but she understood he had much more to say.

"I need to take a few days off, sir," she said.

"Not happening." Maddox's voice returned to its usual brusque stride. "You're going to do one of two things. Option one, you come in and consult with the mainland agents running the investigation. Or option two, you wait for Doug Zeller to get there and let him escort you to your family. You can talk to the DC agents, but they're going to have strict instructions to keep you sidelined."

Panic put Megan on high alert. Zeller was a nice enough guy, but she couldn't afford to be shackled to a babysitter.

"I appreciate the concern, sir, but I can work better if—"

"Buddy system or nothing, Luchek. Your choice," said Maddox. "What's it going to be?"

"I'm by Checkpoint 5," said Megan. She took several steps forward to close the distance that had opened during her chat with Maddox.

"He'll be there shortly," said Maddox. "Cooper and Pitman are on standby. Check in with them regularly or I have Zeller turn you over to the nearest police department for safekeeping."

Megan wouldn't put such a move past him.

"I'll be careful, sir."

Maddox spent another two minutes holding her on the line to give Douglas Zeller a chance to find Megan. The lack of trust annoyed her, but she admitted that she would have sorely been tempted to dodge Zeller if the opportunity arose.

She signed off once her minder arrived.

"Do you have a ticket?" Megan asked Zeller.

He waved his ticket in answer to her question.

"You're traveling awfully light," Megan commented, noting that he didn't have a bag.

Security held them back until somebody higher up confirmed that FBI agents could carry guns on commercial flights.

They arrived at the correct gate minutes before the final boarding call.

Megan wished they had time to grab something to eat, but plane fare would have to do. She hoped they didn't charge for it. Airlines rarely accepted cash these days, and she didn't want to risk using a credit card until they knew more about why her sister had disappeared.

After takeoff, Megan remembered her betta fish, Handsome. *Who will feed him?*

She texted Dan announcing she had another favor to ask of him but then promptly sent a follow-up message telling him to forget it.

Sorry, Handsome, the second bloodworm feast will have to wait. Guess we're trying fasting.

Dan replied with some question marks.

Megan explained that she was going to ask him to stop by her apartment to feed Handsome but had changed her mind.

Dan's reply made her smile.

Covered. Kai and I will feed the fish tonight.

After conveying her thanks, Megan sent another text telling him to break into her car and get the file back to Ms. Walker.

On it.

Dan ended his message with a Thumbs Up emoji.

Smiling, Megan teased him about finally joining the modern era and tucked the phone away to preserve her battery. The thing was already hovering near 30% from the workout she'd been giving it this afternoon. She added *phone charger* to her list of things to buy when they landed in Lincoln Airport. Panic set in until she remembered the cell phone Cassandra had sent her. She'd stuffed it into her purse. Digging it out, Megan checked the charge and relaxed when she saw it read 83%. At least that lifeline would remain open today.

Zeller took his buddy system duties very seriously. He would have spent the ten-hour flight watching her from three rows up if the kind soul next to Megan didn't offer to switch seats with him.

The first time Megan got up to use the facilities she spent two minutes assuring Zeller she could handle the errand on her own. Since she'd dragged out the face washing process to bask in the aloneness, she had an even harder time convincing him to stand down when she needed to get up and stretch her legs.

Now that she had nothing to do, the pent-up worry and frustration crashed down upon her with considerable force. Only being in public prevented her from curling into a ball for a good cry. She hoped the resulting exhaustion would help her sleep, but instead, it flooded her with memories of Tara.

Her sister hadn't turned into a star student until the second year of college. High school had been more about managing an endless string of boyfriends. A rough relationship and a pregnancy scare during her first year in college had set her on a straighter path. The six-plus years between their ages and lack of other siblings gave them a strange relationship. Sometimes, it resembled more mother-daughter status than sister-sister.

Growing up, Tara had naturally assumed the protector role. Even though Megan had never truly fit the popular people clique at school, her sister's reputation sustained her during the first two years of high school. The one time a boy had bullied Megan during her freshman year, word spread quickly. Despite having graduated, Tara had enough connections in the junior and senior classes that the matter got sorted during the next football practice. From then on, nobody messed with Megan.

She reflected upon the various times they had leaned heavily upon each other for moral support. As Tara settled into serious studies and worked through law school, Megan blundered into an abusive relationship, then spent a year overseas in the Middle East working on language skills. When Megan got her head screwed on straight and joined the FBI, Tara had suffered a miscarriage. Shortly thereafter, the whole family faced a cancer scare with Dad.

Where are you, Liv?

Tara had never loved her middle name of Olivia, so Megan had always enjoyed calling her Liv. The thought of never bothering her sister with the nickname again made Megan's heart ache. At this point, she'd even love to hear her sister call her Maggie. Typically, that was a privilege reserved for their parents.

Since thoughts of their parents' pain made her eyes sting, Megan forced herself to concentrate on what needed to happen when they landed. She needed to connect with Cassandra, but she couldn't predict the former assassin's reaction to Zeller. Figuring out the scope of his assignment would also be important. Megan would have launched into an interrogation then and there, but her bodyguard had finally dozed off. Besides not wanting to disturb him, she enjoyed the respite.

Where do we start the investigation?

Virginia made the most sense, but Megan still held hopes that Gatton would come through with a vital lead. She realized Eagle Eyes could cross a million legal and moral lines, but if it saved Tara's life, Megan would gladly turn a blind eye to illegally obtained information.

Hang on, Liv. We'll find you.

Chapter 7:
Game Changes

In the early morning hours, Lillian Marquez once again found herself playing peacekeeper for two of her tech guys. Clearly, Vinny and Gary couldn't be trusted to work the same shift. She would deal with the scheduling issue tomorrow after she got some decent sleep.

"Take it down!" Vinny shouted. "She's not playing. She's on the Protected List." He stood behind Gary's chair, looking ready to physically attack any second.

Halting his work, Gary spun his chair around to face Vinny.

"You want to tell C-Team they get to start from scratch?" asked Gary.

The tech boys glared at each other.

"That's what I thought," said Gary, resuming his original position and placing his hands on the keyboard again. "I was told to prep the page, so that's what I'm gonna do. You got a problem, take it up with O."

I intend to, Lillian silently promised.

"What does he have you doing?" she inquired.

"He's prepping a webpage for Tara, but she can't play," said Vinny, still visibly agitated. "Find somebody else." He shot the last comment at Gary by clapping him on the shoulder.

"Man, you're such a hypocrite." A series of frantic clicking noises punctuated the statement as Gary shrugged out of Vinny's hold. "If she wasn't your cousin, she'd be somebody else's. Everybody knows somebody. Get over it."

"The fact that she's my cousin means she's got some hardcore connections," Vinny said.

"Like what?" Gary challenged.

"Her sister's an FBI agent!" Vinny snapped. "We push too hard and every cop and fed on the East Coast will be combing the woods for her."

"If it becomes too hot, we give her to them," said Gary. The look he shot Vinny lowered the room temperature a few degrees. "End of investigation. That's part of the game too. C-Team took a risk by bagging the judge, no question. If the move backfires, they're out."

The deadness in Gary's eyes unnerved Lillian. He wasn't speaking about releasing the judge. From a practical standpoint, his logic made sense. The quickest way to cool a frantic missing persons case was to give the cops the body they sought. Doing so would send the investigation down many time-consuming trails. On the other hand, Lillian did not want to see how Megan Luchek would react if they murdered her sister.

"They're going to be here soon," said Lillian, checking the time. "For now, Gary should carry on. Vinny, get some sleep. I need you to stay away from C-Team and their prisoner."

"But—"

Lillian raised a hand to cut off his inevitable protest.

"I'll call O again and tell him of your concerns," she promised. "You need to concentrate on not being identified by your cousin." She made eye contact with the young man to drive home her point. "I'm sure C-Team has taken proper precautions to keep her ignorant, but if she finds out anything that can be used against us—"

"She's dead." The sing-song, cheerful way Gary spoke the reminder broke the last word into several syllables.

Vinny clenched his fists, set his jaw, and marched out. The rebellious set to his shoulders told Lillian she might have to put a guard on him.

"You want to see the betting page for him?" asked Gary, once they were alone.

"What page?" Lillian failed to keep alarm from creeping into her question.

"V has a betting page," said Gary. "O had me make one for him once he learned of the connection between him and C-Team's vic. It's pretty popular tonight."

Without waiting for permission, Gary opened a new window and leaned back so Lillian could read the words on the page. She skimmed quickly. This small section held several 50-50 polls. People bet two credits for the chance to vote on various choices, which usually consisted of simple yes or no questions. The house received one credit from each bet and the remaining one went to pay the winners.

Lillian didn't bother reading every question as Gary scrolled through them, but a few caught her eye.

Will V get to meet the victim he knows?

Not if I can help it.

Will V be retired because of his connection to a victim?

The question hit Lillian hard. She understood that people would die for this game, but she'd counted on not knowing them. This felt like a direct attack on one of her people. It didn't matter that she had known him for less than twenty-four hours. Responsibility for him still fell to her. The only suitable course became clear even before she read one more question.

Will V be sidelined over this?

Absolutely.

Computer expert or not, Lillian wasn't going to let the kid get himself killed over this. They could limp through with three tech guys until Steel sent a replacement.

"I only know one answer," Gary chattered. "O said you can't bench V."

The phrase "O said" was quickly getting old. Lillian wondered why a punk kid like Gary had an in with O. It had taken her nearly six years of hard work before being entrusted with his number.

"I saved proof this time, if you want to see it," said Gary. Without waiting for her response, he brought up a chat thread and waved to it.

"I believe you," Lillian murmured, more than done with Gary by this point. "Finish the page but wait for my approval before you publish."

Retreating to her private office, Lillian called O and laid out both the situation and her reservations.

"Do your job," said O. His raspy voice added a threat to the words. He had a way of clipping words so that each one sounded like a command.

"I can't if you keep blocking every logical move." Lillian hadn't meant to be so bold, but the late hour and her irritation at everything removed normal inhibitions.

"What do you suggest?" asked O. His tone said he was merely

indulging her.

"Move Vinny to a different operation before C-Team arrives." Lillian spoke swiftly to get her thoughts out before the rare opportunity slammed shut. "And keep the judge isolated a few days before having C-Team return her unharmed."

"That would disappoint many people," O noted. "Our investors want excitement, action, drama."

"I can give you that," Lillian promised, "but not at the expense of my people."

"Too late."

As O's words slapped Lillian, she heard a muffled noise from outside through a crack she'd left in the window.

Ending the call, she dashed for the stairs and slammed through the front door. Halting two steps from the door, she swept her gaze over the scene.

Floodlights had been strategically placed to illuminate a large section of the gravel driveway. Gary stood calmly off to the side with a video camera. Vinny sat on the ground alternately firing curses at Gary and struggling against zip ties. Al, one of the security guys who came with the isolated house, stood behind Vinny. His black, expressionless face mask looked especially intimidating when paired with crossed arms, dark clothes, and a bulletproof vest.

"What's going on?" Lillian could guess, but she wanted an explanation anyway.

"O's orders. Stay out of the way," said Gary.

Lillian looked at the young man more closely. This version came with a surprising amount of confidence, demonstrated by his stiff posture and alert expression. A white plastic full-face mask sat atop his head, ready to be pulled down into position.

Ty, Security Muscleman Two, appeared near Lillian's left shoulder. He said nothing, but his presence spoke volumes. Pulling a mask into place, Ty offered Lillian one. She took it but didn't don it right away. She hated the things. They smelled weird and always made her face itch.

A white van slowly crunched its way down the driveway.

Anger and frustration tinged with fear kept Lillian silent as the four masked members of C-Team disembarked and stood by their van. The driver and front passenger hung back while the other two opened the back and helped a woman climb down. Next, they guided her around to the front of the van. The captive wore a black hood, but Lillian suspected that would go soon. The woman wouldn't be able to see anything beyond the glaring spotlights, but Lillian reluctantly followed the safety precaution of wearing the stupid mask.

As with Vinny, plastic zip ties had been employed to bind the woman's hands behind her back. Unlike Vinny, her legs were free. The men flanking the judge guided her forward. They must have removed her coat because sane people did not normally venture out into cold nights wearing only jeans and a long-sleeved T-shirt with a soup kitchen logo.

The impulse to rush forward and stop everything warred with common sense. Gary, Al, and Ty would turn on her in a heartbeat. Lillian spared a second to regret not having Steel send some guys she knew as backup.

Can I trust Steel?

The thought ambushed her, but she buried her misgivings. There would be processing time after this disaster unfolded.

"Kneel," C-Team's speaker instructed the prisoner. He emphasized the order by pressing down on the woman's right shoulder. By design, each team had only one elected speaker to limit the contact with the victim since in theory at least one would eventually be released.

Once the woman obeyed the order, the speaker whipped off the hood. Blinking rapidly released some tears as the captive adjusted to the onslaught of light. The rigors of rough travel had left the woman's blond hair in a frightful state of disarray and marred her makeup. Despite this, Lillian could easily see she possessed striking beauty. Her brain instinctively compared the lady to her sister. Even with the judge kneeling, Lillian could tell she was probably a few inches shorter than the agent. The two women shared enough facial features to confirm the family connection.

"Don't you have anything to say, V?" Gary prompted.

"No," Vinny said flatly. "That's what he wants. I'm not playing. I won't help you make money off this!"

"Vinny?" The prisoner squinted in the direction of his voice. "What are—"

The handler for C-Team shoved the woman to the ground, knelt on her back, and pressed a gun to the back of her neck.

"No talking," scolded the team's speaker.

"Get off of her!" Vinny's anger nearly brought him to his feet despite bound ankles.

At a nod from Gary, Al plucked Vinny off the ground and

shoved him into the pool of light. He landed awkwardly on his side with his face pressed into the stones.

The handler soon had the judge back on her knees, facing Vinny.

Leaning down, the speaker brushed dust and bits of gravel off the woman's face.

"Take a long look," said the speaker. "You now have two reasons to obey us. Your safety and his. Am I clear?"

The judge's expression cycled through fury, fear, and confusion. She settled on confusion but managed to nod curtly.

"Great footage," said Gary. "Your entry will be updated shortly. A bonus for making the first entry will hit your accounts soon."

"We're not leaving," said the C-Team speaker. "We're staying to guard our investment."

"You have to leave." Gary's voice turned frigid again. "Those are the rules."

"We're changing the rules," said the speaker.

"That's unfortunate." Gary's words and tone didn't match. He sounded excited.

Four gunshots rang out, two from Al and two from Ty.

Lillian flinched.

The prisoner screamed.

Four bodies hit the ground, two by the van and two flanking the judge.

"Looks like the house gets the first entry," said Gary with a shrug. "Get her cleaned up and stored properly. Then, get the bodies into bags and throw them in the freezer."

"What about him?" asked Al, pointing to Vinny.

"Keep him locked somewhere away from the prisoners for now," said Gary. "I have to make arrangements for gathering one more special guest."

As she watched him leave, Lillian determined to find out everything worth knowing about Gary Sheffield.

Chapter 8:
High Roller Advantage

A very long week dragged by before Officer Rathberger directed James Turner to the storage closet for another illegal communication with the outside world. A shipment of toilet paper must have come in because the large rolls took over every flat surface, including much of the floor. Only the beautiful sight of a cell phone sitting atop a pile of toilet paper rolls on the lone stool let James endure the tight space.

Picking up the phone, James found one short text message awaiting him. It consisted of three letters: HRA. Tapping on the hyperlink, James found himself on a simple website. The font choices and graphics screamed amateur, but he guessed some of that might be on purpose to avoid drawing unwanted attention to the site.

A popup window asked him for a username and password. Both had been autofilled.

The username read: jet25716

The password box showed only nine asterisks side by side.

Hitting enter brought him to a welcome page. The long-winded passage worked out to be a "thank you for your generous support" missive combined with a generic "enjoy your time" message.

Below this, James found another innocuous hyperlink that read: Popularity Contest. Following the link brought him to a page with four titles: Judge, Teacher, Physician, and Waiter.

Clicking on the first profession showed him a woman's picture and a brief profile.

Name: Tara Olivia Sidell
Profession: Family Court Judge

Age: 36

Description: Tara is a loving sister, daughter, wife, and pet parent. As a pillar for her community, she enjoys helping those in need. Vote for Tara if you want her to survive.

A warning after the description told him to read every profile before casting his vote because he could only support one person each round. If his candidate survived to the end from Round One, he would earn a bonus of $10,000 on top of the credit earnings, which would be evenly split among the winners.

The first picture posted obviously came from social media. It showed a beautiful blond woman in a wedding dress. The two pictures below the warning were much more recent. These featured the same woman at varying stages of captivity. The left image showed her sitting on a cement floor bound hand and foot and staring up at the camera with haunted eyes. The right picture showed her sleeping on a blue blanket.

Links clustered at the bottom would bring James to the other contestants' pages and the main game page. Since he didn't have a great grasp on the game, James opened the Popularity Contest main page and speed read the description and rules.

The game consisted of three rounds with one person being eliminated each round. The loser from a given round would be subject to the Tribunal, a panel of randomly chosen High Rollers, who would decide his or her manner of death. Standard level gamblers would be able to spend credits to vote on which three kill methods went before the Tribunal. They would receive a payout if the method they voted for was employed.

James thought it might be more interesting if the contestants had to do tasks to survive. To his pleasant surprise, the game addressed that in later rounds. Round One would be determined by High Rollers only. Round Two was controlled mainly by Standard and Premium players. The three surviving contestants would also have a hand in their fate. They could earn points by creating fundraising videos, winning games of chance, and competing in various trivia challenges and funfair-inspired games. Families and communities for each contestant could also earn points for their favorites by posting video pleas for the gamblers to watch. High Rollers would be relegated to a support role for Round Two. Round Three amped up the competition between the players. All levels of gamblers would get one vote to spend on their favorite contestant.

Now that he understood the game better, James scrolled down

to the bottom and found the link for the Teacher.

Name: Fredrick August Davy

Profession: Middle School Social Studies Teacher

Age: 31

Description: Fred is a devoted husband and the father of twin boys. His interests include mountain climbing, visiting battlefields, traveling, and photography. Vote for Fred to send him back to his kids.

The pictures below the standard warning not to vote right away mirrored the same poses as for the judge. In the left one, Fred sat on the floor and gazed into the camera, and in the other, the man lay on his back fast asleep.

Rathberger knocked to give James a one-minute warning.

Wanting to be thorough, James checked the profiles for the Physician and the Waiter.

Name: Michelle A. Deel

Profession: Pediatrician

Age: 41

Description: Dr. Deel works tirelessly for her patients. She has won numerous awards for her kind, compassionate approach to pediatric medicine. The world wouldn't be the same without her. Give Michelle your vote today.

Given the doctor's age, James removed her from consideration. Odds were great she would be the first to die.

Name: Jonathan David Palatros

Profession: Waiter

Age: 18

Description: Jon doesn't know what he wants to be. He enjoys video games, movies, and hanging out with his friends. Vote for Jon if you want the kid to live.

James figured the kid might have a good chance if he made it to Round Two, but his chances of impressing enough High Rollers to get him through Round One weren't great. The judge and the teacher would likely be the top contenders because they were by far better looking than the doctor and the pimply kid.

Rathberger swung the door open.

"Time's up, Turner," he announced.

Flipping back to the judge's page, James cast his vote for her.

***

An alert box opened, letting Jeffrey Gatton know at least one query had an answer. The bot reported a match for Tara's picture. He had submitted a picture from Megan's social media page to one of his private facial recognition software programs. It translated the shape of somebody's face to a mathematical algorithm and then roamed the internet looking for close matches. Once the program identified a likely candidate, it conducted surrounding and keyword searches. If a picture showed up in more than one location, the program would catch duplicates then compare the websites. It sent Jeff an alert if there was a discrepancy in site ownership.

Further digging brought him to cyberleaguesports.com on the Dark Web.

Within minutes of poking around, Jeff knew he'd come to the right place. The surface version of the site displayed a wide variety of entertaining gambling opportunities fit for every budget. These mostly consisted of video game scenarios. The layout and wording reminded Jeff of a similar site that had tried to make it on the normal internet, The Keres Legacy.

Getting to the heart of the site required moderate hacking and puzzle-solving skills. Using a program that revealed all hidden text, Jeff found the keystone phrase on one page and the place to input it on another. At first, nothing happened. Another look revealed four sets of passwords and places to enter them. The passwords were each readily available, but they had to be input in a certain order, which changed every three tries. He could have used a program to slice past the clumsy lock, but his mind enjoyed the challenge.

The deeper version of the website looked terrible. Whoever had chosen the childish fonts and ugly color schemes must have failed design school. Jeff might have left the site altogether if he didn't have Eagle Eyes and wasn't in the middle of an investigation. Since he had Eagle Eyes, he adjusted the tint and contrast settings to make the words easier to read.

A page describing how the site worked walked him through the many payment options. He could use one of three dozen cryptocurrencies to purchase credits or become an investor. The latter option required a bank account transfer. Those who invested heavily enough were automatically granted high roller status. Curious, Jeff followed the link to find out more about becoming an investor. The minimum acceptable investment was hard to pin down, but hints around the site gave him 2.5 million as a ballpark number.

He sat back to think, tempted to call Cassandra for another pep talk. If he went for it, calling her would be the next step, but he wanted to have a plan laid out before speaking with her. The idea of betraying her someday weighed on his conscience. For the last week, he had been maintaining a fine balance between working with her and keeping tabs on her. Someday, he would have to pick a side.

Focus. You need her help.

The monetary input alone didn't bother him. Being able to play with large amounts of money was a perk of being a billionaire. The idea of supporting a very shady site raised some moral questions. He knew with certainty that Tara was recently connected to the site. From an investment standpoint, it looked risky, but he would likely earn the initial payment back and make money too.

The website wouldn't show him more without him laying down some money. Hacking in might tell him the information he needed but doing so quickly would involve some blunt techniques. The site owners would find the problem, address it, and block his access instantly, forcing him to start from scratch to find it again.

His black phone rang, making him cringe.

"Gatton," he said.

"Jeffrey," greeted his handler. "I saw you active and wanted to ask you for an update. How are our two little side projects coming?"

The man had been harping on the need to control Cassandra. Gatton had never agreed to help, but he had to be cautious about his refusals.

"We've never met in person," Jeff said. "I can't track her all the time if she's not using Eagle Eyes."

That was a little white lie.

He had managed to develop a method of tracking Agent Luchek's prototype through passive means. The need to deploy the method hadn't come up because she had actively started using Eagle Eyes.

"I believe in you," said the handler. "I may have another angle to exploit but stand by for instructions. It could require your expertise. And I want my prototype now. Have one of your people deliver it to Dead Drop 44 within the hour."

"I need more time than that," Jeff protested. "Prototypes are kept in a secure location. It's well after business hours. My people won't be able to get it for at least—"

"Make it work," said the man. "If you give me the woman's location, I can have my people move in and acquire the prototype you left with her."

The connection ended abruptly as usual.

No way, Jeff argued silently. *She's my one ticket off this ride.*

Renewing his vow to cast off his CIA shackles, Jeff wrenched his thoughts back to the current crisis. He would have to push off the issue of getting his handler a defective version of Eagle Eyes until later.

Which identity do I use?

Bank transfers took time and involved real names. When he'd been young and bored, he had created several ghost employees for Gatton Technologies. Many were true ghosts with hardly any digital footprints. A few were what he thought of as fleshy ghosts. These personas had social media accounts, social security numbers, bank accounts, and documented allergies. Unfortunately, Jeff had already burned Lester Malik, the disgruntled Integrity Analyst, in the first battle with the Club. He considered recycling the identity, but that would be risky. The chances of the Club having its paws on this scheme were disturbingly high.

Thoughts of the Club made him think of Megan. Opening a new window, Jeff checked the status of her flight, then ran a background check on the other passengers. That could run while he wrestled with the infiltration issue. The agent used her nickname to purchase the ticket, but Jeff's programs always used every permutation and several misspellings of a name.

Adding the creation of more fleshy ghosts to his mental to-do list, he pondered his current problem. A review of the personas left showed him only one candidate associated with a big enough bank account, Moira Jethro. His voice masking programs could successfully hide his identity, but he'd yet to teach them to make him sound like a woman. The prototype voice creation program still lacked much in the way of a personality, so that was out. To pull this off, he would need a real live lady. Moira's age put her in range for Megan Luchek or Cassandra Mirren, but Jeff had enough sense to ask the assassin first.

Sending the call through before he lost his nerve, Jeff accessed Moira's accounts to see if she had enough funds to become an investor in cyberleaguesports.com.

Once again, Cassandra answered before the first ring sang its last note.

"What can I do for you, Gatton?" The assassin sounded fully alert, despite the late hour.

Does she ever sleep? Is she even human?

"I think I found her," said Gatton. The details poured out of him in a rush. "There's a Dark Web gambling site linked to crimes, but I can't see more information without investing in the site and the only personality prepped with that kind of cash is a woman. I need your help."

"Play the part of her hired help," Cassandra suggested. "Most rich people keep plenty of assistants around for these situations."

"I don't know the minimum investment, but it's over two million dollars," said Gatton. "They're going to want to speak with the lady for a transaction that large. I've started on something that could simulate the right voice, but it won't be ready to test for a few months. I can handle the bank transfers and computer work, but I need you to do the talking."

Jeff caught his breath while Cassandra considered the proposal.

"It might not be fast enough," said Cassandra, after a slight pause.

"What do you mean?" asked Jeff. "Once I'm in, I can set some programs to work analyzing every query sent to and from the site. They're probably using proxy servers, but even those have to receive the information from somewhere before spoofing others."

"And how long will that take?" Cassandra's tone implied she already had a guess.

"A week? Maybe two." Jeff's tone became hesitant as the point sank in. "More if they use multiple proxy servers and have decent cybersecurity," he admitted.

"It's too long," Cassandra repeated. "We should certainly use the plan, but we can't rely on it to help us get to the agent's sister."

"What can we do?" Jeff asked, letting his shoulders dip at the setback.

"I'll offer them my services and something I know they'll want," said Cassandra. "Megan."

Chapter 9:
Most Logical Move

Jeffrey Gatton laughed nervously to fill the space while he reviewed the assassin's last statement. People who thought he had a scary mind had clearly never met this woman. Using Agent Luchek as bait to get the location for her sister was crazy enough to work, but it hinged on an astronomical number of things going right.

"You're not serious," he said. "You can't be." A thought sailed in out of nowhere, halting the stream of denials. Jeff sucked in sharply. "This was your original plan. That's why you let Megan come to the mainland."

Eagle Eyes had recorded their original exchange, and Cassandra had also called to convey the pertinent points and pass on Megan's request to hear from him. He'd been putting the task off until he had something to say. Now, he didn't know where to begin.

"I was hoping you'd give me another option," said Cassandra.

"Does she know?" asked Jeff.

"Not yet." The assassin sounded weary. "I didn't want to worry her needlessly."

"What makes you think she's even a target?" Jeff tried to stop his mind from exploring the possibilities if the people behind the website didn't agree to take the FBI agent.

"It's the most logical move," Cassandra said.

Jeff did not like the confidence in her voice.

"*If* they agree and *if* they give you a place to take Megan, what makes you think it'll be the same place they took her sister?" He liked absolutely nothing about this plan.

Cassandra sighed.

"I don't have all the answers, Gatton," she said quietly. "What I have are the facts of the case, the information you just gave me, and a working knowledge of how these people think. The highly organized kidnapping said they intended to make a profit. That means gambling, human trafficking, or ransom. You confirmed gambling."

"I could be wrong," said Jeff. Given the timing of Tara's information posting to the website, he wasn't wrong, but statistically, the possibility existed. "We still don't know how the site will exploit the situation. And you never answered my earlier question about helping with that."

"I'll help you," Cassandra promised. "There's no guarantee that saving Megan's sister and whoever else is being held with her will end this thing."

"What makes you think that?" Jeff asked.

"Hurting people for sport is an ancient human pastime," Cassandra noted. "As is betting on the outcomes. The internet has simply provided a way to reach more people. If not the whole, this is at least part of the big happenings with cybercrimes."

Jeff forgot discussing that with Cassandra. At this rate, he should hire the woman as an advisor. One more question nagged at him.

"What if Megan doesn't agree to the plan?"

"She will," said Cassandra. "She'll know it's the quickest way to reach her sister."

"Fine." Jeff knew Cassandra wasn't asking his permission but felt the need to close that discussion section before moving on. "Do you want to update her or shall I? I still owe her a call."

"I can handle the update," said Cassandra. "You should get things ready for our big investment. I'll reach out to my contacts and get a feel for the Freelancer jobs available."

"Why would that matter?" Jeff was tired of asking questions, but Cassandra rarely divulged extra information for fun.

"It will tell me if I'm going to have any competition trying to collect the agent," Cassandra explained.

Her statement reminded Jeff to check his passenger searches. The program wasn't done checking everything, but it had already highlighted one name: Douglas Zeller, FBI. The seat assignments for the two agents were several rows apart, which made sense given the last-minute nature of the purchases.

"You do have competition," said Jeff. "I think there's an agent traveling with her."

The assassin let a few beats pass before speaking.

"Send me everything you know about the other agent," she ordered.

"What will you do?" Jeff tried to mask his alarm.

"That depends on what your report says and how the agent responds to instructions," said Cassandra.

Will you kill him?

He had the decency to hold the question in, but she answered it anyway.

"I won't kill the other agent without cause."

She left unsaid the course of action she would take if the agent posed a threat to Megan.

Not daring to pry further into that line of questioning, Jeff waited until the line fell silent.

He should get some sleep, but the prospect of checking into this new agent excited him. The only other option was to sit and stew in his worry. Confidence in both Megan's and Cassandra's abilities didn't make it easier to watch—and help them plan—how to march into danger.

Maybe he could try the phone hacking program to see what messages the agent had been receiving the past few days. Once he knew the customer name, the phone number, and the carrier, he could let the baby program out to play. Getting her into the correct server might take some doing, but Jeff had never met a firewall he couldn't climb, dig under, or drill a tiny hole through.

***

"Where to now?" asked Doug Zeller, when they finally landed in Lincoln Airport.

"Restroom. Then shopping," Megan answered. She needed a moment alone, and she wanted to wash her face. Leaving in a hurry had left several significant gaps in her equipment. Most notably, she needed a phone charger for both her iPhone and the phone Cassandra sent her. The assassin never sent chargers because the amount of time she used a given phone could be measured in days at most.

"Sounds great," said Zeller. His cheer sounded forced, and he looked exhausted.

Megan understood the exhaustion, but the nervous way Zeller kept checking their surroundings didn't bode well. The man would never win a chatterbox award, but midway through the flight, he had turned exceptionally quiet. She didn't know him well enough to know if she should attribute the behavior to jetlag or something else. The mysteries of time zones had them leaving Hawaii around 5:30 p.m. and landing in Nebraska at 9:32 a.m. the next morning.

Following the signs, Megan made her way to the restrooms with Zeller on her heels.

"This is where we part ways for a minute," Megan said, stopping in the short hallway that would lead to the Women's room.

Zeller appeared ready to follow her to the bitter end.

A woman dodged around him and gave him a sideways look as she passed.

"Don't leave this area without me."

Megan accepted Zeller's order with a nod. Every good intention to hurry left her head as she enjoyed the blissful solitude. Strangers surrounded her, but the knowledge that they would never cross paths again still counted. As she put soap in her hands to wash up, one of her phones buzzed. After rinsing off quickly, she dried her hands in her hair because the two air dryers were being monopolized by children sticking their heads under the blowers.

Not my monkeys. Not my problem.

Diving into her purse, Megan located the buzzing phone, accepted the call, and shouted a greeting. If the person on the line said anything, Megan completely missed it.

"Sorry, I'm leaving a public restroom. I'll be able to hear you shortly." She spoke loudly in the hopes something would make it through, earning a few glares from weary travelers.

As she rounded the corner, the speaker's next words stopped her cold.

"Don't leave the restroom," said Cassandra.

Megan spotted Zeller pacing in the short hallway. Instinctively, she backed up a step so he wouldn't see her.

"Why am I dodging my help?" Megan lowered her voice so she wouldn't attract too much attention.

"The line's back here," called a woman.

Megan moved toward the far end of the restroom to get away from the blowers. The ladies glared and grumbled, but nobody else said anything to her once they realized she wouldn't steal their precious place in line.

"Because he's compromised," Cassandra explained. She spoke quicker than normal. "Somebody threatened his family."

"That's … bad," said Megan. She had so much more to say, but she also had an audience.

"I'm aware you're in public, so just answer 'yes' or 'no,'" said Cassandra. "Are you willing to try a similar plan to our second Tantalus meeting?"

The one where you shot me with a blank?

"That seems … extreme," Megan commented. "Why would that be necessary?"

"Gatton has a plan for finding the people behind your sister's kidnapping, but it could take weeks or months to work," Cassandra reported.

Tara doesn't have that long.

"There's also a capture bounty on your head," Cassandra announced. "If I don't kidnap you very soon and very publicly, somebody else will."

"Why would anybody bother?" Megan struggled to wrap her head around the bounty news. She leaned against the wall, closed her eyes, and rested her head back on the cool tiles.

"$25,000," Cassandra said. "It's a generous price for a job of this nature where the hunter doesn't have to keep you for long. I'm hoping the meeting will be wherever your sister is."

Pushing away from the wall, Megan gripped her head with her free hand. Her mind raced.

"I'll do it," said Megan, dropping her hand. "What do you want me to do about Zeller?"

"Slip away from him," Cassandra said. "That will be the safest for both of you. After that, make your way down to the rental counters and wait."

"What am I waiting for?"

"I'm going to apologize in advance," Cassandra said, dodging the question.

"Dare I ask why?" Megan inquired.

"There may be many more eyes upon you than you know," Cassandra explained. "This needs to look genuine."

Megan acknowledged the grim news with a low noise while she questioned her sanity. Her mind scrolled through the people in her life and predicted what their stance would be on undertaking this crazy scheme. Tara, Mom, Dad, and Dan would give her a firm "no" in answer. Gatton and Ophelia Pitman would likely say "yes" reluctantly.

"I'm on my way," said Megan.

Off to get myself kidnapped again.

Chapter 10:
Run

"Did you look at any of this?" asked Lillian Marquez.

"You said not to," Ashton replied.

The petulant note answered her question.

"I also said it was dangerous," Lillian muttered, realizing her mistake.

"What is it?" Ashton asked, failing to downplay his curiosity. "I only read a little!"

"Did you cover your tracks?" Lillian demanded, letting the anger sharpen her tone.

"Always do," said Ashton. "Who's this Sands guy? These articles are ancient history. He sounds cool."

The comment told Lillian the tech guy's definition of "a little" must be faulty, but she couldn't waste more time worrying about something already done.

He's dangerous.

"A friend," Lillian answered.

A friend who will kill you if he thinks you're a threat to him or the Club.

Lillian knew she should warn the kid, but instinct told her it was already too late for him to escape cleanly.

"Where's V?" asked Ashton. "He's usually a slacker but not by this much. Shift started an hour ago."

"Something came up," Lillian answered vaguely. "You're on your own for a few hours, but Gary and Eddie are around if you need help."

"I'll be fine. Two people this early is always overkill," Ashton said, shrugging. "The guests keep weird sleeping hours so there's not much to monitor."

"How many events have you done?" Lillian wondered. She had errantly assumed this was the first such undertaking.

"Four or five," Ashton said. "They've been much smaller scale. Single event. One vic. One handler who stays on for the whole show. Steel said to keep everything in-house this time, except the initial drop off, of course."

Lillian adjusted her perception of the tech guy. His casual attitude could have two meanings: one, painful naiveté or two, immunity.

"Did you tell anybody about the research?" Lillian wished the question didn't sound so breathless.

"Not exactly," the kid mumbled, looking uncomfortable.

A hard stare from Lillian shook the confession loose.

"I was careful and good, but the computer had a passive alert system in place. It's not my fault! Steel called almost immediately. I couldn't even lie about it."

"Forget it," said Lillian.

"You're not mad?" the tech guy sounded hopeful.

"Show me what you found," Lillian instructed. If she was going to get into trouble over this, she might as well know why.

"Steel said you should call him," said Ashton.

A sinking feeling stole over Lillian. Kicking the kid out and locking the door behind him, she sat down in his chair and pulled out her phone.

Do I get on board or get out of the way?

If she left, Vinny would die. The flash of concern surprised Lillian. She had met him yesterday. His connection to one of the victims couldn't be an accident, which meant somebody had carefully planned this. The obvious candidate for master manipulator was Steel, but the risk versus rewards math wasn't working for Lillian. Over the years, Steel cultivated a reputation as an honest mobster. Endangering an employee for a job didn't fit right.

I'm missing something big.

The articles Ashton had retrieved from the internet sat before her. One spoke about Lou Sands being arrested and charged with murder and racketeering. Another mentioned the prosecutor's frustration at witnesses disappearing or recanting. The third article, barely more than a footnote, covered a brief stay at Parkridge Behavioral Healthcare Hospital. Ashton had put a note with this article that records from before 2013 weren't available electronically. The fourth and fifth articles concerned a wedding and a birth.

One of the many discussions—fights—between her parents came back to Lillian in bits and pieces. Mother had been adamant about keeping Steel out of her house, and Father wouldn't hear of it. She didn't want the "loon" anywhere near the children. Father had agreed to conduct more business away from the house, but in an act of defiance, he'd started taking Lillian—the eldest of her siblings—with him to the office. That's where she first encountered Club business, though she didn't know or understand it at the time.

She had never questioned her status in the Club or their relationship, but now she suspected she finally understood his lack of meaningful promotions.

Heart heavy, Lillian called Steel.

"Is O real?" Lillian asked, skipping over pleasantries.

"As real as you or me," Steel answered instantly.

"But he is you," Lillian insisted.

"He's *part* of me," Steel corrected. "There's a difference. People only call it a mental illness because they don't understand."

"Help me understand." Lillian's tone started as a plea and edged quickly toward anger. "How did you pull it off? Why not take the position of power yourself?"

A short silence fell before a new voice addressed Lillian.

"Nobody trusts a crazy man for long." The speaker delivered the coldly factual words in a harsh whisper.

Lillian's whole body went rigid. Dealing with O had always unnerved her, but she attributed that to normal fear of speaking with somebody so far above her bosses as to be untouchable.

Steel spoke before Lillian could muster a response, and he sounded upset.

"Get out of there, Lil!" he cried. "He wants to kill you. We're on the way. Run! Now!"

Disconnecting the call, Lillian raced for the door. She needed to grab her gun from her room. She didn't use it often in her position, but one did not climb anywhere in the Club without a working knowledge of firearms.

Do I take the kid?

Lillian dismissed the idea immediately. When the teams dropped off the remaining victims, O had put extra security in place. She'd be lucky to get to her car.

***

Instinct sent Cassandra Mirren into a dive before thought caught up. Something smashed into the cement pillar next to her, sending fragments in several directions. One nicked her left cheek as she pivoted to face her attacker. The force the man put into the blow that struck the pillar had left him flatfooted. Since she was already low, Cassandra swept her attacker's legs.

A crowbar hit the ground near her.

Ignoring the weapon, Cassandra drew her gun and pointed it dead center of the man's chest.

A tense second passed.

She wasn't comfortable with the distance. If the man had any significant training, he could have her gun in a heartbeat. Rising, she backed up against the pillar.

"Put your hands on your head and lower yourself to the ground," Cassandra ordered.

The man hesitated.

Recovering the step, she slammed the gun into the side of his neck. He would never have surrendered. The order was only meant to occupy his brain cells while she moved.

Activating Eagle Eyes, she turned on proximity alerts, switched the view to thermal, and swept her gaze over the garage. She saw several groups of people moving about, but their pace and posture indicated they were dragging luggage. Two more people operated vehicles. Three sat in the back seats of vehicles. As she looked in the other direction, she found a figure seated in a van. The size and mass readings indicated an adult male.

Glancing toward the main part of the airport hurt her eyes, so she switched off the thermal view.

Keeping her gun in hand, Cassandra had Eagle Eyes locate and call Megan Luchek.

"Change of plan," she said when the agent answered. "Find the nearest security checkpoint and wait for me. There's at least one team here for you. Do not leave public areas, and do not go anywhere with them."

She ended the call before the agent could respond. That would only end in an argument.

Concealing her gun again, Cassandra flipped to thermal and sprinted across the parking garage. Upon reaching the black van, Cassandra dialed down every reading except electricity. The van lit up like a Christmas tree. Eagle Eyes estimated a 78.68% chance the man would pose a threat to her eventually. Reasonably certain of the conclusion, she turned on the combat display, wrenched the van door open, and leapt inside.

Panel lights provided soft illumination to see by.

A man swiveled to face her and started to rise, but Cassandra's hard slap knocked him back into the seat. She refrained from punching him because she wanted to have a chat and breaking his jaw would make that difficult.

Needing the privacy, she shut the door.

When she turned back to the man, the combat package warned her he had a small canister in his right hand. Grabbing hold of the wrist with both hands, Cassandra exerted enough pressure to make the canister fall free, then kicked it aside.

The man leaned back in the chair, moaning and clutching his sore wrist to his chest.

"First, last, and only warning. Try something like that again and I'll break your wrist," said Cassandra. "I have some questions. If you have decent answers, you get to live. Lies do not qualify as decent answers. Nod if you understand."

The man glared at her but nodded once.

"Question one: where are the zip ties?" While she waited for an answer, Cassandra had Gatton's nosy computer program isolate everything that could be plastic, based on the density range for standard zip ties. She located them a second before the man helpfully pointed them out.

Retrieving three, Cassandra shoved the rolling chair until it bumped into the driver's seat. Next, she secured the man's wrists and ankles before using the last tie to attach his hands to the driver's seat headrest.

"Good start," she commented. "How many people are on your team total, including you?"

She let a few seconds pass before drawing her gun.

"I don't have time for a long interrogation, so we're going to have to skip straight to answer or die." Cassandra pressed the gun to the man's head. It wasn't the most practical place to shoot somebody, especially in such tight quarters. However, it did have a powerful psychological effect.

"Four," said the man.

"Who's your target?" She needed the confirmation.

His answer surprised her.

"Both of you."

"If you succeeded, where were you supposed to take us?" asked Cassandra.

"I don't know."

She weighed the negative answer. The technical support for a team like this should be the one to have such information, but occasionally, the leader revealed details at the last minute.

"You're doing well so far," said Cassandra. "The last two things I need from you are a rundown of who's who on your team and a description of the plan."

Many more questions zipped through her mind, but she needed to wrap this up and get to Megan immediately. Cassandra trusted the agent to follow directions to a point, but she didn't like the woman's odds against a rogue FBI agent and half a team of professional kidnappers.

Chapter 11:
Competition

"What's your hurry?" asked Gary, holding out his arms to prevent Lillian from crashing into him.

Ty and Al stood behind him.

Now that she concentrated, Lillian saw the faint family resemblance in the shape of his jaw and nose. His glasses changed a lot about his looks. Plus, his slight build must have come from his mother because there wasn't one trace of Steel there.

"Get out of my way," she said, struggling to keep calm.

"I'm in charge now," said Gary. "And Dad said he wants to see you."

"Then let me know when he arrives." Lillian used a frosty tone to mask her fear. She ignored his statement about being in charge.

Gary's grin looked predatory.

"You're very good," he said. Next instant, his expression clouded. "That's why he likes you."

The words reeked of jealousy.

Seizing her upper arms, Gary turned and slammed Lillian against the wall.

Her breath rushed out, but before she could react, Ty and Al pointed handguns at her.

Gary leaned uncomfortably close. The height difference between them had him looming over her, which made her claustrophobic. His sour breath moved across her senses, twisting her stomach.

"Before we left my dad, hardly a day went by without a Lillian story." Gary's voice lacked emotion. He took a small step back. "I'd never even met you, and I hated you."

"You want a tissue for the sob story?" asked Lillian, inserting as much contempt as she could gather. "Get those guns out of my face. I have a job to do."

"When we reconnected a year ago, I begged him to let me kill you," Gary said, as if she hadn't spoken. "Maybe I'll get my chance soon. Guess we'll have to wait and see who's in control today."

Lillian gasped. Her eyes darted to Al and Ty.

"Don't worry. They know," said Gary. "They've been my personal bodyguards for months now. Dad insisted they know the truth."

"Who else knows?" asked Lillian.

"I'm touched you care," said Gary.

She needed to change tactics fast.

"He's unraveling, you know," said Lillian. "Making reckless decisions. If we don't stop him, we're all headed for prison."

"You'll never make it to prison," Gary promised.

A nod from the young man set the goons into motion. Ty adjusted his position to keep a close watch on Lillian while Al pulled her away from the wall and bound her wrists behind her back.

"Toss her down with the others," Gary instructed. Tilting his head toward Al, he spoke in a stage whisper. "Make sure they know who she is."

Horror weakened Lillian's knees. She leaned against the wall for support.

They kept the prisoners together in the basement and left them unbound in case any of them wanted to directly improve their odds of survival. So far, the cameras had shown a lot of talking but little else. Mostly, the prisoners stayed in their respective corners. If they knew she worked for the kidnappers, there's no telling what they would do.

Ty chuckled, but Al shook his head.

"Too risky," said Al. "Boss wants to see her."

"It's not that risky," Gary countered. "We could cut the ties and watch the fight. Bet the viewers would love it."

Thankfully, Al stood firm on the issue.

It didn't improve Lillian's situation by much, but she wouldn't be lynched before getting to see Steel. She fervently hoped he was himself today. O would be much harder to reason with.

***

Megan Luchek stared at her phone and mentally replayed Cassandra's short message. The assassin sounded more rushed than panicked, but from where Megan stood, either was bad. Cassandra's confidence when speaking of a collection team said she must have met at least one of them. With luck, the person would be alive but unconscious.

Megan disliked changing plans on the fly but admitted this one was more direct than the instruction to wait for Cassandra's fake kidnapping attempt to unfold. Checking signs, she got her bearings and turned around.

Her phone buzzed for the ninth time as Zeller frantically tried to find her again. She'd only recently managed to duck out on him by weaving through tight aisles in an airport gift shop. Her new path would take her back in that direction. Right now, he was a low priority.

Would he help?

The tricky question occupied her thoughts as she wove through the airport crowd back to the security checkpoint in this zone. If Cassandra's claim about Zeller being compromised held truth, he had an agenda to fulfill. Whatever his plan, it likely didn't include letting another team walk off with her.

Upon reaching the security lines, Megan froze. She felt very exposed. Standing near a wall gave her a small sense of security, but the tension hurt her head.

Five minutes dragged by. Then ten.

The ache in Megan's head intensified as she scanned the crowd for possible threats, hoping to see Cassandra.

Her phone pinged to announce a text message. Seeing Zeller's name, she almost put the phone away, but the first few words sank in.

The agent needs you …

The message had an attachment that didn't show up in the preview.

A chill swept through her as she opened the full message.

The picture showed Zeller lying on a tiled floor bleeding from the head. The rest of the words gave Megan specific instructions to follow.

Cassandra's warning to not leave public places fired through her head.

Indecision kept her rooted in place. Following the instructions would be pure madness. Ignoring the instructions would likely get Zeller killed. The knowledge that he might try to turn her over to dangerous people didn't make her his biggest fan right now, but his status as an FBI agent and a father meant something.

A new message arrived.

You have 2 minutes. Then, he dies, and we take a new hostage.

This was followed by an alarm clock emoji.

A call from Cassandra arrived.

Megan scrambled to answer it.

"Go to the meeting and stall," Cassandra instructed.

"How do you even know about it?" Megan wondered.

"Eagle Eyes is tapped into your phone," Cassandra explained. "I'm close, but I need a few minutes to prepare something."

"Want to tell me about this something?" Megan knew the answer before she asked. Flipping back to the earlier text from Zeller's phone, she plotted a path to the restroom described.

"No time," said Cassandra. "You're going to have to sprint to make it."

I can run and talk.

Megan didn't bother saying the words aloud since Cassandra had already left the conversation. Instead, she poured her energy into running. She'd abandoned her duffle bag and purse ages ago, taking only her ID wallet, most of the cash, and her driver's license. Hopefully, a Good Samaritan would drop the purse off at the lost and found.

Hopefully, you'll be alive enough to care tomorrow.

When she reached the correct restroom, Megan grabbed hold of the cleaning cart somebody had placed across the opening. Taking out her gun, she paused to draw several steadying breaths. If she stormed in with this many nerves frayed, she would be useless in a shootout. Raising the gun, she approached the corner cautiously.

"Come on in," invited a male voice. "You're late, but I forgive you."

Peeking around the corner, Megan took in the scene. Zeller sat propped up against the far wall, clutching his head. One man stood to the right of Zeller near the sinks and another stood in the handicap stall. Both had handguns pointed at the subdued agent.

Pulling her head back into the protected area, Megan leaned into the wall nearest the hostile men to cut down on the angles they would have to shoot her.

"Enter before I lose patience," said the same speaker as before.

If Megan had to hazard a guess, she would say the speaker stood to Zeller's left by the sinks.

"I can hear you," Megan argued.

"Yes, but shouting could draw unwanted attention," reasoned the man. "That could get messy."

Conceding the point, Megan pushed off the wall and spun to face the man holding Zeller hostage. Keeping her weapon aimed at the man's chest, Megan calculated the odds. She didn't need Eagle Eyes to tell her that a shootout would kill her, Zeller, and the speaker. The assailant tucked into the bathroom stall would be very hard to hit.

"Before we continue, I'm obligated to tell you that assaulting a federal agent carries some stiff penalties," said Megan. "You should let him go."

"And you should put down your gun before I hit him again," the speaker countered.

Fighting every instinct, Megan stooped and set her gun on the ground. Rising, she kept her hands out from her sides, palms open.

Hurry up, Cassandra.

"All right. Gun's down. Now what?" Megan spoke slowly and clearly, trying to defuse the situation. "You can't exactly knock me out and carry me through the airport."

A small part of her argued that they probably could if the public stuck to normal levels of apathy.

"We're going to walk to the parking garage together while my colleague waits here with the other agent," said the speaker. "When you're secure, I'll call him."

"What's to prevent you from killing Zeller once you have me?" Megan asked.

"Nothing. But he's not worth the bullet," said the speaker with a shrug. "You should want to come with me. I'll be taking you to Tara. Isn't that why you're on the mainland?"

Megan bristled at the use of her sister's name. Her open palms became fists.

"Guess we have a walk to take," Megan commented grimly.

The man made a show of calling his colleague.

"This line will be open for the duration of our travels. If anything goes wrong, he'll know to kill some people, starting with the agent." The speaker gestured for her to turn around, and added, "Keep to a normal walking pace."

***

Dressed in custodial coveralls, Cassandra whistled a tune and backed into the main area of the restroom, dragging the large cart of supplies with her. She had Gatton's toy block the cell phone signals to be on the safe side.

"Hey, you can't be in here!" cried Sid Morton.

She knew the name thanks to Nigel, the chatty technical support for D-Team. They'd been responsible for capturing the doctor for their entry into some bizarre gambling thing. She supposed she would know more if she'd had time to help Gatton infiltrate the investor ranks for the website. This gig to capture Megan was purely mercenary in nature. Ted Summers, the man walking through the airport with the agent, had led this merry band for two years. Orin, the first guy Cassandra encountered, rounded out the team by taking on the thug role.

"Are you deaf?" demanded Sid. "I said—"

Selecting a mop from among the supplies, Cassandra whipped around and swung upward, connecting with Sid's head.

Cursing, he stumbled back and fumbled for his gun.

Charging forward, Cassandra rammed his stomach with the mop handle, then punched him for good measure.

Zeller tried to rise, but Cassandra stilled him by laying the handle on his chest.

"Stay here and get in touch with your bosses," said Cassandra. "Give us a head start of about a half-hour and then pursue. Bring a lot of help."

"But my wife," said Zeller. "My boys."

"Have your boss arrange for protection," Cassandra instructed. "The threat's probably empty. This is a very rare second chance. There will not be a third."

Without waiting for Zeller to verbalize his decision, Cassandra ripped off the coveralls and left the restroom at a run. Using the stolen employee badge, Cassandra followed directions from Eagle Eyes. She needed to reach the parking garage first.

Chapter 12:
Too Easy

Waiting for Cassandra to make a move did nothing nice for Megan's nerves. By the time she reached the parking garage with her captor a step behind, her heart ached with each frantic beat. As they passed the rental counter, Megan slowed, unsure of where to go.

"Make a left," directed her escort.

A hand landed on her elbow and steered her in the indicated direction.

Megan jerked her arm free, rotated her shoulders to face the man, and gave him a dirty look.

"Not a great place to cause a scene, agent," said the man, leaning forward and lowering his voice. "Get moving."

Megan imagined smashing her head into the guy's nose. It would hurt but be completely worth it. Leaning back, she retreated a half-step to keep from turning the vision into reality. As satisfying as breaking the man's nose would be, Megan didn't want to be responsible for Zeller's death.

"This would go a lot faster if you took the lead," said Megan.

"Keep stalling and I'll have—"

"I got your message," Megan said, cutting the man off. "I'm not going as fast as you'd like because I don't know where I'm going. Either give better directions or show me the way."

The man studied her for a few seconds before nodding curtly and stepping around her.

Dutifully, Megan fell into line.

As predicted, they traveled much faster under this arrangement.

Too fast.

As Megan started to panic, the man in front of her disappeared. She blinked stupidly at the empty spot until sounds of a scuffle captured her attention.

Cassandra had buckled the man's right knee with a crowbar and shoved him into a cement pillar. When she tried to use the crowbar again, he caught her wrist.

Triumph and fury gleamed in his eyes.

She'd never win a straightforward contest of strength.

Letting the weapon tumble from her right hand, Cassandra snatched it out of the air with her left and rammed it into the man's gut. The strike didn't carry much force, but she followed this by rotating her wrist upward, bringing the crowbar's curved end into the man's mouth.

Stunned, he cried out and released her wrist.

Dropping the crowbar completely, Cassandra grabbed the guy's arm and used it as a lever to flip him forward over her shoulder into a car bumper, ending the fight.

Both impressed and horrified, Megan looked from the assassin to the unlucky kidnapper.

"That was … exciting," she commented.

"That was too easy," Cassandra countered, "but we need to leave."

Without further explanation, Cassandra efficiently plundered the man's pockets, relieving him of his gun, a pocketknife, several zip ties, and a phone. She dropped the ties by the man's unconscious body, broke the phone, and tossed the gun to Megan.

"We could have used that," said Megan, protesting the phone's demise. She caught the gun and checked to see if it had bullets. The weapon was a Beretta M9, but Megan decided not to be picky. She felt infinitely better simply being armed.

"Too easy to track," Cassandra explained, picking up the crowbar. "I have the address we need and a supply kit waiting for us."

Climbing to her feet, the assassin closed her eyes and bowed her head like she was observing a moment of silence.

Before Megan could question the odd behavior, the sound of a car unlocking caught her attention.

Jogging four cars down the row to the right, Cassandra opened the driver's door of a white Toyota Corolla and tossed the crowbar to the floor of the passenger's seat.

"Get in," she ordered.

Megan hesitated only a split-second before racing for the passenger door.

"Maddox is going to murder me," Megan muttered, snapping the seat belt into place. "Why are we stealing a car?"

"Because we can, and it's faster than explaining things to security," Cassandra answered. Throwing the car into reverse, she expertly maneuvered out of the parking spot and drove toward the exit. "And technically, I'm kidnapping you, so your conscience should be clear."

The assassin's tone gave little away, but a small smile underscored the humor.

The rapidly dissipating tension left Megan giddy, so she laughed.

"That might be the first normal thing I've ever heard you say," she noted.

"Agent, given the past two weeks, this *is* our normal."

"Someday, we have to change that," Megan said, acknowledging the staggering amount of truth in the assassin's statement.

Cassandra sent her a sideways glance that held a question.

"It means we have to do something normal people consider normal, like coffee," Megan explained. It struck her that she didn't even know if Cassandra liked coffee. "Or tea. Or water. Or heck, just a conversation that doesn't revolve around a crisis."

"Maybe someday," said Cassandra. "Let's deal with the current crisis first."

"Agreed, but I am going to hold you to that," Megan insisted. She left unsaid the obvious point that such a mythical meeting would require them both surviving the next few hours. The thought stole any levity left in the moment. "How's Zeller?"

"Alive," said Cassandra. "Hopefully, calling your boss and arranging for backup."

"How will anybody find us?" asked Megan.

"Since I wasn't sure what Zeller would say, I also notified Gatton, Cooper, and Pitman," said Cassandra. "I sent them the address I received from Ted's teammate. Ted was your guide through the parking garage."

"Should we wait for backup?" asked Megan.

Cassandra stayed silent a beat longer than Megan was comfortable with.

"No, it was too easy," said Cassandra. "That means there could be a second or third location beyond the initial meeting place."

"None of that seemed easy," Megan argued.

"One team of four means they wanted your attention," Cassandra explained. "They would have sent three or four teams if they truly wanted the kidnapping to succeed, but they knew it wouldn't be necessary."

"Either the team would grab me, or I'd find out where to go," said Megan, following the rest of Cassandra's logic.

"And if that failed, you'd receive a more civilized invitation."

"Why not start with a civilized invitation?" Megan inquired.

"It's not exciting enough," said Cassandra.

"Why does that matter?" asked Megan, rubbing her forehead wearily.

"There's a good chance your sister's kidnapping is related to an online gambling ring," said Cassandra. "Gatton's looking into that angle. Gambling requires risks and rewards. Danger is appealing, and therefore, good for business."

Hot flashes of anger sent pain through Megan's head. Her life and career had shown her much of humanity's dark side, but the callousness of gambling with people's lives left her momentarily speechless. She considered the trauma inflicted upon her family in the last twenty-four hours.

"Business." Megan finally managed to utter the word like a curse.

"Gatton and I will deal with the ring leaders in time," Cassandra promised.

"Do you trust him?" Megan honestly couldn't answer the question herself. Jeffrey Gatton had saved her life several times recently, but he had also manipulated and endangered her at least the same number of times.

"He's in an awkward position," Cassandra reported. "We're working on that problem, but for now, we can only trust he'll do what's best for his company. Proving Eagle Eyes has extensive applications is good for him."

Megan wanted to dwell on the question of Gatton's loyalty, but other matters needed to be addressed.

"Where are we going, and do we have a plan of action when we get there?" asked Megan.

"We're going to a small airport nearby and then on to Pennsylvania," Cassandra said. "The plan beyond that involves driving to an isolated house near Lake Erie, securing your sister and anybody with her, escaping, and not dying in the process."

"I was hoping for a bit more detail," said Megan with a frown. "And I feel like 'not dying' is misplaced on that list."

"We don't have many options," Cassandra reminded her, shrugging. "We'll be outnumbered, outgunned, and walking straight into a trap. Our only advantages are knowing this ahead of time and splitting up. They'll control almost everything else. You should try to draw them into the woods, but if they insist, go with them."

"Where will you be?" Megan asked. "And how is knowing it's a trap an advantage?"

"It means they'll want you alive for a while," said Cassandra. "And it's best you don't know where I am."

Megan agreed with the assassin, but that didn't make her feel much better about the plan.

***

Jeffrey Gatton scowled at the Eagle Eyes readings. Since the business with Megan in Dallas, he had worked on several ways to track anybody with an active prototype. Currently, he had the program pinging nearby cellphones to piggyback off their GPS.

His CIA handler had ordered him to cease communicating with Cassandra until matters settled, so naturally, the only thing Jeff could think about was ways to safely disobey. He should be sleeping, but the problem fascinated him.

How can I get Eagle Eyes to not report a call?

By design, the program recorded, catalogued, and dated everything down to the nanosecond even while in standby mode.

How do I stop time?

If he had a month, he could code a proper time-loop for the program.

The answer carried him up out of his chair. He didn't need to stop time. He needed to change it. If Eagle Eyes ever made it past the prototype stage, Jeff would have to address each loophole, but right now, he was happy to exploit it.

Calling Cassandra would prompt Eagle Eyes to keep a record of the conversation. He couldn't stop that reaction. However, if he changed the date, the program would automatically file the data away in the correct chronological order. It would raise red flags eventually, but until then, it would disappear under a mountain of data.

Soon, he successfully connected with Cassandra.

What is your status?

En route.

The assassin's response was surprisingly prompt.

CIA trap! Abort mission.

Thanks. I know the warning cost you.

I can't help. He's monitoring the Eagle Eyes reports too closely.

Did you fulfill my shopping list?

Yes. Everything's on the plane.

Then you've helped enough. Stand by. When this is over, we'll revisit the idea of freeing you.

The assassin closed the connection from her end.

Jeff wanted to believe she could keep that promise. He had stopped her the last time she made that offer because he had figured life would be easier dealing with the known evil. If something happened to the current handler, a new one would spring up like a stubborn weed. Still, this model had long since spent his last shred of humanity and breathed threats against everybody from Mr. Pudges to Luciana to Gatton's mother.

Thinking of the handler reminded Jeff he needed to check in again. Though circumstances obligated him to help the man, he was rooting for the agent and the assassin.

Why are you after them?

Jeff decided a little research was in order. It would probably get him in trouble, but at this rate, they would reach a breaking point very soon anyway.

Chapter 13:
Fans

Of course, the assassin is also a pilot.

"Where'd you learn to fly?" asked Megan, climbing into the tiny airplane. She took her time. The car ride had been long enough to let her legs grow stiff, and she wasn't eager to hop into another seat.

"Assassin school," replied Cassandra, tossing a headset at her and turning on the plane's engine.

The noise level startled Megan. She quickly donned the headset

"I can't tell if you're making fun of me," Megan complained. She adjusted the copilot's seat to give herself more legroom. "It's annoying and encouraging."

Cassandra continued her flight preparations.

"Get some sleep, agent. Flight time's over three hours. I'll wake you when there's a half-hour left, so you can eat something."

"What are you going to do?" Megan asked, hoping to hear the assassin also planned to rest up.

"Prepare some contingencies," Cassandra answered. "It's—"

"Best I don't know," Megan finished. "You know, there's a chance I could help if I understood what you needed."

"You're safer not knowing," said the assassin.

The plane started moving forward, giving Megan an excuse to not respond. She leaned forward to watch the world whiz by outside the cockpit.

When they reached their cruising altitude, Cassandra let the autopilot take over and picked up the conversation where they had left off.

"There are reasons I don't let many people close."

"Like what?" Megan pressed.

"They tend to die," said Cassandra, turning to face Megan.

"Hey. This isn't your fault," Megan protested.

"This is somebody you've impressed on your own," Cassandra agreed with a nod. "Dallas was not. That one was my fan."

"You don't know that," Megan argued. "Somebody manipulated him."

Facing front again, Cassandra leaned back against the headrest.

"There's also the things I've seen and done." Her tone didn't ask for pity or forgiveness. "It's a lot to take in for anyone."

"I'm not trying to pry, but burdens are easier once shared," Megan pointed out. "You have an open invitation to unburden yourself any time."

Cassandra made a low noise of agreement and repeated her earlier sentiment.

"Get some rest. We won't get the chance to share burdens if this goes wrong." Letting that sobering statement linger, she carefully got up and maneuvered into the tiny back compartment.

Megan didn't think sleep would visit her, but as soon as she relaxed, exhaustion took over.

***

Once certain the agent was asleep, Cassandra called Gatton from one of the burner phones she had requested.

"Is everything ready with the money?" she inquired.

"Sending the account number now," Gatton said. "Are you sure you don't want to use Eagle Eyes for this? I can make the line secure for a few minutes."

"Do it," Cassandra said. Until they sorted the matter of Gatton's overbearing handler, Cassandra wanted to keep phone calls far away from the nosy program, but she doubted she could justify plane engine noise in the background. Besides, she wouldn't put it past Gatton to be able to monitor her calls even with the program in a sleep mode, and she hadn't thought to ask for a holding case for the contact interfaces.

A string of numbers appeared in a text message.

A second message told her the balance in the account was 4.8 million.

"What's my backstory?" asked Cassandra.

"Your name is Moira Jethro, and you're a data analyst for GT three days a week. Otherwise, you're mostly a bored housewife looking for excitement," Gatton reported. "You live in Reno but visit the Hawaiian Islands several times a year."

"How did I hear about this exciting opportunity?" Cassandra asked.

"Your cousin's husband heard a rumor floating around the Kulani Correctional Facility," said Gatton. "He was recently released but can't move money anywhere safely. He passed on the tip in exchange for a future payout."

Cassandra spent the next several minutes grilling Gatton on her new identity before letting him place the call to the cyberleaguesports.com customer service line. A machine picked up, so Cassandra pressed 0 to request a real human. As she waited for someone to answer, she considered altering her voice and concluded it wasn't worth the effort.

When a young female voice answered, Cassandra did her best to channel "bored housewife looking for excitement." The customer service representative transferred her to a service agent who ran her through the standard investing opportunities.

"You are wasting my time," Cassandra said imperiously. "Get me somebody who can make real decisions, right now."

The request earned her a transfer to a service manager, then an investment manager. Finally, the call made it through to a young man named Gary. After the customary small talk and some probing questions about her morals, he described some of the private investment options the company offered.

Several minutes into the conversation, Eagle Eyes informed Cassandra that Gary's approximate location happened to be right where her travels would take her today. The revelation changed her perception of him, but she rolled along with the chat. She bid the program to dig into Gary, starting with his phone activity.

"What are the prospects if I lent you a million dollars?" Cassandra asked.

"Not much better than petty transactions," said Gary. "We want to see you succeed fast, so we insist on investments of 2.5 million or more. These aren't stocks. They don't grow over time. We take your money, multiply it, and give you a payout. After that, it's your choice to reinvest for a new project."

Cassandra hesitated, letting Gary ramp up the sales pitch.

Gatton ran a statistical analysis on how long she should string the man along.

Gary's passion for the business came through clearly as he described how the betting schemes worked and explained the differences between various high roller accounts. When asked how far beyond the legal line she wished to travel, Cassandra honestly answered that she had no idea. Gary promised to forward a survey that could measure her feelings and set her up with appropriate gambling opportunities.

If it had been up to her, the verbal dance would have been much shorter. Cassandra feared Gary would get fed up and disconnect before they got anywhere, but eventually, she received Gatton's blessing to accept Gary's terms.

"Congratulations, Ms. Jethro," said Gary, once they'd concluded negotiations. "If you can send me the account information, I'll get things moving. Normally, we wait for things to clear, but because I have a good feeling about this, I'll get you set up with a hundred thousand credits so you can dive right in."

Cassandra absently accepted the congratulations while she prepared the account details. As she hit send, she hoped they could follow the data trails swiftly enough to stop whatever had Gary so excited.

Gatton too congratulated her but for different reasons.

"I'll explore the site and give you the highlights when I can," he promised. "In the meantime, I'm sending you IRA's report of possible victims you might encounter."

***

The nap refreshed Megan's body and renewed her spirits. As promised, Cassandra woke her with plenty of time to eat a turkey club sandwich, which had been suggested by Eagle Eyes. A proper washing up would have to wait until they arrived at the tiny Pennsylvania airport, but Megan filed germs away as the least of her current worries.

Cassandra brought the plane down to a safe, somewhat bumpy landing.

It took them fifteen minutes to wrap up business at the airport, pack the waiting car, and get on the road again. Megan paid little attention to the scenery because Cassandra had spent most of the ride outlining the steps she should take upon arrival.

By evening, Cassandra dropped her off about a half-mile from the destination.

Megan questioned her sanity as she charged through the forest following Cassandra's cryptic instructions and directions. The sprint warmed her up, which was good because this adventure had left her no time to be properly equipped for the chilly February temperatures. The special blouse she'd borrowed from Cassandra helped, but it couldn't do anything to protect her hands. Determination let her ignore some of the cold, but if she stopped too long, she'd have serious movement issues.

When she caught sight of the house, Megan drew her gun and took out the black cell phone the assassin had left with her. It came preloaded with five numbers. The third was eventually answered by a young man.

"Hello?" He sounded confused. "How did you get this number?"

"This is Special Agent Megan Luchek, FBI. Who am I speaking with?"

"Are you here?" Surprise and excitement made the man sound even younger. "Please tell me you're here!"

"Let me speak with Tara Sidell, Fredrick Davy, Michelle Deel, or Jonathan Palatros," said Megan, working from Cassandra's list.

"I know who you are, Agent Luchek," said the young man. "My dad's been wanting to meet you for a while. You're in luck. He's supposed to arrive shortly. He'll be so excited."

"What do I call you? And how does your father know of me?" asked Megan. That question wasn't on her script, but she couldn't help it.

"Come on in," invited the friendly young man. "You can call me Gary. The others will be relieved to see you."

His use of the word *relieved* disturbed her as did the fact that he gave her a name.

"The timer's been ticking down steadily. If you delay much longer, you still might be too late."

Megan wanted to demand an explanation, but Cassandra had warned her to avoid predictable questions.

"Don't you want to know what happens?" prompted Gary.

"I'm listening." Megan shored up her emotional defenses in anticipation of his next words.

It didn't help much.

The unease and cool temperatures combined, making her shiver.

"I thought you'd show more concern for your sister at least," said Gary with mock disappointment. "I know the others are strangers to you, and I have to keep everybody alive." He sounded like a kid frustrated with orders to walk the garbage to the curb. "But Dad said I could torture them, just a little. Did you know your sister's pregnant?"

Gary's question blindsided Megan.

She almost dropped the phone and her gun. Instead, she tightened her grip on both. The urge to sit down and spend the next hour processing the information made her legs feel like they were trapped in cement. Fear and anger made her hyperaware. She sensed movement from two sides. Since she couldn't face both threats simultaneously, Megan backed into a large tree and pointed her gun at the man approaching from her right side.

"Focus, Gary," Megan ordered. "State your demands, terms, and threats clearly so I can decide how hard I'm going to punch you when this is over. And just so we're clear, if you harm any of them, I will skip over punching and go straight to shooting, starting with your minions."

"I wonder what electricity does to—"

"Nothing good. Move on," Megan snapped.

"Don't know what Dad sees in you," Gary muttered, heaving an exaggerated sigh. "You don't sound special."

"Gary, what do you want?" asked Megan. She enunciated each word carefully.

"Surrender your weapons to one of 'my minions,' and let them bring you in," said Gary.

"Let your hostages go, and I'll consider it," Megan countered. She knew he wouldn't go for it, but she had to try. Her arm started to ache from pointing her weapon at Minion One.

A gun materialized next to her left ear.

"Give the gun to my partner," said a deep male voice.

A large man sidestepped so Megan could see him. She automatically dubbed him Minion Two.

Slowly, Megan ended the call with Gary, stood up straight, and relaxed her shooting arm, allowing the gun to loop onto her finger through the trigger guard.

Sweeping forward, Minion One plucked the gun and phone from her hands and tucked them away.

"Face me and place your hands behind your back," said Minion Two. "Nice and slow."

He didn't have to finish the threat. The gun still pointed at her head said enough.

Megan knew even a short walk through the woods would be uncomfortable with her hands bound behind her back, but she didn't argue.

A hole in the head would be far worse.

Chapter 14:
The Long Game

When the large house came into view, Megan slowed her steps. The soft glow of many lights from within made it seem warm and inviting.

"Move," said Minion Two, delivering a motivating shove.

Megan stumbled forward, nearly bashing her head on a tree trunk. Righting her balance, she resumed her doomed march. Cozy as it looked, she did not want to reach that house under these circumstances.

Come on, assassin. Do your guardian angel thing.

As they emerged from the woods, two soft swishing noises sounded.

Ahead of Megan, Minion One slapped at his neck. Behind her, Minion Two grunted. Spinning around, Megan ducked and charged, driving her right shoulder into the man's gun hand. The gun popped free and sailed into a tree. Unfortunately, Megan's momentum sent her bouncing off Minion Two. Unable to brace herself, she hit the ground hard. Rolling brought her up to her knees in time to watch the assassin lay into Minion One with the crowbar.

A head blow might have been more efficient, but it also risked killing him. Instead, the assassin struck three times. The first blow buckled his right knee. The second strike was a backhanded one that landed across his shoulders, driving the man to the ground. The third whack struck the back of man's good leg. Without pausing, Cassandra dealt Minion Two a similar hand of hard knocks.

Once certain both thugs would stay down, Cassandra freed Megan's hands with the pocketknife she'd confiscated a few hours earlier.

"Thank you. I think this officially means I owe you two," said Megan.

"More like one." The assassin nodded to acknowledge the thanks. "Dallas squared Reno."

Moving back to Minion One, Cassandra flipped him over and recovered Megan's gun. Next, she dug two phones out of his pockets. She dropped the man's phone onto his chest.

"Take these and get inside," said the assassin. She held the other phone and the gun out to Megan. "It's not over yet, but it will be soon. Remember what I said about this phone."

"Where are you going?" Megan asked, not really expecting an answer.

"More preparations for the long game," said Cassandra.

"Cryptic. Figures," said Megan, slipping the cell phone into her left pants pocket.

"Before I go, I have one more gift for you. Compliments of Gatton," said the assassin. Pulling a small plastic container out of a pocket, she bent down and placed it carefully in front of Megan. "It comes with strings attached, of course, but it should give you the edge you need. It's also a more official invitation to join us in taking down the people responsible for this mess."

"Noted and accepted," Megan said. Shoving the gun into her shoulder holster, Megan picked up the container without hesitation. Strings or not, Eagle Eyes would improve her chances of surviving this lone raid. Reaching out, she grabbed the assassin's right hand and squeezed to convey her thanks. If she thought deeply about how much she owed the assassin, she might get weepy.

"I'll be in touch, agent," said Cassandra, briefly increasing the pressure on their clasped hands.

"Any word on official backup?" Megan asked, letting Cassandra's hand slip free.

"They're going to arrive too late," Cassandra reported. "There's already chatter about a bigwig coming. Much as I'd like to have it out with him right now, I doubt he's coming alone, and we are ill-equipped for a siege. One thing at a time. Go get your sister."

Megan looked down at the container holding Eagle Eyes. By the time she looked up again, Cassandra was gone.

Farewell, assassin.

Without further ado, Megan took out the specialized contact lenses, put them in, and closed her eyes to absorb the influx of information. This time, her username and password were already preloaded, so she had full access right away. Megan spent twenty seconds getting reacquainted with the display controls and toggling through various modes. Gatton had made some cosmetic changes since she'd last used the program.

A pre-recorded version of Jeffrey Gatton's voice sounded.

"Welcome back to Eagle Eyes. I see you are preparing for armed conflict. Are you sure that's wise?"

"Don't have a choice," Megan muttered, retreating a few steps back into the line of trees. Aware of how much time had passed, she wanted to storm in, but she needed to know exactly what she faced. That required getting properly reacquainted with Gatton's miracle computer. "How many people are inside?"

"Eleven," the program reported instantly.

"Isolate friend from foe and mark these please," said Megan.

"How shall I make that distinction?"

Megan considered the program's question. She couldn't categorize all men as hostiles because at least two victims were male. She knew of four victims, but nothing guaranteed that there would be only four held in this house.

"Check them for metal," instructed Megan. "Disregard key shapes and pocket change. Focus on gun shapes and cell phones. If a figure has one or both, mark it hostile."

"Done."

A see-through virtual version of the house formed for Megan. It showed her five red dots and six gray dots. Two red dots occupied the top floor and three red dots hovered near the six gray dots which were located below ground.

"Also, track movement," said Megan. "If a figure moves freely, mark it hostile. If it hasn't moved or is moving slowly in a regular pattern, give it a question mark. Can you identify thin plastic strips like zip ties?"

"I can identify over three thousand shapes and substances," answered the program. **"And done."**

The six gray dots now had question marks over them.

"Show me biometrics," Megan ordered. "Check files for the known victims and compare them to the question marks. If you find a match, change the icon to friendly."

Four gray dots morphed into green ones. A second later, the dots changed into miniature human figures, two female and two male. By concentrating on a figure, Megan received each stat Eagle Eyes had estimated for the person. She narrowed the scope to height, weight, and approximate body shape. The two remaining question marks appeared to be one male and one female.

Megan wanted to analyze the situation from every angle, but too much time had slipped away already. Gary would be growing impatient.

"Please prioritize the hostiles," said Megan. "Mark the ones closest to the victims as the highest priority. Place a movement alert on the two on the top floor. Hopefully, they'll stay out of it."

"Finished."

Her heart sank.

The three top priority hostiles changed from red dots to little male figures. Two stood still near the four victims and the unknown woman. The third paced a short distance away.

How am I going to deal with three of them?

"I sense you have a question. If you type it out or verbalize it, I may be able to assist you," said Eagle Eyes.

Megan threw the thought into the text box for the program as she drew the gun and jogged toward the house.

"I can help," offered the program.

By the time Megan gingerly stepped foot in the house, Eagle Eyes had explained its plan. As far as plans go, it wouldn't be the craziest one she ever tried, and it might work well. Even though the computer program didn't report any people, Megan cleared each room she passed through. Her swift tour of the first floor brought her to the steps leading down to the basement.

Pausing at the top, Megan checked in with Eagle Eyes to clear up a few lingering questions about the assassin's plan.

Slipping the gun into her holster, Megan took out the cell phone Cassandra had modified and cradled it to her chest. Next, she slipped earplugs into place.

Now or never.

Taking the stairs three at a time, Megan landed at the bottom and dove left.

Alarmed shouts rose.

Two men reached for guns.

A third stood defiantly and glared at her. This must be Gary.

Pain shot through Megan's left shoulder, but she concentrated on sliding the cell phone towards the three men. Clamping her hands around her ears, she ducked her head toward her chest, clenched her eyes shut, and rolled to her right.

"Now!"

Megan's shout triggered two things.

First, each man's cell phone vibrated and emitted a high-pitched, loud chirp courtesy of a video virus delivered by Eagle Eyes. A split-second later, the modified phone exploded into a brilliant white flash and an ear-assaulting noise.

With the aid of Eagle Eyes, Megan monitored the situation while her body recovered from the sensory overload.

The two men guarding the prisoners weren't so lucky. They dropped to their hands and knees.

Gary escaped the full effect of the improvised flashbang grenade by being behind one of the men. Staggering back, he stumbled into the wall and leaned against it.

Leaping to her feet, Megan rushed to subdue the dangerous men. Wishing she had that crowbar, Megan knocked the man on the left down the old-fashioned way by clocking him with the gun. It was crude, but time did not favor her. Already, the two red dots upstairs scurried in her direction.

The middle guy threw up, making Megan glad she'd chosen to deal with the left guy first. A search revealed keys to the large makeshift cage taking up the entire second half of the room.

"Not over," Gary mumbled. He gave her a long look as if calculating his chances of rushing her.

She didn't hear the words so much as read them on his lips.

The middle guy struggled to his feet.

If this devolved into a barroom-style brawl, Megan would be in trouble. The basement suddenly seemed very crowded.

Backing into the corner, Megan assumed a shooter's stance and pointed her gun at the middle guy since he seemed like the most immediate threat.

The men still looked woozy from their flashbang experience.

"Let's go," Gary ordered the middle guy.

Reading his lips again, Megan kept her gun leveled at the middle guy but decided to let them go. She might regret the decision later, but if she delayed too long, nobody would be leaving. She couldn't do that to the others and waiting for Gary's father—her big fan—to arrive would be suicidal. She could try to force the men to stay, but that would require shooting them. In the grand scheme of things, Gary was a tiny, sadistic fish. Cassandra had been insistent about letting the rats flee in favor of the long game.

Once certain Gary and the one guard posed no threat, Megan asked Eagle Eyes to delay or deter the two upstairs with spoofed messages and prank calls.

Beg, bribe, or threaten. I'm on it, agent.

The voice quality told her she had the real Jeffrey Gatton in the computer program's pilot seat.

Are we safe?

Reasonably so but hurry up.

As Megan approached the gate, she realized the people crowding behind the gate were all speaking. Gesturing for them to wait, Megan removed the earplugs. Next, she asked Gatton to monitor the guy on the ground and find her the key. Fortunately, the key part was easy since it hung on a hook near the gate.

Finally daring to put her gun away, Megan guided the key into the lock. The gate swung open, and her sister tackled her with a tight hug.

"Maggie!"

Megan's rational side told her to hurry this up so they could leave. Nevertheless, she indulged her emotional side a hair longer, letting her sister channel the worry and relief into the long embrace.

"It's good to see you too," said Megan. "Easy on the back. I've had a heck of a time finding you."

"Finish your reunion later," said a familiar female voice.

Pushing away from Tara, Megan stepped in front of her sister.

"Lillian, why do we keep meeting this way?" asked Megan. "You were supposed to take the out after Reno."

"The Club is a part of me," Lillian replied. Her stiff expression flickered, pierced by pain. "The Club was a part of me."

"They're not subtle about turning on you," Megan commented. "Feel like taking them out properly?"

Lillian tensed, looking ready to fight. She regarded Megan with an expression that mixed hope, fear, and suspicion.

What are you doing? Gatton demanded through Eagle Eyes.

This entire rescue operation crossed so many lines, I'd never get a conviction on any arrests anyway. You know that. I might as well flip Lillian if I can. This is the second time somebody Club related has betrayed her big time.

"I'll think about it," Lillian said at last. "Are you going to try to stop me?"

"I will," said an angry young male voice.

Cousin Vinny appeared by Lillian's side.

"You're just as guilty as I am," said Lillian.

"You both belong in prison," said Fredrick Davy, "but I think we've all had enough of cages. Let's get out of here."

Every eye turned to Megan for a decision.

Gatton, do we have escape options?

There's a big, ugly van out front that might suit your needs.

"Get in the big, ugly van that's out front," said Megan. "We'll continue this discussion on the road."

Where are the keys?

You could remote start it with Eagle Eyes. It's perfectly equipped for that.

Key, Megan insisted.

Not as fun. It's on the kitchen table.

"I'm not going anywhere with her," said Vinny, waving to Lillian.

"I'm not going anywhere with you either," Lillian snapped.

Megan sighed.

"I'm leaving," she said. "If anybody wants to come with me, get in the big, ugly van. We're headed south and east." Not waiting for a response, Megan took her sister's elbow and headed for the stairs. "Except you. You don't get a choice. I'm taking you home and turning you over to Jason. And Mom. And probably half the family."

"Vinny's coming too."

Vinny groaned at Tara's announcement.

Megan quirked an eyebrow at her sister.

That's going to be an interesting family discussion.

Epilogue:
Lost Cause

"Burn it. Burn it all."

O's order haunted Steel. He stared at the empty house, then contemplated the lighter in his right hand. He didn't have to set the house on fire. His people had less dramatic ways of cleansing a place, but O insisted they start fresh.

Overall, the collapse of the Popularity Contest was a modest setback. The site might owe a few more payouts than expected to people who predicted such disaster, but they could even things out with the next game. The loss of equipment could be absorbed easily, most of the personnel could be replaced, and the Club owned numerous properties in many states.

Steel thought about his son. Gary didn't react well to challenges. Steel would have to contact the boy soon to ensure his plans aligned well with Club interests. Otherwise, Gary would seek revenge in his own way. While satisfying, his methods always proved messy and unprofitable.

Flipping the lighter open and closed produced a satisfying click. Lil had given him the lighter as a birthday gift a few years ago.

"Lillian is a lost cause. Kill her."

Though he wanted to argue, Steel hesitated. This project represented his last-ditch effort to give Lillian meaningful Club work. Maybe that's why burning the house was so important to O. It would signal Steel's agreement with O's conclusion.

Flicking the lighter on and locking the flame into place, Steel tossed it onto the trail of lighter fluid. A blue flame zipped down the line and disappeared into the house. The place wouldn't explode instantly, but Steel understood he should probably step back. Once the open gas lines from the stove caught, the fire would tear through the place.

"If you put down Lillian, do the same for her father," said Steel. "Carlos deserves to die remembering his daughter fondly. He can't know of her failures."

A deep sense of satisfaction crept over Steel as he received O's approval of the plan. It righted something in his soul. Maybe he'd do the hit himself. Carlos would understand.

"The FBI woman. She's been trouble. Kill her too."

Steel thought about O's order. Megan Luchek wasn't the first law enforcement person to give the Club trouble. In fact, they kept a list of troublesome officers and agents.

"The Hero Contest is up next, right? That requires some special guest stars," he mused. "Maybe she'll get to be one. I saw her on the list. We'll have to see who has been nominated."

He wanted to remain noncommittal, but he knew O would push Megan's name through the election process.

Excitement lifted Steel's spirits as he jogged to his truck. He had a lot of plans to set in motion. Hopping in, he drove backwards until he could turn around. As he completed the K turn, a flash of light reflecting off the rearview mirror dazzled his eyes. A muffled boom quickly followed.

Sleep well, agent. Tomorrow's a big day for you.

Cyber League Crimes Book 2:
The Hero Contest

By Julie C. Gilbert

Table of Contents:

Prologue:
Champion Candidates

"You will follow orders." Lou Sands—better known as Steel—usually reserved the deadly calm tone for subordinates standing a hairsbreadth from a bullet.

"Why can't I kill her?" Gary Sheffield whined. Three quick steps took him to the door where he turned around and retraced those same steps.

If you weren't my son, I'd kill you to stop the noise.

Consciously not drawing his gun, Steel placed his hands across the young man's shoulders, guided him over to the sorry excuse for a lounge chair, and forced him to sit down. The cheap threadbare carpet couldn't take much more of the pacing.

He's a lot like his mother.

O's thought sent a jolt of resentment through Steel. His ex-wife hadn't been up to the rigors of dealing with him and O. While dating, O had been on his best behavior and let Steel handle everything. Once married, the second personality was hard to hide. Tonya never bought his argument that twice the personality meant twice the love. She barely tolerated the pair of them for two years. He couldn't blame her for that part, but she took his kid when she left. He'd had to waste precious resources tracking her down.

Should have killed her back then. Raised the boy alone. He wouldn't be such a whiner.

"Personal vendettas have no place in business," said Steel, speaking as much to O as to his son. He stepped back to counter the rising tension.

"Then why'd you send for Branson and Antonio to go after Lillian?" Gary demanded.

Despite everything, pain shot through Steel's chest at the mention of Lillian Marquez. As the daughter of his best friend and Club co-founder, Carlos, Lillian had been raised in the business. In addition to watching her grow up, Steel had helped teach her Club affairs.

"That is also business," Steel said, after a brief pause. "Lillian knows too much about how we work. She could cause the Club a lot of trouble."

When Carlos's mind started going, Steel had stepped in as Lillian's right-hand man, letting O continue the role of mysterious boss alone. She was much more than his protégé. He knew her better than his own son.

"The FBI agent has already caused a lot of trouble." Gary slumped in the chair and crossed his arms. "The Popularity Contest—"

"Is no longer our concern," Steel interrupted. "The debts have been paid and the losses minimized. It was always meant to be a dry run for this anyway. If you can't handle—"

Gary shot to his feet.

"You know I *can* do the job," he said. "I'm still waiting for a reason I *should* do it."

Maybe the boy has a backbone after all.

Even straightened to full height, Gary barely came up to his shoulders.

"She's one of the top nominees," Steel said, meeting his son's challenging gaze. "You said you wanted a mission with real responsibilities. Here it is. Take it or grab your laptop and get comfortable providing tech support for the rest of your career. Is that what you want?"

"No, sir," Gary mumbled.

"BB has the team assembled and waiting for you in Falls Church." Steel leaned around his son to pick up the handgun sitting on the end table's scratched surface. He held the gun out to Gary. "You'll have to drive through the night to get some time to rest and debrief with the team."

A spark of delight brought a broad smile to Gary's face as he accepted the weapon with two hands. A second later, the joy vanished.

"I want a job where I can use this." Gary's green eyes begged Steel to understand.

"If you handle yourself well with this job, we can talk about future ones," said Steel.

"Send me after Lillian," Gary said, admiring the gun in his hands.

"Nobody's going after her yet," said Steel. "The two I sent will track her so that when we're ready, the kill will be quick and clean, but I won't order it yet. I still have business to take care of in Vegas."

"I can do that," Gary offered.

"You already have your assignment," Steel reminded him. "You'll receive more details when you reach the safehouse, but I want to emphasize that we need the FBI agent alive and functional. Do not break any of her bones."

Gary looked like he might argue that the incident referred to was only once and the instructions weren't clear. Instead, he grunted and left.

When the sound of the closing door faded, silence settled into place. Steel looked around the bare, lifeless hotel room and frowned. If he hadn't gone to a lot of trouble to arrange the next meeting, he would leave and happily forget this place.

Flipping TV channels to confirm nothing good was playing killed five minutes. Since Steel had at least another hour until his contact would arrive, he decided to get some work done. Digging out his notebook, Steel flipped back a few pages and re-read the notes to jog his memory. Most of the new generation would scoff at that, but the act of putting thoughts on paper helped him process. He liked to review facts before launching big endeavors.

Some people worried he would lose the notebook, but not Steel. He'd die of old age before anybody cracked his personal code.

The Hero Contest should work much like the Popularity Contest with a few added incentives and complications. Once again, only four teams would be allowed to participate, but this time the handlers had a bigger role. Only qualified teams who successfully acquired a champion would earn a spot in the game. As the House Team, Gary's crew should get a few extra hours to prepare. The others would receive the list of possible targets at 5:00 a.m. Eastern Standard Time.

Many Dark Web forum threads had generated a list of people in four different categories: Law Enforcement, Soldier, Firefighter, and Emergency Services. If Gary's mission proved successful, the FBI agent would fulfill the law enforcement slot.

Gamblers had already placed bets on the candidates they thought would become champion of each category. Limiting the number of champions to four automatically meant the House would reap a tidy profit on the selection round. If two people in the same category got snatched, there would be a tiebreaker round. Steel hoped for at least one tiebreaker. If one didn't happen naturally, he'd have a security team find a last-minute entry. The beautiful thing about being the House in a Cyber League event was the ability to make, break, and modify rules as needed.

Choosing a champion candidate was no easy feat. The person had to have a good reputation at their job. He or she also had to have family, close friends, or a significant other to threaten. Ideally, the collateral control and the candidate would be acquired at the same time, but if the teams didn't plan things right, two incidents would have to be arranged.

Assuming the game launched, the champions needed tasks to do. Having to rescue the hostage was a given, but that could not be the first task. Such a predictable move would bore the gamblers. They needed to be constantly impressed.

Steel scanned his notes for possible events. Most of the early task ideas would be more suited for Bloody Bingo or the Scavenger Hunt, but those wouldn't work with hero types. It might be interesting to see how far the heroes could be pushed, but they should start out on a lighter note.

"Have them rescue something. Not the control, but something," O suggested.

His voice startled Steel since he usually never got involved at this stage.

"Do you have any suggestions?" Steel wondered.

"A baby."

At first, Steel couldn't fathom why O would choose that target, but the many reasons slowly came to him. Acquiring the target should be relatively simple. Even during cold weather, cooped up mothers often took their infants on strolls through cities and parks. Besides, the work of cleanly snatching the babies could be a separate assignment. The team didn't even have to keep the kid, just stash them well in a specific location: a church, a cemetery, a school, and a bank. Random drawing could then determine which of the other three babies their champion had to find based on a few clues. The media attention would stoke the betting fervor. Law enforcement would be frantic.

"Babies don't fight back," said O.

Steel understood the implication. Even with somebody to control the hero, he or she would constantly search for a way to sabotage the game. If a champion rebelled, the entire team would face the

Tribunal. The thought worried Steel because the agent didn't have high marks for projected levels of compliance. He fought off the instinct to phone the House Team and send them after somebody more predictable. Most of the Emergency Services candidates had high compliance scores.

A knock interrupted Steel's thoughts.

A time check said the contact was early.

Rushing to the door, Steel stepped to the side and prepared to open it a crack to confront his visitor.

"I know exactly where you're standing and that you have a gun. I can tell you the model number if you'd like, but if you want this deal, open the door."

Cautiously, Steel removed the security latch and opened the door wide enough to shove a gun in the man's face.

"Who are you?" Steel demanded. "I was expecting somebody else."

"Call me Bob," said the man. He seemed unfazed by the presence of a gun hovering near his face. "I hear you're in the market for Eagle Eyes."

"That ship has sailed," Steel replied.

"That would be a pity," said the man, who was obviously not named Bob. "My employer is still working on getting another few units. Meanwhile, I'm here to change your mind."

"What's to prevent me from killing you and—"

Steel stopped speaking when he found his own gun leveled at his gut.

"I'm good at what I do," said the man mildly. Flipping the gun around, he offered it back to Steel. "And once you see what this product can do, I guarantee you'll want more than one."

"All right, but I don't deal with unknown people," said Steel, holding out his right hand for a shake. "What should I call you? A working alias is fine, but you don't look like a Bob."

"Curtis D'Angelo. Freelancer," said the man, accepting the handshake. "May I come in?"

Chapter 1:
Food and Family

The drive from the creepy house in the Pennsylvania woods back to Tara's apartment in Fairfax, Virginia should have taken about six hours. Megan Luchek made it in a little over four hours by breaking every speed limit along the way. She did so safely by using Eagle Eyes to monitor and divert patrol officers as necessary.

Once upon a time, the misuse of Jeffrey Gatton's powerful computer would have bothered her. However, she needed to end this nightmare as quickly as possible for the sake of her entire family.

Less than forty-eight hours earlier everything had been fine. Megan's first day back from a very eventful vacation was the epitome of normal. Her boss had handed her a new case, and next day she had attended an assembly for some at-risk youth. Then, life threw her multiple curveballs, including learning of her sister's kidnapping and almost suffering the same fate. Freeing her sister and the other hostages had taken a lot of effort.

Thoughts of the others prompted Megan to simultaneously wish them well and good riddance. The first hour of the drive had been miserable. The social studies teacher had complained non-stop. The young waiter had alternated sulking and whining, and the doctor had threatened to sue Megan several times for one of the rough patches involved in the rescue. Dumping the lot of them on the outskirts of a tiny town had been the best decision Megan made all night. She felt bad about making them walk a few miles or hitchhike to the police station, but she wanted no part of talking to cops until she reached her destination.

During the drive, Megan insisted Tara and Vinny sleep, but her sister only took a short nap. They had spent the remaining time catching up, comparing stories, and talking with most of their relatives via Eagle Eyes, which Megan explained in only the vaguest of terms. She had considered not sharing anything, but that would only have caused Tara to pry, something she excelled at.

The only things they hadn't shared with the family were Tara's pregnancy and Vinny's presence. Tara deserved to give the news to everybody in person, and Vinny's role in the kidnapping was a huge unresolved issue. After several attempts to get him to open up, Megan and Tara had decided to delay the interrogation until they had backup, namely their mother and Aunt Silvia.

Pulling up in front of Tara's apartment, Megan put on the flashers and parked so her sister and cousin could disembark.

"There's usually good parking around the corner two blocks up," said Tara. "Thanks for everything. I'll see you in a few minutes."

"I need to make a few phone calls first," Megan said. "Tell the folks I'm coming."

"Don't be long," said Tara. "They need to see you too."

"You're the one officially missing," Megan pointed out. She made a shooing motion. "Be gone."

"Let's go, Vinny," Tara ordered.

"Coming," he mumbled, hopping out of the van.

As predicted, Megan found several metered parking spots a few blocks up from her sister's apartment. Choosing one near a fire hydrant so she'd have some leeway, Megan guided the stolen behemoth into the space. Lacking a quarter to pay the meter, Megan wondered if she'd get a ticket before rational thought caught up.

The van being stolen is a bigger concern.

Most of her wanted to hit the recline button and nap for a few days, but she needed to update the local law enforcement officers. Depending on how efficient the other police department was at debriefing the liberated captives, the Fairfax police may be looking for the van. Her boss and Daniel Cooper also deserved calls.

The first call went surprisingly well. The desk sergeant informed her officers would stop by soon to collect the van. Megan gave them her sister's address and told them she would wait there. The policeman initially questioned her on leaving the van but backtracked when reminded of the circumstances. Megan's family needed to see her in person very soon for everybody's peace of mind.

Bolstered by the success, she locked up the van and ran toward her sister's apartment. Nobody else was stirring at this hour. Finding the solitude peaceful, Megan might have slowed her pace if she wasn't so cold. The light suit jacket had been perfectly fine for February temperatures in Hawaii. It was not up to the rigors of East Coast winter weather.

Since Hawaii's time was five hours behind Eastern Standard Time, Megan assumed her boss would still be awake. She put the call through once somebody buzzed her into the front entrance to the apartment complex.

Special Agent in Charge Bryan Maddox accepted in record time, telling Megan he had probably been waiting for the call all evening. That stuck her with a needle of guilt.

"Luchek? That better be you confirming you're alive," said her boss.

"It's me, sir," Megan assured him. "I'm alive, and I found my sister. She's safe."

"Glad to hear it," said Maddox. "That's all I need now. Given the hour here, you must be exhausted. A full report can wait until business hours. Spend some time with your family and get some sleep. We can discuss your return later."

Megan barely had time to thank him before the call ended. Next, she dialed Dan Cooper's number.

"You're alive! Oh, thank goodness!" shouted Bethany Cooper.

Beth's volume caused Megan to flinch, even though there was no chance of being overheard.

Eagle Eyes adjusted the volume accordingly.

The sound quality from Beth's side told Megan the phone was set to speaker mode.

"Daniel! It's Megan!"

"It's great to hear from you," said Dan, sounding slightly winded.

"Why does everybody sound so surprised?" asked Megan, wondering if she should feel insulted.

"It's not surprise. It's relief." Dan's voice hitched. "Ya scared us. We didn't know if we'd ever hear from ya again."

"Sorry," said Megan, leaning heavily against the wall for support. "It's not like I try to find these situations."

"You've got nothing to apologize for," Beth said fiercely. "Did you find your sister?"

"I did. She was being held in a house in northwest Pennsylvania," said Megan. "I got her and three other people out, but I couldn't make any arrests."

She consciously omitted freeing Lillian Marquez. That woman had yet to truly pick a side.

"Saving lives matters most," said Beth. "Everything else will sort itself in time."

"Will you stay for the investigation?" Dan's voice sounded stronger.

"If Maddox lets me," Megan answered.

"He will," Dan said.

His confidence piqued Megan's curiosity.

"Did something happen that I should know?" she asked.

"Not sure, but Zeller's call kicked up a mess of activity this afternoon," said Dan. "Since he was with you, I'm guessing it's something to do with your sister's case."

"I'll tell you about it later," Megan promised. "I've got to get up to Tara's apartment before my mother organizes a new search party."

The farewell exchange took place as Megan trudged up the four flights of creaky stairs.

They have got to upgrade soon.

A fourth-floor walkup in a bustling little city had seemed the perfect place for a young newlywed couple. It let them save money and exercise at the same time. Six years later, the charm had worn off.

As her feet touched the top landing, Megan heard the drone of voices and high-pitched, yappy contributions from Charles. The noise conjured an image of the impish Maltese. Megan had always thought Tara and Jason would be better suited for a large dog, but she admitted that the tiny white furball was cute.

Enjoying a last few seconds of calm, Megan knocked twice and rang the doorbell.

The door whipped open so hard it slammed against the wall.

Her mother—Susanne—tackled her with a hug that cut off her ability to breathe.

"Grazie! Grazie!"

Megan lost track of the number of times her mother thanked her. The rest of her mother's words—a stream of Italian and English— were lost in sobs and drowned out by dozens of questions from other family members.

"Let her in!" Her father's exasperated cry barely reached Megan, but it opened a hole in the crowd of relatives.

Soon, Megan and her mother were joined by her father. For a sweet moment, Megan blocked out everything else and enjoyed feeling like a kid again, safe in her parents' arms. When the group hug finally ended, Megan let the family current wash her into the living room where she found more people.

The volley of questions and comments resumed.

A whirlwind tour of greetings ensued. Most of the greetings were heartfelt but brief until she reached her brother-in-law. Jason gave her a rib-crushing embrace and whispered his thanks before returning to Tara on the couch.

Great Aunt Celia presided over the controlled chaos from the large leather recliner. Charles expertly wove in and out of people's legs, leaping over limbs as necessary. The entire room buzzed with chatter from aunts, uncles, cousins, and their significant others. Cousin Davy held his infant daughter, but other than that, the room mysteriously lacked children.

Cousin Vinny stood sullenly in the corner. For now, Megan was content to let him continue sulking. That discussion would likely be best without such a large audience.

Mom's sisters—Aunt Sophie and Aunt Silvia—argued with each other over what Megan should do next. Aunt Sophie said she should shower and sleep, and Aunt Silvia insisted she eat something first. The delicious scents filling the whole apartment caused Megan to favor Aunt Silvia's plan. A peek into the tiny kitchen confirmed that a feast awaited.

Grabbing a plate, her father gathered giant helpings of her favorites. She could have collected the food herself, but she also understood his need to do something for her. A stool was cleared so she'd have a place to sit.

After accepting the plate of spaghetti Bolognese and balsamic glazed salmon separated by a thick piece of bread, Megan set it on the stool and gave her father a proper hug.

He didn't say anything, but his return hug conveyed his worry, relief, and gratitude many times over. Andrew Luchek wasn't known for displaying his emotions, but Megan noticed that he didn't attempt to hide the tears in his eyes.

She wanted to reassure him, but every comforting phrase that popped into mind felt hollow. Squeezing his hand, Megan let a sad smile communicate her mixed emotions. Although pleased to see her family, the circumstances were far from ideal. Finding Tara without arresting the guilty parties meant the danger lingered, but what could she do?

Instinct told her to stick near Tara, but she couldn't always safeguard her sister. Eventually, she would fly back to Hawaii and resume the life she'd built there.

Before she could start eating, a knock announced the arrival of police officers. Since the apartment couldn't bear more people, Megan guided the officers down to the third-floor landing and gave them a brief statement and a promise to stop by the station later to give a longer statement. She also handed over the keys to the big, ugly van she'd commandeered to transport the freed captives.

Once finished with her interview, Megan pried her sister away from Jason long enough for her to speak with the officers. By this time, Megan felt faint with hunger, but she wasn't quite ready to let Tara out of her sight. When they finally returned to the apartment, Megan dashed back to her abandoned meal.

Knowing people would disperse soon, Megan dispatched her father to tell Aunt Silvia and Cousin Vinny to stick around. He gave her a quizzical look but did as bid.

As Megan finished the oddly timed meal, much of the extended family had left. Even Charles settled down. Freshly showered and robed, Tara leaned back against her husband, cradling the dog.

The sight reminded Megan of her sister's pregnancy. She quirked an eyebrow at her to ask if she was going to say something.

Nodding, Tara stood and gathered everybody's attention to deliver the news.

Even with a quarter of the previous crowd, silence took a while to achieve.

"I know you didn't come here for this news, but thanks to Megan, I get to make an important announcement," said Tara. She looked fondly at her husband before continuing. "Jason and I are going to be parents."

The news sparked a storm of words as everybody rushed to offer their congratulations, give unsolicited advice, and fuss over the couple.

Taking advantage of the distraction, Megan dumped the paper plate in the garbage, dropped the silverware in the sink, stole a towel from the closet, raided Jason's stash of sleepwear, and slipped into the bathroom for a much-needed shower.

When Megan emerged from the bathroom, she found the entire apartment changed. It looked like a scene from a hurricane shelter. The couch had been transformed into a bed. An air mattress had been stuffed into the short hallway by the door. Two sleeping bags had been pressed into service as bedding. One lay across the recliner. The other was piled in a heap near a beanbag chair.

"That one's yours," said Tara, pointing to the only free sleeping bag. She sounded apologetic. "Put it on the beanbag chair. It's surprisingly comfy."

Megan grunted and suppressed the urge to ask why Cousin Vinny got the air mattress. At this point, she could sleep on a cement floor with ease. Her parents had claimed the pullout couch, and Aunt Silvia occupied the sleeping bag on the recliner.

"Should we wake them?" Megan asked.

At some point, they'd have to squeeze the whole story out of Vinny.

Tara shook her head.

"Get some sleep," she said. "When everybody wakes up naturally, I'll send Jason and Dad to fetch breakfast. That will give us enough time to shake Vinny's story out of him."

Agreeing to the plan, Megan collapsed onto the beanbag chair and used the sleeping bag as a blanket. Since Tara favored silky pajamas and nightgowns, Megan had borrowed a baggy sweatshirt and fuzzy pants from her brother-in-law. Still warm from the shower, Megan slipped into a comfortable sleep before her sister turned off the lights.

Chapter 2:
Priority Order

Since starting Gatton Technologies as a young teenager, Jeffrey Gatton had invented some amazing things, rubbed shoulders with the world's elite, employed thousands, and made billions. The journey had taken him through several highs and lows, but he'd never felt such extremes of disgust, helplessness, fear, and rage. People had certainly tried to steal from him before, but never like this.

He couldn't even think of a proper curse to capture the situation.

Six units of Eagle Eyes were gone.

The entire stock of prototypes in the Kansas black site had been checked out. The only person besides Jeff who had the clearance to do so was his CIA handler. A thorough sweep of the security showed a man walking in with nothing and leaving with the case of prototypes. If the removal had any legitimacy, Jeff would have received a call by now.

As the thought crossed his mind, his black phone rang.

Jeff couldn't answer fast enough.

"What are you doing?" he demanded.

"Good evening, Jeffrey," said the CIA man. "I need the activation codes for certain Eagle Eyes prototypes. The ones from Kansas. You should have the model numbers, but I'll text them to you anyway. Your mother sends her love."

"Prove it," Jeff said tightly.

"She's sleeping right now, but I'll send you a picture momentarily," said the man casually. "Give me the codes."

"I don't have them memorized," Jeff protested. "I'll have to look them up."

"I can wait," said the man.

"I put them in a vault somewhere," said Jeff. "It'll take me a while to get them."

"One hour," said the man after a lengthy silence. "Or your—"

"You'll have them," Jeff promised, interrupting the man's threat. "Then, I want my mother delivered to my apartment in Houston."

"I'll think about it." The CIA man ended the call.

The Houston apartment, like every one of Jeff's places, offered top-notch security, but that wasn't the reason he wanted her taken there. If he could arrange things right, he might be able to get her swept off to a remote farm with a trusted bodyguard or two.

Finding the codes the man wanted as a ransom took three minutes, but Jeff needed the rest of the time to prepare a unique patch for each access code. The modification would trigger an update once each prototype dumped data onto the main Eagle Eyes cloud server. The update should insert some exploitable vulnerabilities, which would, in turn, give Jeff greater access to the prototypes. Jeff couldn't believe he was working so hard to sabotage one of his best inventions, but it beat letting the CIA rogue hand them over to the highest bidder.

When he finished his coding sprint, Jeff duplicated the work and tucked everything in place. He should be notified once his plan started to unfold. He would have to prepare a more robust viral attack later if he wanted to completely cripple the prototypes, but the units represented many months of work for his company. For now, he wanted to entertain the notion of recovery being possible. Next, he dug out one of Cassandra Mirren's phones and pulled up the single contact.

It took her three full rings to answer.

"Go ahead, Gatton," said Cassandra.

"He has Eagle Eyes and my mother!" Jeff shouted.

"I assume you mean the CIA thorn-in-your-side," said the assassin. "Do you know where he's keeping her?"

"No, but I can find out," Jeff said rapidly. "It doesn't matter. I'm giving him the access codes to unlock the six prototypes' full potential. He should free her once he has those."

"Not if he expects a clean getaway," replied the assassin. "Find out where he took her."

"You need to get the prototypes back," said Jeff. His heart pounded, making his head hurt. He couldn't believe the words coming out of his mouth. If the assassin accepted them, he could be dooming his mother. "I've … taken some steps to slow the prototypes, but Eagle Eyes was designed to defend itself. It can't get into the wrong hands. It's too powerful!"

"I'm aware, Gatton," Cassandra said. "Get me the addresses and details. I'll call in some favors. See if the agent can help."

"She might be … busy," Jeff said uncomfortably. One way or the other, he would have been calling Cassandra. His research into the Club's connection to the Cyber League had yielded some disturbing revelations.

"They're still after her," Cassandra concluded, correctly interpreting his hesitation. "Did you pass on the warning?"

"There wasn't time!" Jeff shouted. "I discovered the missing prototypes, wrote a patch to make them trackable and limit their uses, and called you. She doesn't even have her cell phone, and Eagle Eyes calls won't work if she's sleeping."

"Leave a message for her," said the assassin. "Then, get me the rest of that information. I also want everything you have on the threat against the agent."

"One of the forums is buzzing with chatter about a new contest," said Jeff. "It's something about heroes. When I asked Eagle Eyes to compile a list of people they might target, Megan came out near the top. That's all I've got."

"Is this like their last venture?" asked Cassandra. "Kidnapping, gambling, and so forth?"

"From what I've read, yes, exactly like the Popularity Contest," said Jeff. "That fell apart a few hours ago. The payouts came through maybe an hour after you dropped off the agent. I'm assuming she's responsible for that."

"Keep searching for details," said Cassandra. "If we can stop this new threat, we do so. If we can't, we start moving pieces to get her back."

Hearing the line disconnect, Jeff dropped the phone and reached for his keyboard.

***

How many lives do you have, agent?

Cassandra Mirren contemplated the new threats and problems in priority order from highest to lowest: Gatton's mother, the rogue CIA man, the prototypes, and the FBI agent. Though she would do everything in her power to send the agent a timely warning, real help would have to wait. To start, Cassandra tasked Eagle Eyes with preparing a list of phone contacts for Megan's immediate and extended family. Somebody would know how to reach the agent.

Freeing Gatton's mother topped Cassandra's to-do list because she needed the young tech genius thinking clearly throughout the rest of their mission to sever the ties holding them to the United States government.

For several weeks, her goal had been to secure a quiet retirement. Events in Dallas had convinced her that wouldn't happen until certain CIA staffers ceased sending former colleagues to kill her. Eagle Eyes could eventually access the information she needed, and nobody knew the computer gadget better than its inventor and lead programmer.

The rogue CIA man had to be identified and neutralized. Gatton would have to handle those searches, since they would certainly be more complicated than her surface queries about phone numbers for the agent's family. Normally, *reasoned with* would also be an option, but the CIA man's actions had revealed his moral flaws. In Cassandra's experience, people whose first instincts involved taking a hostage rarely negotiated well.

With Lia in California and Owen Ramsey in Florida, Cassandra figured she could address two of the issues from afar. Responsibility for retrieving and safeguarding Gatton's mother would go to whoever was closest once the location came through. She usually handled extractions herself due to their tricky nature, but she trusted Lia and Owen more than anybody else, except maybe her former master and the agent. She wouldn't know the first place to begin finding Smith and contacting the agent might be a more daunting task than anticipated, given the size of the growing contacts list.

What else should be outsourced?

Since the CIA man presented the largest threat, Cassandra wanted to personally handle the job, but honesty forced her to admit that Owen had more experience as a tracker. He'd spent some time chasing her before they had sorted the details of being on the same side. Early in her career, the various shady government organizations didn't communicate well. Somehow, the Shadow Council had decided a certain Saudi businessman needed to die to cut off a terrorist cell's funding about the same time the CIA drew the same conclusion.

Cassandra and Owen had nearly killed each other finishing that job. Over the years, they had cautiously passed each other helpful information. The mutually beneficial arrangement eventually became a friendship.

Have all my friends started as enemies?

Since the list of trusted friends started with Owen and ended with Megan, the answer was yes. Lia hadn't, but the Shadow Council's master-apprentice system hardly counted.

I still owe Owen a solid answer.

He wanted to turn their friendship into something much deeper. She had tentatively agreed, but the recent threats had kept her too busy to consider anything except survival. Retiring with somebody would be nice, but Cassandra struggled to picture a life of domestic bliss.

What would I do?

Sighing, she admitted a peaceful and calm existence might as easily be the death of her. Owen's suggestion of joining the CIA proper didn't hold much appeal considering the current job of dealing with a rogue from within those ranks. With effort, Cassandra focused her thoughts.

Owen can track the CIA ghost. Lia can find Gatton's mother.

Guilt welled up at having to call her apprentice into the field again so soon after letting her take some time off to be with family.

That leaves the prototypes for me.

She'd have to work fast. If the CIA man sold the Eagle Eyes units to different bidders, retrieving them would become many times harder.

The list of people connected to the agent was still growing slowly, but the strength of those connections waned. Starting at the top, Cassandra tried the first one.

Nobody answered.

Given the late hour on the East Coast, where most numbers originated, that wasn't surprising. Cassandra also worked from a blocked number, which people usually ignored unless they expected a call from her. When the first offer to leave a message surfaced, Cassandra ended the call without saying anything. Passing on a cryptic, second-hand threat to the agent would be bad enough without involving a third party's voicemail.

When the ninth call ended fruitlessly, Cassandra found the login credentials for cyberleaguesports.com. She had purchased the pricey access with Gatton's money on his behalf so they could better understand their opponents. The FBI had contracted Gatton Technologies to form and work with a task force meant to deal with the growing Dark Web problems. To her knowledge, the task force hadn't even met as a whole entity yet.

On her own, breaking into the Dark Web would have been difficult, but Eagle Eyes came equipped with a hacking tool good enough to create an opening to slip into the first ring. Gatton had babbled a long time about the various levels of the Dark Web. Cassandra had only half-listened to the details after he told her she wouldn't have to do any hacking to get in.

The High Roller status brought her past the low-end gambling options and gave her access to exclusive pages. A tour showed her that most pages were incomplete but confirmed Gatton's earlier summary. The new game revolved around heroes.

Cassandra read the main points outlined on the contest's summary page.

- Heroes make life-altering decisions every day, but who's the best of the best?
- High Rollers get to choose which situations to present to our brave volunteers.
- Get rich making predictions.
- Sponsor a hero and improve your overall chances of winning the grand prize.
- Losers perish in shame. Winners get a hero's send-off. Join the Tribunal today and decide their fate.
- Have you ever wanted to hold the power of life and death in your hands? New and exclusive to this contest: Select Tribunal members can purchase the Ultimate Power Package. Come join us on the set and participate. **Warning**: Vetting process required. Not all applicants may qualify. Must be in good physical health and willing to sign multiple waivers.

The last note caught Cassandra's attention. She should probably consult with Gatton before doing anything rash, but she couldn't let an opportunity like this slip by. Without hesitation, she applied to see the set and participate in the potential murders.

Whether the organizers chose to harass the agent or not, clearly at least four people were due for a bad day. If Gatton had set up the backstory for Moira Jethro well enough, Cassandra stood a good chance of gaining an invite to participate. She would love to have an exclusive chat with the sick minds conjuring these contests.

A search through the popular polls thread of the forum brought her to one that confirmed her fears.

Law Enforcement Candidates:

- Female FBI Agent – 39%
- Female Police Officer – 25%

- Male FBI Agent – 18%
- Male Police Officer – 8%
- Male Security Officer – 7%
- Female Security Officer – 3%

Hovering over the line for female FBI agent brought up an old photograph of Megan. Cassandra looked at the pictures of the others but didn't recognize any other face.

Agent, you better have a few spare lives left because even if I can warn you, I can't stop what's coming.

Chapter 3:
Vinny's Problem

Tara's plan unfolded beautifully. Jason and Dad didn't want to leave, but Tara insisted they get biscotti and breakfast pastries from her favorite bakery, which happened to be a fifteen-minute drive away. As soon as the door closed behind them, Megan changed back into her suit, rearmed, and helped her mother right the living room furniture while Aunt Silvia made coffee. Upon receiving Tara's signal, Megan grabbed Cousin Vinny from the bathroom where he was brushing his teeth.

It's a good thing Tara stocks toothbrushes like a hoarder.

Megan made a gesture that told her cousin to finish his teeth scrubbing quickly.

Vinny Carbonelli spit one more time and wiped his mouth on his sleeve.

"You waited this long, what's the rush?" he asked.

"Dad and Jason just left," said Megan. "It'll be better for everybody if we have this discussion without them."

Vinny reluctantly followed Megan into the living room where Tara had already herded Aunt Silvia and their mother.

"What are you girls up to?" asked Mom. She gave them each a measuring look.

The likely target to spill a story had changed over the years. Their mother had a knack about sensing who to question first. Megan and Tara exchanged a glance to decide who would open the interrogation, but their mother beat them to it.

"What did you do?" she asked. Her eyes drilled a hole through Cousin Vinny.

"Nothing! I—"

"Sit down," Tara ordered, cutting off Vinny's protest. She pointed to a kitchen stool she'd moved into the room for the purpose.

"How did you end up in the same house Tara was taken to?" Megan asked, aware they had a time limit for the question-and-answer session.

Aunt Silvia looked ready to cry. Reaching out, she clasped hands with Megan's mother.

"Start at the beginning," Tara prompted.

Megan had forgotten that before finding her true passion in family law and becoming a judge, her sister had done a short stint as a prosecutor.

"I played a few games online," said Vinny, shifting uncomfortably on the stool. "One thing led to another, and before I knew it, I owed the company $60,000."

"What company?" Megan fired the question but suspected she'd only narrowly beaten Tara to it. Her mind tried to wrap itself around the gambling debt.

"Cyber League Sports," said Vinny. "It's only on the Dark Web for now."

"Vincent." Aunt Silvia filled the name with sorrow and disappointment. "Why?"

"Why can wait," Megan said, keeping her gaze locked on her cousin. "I assume they offered to let you work off the debt. Tell us about the website."

"It's a gambling site," said Vinny. He shrugged helplessly. "That's all I know. I wasn't there long. They had me code some pages for a few events. I moved around to a couple different houses, but it's not like they showed me the inner workings of the organization. I figured out it had mob connections and stopped asking questions."

"How did you end up as a prisoner instead of an employee?" Megan asked.

"One of my jobs was to prepare a list of people to avoid," said Vinny. His expression turned indignant. "Somebody else had already started the list, but I made a program to expand it. I made sure you and Tara were on that list. When I learned a team went after her, I confronted Gary. He had security guys jump me later."

"Is he in danger?" asked Aunt Silvia, looking to Megan for an answer.

"Probably," Megan admitted. Ignoring a razor-sharp look from her mother, she turned back to her cousin. "Do you have a safe place you can go for a few weeks?"

"Not really," said Vinny with another shrug.

Tamping down the urge to shake her cousin, Megan hosted an internal debate about the wisdom of giving him money. Giving a gambler cash was the fastest way to get him to dig deeper into debt. On the other hand, his former overseers wouldn't want him running around ready to testify. He might claim to know little, but Megan guessed that a long sit-down chat with a detective who knew computers would be very fruitful.

"Let me see what cash I have," said Tara, stepping toward her bedroom.

Megan held up a hand to stop her and withdrew the wad of cash she'd borrowed from Cassandra Mirren.

Vinny's eyes lit up with interest when he saw the money.

"Where did you get that?" asked Tara.

"Borrowed it from a friend," said Megan. The thought of Cassandra set a wave of worry loose in her. She acknowledged its existence then shoved the feeling aside.

Worry can wait. Bigger fish to fry.

Coming to a decision, Megan crossed over to the couch, knelt, and folded the cash into her aunt's hands.

"Aunt Silvia, I need you to listen carefully. There's a small but very real chance Vinny's employer comes after him," Megan explained. She spoke slowly, trying to penetrate the shock surrounding her aunt. "I need you to do three things for me. One, take Vinny to the police station and have him give a statement. Two, buy a pre-paid cell phone and program it with my number and only my number. I don't have my phone on me today, but I should be able to get it by tomorrow. Three, get him checked in at a cheap motel under a false name. Pay for everything in cash."

She made a mental note to call the Lincoln Airport about getting her purse back. It had been a victim of yesterday's craziness.

"Is this necessary, Maggie?" asked her mother. "You're scaring her."

"Why not give me the money?" asked Vinny. "I'm not a child. I can do those things."

A series of loud knocks prevented Megan from answering. Leaping to her feet, she shot her sister a questioning look.

Could they be back already?

Color drained from Tara's face, but she stiffly shook her head negative.

"Lock him in the bedroom with Charles," Megan ordered her sister.

They had exiled the dog to make sure the interrogation ran smoothly.

Vinny started to protest, but a fierce look from Aunt Silvia knocked the fight out of him.

Cautiously approaching the door, Megan drew her gun.

The door burst open and slammed against the wall.

Megan threw her body left to minimize the chance of being shot while she processed friend from foe. Recognizing the first man as her brother-in-law, she changed her aim.

Her eyes absorbed details before she had time to think about them. Jason raced straight past her to Tara who was returning from the hallway leading to the bathroom and bedroom. Megan's father rushed over to her mother. Aunt Silvia clutched her chest and breathed rapidly.

Another man charged Megan and shoved her hard into the wall. Her gun fell and skidded toward the kitchen. Twisting before he could pin her in place, Megan brought the heel of her hand up hard under the man's chin, snapping his head back. Seizing the freedom, she dove for her gun, scooped it up, and scrambled to stand.

Activating Eagle Eyes didn't help. It only bombarded her with late messages warning her of danger and confirmed the sinking feeling in her gut. Overwhelmed, she shut most of the displays down.

The man who had pushed her into a wall drew a gun and stepped away from her, but she ignored him in favor of aiming at the last man to enter.

Gary gave her a friendly wave as he stepped in and closed the door gently.

Megan backed up into the corner so she could get a better perspective.

The other two assailants had taken full advantage of Megan's momentary fixation on Gary. One had pulled Megan's mother off the couch and maneuvered her into the center of the room. The other man did the same to Tara. Jason, Megan's father, and Aunt Silvia sat unmoving on the couch. Their expressions reflected the abject horror coursing through Megan.

In a coordinated move, the men turned the hostages to face Megan and pushed them down to their knees. They huddled together, locked in an embrace, quietly weeping.

"Put the gun down. You're not going to shoot me," said Gary. "That would get everybody killed."

"Don't tempt me." Fueled by anger, Megan's voice was surprisingly strong.

Gary shot her an impatient look.

"Come on," he whined. "You know how this is supposed to work. Drop the gun and they get to live."

"Negotiations take trust, Gary," said Megan, "and—news flash—I don't trust you. If you want a private chat, call off your goons, and we can discuss things outside. I'll even leave my gun behind."

Touching his chin thoughtfully, Gary hummed and pretended to consider the proposal.

"How about I shoot that lady to prove my point?" Drawing a handgun, Gary pointed it at Aunt Silvia.

Several people shouted at once.

Megan's father wrapped his arms around her aunt and glared at Gary.

"Fine. Give us your speech. Then, get out," said Megan. Straightening out of the shooter's stance, she let the gun drop to the carpet.

Gary paused dramatically before nodding to the men.

"Better," he commented. "Please hold still for this next part."

Both enforcer types stepped away from her mother and sister. The one man kept his gun aimed at them while the other holstered his weapon and took out a plastic zip tie.

Fending off the instinct to fight, Megan stood still while the man she'd struck earlier bound her wrists tightly in front of her. The choice surprised her. If she intended to renew the fight, having her hands in front presented many options.

"Why are we still here?" asked Megan. "There are much easier ways to kidnap people."

"You're a hero," Gary announced.

Megan didn't know how to respond to that.

"Heroes have to make hard decisions," he continued, waving to her mother and sister. "Choose."

Alarm stabbed her multiple times in the gut.

"What am I choosing?" Megan barely had breath for the question.

"One of these lovely ladies is going to come with us," said Gary.

"Me. Take me!" said Megan's mother. Dashing away tears, she tried to disengage from Tara.

Megan nodded numbly.

"Is that your choice?" Gary asked. "I need to hear you say it."

Tara locked eyes with Megan and shook her head. The message was clearly along the lines of: *Don't you dare.*

"Tara," Megan said softly, dropping her gaze. She couldn't bear to look at either of them.

"Maggie, no!" cried her mother.

Something hard struck Megan's head, knocking her onto her side.

Several people screamed.

Her father and Jason leapt up but stopped when Gary lowered his gun to Megan's head.

Once certain he had their cooperation again, Gary knelt, rolled Megan onto her back, and moved the gun into her line of vision.

"Sometimes hard decisions matter and sometimes they don't," Gary said. "Fortunately, your choice matches the poll today. Your sister will indeed be coming with us."

"You don't need her," said Megan. "I'll go with you."

"Didn't you just hear me?" Gary scolded. "The poll says she's coming. We're leaving soon. I need you to say a quick goodbye to your family and—"

"I called the cops!" Vinny's announcement cut off Gary's instructions. He had Megan's gun in his shaking hands.

The smile that formed on Gary's lips frightened Megan.

Twisting her head around, Megan saw her cousin framed in the doorway.

Perfect target.

As Gary lifted his gun toward Vinny, Megan rotated her right wrist so that her hands faced each other. Clasping her hands together, she slammed them into Gary's arms just as he fired.

Chapter 4:
The Nightmare Resumes

The bullet slammed into the wall next to the kitchen doorway. The gun flew out of Gary's hand, bounced off the wall, and landed a couple of feet from Megan's head.

Vinny dropped into a crouch, barely holding onto Megan's gun.

Surprise flipped to murderous rage in Gary's eyes. His hands closed around Megan's throat and started squeezing.

The sudden pressure caused flashes of light to burst behind her eyelids. She managed to catch his wrists and squeeze, but her strength declined rapidly as the lack of oxygen weakened her.

The pressure ceased as suddenly as it began.

Megan drew deep, gasping breaths and watched as the man who had shoved her into a wall earlier whacked Gary hard across the shoulders.

"No," said the man. His sharp tone made it sound like he was scolding a dog. "Stick to the plan."

Gary spun to face the man.

The prone position made Megan feel extremely vulnerable, so she sat up and scooted back. The situation hadn't improved much, but she wasn't dead yet. The move put her in range of Gary's gun.

Before she could roll to recover the weapon, Gary bellowed in frustration, whirled again, and kicked the gun. It skipped across the floor into the kitchen.

The goon grabbed Gary by the shoulders and held him back.

"Drop the gun," ordered the other attacker, speaking to Vinny.

Please, do it.

Having Vinny armed wasn't much of an improvement. His stance didn't inspire much confidence that he'd ever held a gun before, and if he fired, his shaking arms were as likely to direct the bullet into a family member as into an attacker.

Multiple people shouted conflicting statements. Without the guns, Megan might have believed it a typical family meeting.

Another gun went off. This bullet hit the wall above Vinny's head.

The room plunged into silence.

The man who'd fired—the one standing by Tara and Mom—centered his aim on Vinny's chest.

Vinny threw the gun to the ground.

"Get your gun. We're leaving," said the man standing near Gary.

Scowling, Gary marched into the kitchen, presumably to retrieve his weapon.

Moving to Megan, the man hauled her upright and pushed her toward her mother who stood alone in front of the coffee table. Tara had been bound similarly to Megan and pulled off to the side.

"Thirty seconds," called the man who had picked Megan up. He sounded like he'd be counting each second in his head.

Megan stumbled into her mother.

"Don't let this happen, Maggie!" her mother cried, catching hold of her shoulders. "Not like this!" Frustration put some force behind her mother's words. "Don't go!"

The pain and panic reached out and seared Megan. Her bound hands made giving a hug impossible. Drawing her hands close, she reached up and gripped one of her mother's hands.

"We'll be back soon," she promised, fervently hoping it would happen. Her voice sounded wispy and dazed as the calm moment let shock creep in. Clinging to the anger at everything happening to her family, Megan straightened.

Pulling her hand free, Megan's mother hugged her tightly.

"Hey. Do you remember that extreme sports camp I went to when I was fifteen?" asked Megan in a desperate attempt to distract her mother.

She felt her mother's nod.

"You were convinced I'd break my neck and never return, but I did," Megan continued.

Pulling out to arm's length, her mother met her gaze.

"You broke your arm," she said, chuckling even as tears flowed down her face.

"Beside the point," Megan said. "I kept my promise to return, and I'm making a similar promise now. I will bring Tara back from this, I promise."

"Time's up. Step back." The order came from Gary who sounded fully in control this time.

After planting a final kiss on her mother's cheek, Megan leaned back, but the gentle pressure failed to break her mother's hold.

"You have to let go," said Megan.

Her mother shook her head violently and tightened her grip on Megan's shoulders.

A sharp cry from Tara caused Megan to whip her head around, letting her see Gary's gun hovering near her head. The man handling Tara had knocked her down again. He didn't point his gun at her, but he had one in hand and seemed very comfortable with the weapon.

"You can either let them go with us or bury them both," said Gary.

At a gesture from Tara's guard, Megan's father leapt up from the couch, dodged the coffee table, and embraced her mother. Leaning down, he whispered something that brought forth a fresh wave of tears and broke Susanne's hold on Megan.

"Go then." Andrew's shoulders dipped as the words weighed upon him. Then, making eye contact with Megan, he stiffened his stance and spoke in Italian. "Abbi cura di tua sorella e ritornate da noi."

Take care of your sister and come back to us.

The strain of not lashing out made his skin go pale with red patches. Megan had only seen that reaction a few times in her life, and she never wanted to see it again.

As calmly as she could, Megan walked over to her sister and helped her up. She looked at Gary to see how he wanted her to proceed.

"Ladies first," said Gary.

When Megan reached the threshold, another gunshot made her jump.

Screams, shouts, and curses rang out in English and Italian.

Instinctively, Megan turned and sidestepped to block anybody from approaching Tara. The new vantage point let her watch Vinny hit the floor.

"His debt is now the family debt," Gary announced. "With interest, it's now $85,000. Start pooling your money. I'll be in touch in a few days. If you can't deliver the payment, expect the next bullet to be several inches closer to his heart."

The last thing Megan saw before Gary prodded her to step outside the apartment was Aunt Silvia collapsing to the ground beside Vinny, sobbing and leaning across his left shoulder.

"What was that for?" Megan demanded.

Ignoring the question, the three assailants put their weapons away and guided Megan and Tara down the four flights of stairs.

A white van with a random construction company logo sat near the front door in a space kept clear by a fire hydrant. Tara's guard opened the back door and helped her climb in. Gary hopped into the front passenger seat. Megan's guard let her struggle to get in before directing her to sit in the back row.

The interior light came on and the door slammed shut.

Tara's guard had already strapped her in with the seat belt. He held a black cloth hood.

"Drink this." The man hovering near Megan handed her a small cup filled with a clear liquid.

"What is it?" Megan asked, though she could guess.

"Water laced with GHB and a faster sedative," replied the guard.

Is mixing that stuff safe?

Ingesting gamma-hydroxybutyrate and a mystery sedative did not strike Megan as a good idea, but it wasn't a request. Still, she hesitated. Eagle Eyes could probably keep track of their location, but the thought of being drugged to the point of senselessness terrified her. At least while conscious, Megan could pretend she had some control over the situation. To be safe, she set the computer program to start tracking and continue until she manually turned off the feature.

"Don't drink that!" Tara twisted around in the seat and fumbled blindly for the latch to free herself.

The guard with her rolled his eyes and pinned her shoulders in place.

"Stop struggling," he commanded.

"I'm not going to let you drug my little sister!" Tara said hotly, twisting her shoulders to shake off his hold.

"It's the drug or we knock her out some other way," replied the man, pressing harder. "Would you prefer that?"

"Of course not, but what's the point?" Tara asked, ceasing her struggle.

Her guard took advantage of the calm to slip the black hood over her head.

"It's all right," Megan lied. She wanted to argue but didn't see much of a point to fighting free this second. Quickly, before rising resentment made her do something stupid, Megan drank the cup's contents. "It's done."

"Good girl," Gary mocked. "Try to relax. We have a bit of a drive ahead of us. You should be grateful. I got you the good stuff."

Grateful is not the word I had in mind.

"We'll be fine," Megan said, ignoring Gary.

Oddly, the feeling washing over her matched the statement.

The van's engine rumbled, and the vehicle started moving.

"Nothing about this is fine." Tara's frustration rendered the sentence in three distinct clauses. "That's the drug talking."

"It's better than the last drug I was given," Megan said wearily. "So far anyway."

Whatever Curtis D'Angelo had used on her in Dallas came paired with a killer headache.

Somebody reached around Megan and snapped the seat belt buckle into place. Part of her brain tried to raise an alarm at having the guard in her personal space, but a few seconds later, she stopped caring. She just wanted to sleep.

"When were you drugged before?" Tara demanded.

"Vacation," Megan answered.

She missed Tara's reply as a fuzzy black cloud settled over her mind and eased her into an inviting sleep.

***

Upon entering his workroom, Jeffrey Gatton noticed a series of alerts bunching in the bottom right corner of the main screen. Despite the early afternoon hour, he had just woken up. Having a lot of alerts after several hours away from the internet was normal, but he'd asked Eagle Eyes to monitor the current crises. Racing across the room, he dropped into his favorite chair and checked the messages.

The first three alerts merely informed him of the weather conditions, a dental cleaning, and Luciana's two-week vacation. He would have to check the kitchen to see if he had fresh food. The housekeeper usually handled his day-to-day affairs. She even did the hiring and firing of household staff, though that wasn't too difficult since the fulltime staff numbered two: housekeeper and groundskeeper. They'd had some trouble keeping a reliable maintenance manager in recent months, but Gatton didn't care while everything worked properly.

125

The fourth note came from IRA. The Incident Report Analysis program said there was an odd uptick in the number of Amber Alerts in Pennsylvania, specifically in or near the city of Philadelphia. On average ten to fifteen such alarms would go out in a month. Five had happened today. Accessing IRA's full report, Jeff absorbed the details. The missing children ranged in age from four months old to ten months old. Another police report of an attempted kidnapping mentioned a newborn baby.

Are the incidents related?

Jeff guessed they were, but he couldn't begin to guess at why anybody would target infants. He instructed IRA to keep a closer watch on that situation and moved to the next message.

The fifth alert—Mom's birthday is in two days—made his stomach twist. Jeff closed that one immediately. The series of flowers Luciana had ordered on his behalf should be almost fully delivered. The thought of the flowers slowly dying without being seen by his mother sent a surge of anger through him. A few keystrokes told him Eagle Eyes still believed Mom was in Austin, Texas, but he wasn't ready to trust the information. It only indicated that her phone never left her apartment.

Setting a program to access the security cameras in the complex, Jeff considered remotely hacking his mother's phone. He'd put the proper pieces into place ages ago in case something terrible happened, but common sense had prevented him from trying it before. Deciding he'd rather have her alive and livid, Jeff entered the commands to let the hack happen.

The sixth notification showed him that the Eagle Eyes unit currently being used by Megan Luchek had drastically changed locations. Thankfully, she had activated the GPS locator. Pulling up the ping log, Jeff tracked her progress from Fairfax, Virginia, where her sister lived, up to Philadelphia.

100% related, Jeff concluded.

He still didn't know how the bizarre number of Amber Alerts and Megan's move were connected. Jeff paused with his hands poised above his keyboard. If he connected directly to the Eagle Eyes unit Megan used, he might learn something useful, but that would leave a record of everything on the EE cloud server. The CIA man had access to that information.

The seventh notification told Jeff that one of the missing prototypes had been used last night in a motel in western Pennsylvania. Since the motel was the only point of reference, Jeff couldn't tell direction yet, but he'd bet anything the next location lock would be further east.

The agent, the kids, the prototypes. Is everything related?

The CIA man had to sell the prototypes to somebody, and presumably the people behind cyberleaguesports.com had a vested interest in cutting-edge computer technology. Having his problems be interconnected would be convenient, but it also ratcheted up the danger factor for everybody.

Luchek, I hope you're conscious because we have a lot to talk about.

When his first attempt to establish a connection failed, Jeff set up a program to reach out to her every five minutes until she answered. Then, he dove back into the task of locating his mother. If he could get the assassin the right information, everything would work out well. He refused to believe anything else.

Chapter 5:
Left in Play

"I found one of the prototypes," said Cassandra Mirren. "Shall I recover it?"

"What's the other option?" asked Gatton.

"I can leave it in play in the hopes that the criminal wearing it eventually returns to a base of operations where the rest are located," Cassandra explained.

"Why don't you sound confident in that plan?" asked Gatton.

"Because I'm not," she answered. "This is probably a test run."

"You don't think he has the rest," said Gatton, after a brief pause.

"I doubt a sale this big would go through right away," said Cassandra. "The buyer probably demanded proof of its capabilities. How many systems did you leave them?"

"I had to leave most of them in place," Gatton admitted. "I only had time to take the most dangerous programs offline and give it an MP Protocol."

"You'll have to explain that later, but I need an answer now," said Cassandra. "If you want this one back, I have to move soon."

"Leave it in play," said Gatton. "Can you stay close to the unit?"

"Depends on what you mean by close," answered Cassandra. "I'm probably—"

"You're 647 feet from the target unit," Gatton said, cutting in. "I need you to be within 100 feet. Turn on the proximity gauge. I'll send your unit the signal code to track."

"Moving now," said Cassandra. "I'll check in later."

Heading for the stairs at a fast clip, Cassandra activated more of the Eagle Eyes displays. The proximity gauge's number jumped around as interference disturbed the accuracy of the reading. She steered clear of the thermal display for now since it was one of the most disorienting views. The computer offered dozens of options. In the few days of using Eagle Eyes steadily, she found the bullet counter, the health bar, the person identifier, the breaths-per-minute counter, and the threat assessor most useful.

Upon reaching the bottom, Cassandra slowed her pace. Once outside, it wouldn't be that unusual for her to run, but she wanted to exit the building with some decorum. This neighborhood didn't have a lot of foot traffic, but she wasn't dressed properly to pass as a jogger. Taking out her cell phone and avoiding eye contact, Cassandra strode purposefully after her quarry.

It felt great to be the pursuer on a clear-cut retrieval mission, even if she had to pass by a dozen cops in the process. One could barely go a block without seeing an officer.

The quarry—Gordon Mullins, according to Eagle Eyes—stepped into a church. That seemed like an odd mid-day destination for a Club man, but since he didn't stay long, she didn't spend too much thought on it. On a whim, Cassandra flipped to thermal mode to count the people in the church. The handful of adults didn't surprise her. The tiny lone figure at the back of the attic did.

Focusing on the figure, Cassandra asked the computer to give her every reading possible. The information overload had made her momentarily forget that the people identifier program relied on cell phone data to gather names, important dates, and financial information. It ignored most children.

The figure in the attic was approximately twenty-five inches long and an estimated fifteen pounds.

It's a baby.

The proximity counter started rising. It flashed at her.

Is the baby safe?

She directed this question to Eagle Eyes by sticking it in the text box in the corner. The program had improved its ability to predict and read certain thoughts, but that part still had a long way to go.

"The target in question is reasonably safe for the next six hours," reported the program. **"The temperatures may be problematic after that."**

Is the baby one of the missing ones?

"Unknown, but likely."

Reasonably certain she could leave the child in place, Cassandra resumed her chase. Gordon made two more stops: a coffee shop and a bank.

The coffee shop stop was brief. The man must have ordered something ahead of time because he walked right in and out again. He spent more time in the bank.

"Congratulations. You're within range. Shall I commence the upload?"

Cassandra gave permission, aware that she would need to stay within range the whole time or risk having to restart.

How long is this going to take?

"Approximately two minutes."

It didn't sound like a big number, but Cassandra knew it might be impossible. If Gordon got into a vehicle, she'd be hard-pressed to stay in range.

What are you sending the other unit?

"Clone Code, the MP Protocol, and a pay-it-forward command."

Cassandra asked Eagle Eyes to elaborate.

The program dutifully gave her a sales pitch on each. The pay-it-forward command would attempt to send Clone Code and the MP Protocol through to the other prototypes once it got within range of them. Both programs were straightforward, but the Clone Code intrigued her more right now.

Show me what he's doing, she ordered, once informed Clone Code was successfully installed in the other unit.

The man sat in the waiting area scribbling on an application. Meanwhile, his Eagle Eyes unit scanned nearby customers looking for vulnerable credit cards.

Almost infinite electronic power and he's using it as a card reader?

She hardly believed it. The application struck her as insulting.

"Mr. Mullins is also casing the bank, its customers, and the employees," Eagle Eyes reported.

Alarm shot through Cassandra.

"Don't worry. You are currently projecting Samantha Rigby, a waitress at a high-end restaurant downtown. Every Eagle Eyes unit has the ability to conjure plausible projections as needed."

Is Mullins himself or is that a projection?

"I'm not sensing a projection, but Mr. Mullins is a very new user. I doubt he grasps the depths of the power he holds."

Cassandra wondered how much of the program's arrogant attitude was organic and how much it channeled its maker.

A triumphant ding announced the completion of her mission. Slipping her phone into a pocket, Cassandra exited the bank. As her feet hit the sidewalk, she decided to call Gatton. Taking out her phone again, Cassandra called to let him know the program transfer went smoothly.

"I have another job for you," said Gatton, when she finished her brief report. "The agent is there. In Philadelphia."

"Where?" Cassandra asked.

"Before I tell you, I need to say you can't go after her right now." Gatton's words flowed even quicker than usual. "There's a good chance the Hero Contest will take place in that city. Five children were kidnapped this morning. I think they're going to send the contestants after those kids. If you bust in now, the kids could die."

"That's a lot of assumptions, Gatton," said Cassandra. "Walk me through your connections if you want my help."

"Amber Alerts are relatively rare. Maybe one goes off every other day somewhere. They're localized to states and regions," Gatton explained. "Five in a day would be a big coincidence. Five in one area in a day is a law enforcement nightmare. That whole city's on edge."

"Clearly," Cassandra acknowledged, "but that doesn't explain this other job or why you think it's related to the rash of missing children."

"You can check the website later," said Gatton. "The latest post rambles about heroes rescuing society's most vulnerable members."

"How do you know the agent's here?" asked Cassandra. She guessed Eagle Eyes had told him.

"I can only say that the unit assigned to her is there," said Gatton. "The GPS was activated manually this morning. The agent would only do that if there's a problem. I need you to deliver a similar package to her unit."

"Getting in range for the necessary time might be difficult," said Cassandra. "Can it wait until tonight?"

"She could be dead by tonight!" cried Gatton.

"How is Clone Code going to prevent that?" Cassandra tried to tamp down her irritation, but Gatton wasn't making that easy.

"It's not just Clone Code. You'll also be sending her a Stealth Mode suite to hide the unit from the other Eagle Eyes prototypes,"

Gatton reported crisply. He drew a deep breath and continued in a softer tone. "And to answer your question, the patch may not prevent her death. But it can't hurt, and it should help."

He sounded lost.

"All right. Walk me through the delivery," said Cassandra.

"I tried to send the patch remotely, but I think she's unconscious." Gatton sounded grim. "Her unit's in standby mode. You'll have to get close enough to somebody who might interact with the agent when she wakes up. I modified your delivery suite to give it a bunny hop option."

"Do I need to know what that is?"

"It's like pay-it-forward, only more powerful. It will let the program hop from cell phone to cell phone until it gets close to its true target," Gatton explained. "The transfer range is usually a hundred feet, but it gets shorter inside most buildings if the signal needs to pass through multiple layers of concrete and compete with other signals."

"I'll get it done," Cassandra promised. "Tell me where to go." She wanted to say something reassuring, but comforting sayings eluded her.

Gatton sent her the address of a large office building across the city. Hailing a taxi, Cassandra pondered which approach she should take. If she rumpled her clothes and bought a bottle of liquor, she might be able to pull off *rambling drunk*. Since she didn't want to ruin a perfectly good suit, Cassandra chose to try *lost, clueless woman*. They arrived at the destination before she made a final decision on the matter.

The glass windows along the front showed her three men sitting at a security desk. She could try them, but Cassandra had her doubts they would interact much with any prisoners. Slipping around to the side of the building, she found a maintenance door. The electronic lock looked complicated, but Eagle Eyes made short work of it.

Once inside, Cassandra turned on the thermal view and looked around to get a feel for where people were located. The fifth floor held the most warm bodies. Overlaying a scan for metal confirmed that at least four sets of people were confined to makeshift cages made with common wire fencing. Several men wandered the building, likely patrolling for intruders.

This would be a whole lot easier if you were awake, agent.

Cassandra directed the thought up to a still figure in the last cage on the right from her current perspective. Another figure paced within the same general area. Gatton's nosy computer program had identified the prone one as having an unusual electronic signature. Height and weight estimates were within range for those in the agent's FBI file. Cassandra assumed the other figure was Tara, but she had no conveniently hackable work files to compare with.

Asking Eagle Eyes to identify every possible target cell phone, Cassandra spent the next few hours sneaking floor to floor to get within range while simultaneously avoiding patrols. She longed to take a more direct approach, but if she stirred up too much trouble, the organizers might take their frustrations out on the captives.

Chapter 6:
Bad Penny

Megan groaned as she slowly crawled her way back to consciousness.

"Maggie, are you awake?" Tara's voice sounded from behind her.

Arms wrapped around Megan's stomach tightened.

Pain shot through her head.

She stiffened, preparing to cast off the hands.

"Calm down," said Tara. "It's me. Relax. You're probably still drugged."

Mention of being drugged sent a cleansing shot of adrenaline through Megan's system. It didn't completely drive off the headache, but most of the fog lifted. She remembered getting into a white van and drinking a clear liquid. Everything before that blurred.

"Please say something," Tara pleaded. "I know you're awake."

"Don't call me 'Maggie.'" She shifted restlessly.

Tara's soft laughter moved through her chest.

"I get to call you whatever I want," said Tara, kissing the top of her head. "It's my right for being older."

Megan considered getting up but concluded that it wasn't worth the effort. Besides, Tara made a fine backrest. They hadn't embraced like this since they were kids. When Megan was eight, a flu had flattened her for three days. Their mother tried to keep Tara away so she wouldn't get sick too, but at night, her sister snuck in and stayed with her anyway.

"How long has it been?" Megan voiced the question softly.

"You've been out for almost five hours," said Tara.

"I was talking about us catching a quiet moment together." Megan couldn't tell if she was making much sense. "I miss this."

"Do you always get sentimental when you get kidnapped?" asked Tara. She sounded weary.

"Only when there are drugs involved," Megan replied, patting her sister's arm. The move made her glance down, which showed off the irritated rings where the zip ties had left their mark on Tara.

"Don't joke about that." Tara's voice quality indicated a battle to control her emotions. "I can't take a fright like that again. I didn't think you'd ever wake up."

Breaking free, Megan sat up and twisted around so she could face her sister. The uncertainty in her expression was new. Megan suddenly missed the cool, confident, lecture-prone version of Tara. Shifting to a more comfortable position on the cot, Megan opened her arms and let her sister curl up beside her.

After a good cry leveled their emotions, Tara sat back and looked at Megan earnestly.

"Megan," she began. She brushed the last of her tears away.

"No," Megan said, reacting to her sister's resigned tone. She raised a hand as if that would stop the flow of words. "We are both getting out of this."

"They're probably going to release you to do something. When you get that chance, run." Tara reinforced her message by latching onto Megan's hand and squeezing tightly.

"I'm not running," Megan declared.

I'm going to take these people down so hard their—

"You have to," Tara argued before Megan could finish her thought.

"They'll kill you."

"And if you stay, they'll kill us both." Tara lowered her voice to a harsh whisper. "How is that an improvement?"

Megan conceded the point while maintaining absolute conviction in her chosen path.

"Look. At least if our parents have you, there might be a chance for them to heal," said Tara.

"Liv, Vinny got shot before their eyes," said Megan. "The only way our parents and Aunt Silvia get to heal is if we prove the people behind this are no longer a threat. And that only happens if we destroy them, so that's the plan."

Releasing Megan's hand, Tara leaned against the wall and regarded her carefully after the mini speech.

"You're really scary when you're passionate about something."

Tara's statement coaxed a sad smile from Megan.

"I've had to deal with some unpleasant people lately." Flashes of scenes with Derrick Belmont, Keith Danielson, and Martin Cantrell zipped through her mind. Shoving the personal demons back into their little box, Megan continued, "It helps to be passionate about destroying their schemes."

"Be careful. This isn't an isolated nutcase," Tara said. "There are a lot of unpleasant people involved in whatever this is." She gestured to the cage around them and, by extension, the building.

Megan took the opportunity to take in the surroundings. High above, bright LED lights cheerfully mimicked daylight. The only furniture was the cot they sat on. The place had been converted from office space to a temporary prison by combining two cubicles, knocking out a wall, and lining the resulting box with chain link fencing. To her surprise, she saw no lock on the gate. The sight brought her up off the cot and across the tiny cell.

"Don't bother," said Tara. "There's no lock, but there's a guard. I got the tour when I used the restroom earlier."

"How does one arrange for such a tour?" asked Megan.

"By asking nicely," said a familiar male voice. "It's good to see you, Agent Luchek."

Megan recoiled in surprise.

"Curt." She completed the formalities with a short nod acknowledging his presence. "You're a bad penny. What are you doing in this place?"

"My employer asked me to safeguard something he's hoping to sell," said Curtis D'Angelo. "The prospective buyer wanted a demonstration. Hence, my presence. I got curious about the operation and asked some questions. They were kind enough to explain the contest. Once I learned you were here, I offered my services as a consultant. They have a fascinating business model."

Megan tried to scrape together the wits to enter a verbal duel with D'Angelo.

He looked at her expectantly.

"Aren't you going to introduce me to your sister?"

"There's no need. You know who she is," Megan said stiffly.

"Ah, but does she know me?" Curtis's voice bounced playfully. Leaning left, he waved. "Hello, Mrs. Sidell. You'll have to excuse Megan. She can be rather prickly sometimes."

Stepping forward and right, Megan forced Curtis to focus on her.

"I get 'prickly' when people threaten me or my family," she said evenly.

"How do you know my sister?" Tara asked.

"It doesn't matter," said Megan.

"You didn't tell her?" Curtis asked in mock horror. "I'm hurt."

"Find somebody who cares." Megan hadn't spoken with her family about Dallas because she had wanted to move forward.

"I think I did." With a charming smile, Curtis talked through her. "Mrs. Sidell, my name is Curtis D'Angelo. I'm a Freelancer. That means I pick up odd jobs from time to time. Last week, your sister was my job. I almost killed her, but now, I'm so glad I didn't."

"You're remembering a lot of details wrong," Megan pointed out. "Last I saw you, a cop was helping you into a cruiser."

Anger twisted Curtis's expression.

"Your friends aren't coming to save you this time," he hissed. The mood faded and he recovered his good cheer. "Good luck in the contest. I think I'll stick around to see what happens. Consulting gigs are easy money. Would you like the tour now?"

"I would." Much of Megan's willpower shifted to the cause of not punching Curtis as he gallantly swung the gate open.

"Step this way." Curtis accompanied the statement with a sweeping, exaggerated wave.

"I'll be right back," Megan called to her sister, trying to drive the worry from her eyes.

"Maybe," said Curtis, "but only if we keep the tour short. I think the first round's set to begin soon."

Curtis guided Megan to the restroom and politely waited outside the main door. On the way back, he introduced her to the neighbors. The room held eight prison cells, but only four were doubly occupied.

"Behind gate number one, we have Shanice Nevins and her son Andre," Curtis announced the names with an announcer's flair. "Sergeant Nevins is a highly successful recruiter for the United States Army."

The dark-haired young woman sitting on the cot cradling a slumbering child glared at them. Megan imagined she could feel the woman's hatred pull tight around her chest like a rope. Mother and son shared the same shade of light brown skin. The boy looked unnaturally still.

They drugged the boy.

Suddenly, the hatred made sense, but before Megan could

comment, Curtis ushered her over to the next cell.

"Gate number two holds Jacob Chantry and his little brother, Robbie," said Curtis. "The Chantry brothers come to us from far-off California where Jacob tackles the noble task of fighting fires."

A young man slumbered on the cot while a slightly older man paced the cell. The sleeper had light brown hair, and the watcher had dark brown hair. Spotting them, the watcher rushed over to the gate and shoved hard, rattling the fence. This gate bore a lock, which Megan was suddenly grateful for. The firefighter stood a head taller than her, glowering. He didn't speak, but Megan finally understood Curtis's angle with this tour.

"You're trying to make them hate me," she murmured as they stepped toward the last cell before the one she'd been in earlier.

"I don't have to," Curtis said. "I'm told you're the House Favorite."

"Should that mean something to me?" Megan faked a calm she didn't feel.

"It means you're the one to beat."

He gave her an expectant look which she answered with a blank stare.

"Clearly, you're not a gambler," Curtis complained. "It's less fun when I have to explain."

"Explain or don't," Megan said with a shrug. "I'm sure I'll find out soon anyway."

"First, the last introduction," said Curtis, clearing his throat. "The final hero contestant has been an Emergency Medical Technician for three years. Brett Ringo is joined today by his lovely mother, Alice."

Alice had the cot while Brett sat on the floor holding his head in his hands. Blond hair pooled through his fingers. His expression held no hatred, only shock and fear.

Lost in thought, Megan let Curtis escort her back to the cell with Tara.

Only it was empty.

Megan stared at the cot. The sheet and blanket had been straightened, and the pillow had been carefully placed.

"Guess it's begun," said Curtis as he swung open the gate and pushed Megan inside.

"You knew." Megan didn't bother turning around.

"I told you before, I know many things," said Curtis.

Needing to sit down, Megan sank onto the cot and picked up the pillow. It was still warm.

"Explain House Favorite," Megan prompted. Hugging the pillow, she waited for Curtis to answer.

"The team sponsoring you belongs to the organizers," Curtis explained. "The House, if you want to go with the gambling analogy. That means you'll get certain advantages and disadvantages. It also means that some gamblers may spend credits on things that can hinder you."

"Why move Tara?" Megan wondered.

Every other hostage was safely ensconced in the cell with the contestant.

"Gary only said he needed her for an illustration," Curtis said casually. "He wanted you out of the cell so there wouldn't be too much drama at an inopportune time. Something about maximizing impacts. Don't worry. I think the real party will kick off soon."

Every pounding heartbeat sent blood surging through Megan's head, kicking her headache into a higher gear. The cadence tapped out the urgent order filling her mind.

Get her back!

Chapter 7:
Stealth Mode

Eventually, Curtis wandered away. The return of silence gave Megan's headache a chance to go back into dull-ache mode.

A random guard delivered an evening meal by tossing a bottle of water over the gate and shoving two power bars through the links in the fence.

Megan didn't want to get up, but she hoped the food and water would help kill the headache.

Unless it's poisoned.

She wouldn't put it past the organizers to drug her again, but if they wanted her to do anything tonight, they'd have to refrain from knocking her out. Annoyed she even had to question whether the food was safe, Megan checked the packaging for signs of tampering. Finding nothing, she cautiously opened the first bar and ate it. The chocolate mint flavor tasted good until she followed that with the second bar, which was vanilla. The mixture wasn't pleasant, but she forced herself to finish both. Since the water bottle had been severely dented by its rough landing, it refused to stand upright. Megan drank about half the bottle then screwed the cap on carefully and set the bottle on the floor.

Bored, she played with the wrappers by folding them into tiny accordion shapes and weaving them between her fingers. The mindless activity gave her a chance to think. She had been in some tough spots before and successfully survived, but this kidnapped-for-a-bizarre-game thing was a new flavor of crazy.

It's a game.

The realization made her think of Jeffrey Gatton. Almost

everything the man did revolved around games.

Eagle Eyes!

Megan couldn't believe she'd forgotten about Gatton's ingenious, highly invasive computer tool.

That drug did a number on my head.

She eagerly activated the program.

The program answered promptly with a perfect imitation of Gatton's voice.

"Welcome to Eagle Eyes. Please note that your administrator has placed this unit in Stealth Mode. This will keep the device from being detected by other units. During this time, you may experience some loss of functions. If you believe this was done in error, please contact your administrator. How can I help you today?"

Questions crowded Megan's head, but she understood that she might only have time for a few before the next interruption. To save time, she conjured the question as a whole thought before popping it into the message box that would allow the program to read and respond.

Where am I?

"Information unavailable. A GPS confirmation check would require pinging a satellite. Such an activity is forbidden at this time."

Mention of GPS reminded Megan that she'd activated the unit's tracker upon leaving Tara's apartment.

I had the GPS running. Give me the last recorded location.

"Philadelphia, Pennsylvania, United States."

What do I have access to in Stealth Mode?

"Most modules should work fine unless they require fresh data."

Is there any way out of Stealth Mode?

"I am authorized to lift Stealth Mode if I can mask the data use as something else."

What does that mean?

"Crowds. You will need to find a crowd of people using electronic devices accessing Wi-Fi."

There must be a lot of cell phones being used in this building. Why am I still in Stealth Mode?

"This is a quarantine zone."

Before Megan could ask for a better explanation, Curtis appeared outside the gate.

"They're ready for you." He made the announcement cheerfully and pulled open the door.

When Megan looked at him, Eagle Eyes automatically identified him.

"Stand and step forward. Hold out your hands. The more you cooperate, the nicer they'll be to Tara."

Standing, Megan followed Curtis's instructions, drawing comfort from a mental image of slugging him. The two men who'd helped Gary pull off the kidnapping entered the tiny cell. Eagle Eyes identified the first man through as Timothy Lyra and the second as Randall Fuller. A second later, the program adjusted their names to Tim and Randy. The slightly taller guy—Tim—was the one Megan had taken to thinking of as Tara's guard. Randy rated a spot above Tim but below Curtis on Megan's to-punch list since he'd been pushing her around during the kidnapping.

How are you doing that without a satellite? And why the nicknames?

"They were identified upon sight by their cell phone data. Social media analysis indicates these are their preferred names."

Don't you need a command to do things like that?

"Normally, yes. But if I deem a person a threat, I am allowed to initiate data harvesting protocols to expand the defense package."

The miniature Q&A session distracted Megan enough to let her stand still while Tim invaded her personal space and Randy applied handcuffs. This time, the bindings locked Megan's arms behind her back.

Gripping the short chain between the handcuffs, Randy propelled Megan forward.

Curtis swung the gate as wide as it would go to give them room to exit. Once clear of the gate, Tim took the lead.

The trip up to the seventh floor went smoothly. The room they entered appeared much bigger than the previous one because it lacked the cubicles and fencing. It looked more like a film studio than an office. Mounted lights and cameras focused on four wooden stools arranged in a line spanning the room. About ten feet separated the stools from each other. The first three seats held one of the hostages. The other half of each pair stood behind the stool, also wearing handcuffs. Three men flanked each standing captive.

Apparently, Megan was the latecomer. Her escorts led her to the far right stool, which stood empty. After moving her into position, they stepped back, assuming positions similar to the other teams of captors.

Every eye focused on the room's center where Tara sat on a metal folding chair with her hands in her lap. The position indicated her hands were bound. Somebody had tied a red cloth around her mouth to serve as a gag. Gary stood behind her, resting his hands on Tara's shoulders. A subtle shift of his left hand let the overhead lights glint off something metal.

Megan's muscles tensed when she recognized the object as a knife. Realizing Gary wanted her to react, Megan kept silent and as still as possible. Since she couldn't stop all movement, she balled her hands into fists.

Frowning at her, Gary lifted the knife and admired it.

The better view showed Megan that the weapon was an ordinary serrated steak knife.

Soft whimpers drew Megan's gaze across the room to where the child sat. Gary glared at the disturbance.

"Deal with that," he ordered.

One of the men standing behind Shanice stepped around her and reached for the boy.

"Don't touch him!" she cried.

The two other men with Shanice each took an arm and held her still while the first guy put the child in a headlock.

Shanice struggled, nearly throwing off the hands holding her, until one man said something Megan missed. The child stilled about the same moment the soldier did.

Megan asked Eagle Eyes to identify the men. The program promised to record their faces and search later but reminded her that she was in a quarantine zone.

The other sets of prisoners remained eerily still, not even looking at the scene.

"Now that we can think, allow me to personally welcome everybody to the Hero Contest," said Gary. "Each of you qualified for the honor by excelling in your chosen fields. Before we begin, I have some ground rules and instructions to go over, as well as an illustration to make. Tara is going to help me with the demonstration."

Megan hardly dared to breathe and completely stopped paying attention to Gary's words as he pantomimed stabbing her sister in the neck and side. She didn't realize she'd moved until hands pulled her to a halt a few feet from Gary. Internal heat rose, making her face and ears burn.

"Make your point," Megan said, enunciating carefully. "Spell out the rules and let us get to the contest part. I'm sure your audience wants to see more than you rambling."

"Weren't you paying attention?" Gary asked, feigning surprise and disappointment. "No talking out of turn. I expected better of you, but perhaps I'll let it slide this time if you return to your assigned location." He made a shooing motion.

"I have recorded his words and can summarize for you," Eagle Eyes offered.

The program provided her with a bulleted list of ridiculous rules that covered everything from not interacting with the other hero candidates, keeping quiet unless addressed, not resisting the handlers, not talking to anybody from the outside, and not attempting to escape.

Megan thanked Eagle Eyes and let her handlers drag her back behind the empty wooden stool.

"Your first task will be to rescue an infant hidden somewhere in the city," said Gary. "You'll be given the location and a time limit."

"What happens if we don't make the time limit?" asked Jacob Chantry, the firefighter.

Gary glared, then shrugged.

"You're disqualified," answered Gary.

"And what happens if we're disqualified?" Jacob pressed.

"You and your control die," said Gary. "The only way to live is to win."

Something about the way his eyes shifted bothered Megan. Eagle Eyes chimed in with a notice that there was a 73.35% chance of Gary's last statement being a lie.

We're not getting out of this, are we?

"Information unavailable at this time, but analysis of the website associated with this endeavor shows a high probability the organizers wish to give the winner a hero's sendoff."

"We're prepared to offer you up to three tasks with the assumption being each round has one loser," Gary explained. "However, there's an easy way to win. Would you like to hear about it?"

Megan shook her head no, but the others said or indicated yes.

At an imperious wave from Gary, Tim and Randy moved Megan to the chair occupied by Tara and had them switch places.

Megan sat on the edge, trying not to crush her hands.

"Candidates, it's my pleasure to introduce you to the House Favorite: Megan Luchek," said Gary. "She works for the Federal Bureau of Investigation. Before we get to the first official task, the audience asked that we run a preliminary elimination round."

"What's that?" asked Brett Ringo, the EMT.

His tone told Megan he was merely a mouthpiece. A glance at each of the other contestants told her they already knew what Gary would say. This show was for her benefit.

"In a moment, every candidate will be given the chance to eliminate one competitor," said Gary. "Your handlers will move you into position, release your hands, and give you a knife. If you kill the control you stand by, you will send your competitor to the Tribunal who will decide his or her fate. If everybody kills their control, we'll host a battle royale to determine the victor."

Uncomfortable silence lingered until one of Shanice's handlers nudged her.

Randy pulled Megan up out of the chair and hustled her over to the wall where Andre had been propped up. Tim released her hands and handed her a steak knife.

"What happens to the children taken for the first task if we never make it there?" asked Megan.

"Without a hero to rescue them, they'll die," Gary answered. "Any other comments or questions?"

"I'm not killing a child for you or for anybody," said Megan, stepping away from the boy.

Turning to face the others, she placed the knife on the empty stool. Megan studied her competition. Shanice's shoulders sagged with relief. The two men eyed the knives in their hands uneasily.

"You can't force us to be killers," Megan informed Gary.

The fierce way Shanice looked at her son contradicted Megan. She tried not to think about the fact that with the right threat against Andre, the young mother might do anything.

"Are you sure about that?" asked Gary. "All right, new way to win. First one to kill the House Favorite walks out free and clear with their control."

Chapter 8:
Gifts from Gatton

Following the adventures in the office building holding Megan, Cassandra spent a few hours killing time in a nearby coffee shop, a park, and a diner. She needed to stay close to the target building to monitor the situation. Eagle Eyes made the stakeout much easier on her, but it still stretched her patience.

To pass the time, Cassandra set several alarms and a timer before closing her eyes to do some research via Gatton's fancy toy. She stuck in earbuds, fiddled with her phone from time to time, and moved every thirty to forty minutes to avoid suspicion.

Eagle Eyes had narrowed down the CIA man's identity to 416 possibilities. Although far too many to be a useful number, the progress encouraged Cassandra since they'd started with at least twice that.

Nothing much changed on the Cyber League pages devoted to the Hero Contest, but Cassandra explored other parts of the website. It would be nice if Gatton could deliver a computer virus or break into their shady bank accounts and drain the money away, but unfortunately, the monster had many heads. Lopping off one or two would do precious little to stop the beast.

We need to strike at the heart.

The sentiment was easier said than accomplished. Since unraveling tangled internet intrigues wasn't her strong suit, Cassandra had to wait for Gatton to point her in the correct direction. For now, his priority—and hers—remained the recovery of the stolen Eagle Eyes prototypes.

As she started eating the salad that came with her dinner,

Cassandra received a call from a blocked number. She answered, expecting it to be Lia or Owen.

"It's done," Lia reported. She sounded tense.

The call ended before Cassandra could thank her apprentice. The young woman would send a more thorough account of the mission to the encrypted email account later. The length of the verbal summary was on par for her, but the tone was unusual. Nevertheless, Cassandra called Gatton to pass on the good news.

"Gatton," he answered.

The hoarse, strained tone immediately caught Cassandra's attention. Rising from the booth, she rushed into the Women's room. This was not a conversation she wanted to hold in a crowded diner.

"I assume you have company," said Cassandra. "Give him the phone."

"He's listening," said Gatton.

"Jeffrey was just telling me about you, Ms. Mirren," said the CIA man. He had the smooth, arrogant voice of a man who'd made a career manipulating others. "You're a legend in the agency, but you're a tad predictable. That's a dangerous trait in our line of work."

Ignoring the insult, Cassandra asked Eagle Eyes for the location of Lia's current burner phone as well as the current connection with Gatton. Eagle Eyes promptly gave her a series of latitude and longitude numbers and overlaid the information on a map of the United States. The data sets corresponded to a remote area of Texas, and more importantly, showed that the locations were identical.

"Whom am I addressing?" Cassandra's mind flipped through options. The CIA man likely wanted her to walk away. The move would strike her personal and professional pride the hardest but be the safest for Gatton and any other hostages. She could stay on target without Gatton's support, risking his life for the sake of his work.

"Jeffrey said you call me 'CIA Man.' I like it. Let's go with that."

"What can I do for you, CIA Man?" Cassandra asked, knowing he expected it.

"I want you to go to that building you're so interested in and surrender to Mr. D'Angelo," said CIA Man. "He'll keep an eye on you until the transaction completes."

"What do I get for my cooperation?" Cassandra inquired.

"You get the chance to control how many happy endings happen," said the man. "I'll even throw in the girl's life and Jeffrey's, if he doesn't do anything foolish. Your FBI friend isn't mine to bargain with right now, but she may be in the future."

"I'll need some time to think," said Cassandra. She felt better knowing that Lia was with Gatton. The CIA man might keep her unconscious, but he would keep her alive to use as a threat. If he was stupid enough to let Lia awaken, she'd make him regret it.

"Take your time. I understand you're not far from the building. You have an hour to comply." CIA Man spoke with a friendly, understanding tone. "Please understand, I am merely protecting my investment. Once the sale of Eagle Eyes goes through, I will retire peacefully."

They both knew he would have to kill her to ensure his happy ending. Depending on how paranoid he was, the safest option involved killing everybody involved, including Gatton and Lia.

"You don't have to do anything," said Gatton. His voice shook with anger. "Eagle Eyes will fight back."

"Gatton, I need to speak with the CIA man alone for a moment," said Cassandra. She needed him to stop talking before their adversary started listening to him.

"I'm intrigued," said the man. The voice quality changed enough to tell her he'd disabled speaker mode. "What can't be said for Jeffrey's sensitive ears?"

"You can't afford to kill him. He's the only one who can get the prototypes to reach their full potential," Cassandra explained.

"Not my problem," said the man dismissively.

"It will be," Cassandra promised. "When your buyer runs into the first technical difficulty that requires Gatton's level of genius to solve, they're going to come to you for the solution."

"They'll never find me."

The defensive quality to the man's tone told Cassandra she'd scored a point.

"They will if they're motivated enough," said Cassandra. "Given that this is your retirement plan, I'm guessing your asking price is high. They might even use the prototypes against you. How long do you think you can hide from Eagle Eyes?"

Her reward consisted of a few seconds of silence while the man formulated his response.

"I appreciate your concern. You've given me much to think about," said the CIA man, "but this changes nothing. You now have less than an hour to surrender, or I will express my displeasure through dear Lia."

"Let me speak with Gatton," said Cassandra, not gracing the threat with a response.

"He's been through enough today. Go do your thinking."

The call ended.

Cassandra gripped the phone tightly but refrained from breaking it. She might need it later.

A cold calm settled over her as she set a timer for 58 minutes.

An alert popped into the lower right side of her vision.

It read: **Gifts from Gatton.**

A text box opened then disappeared. A new one opened and flickered several times before disappearing. This process continued long enough to make Cassandra wonder if Eagle Eyes was having a meltdown.

What's happening?

She slipped the question into the box so the computer program could access it.

"Processing. Stand by."

Hearing the program use Gatton's voice pattern reminded her of the mission's newfound urgency.

Cassandra used the waiting time to wash her face, inhale some of the food, and settle the bill. Slipping into her coat, she exited the diner. The chilly night air refreshed her. Needing to further clear her mind, she headed for the nearby park.

For once, the best path eluded her. Protocol would tell her to go to ground and disappear without a trace. She had done it before and could do it again. Logic and good sense told her she should obey the protocol. Curtis D'Angelo was not the most dangerous foe she'd ever faced, but they had recently dealt him a defeat. In her experience, guys like him had fragile egos and long memories. The surrender wouldn't happen smoothly no matter how hard she tried.

Will Curt kill me outright?

Curious, Cassandra threw the question into the Eagle Eyes text box.

"There is a 78.68% chance Mr. D'Angelo will not kill you immediately. His contract specifies that he hold you until given further instructions."

How do you know that?

"After the last incident, Mr. Gatton employed extensive tracking software for everything suspected of having connections to Mr. D'Angelo. The contract was sent to one such email."

The reasonable chance of not dying in the first few seconds after surrender made it a viable option, but Cassandra had a hard time trusting it. CIA Man must have a motive she missed if he didn't sign off on a kill order. One would come eventually, so why the delay?

She checked the timer. It read 47:13 and steadily ticked down second by second.

You can fly away from anything, Little Bird, but there's always a cost and a consequence. Consider your next move carefully.

The thought filled her head, complete with Smith's British accent. Her mentor had excelled at helping her reason through seemingly impossible tasks. He had never told her why he called her "Little Bird," but he'd done so since their first meeting.

I can walk away. The cost would be Lia, the agent, and Gatton. The consequence would be Eagle Eyes going to the highest bidder.

Once upon a time, she'd be able to mentally and emotionally write off the people. Scrapping the mission objective would have been harder. She finally understood Smith's stance on the unspoken policy of avoiding emotional attachments. Among other, more colorful things, he'd called the logic utter, stinking rubbish.

The day you stop caring is the day you quit humanity. Smith had argued. *The trick to surviving will often come down to who and what you fight for. Choose your people and causes wisely.*

It might be more accurate to say the people and causes chose her. The circumstances surrounding Lia's assignment as her apprentice were far from normal. The assassin who had chosen to train the girl disappeared on a mission, and the kid had aged out of the teen training program. If Cassandra had refused the assignment, Lia would have become a rabbit, live prey for a training exercise.

The relationship with the agent started with a gunfight before life threw them into the crosshairs of a madman. The initial shared dangers created a strange friendship. She'd done everything from letting the woman be bait to walking straight into a trap for her.

Gatton had started out as Megan's problem, but since his CIA problem and Cassandra's had similar roots, they'd forged an alliance.

The cause of keeping Eagle Eyes away from the Cyber League might not seem a matter of immediate life or death, but she'd experimented with the programming options enough to know the misuses would only be limited by people's twisted imaginations. Gatton's toy already had a disturbing amount of influence over many types of electronics. It wasn't much of a leap to think of the applications being expanded to controlling other machines.

"My analysis is complete. Would you like a summary?"

The announcement and query interrupted Cassandra's musings. Having reached the park, she sat down and scanned her surroundings, trying to see if anyone was paying attention to her. A man jogged by with his dog, and a cop patrolled along a parallel path to where she'd stopped. Their attention flitted over her.

Go ahead.

"The data packets received contain scripts for Project Meltdown, the Scrapper Protocols, and a Night Owl Initiative."

The meltdown and scrapper programs sound destructive. What's the difference?

"The scripts are self-destruct instructions designed specifically for the six compromised prototypes. Mr. Gatton insisted on personalizing each sequence so as not to endanger other units that might be caught in the blast radius, including this one. We are to be ground zero."

What's the range on the delivery?

"Fifty feet would be adequate, but within twenty-five feet is ideal."

And the delivery time?

"Delivery time will vary based on distance, method, and interference. An accurate estimate is not currently available. If a bunny hop delivery is needed, it will require more time to take effect."

How will I find the prototypes?

She would have to work fast if she hoped to make the deliveries and get to the meeting with D'Angelo.

"Activate the Marco-Polo Protocol."

With everything happening, Cassandra had forgotten about the MP Protocol. If she and Gatton both survived this pitched battle with CIA Man, she'd have to speak with the inventor about streamlining the many additional updates.

As soon as she gave Eagle Eyes the proper permissions, six green triangles appeared and pulsed. Cassandra hardly dared to believe her luck even as the giant coincidence set off internal alarms. She stood. Her objectives lay deep within the very building where CIA Man expected her to surrender to D'Angelo.

She checked the timer again and saw 35:22.

Looks like I have an appointment to keep.

Chapter 9:
Hero Work

Alarmed by Gary's announcement, Megan snatched the knife off the stool and eased to her right to increase the distance from Shanice's son. If the psycho convinced these random strangers to swing at her with those steak knives, she wanted plenty of room to dodge without risking the child's life.

Nobody else moved until the handlers physically pushed the other three towards Megan. None of the handlers spoke, but their expressions showed their eagerness to watch a fight.

Megan tried to step again and felt a hand touch her right shoulder. Her handlers, Tim and Randy, closed ranks behind her.

"There's nowhere to run," said Gary. "And if you're not sporting about this, I'll have them hold you in place."

Yeah, because that's sporting.

"I don't want to fight you," Megan said, addressing the other three people in her position.

"I want to win," said the firefighter. "I'm not letting Robbie die in this place."

"What makes you think Gary will keep his word?" Megan demanded. "If he can change rules that fast, he can—and will—change them again."

"It might be worth a shot anyway," said the firefighter. He held the knife loosely. "I saw the stats and polls. You're favored to win the competition. If we go through with the game, there's only one winner."

"The longer we keep competing, the longer we live," Megan reasoned, meeting each gaze. "Same for our family members." She waited tensely while the words sank in.

Finally, Shanice stepped out of line and moved to her side.

"I agree," said Brett Ringo. The EMT's Southern accent gave the rest of his speech a rolling cadence. "There are five infants out there counting on us to find 'em. Let's get to it, people. Hero work awaits."

The number startled Megan, but she lacked the time to ponder the matter properly.

Why kidnap five infants if there are only four "heroes"?

Each contestant eyed the others suspiciously.

"Why don't we all put down the knives?" suggested Brett. "Together-like, so nobody has an advantage."

He counted to three.

Nobody moved.

"Oh, this is stupid," Megan said. "Can we at least agree to rescue the kids before trying to kill each other?"

After another round of measuring looks, the others reluctantly nodded.

"Fine. I'll go first." Drawing a steadying breath, Megan held the fist clutching the knife straight out in front of her body and dropped the weapon.

Brett stooped and placed his knife near Megan's discarded one.

Shanice's blade clanked down on top of the one Brett put down.

They looked to Jacob expectantly.

He looked from the knife to his brother and tossed the weapon onto the growing pile.

"We have work to do," said Jacob.

"Looks like we have a genuine competition," said Gary with forced cheer. "Heroes, go with your handlers. They'll escort you to the starting locations and explain your task to you. The controls will be returned to their cells to await news of your return. It goes without saying, if you don't return, they'll die. If you wish to say something to your control, do so now."

Tim and Randy looked annoyed by the delay, but they let Megan cross the room to her sister, who perched on a stool.

Tara's eyes pleaded with Megan to be careful, but the gag prevented her from verbalizing the encouragement.

Around them, the murmurs of quiet conversations arose.

Megan reached to remove the gag.

"Leave that," Gary ordered. "You can look but don't touch."

His tone added unnecessary threats.

Megan barely stopped her hand in time. Curling the hand into a fist, she let her arm drop to her side and retreated a step.

Looking deep into Tara's blue eyes, Megan made a dozen silent promises before speaking.

"I'll be right back. You'll barely know I was gone."

"You can do better than that," Gary said scornfully. He stepped up behind Tara, still clutching his knife. Bringing the weapon up, he absently added, "This looks familiar, but something's different. What could be different?"

Walk away.

"I don't need your help," Megan declared. Anger hardened the words even though she knew he craved the reaction.

Take away his audience.

Feeling like she was ripping out her heart, Megan spun away from her sister and stepped between Tim and Randy.

"Tell me how to complete the task," Megan ordered.

I'm so sorry, Liv, but staying would only get you hurt.

A muffled cry from Tara made Megan stumble as the impulse to rush back to her sister slammed into the urge to sprint away.

Randy caught her arm.

Nodding thanks for the assist, Megan finished the trip to the elevators with a shred of dignity.

The other teams had already departed.

She listened carefully as Tim explained what would happen. They would exit the building and walk a block to their van. Once inside, Megan would have to wear a hood until they reached the staging location. She'd be given directions and a marked street map. A timer would be set. Then, it would be up to her to retrieve the package and deliver it to somebody who would transfer the child to the police.

Surprisingly, the plan unfolded as advertised. Megan expected to have her hands bound for the trip, but her handlers didn't bother. The hood was a game requirement. Though uncomfortably hot, the van ride was mercifully short. Megan had been assigned the package hidden in an old church on 2nd St. in the historic section of Philadelphia. The drop off location, allegedly chosen at random, was eleven blocks away.

Tim gave her a tracker and told her not to lose it. They would follow as best they could on side streets. Once done with the task, she could meet them at the corner of 3rd and Market if they didn't find her first.

"How much time do I have?" Megan wondered.

"Fifteen minutes," said Tim.

"Better hurry," said Randy.

Exiting the warm van onto the cold city street, Megan frowned down at her footwear. The boots weren't the worst choice she could have made, but she would have chosen differently if she suspected needing to run a mile in them. The long run warmed her up quickly, and she settled into a swift, steady pace.

Upon reaching the church, Megan found the door locked. She nearly panicked until she noticed a light on in one of the windows. Sprinting over to the lit area, she peered in and saw a young woman vacuuming. Knocking on the window did nothing since the woman wore earbuds.

There must be another door.

Continuing her circuit of the church, Megan found an unlocked side door and slipped inside. Her instructions said only that the child would be hidden in an upper room. It took her several minutes to find the stairs and locate the baby. She expected to find the child wailing her lungs out, but instead, she found the infant fussing softly.

"How long have you been here, baby?" Megan asked, kneeling beside the cardboard box holding the child. The move brought her close enough to get a good whiff. "Phew, okay, so it's been a few hours. Let's get you out of that messy business."

Anger and relief made Megan tremble as she untangled the infant from the sweat-stained, damp blanket. The child's crying intensified.

"I'm out of practice, but I'll try to make this painless."

Finding a clean set of clothes, some disposable wipes, and a fresh diaper tossed down beside the cardboard box, Megan quickly made good use of the items. Not wanting to put the cleaned-up baby back in the ruined blanket, Megan pulled off her suit jacket and wrapped the kid up tightly. As she finished tying off the arms to fix the jacket in place, her fingers brushed something stiff within one of the pockets. Since she didn't have a watch, she couldn't tell how much time remained, but it couldn't be much. She had to undo the knot to open the jacket and retrieve her ID badge.

You're a little young for the badge, but maybe someday it'll suit you.

After tucking away her badge, Megan lugged the baby downstairs, startled the cleaning lady, and explained the situation. It took some convincing, but finally, the woman called 911 and agreed to stay with the child until the police arrived. Megan left the church and jogged to the pickup spot.

She wanted nothing more than to be taken back to her sister and allowed to sleep for a few hours, but when she climbed into the van and turned over the tracker, she sensed something amiss.

Tim and Randy wore broad grins.

"Something happened," Megan muttered, not quite sure she wanted to know.

"The EMT kid cracked," Tim explained. "Walked right up to a cop and started blabbing his whole story. His handler had to shoot the cop and the kid. They're taking the kid back to base for a trial."

"He's so dead," Randy commented.

The van started moving. Thrown off balance, Megan sat down and strapped in.

"Why are you pleased by this news?" she asked, looking from Tim to Randy and back again.

"It means the baby he was supposed to rescue is up for grabs," said Tim. "We're closest too, so we have a good chance of making it. The firefighter found his package and the bonus one, so this is our chance to tie."

"You may have to fight the soldier for the package," Randy noted. "I think they're approaching from the other side."

"You need to get there first." Tim emphasized the statement with a sharp look. "Gary said that since the EMT got disqualified, they're skipping the third round. Two people will face the Tribunal tonight."

Although not certain what that would entail, Megan gathered she should avoid that fate.

The driver stopped the van. Megan disembarked at the gates to a small cemetery. She could clearly see a cardboard box sitting atop one of the graves near the center. Disregarding the paths, Megan darted between the graves to reach the box. Her heart pumped so hard her head hurt, and she silently cursed the cruelty of abandoning a baby in a cemetery on a cold night.

Please don't be dead!

The piercing cries of a baby never sounded so good. Picking up the red-faced infant, Megan tried to comfort him.

"You're singing my song, little man." Cradling the baby, Megan rubbed his back and picked her way back toward the white van. "A good cry sounds wonderful right now. Let's get you somewhere safe."

Suddenly, Shanice stepped in her way.

"Give me the baby." The woman's tone drilled home the command. She held a knife out to the side so Megan could see it.

Tim, Randy, and two other men—Shanice's handlers—eagerly watched the drama unfold.

They planned this. It's probably part of the blasted game.

"Put the knife down, and I'll consider it," Megan countered.

"Don't do it," called one of the soldier's handlers. "Think of Andre. This is the only way he'll have immunity."

Shanice stepped forward. Megan backed up, trying not to trip over a gravestone.

"I don't want to hurt you," said Shanice, "but I must protect my son."

And I must protect my sister.

"Let's do the turnover together," Megan offered. "A three-way tie will get everybody through the round." She wasn't sure the game organizers would agree with the logic. They seemed to do whatever they pleased, but she wanted to believe they followed some rules.

"Or it could get none of us through," Shanice argued. "I'm not taking that chance. Hand it over."

"What's going on here?" The new female voice came from behind Megan.

The handlers subtly reached for weapons.

One of the men who came with Shanice cursed.

"Wait. Let's see what the cop does," Tim said quietly.

"If she gets too close, I'm killing her," said the other man with Shanice.

Making a snap decision, Megan stepped close to the soldier and thrust the baby into her arms. She gripped the hand holding the weapon and leaned in so the others wouldn't hear.

"Give me the knife and get that kid to the cop," said Megan. "Convince her to walk away."

Shanice clutched the knife a second longer before letting Megan pry it away. Once in control of the weapon, Megan stepped out of the soldier's path, placed a hand on her back, and propelled her toward the approaching officer.

"Why did you do that?" Tim hissed the question as he moved to her side. He snatched the knife away.

"To save the cop, obviously," said Randy. His voice rumbled with disgust. "There goes our money." He grabbed Megan's arm in a vice-like grip. "Get in the van."

"It might be all right," said Tim. "We'll have to wait and see how the viewers vote."

Megan shot him a curious look.

Randy used his thumb to point to their right where a young man stood near some video equipment.

Megan tried to conjure a feeling besides bone-deep weariness, but now that she had stopped running around the city and sacrificed her suit jacket for a good cause, she was too cold to care.

Chapter 10:
Grandfather

"Sorry." Jeffrey Gatton grabbed the napkin and swiped at the soup dripping down the woman's chin. Spoon feeding a very attractive woman wasn't a task he had much experience with. Despite the carefully crafted reputation as a party-loving billionaire, Jeff didn't often interact directly with people, let alone pretty girls. Guns and girls both made him nervous. The combination made coordination difficult, even though the gun wasn't meant for him.

"Relax, Jeffrey," said CIA Man. He sat on the guest bed pointing a gun at the girl. "I need some of that soup to make it into her. I may need to keep her alive for a few more days."

Scooping up another spoonful, Jeff steadied his nerves and aimed for the woman's mouth. She said nothing because CIA Man insisted she stay silent. Jeff didn't know why. It's not like she could do much bound hand and foot to the upright chair. Her head tipped right, and her eyes didn't quite focus, thanks to the drug CIA Man kept pumping into her. This time, most of the spoon's contents successfully made it into the woman's mouth.

A soft knock at the door brought CIA Man to his feet. He slipped into the corner behind the door and looked sharply at Jeff, gun trained once again on the young woman in the chair.

"Who is it?" Jeff called.

The response was too muffled to understand.

Jeff gestured to the door, silently asking for and receiving permission to answer it.

CIA Man shifted his gun to the door.

"Keep them out of the room," he ordered softly.

Swallowing hard, Jeff put down the spoon, crossed the room to the door, and cautiously opened it. He only got it open a few inches before it sprang out of his grip and crashed into CIA Man.

Four muffled shots sounded as Jeff stumbled backward, nearly landing in the young woman's lap.

CIA Man grunted and cursed as he too backed away from the door. The way he leaned against the wall told Jeff at least one bullet had hit him in the leg. Murder in his eyes, he raised the gun toward Jeff.

The door continued its journey toward the wall and struck with a crash.

A figure entered and calmly shot CIA Man twice more in the chest.

Jeff caught his balance and flinched as the new bullets hit their mark, who slid to the ground, partially hidden behind the twin bed. CIA Man's gun fell to the floor with a distinct thump.

"Don't kill him," called the young woman, sounding surprisingly alert. "We don't know if they have her yet. His men won't listen to us!"

Kneeling before the fallen man, the newcomer gently picked up his left hand, turned it palm up, and dragged a small blade across the tender flesh.

"Just a mild sedative and paralytic agent for now," said the man, interrupting a new round of curses from CIA Man. "Thought you might be wearing a vest. Bet you're glad you did. Concentrate on breathing. There's a good chap."

His refined British accent struck Jeff as odd. Now that the man had stopped moving, Jeff recognized him as Brady, the new maintenance guy. The few times they'd spoken, there hadn't been even a hint of an accent.

"You there," said the man, addressing Jeff. "Give us a hand with him. I'd like to minimize the blood loss."

"You shouldn't move him then," Jeff mumbled.

"Best to be on the safe side," advised the man. "Let a fellow like this out of sight for a second, and he'll stab you in the back."

Reaching down, he grabbed CIA Man's ankles and dragged him into the room's center. Next, he cut some strips off the man's shirt and bound his hands, feet, a leg wound, and an arm wound. By the end, the prisoner looked like a very strange corpse. As a final touch, the man stuffed earplugs into place.

Jeff stared at him with mixed feelings. He didn't look scary now, but he still held a frightening amount of power.

"Why are you doing that?" Jeff asked.

"Because sedatives don't always work instantly," said the young woman, "and people can fake their effects as I did."

"But the injections—" Jeff began.

"Those worked fine while in my system." The young woman slipped a hand free from her bonds. "I simply misled him about how long each dose lasted."

"Clever, Baby Bird," said the British man affectionately.

"May I borrow a knife, *Grandfather*?" The woman stressed the last word, holding a hand out expectantly. Amusement and affection lit up her eyes.

"Cheeky little git," said the man, placing a switchblade in her hand. Catching Jeff's dumbfounded expression, he explained the exchange. "Cassie was my pupil in the business, as Lia is hers."

"She's in trouble, Smith," said Lia, solemnly handing the blade back. "Real trouble."

Jeff hadn't even noticed her deal with the rest of the bindings.

"Don't count her out yet," said Smith. Retracting the blade, he tucked the weapon into a pocket. "She's as clever as you and as lucky as me."

"What should we do?" asked Jeff.

He didn't want to break up their moment, but every second wasted brought a good chunk of his life's work further out of reach.

"You should finish eating that," said Smith, pointing first to Lia and then to the bowl of soup. Next, he faced Jeff. "And you should get back to your office and monitor the situation with Cassie while I deal with our CIA friend."

"It's cold." Despite the complaint, Lia obeyed the order from Smith.

"I can do that," said Jeff, trying to figure out how to move his legs. "Should I call the police?"

"No!" Lia's sharp answer pulled Jeff in from the dreamy state of shock. She set the spoon down and turned the full might of her intense gaze on Jeff. "Helping my mentor may require doing things you don't want the police involved with."

"We're traveling highly unofficial channels tonight, Mr. Gatton," said Smith. "Best keep this quiet."

"Is my mother okay?" Jeff wondered.

"She's tucked up safe in her flat," Smith reported. "I'll know if anything's amiss."

Jeff tensed.

"It's not like that," Lia said. Abandoning the meal, she stood and placed a hand on Jeff's shoulder.

He jerked free and glared at her.

"How do I know?" Anger hardened the question into a sharp accusation.

"Because *we're* not like that," said Lia.

"Call her," said Smith. "I hired a fellow to watch the area for strange activity. I believe he mentioned introducing himself."

"She could be forced to say anything!" Jeff's hands shook. Even with the CIA problem trussed up at his feet, the helplessness threatened to paralyze him.

"Then, listen to her," Lia suggested gently. Taking his arm, she led Jeff over to the chair she'd been bound to a few minutes ago. Once he was seated, she knelt, placed both hands atop his, and met his suspicious gaze. "Not the words. The tone. You're right, people can be forced to say anything, but unless they're highly trained, you can hear the difference when they say something under duress."

"I think she'd like to hear from you," said Smith. He offered Jeff a phone. "I'd offer you some privacy, but we're short on time."

Lia retreated to check on CIA Man.

Accepting the phone, Jeff called his mother. He pressed the speaker button so everybody could hear the conversation.

"Jeffrey? Are you all right? Are you hurt? What's wrong?"

The barrage of questions broke Jeff's tension, making him laugh with relief.

After assuring her of his own safety, Jeff got his mother talking about her eventful day. A man posing as a flower delivery guy had burst in and held her captive in her own home for several hours. During that time, he had four accomplices come in and share the burden of watching her. A young woman had arrived and fought the men.

Gatton looked to Lia for confirmation and received a nod.

The men overpowered Lia and left, leaving only one man behind to guard his mother. Soon after their departure, an older man came and ambushed the remaining thug.

"He promised a friend would check in and left," Jeff's mother concluded. "I didn't even get to thank him."

"No thanks necessary, madam," said Smith, "but do us a favor and stay in the rest of the evening. That will make safeguarding you easier on my mate."

After exchanging several more assurances with his mother, Jeff finally closed the conversation and returned the phone to Smith.

"How can I help?" he asked, fully invested this time.

"I haven't a clue," Smith admitted, "but I'm sure you'll think of something."

CIA man stirred.

"If you'll excuse me, I have an interrogation to conduct," said Smith. "I dealt with the rest of your houseguests but take the baby bird with you anyway. She can protect you."

Bending down, Smith recovered CIA Man's gun and handed it over to Lia.

"Don't wait up, luv." Leaning down, he kissed her cheek.

Lia hugged him fiercely.

"Be careful. This fellow wasn't working alone," he said.

The statement jolted Jeff.

There could be more rogue CIA agents?

"Come, Mr. Gatton, we still have work to do," said Lia. Raising the gun, she cautiously advanced toward the door, stepping around CIA Man.

"Best stick close to her," Smith advised.

"Thank you," Jeff answered. He meant much more than acknowledgment of the current advice.

"All in a day's work," replied Smith. "Ignore the mess. It'll get sorted. When you speak with Little Bird, tell her 'the Hawk is hunting.'"

Finding the cryptic statement deeply unsettling, Jeff relied on his publicist's training.

Ask no questions. Plausible deniability.

During the trip down to his first-floor office, Jeff thought he saw a body in one of the rooms they passed. The sight quickened his breaths and his steps. The publicist's mantra echoed louder in his head.

Once safely ensconced in his computer chair, a small measure of control returned to Jeff.

Lia stood off to the side, trying to stay out of the way.

Jeff directed her to a spare chair.

"Don't hover," he said. "It hurts my concentration."

"I'll stay by the door," Lia promised. "Smith's very thorough, but they could potentially send a second wave."

"I hope not," Jeff said, absently waking his computer and two spare monitors.

The Eagle Eyes controls spread out before him.

What will keep Cassandra alive?

He had so many options. The hard part would be narrowing down what to send. If he tried to cram too much into any single patch, it would fail or take too long to transfer. A time check said that the hour deadline CIA Man gave to Cassandra had expired several minutes ago.

"Should we call her?" Jeff asked.

"She won't answer, but you can try," said Lia.

He did, but Lia's prediction came true.

Jeff scanned his options frantically. Finally, his eyes locked on the perfect mod to send.

He let a smile form.

Let's try God Mode.

Chapter 11:
God Mode

"Congratulations. God Mode is available," said Eagle Eyes. *"Once activated, you will have thirty seconds to address anybody within range on their mobile phones, computers, or Eagle Eyes units. Would you like to enter God Mode?"*

Not yet.

Cassandra had snuck into the building with ease, but she wasn't quite ready to pick a fight with the security teams yet. She also needed a moment to compose an appropriate speech.

Track the hostiles, identify the neutral parties, and locate Megan Luchek.

"Acknowledged. Please await processing," said the program. *"I've also been instructed to tell you that Siren and Hive Mind are downloading. I will inform you when they are ready."*

You're receiving instructions now?

The program didn't understand the question, so Cassandra reworded it more directly.

"Yes. Mr. Gatton initiated both downloads thirty-three seconds ago."

Call him.

"Calling now."

Cassandra ducked into a supply closet. The building's security cameras focused on the main entrance and elevators, but she needed some privacy to plan, especially if she didn't have to fake a surrender.

"Cassandra, is it you?" Gatton sounded like he was bracing for disappointment. "Are you … safe?"

"Safety's a fluid thing, Gatton," Cassandra answered. "I'm not currently fighting for my life, if that's your question. Have you dealt with your houseguests?"

She brought up the mapping feature and watched as Eagle Eyes populated the basic schematic with multicolored dots. Most figures were yellow, which meant that the program hadn't categorized them as friend or foe yet. As it matched a phone number and profile to the database of known criminals, the program switched their marker over to deep red. Those in close association with red markers were switched to a lighter shade of red with a question mark.

"Yes!" Relief made Gatton's word trail. "A few ... friends of yours cleaned house."

"Good. That will make this a lot easier," said Cassandra. She'd only sent him one friend, but Lia kept her own contacts.

The space Cassandra intended to clear was significantly bigger than any private residence, but the predictable layout gave her more options in setting traps.

"CIA Man won't be a problem," said Gatton, "but your friend said he wasn't working alone."

How would she know?

They'd barely touched upon lessons involving asset development. Lia simply didn't have the field experience to have contacts deep inside the Central Intelligence Agency.

"I think we're talking about different friends," Cassandra commented.

Switching to thermal view, she carefully turned in a slow circle, so the program could map figures not carrying cell phones. Four orange blobs appeared a few floors above her. The program swiftly refined the images as height, weight, and body proportions became clearer. The even spacing between the two women, one man, and single child hinted at them being hostages, but Cassandra confirmed the guess by overlaying a metal simulator.

"Old guy. British accent," said Gatton. "Kind of scary. Please, please tell me he's your friend."

"Not the one I had in mind, but I can confirm he's a friend," Cassandra said. For a man supposedly long out of the game, Smith kept surprisingly well informed. His involvement troubled her. As her mentor, he'd always insisted she handle her own affairs. The few times he had stepped in to help, she'd been in far deeper trouble than she'd realized. "Did he have a message for me?"

"He said, 'the Hawk is hunting,'" Gatton reported. "Don't know what it means, but it didn't sound good."

"It's not," said Cassandra. Having completed her circle, she stopped moving and let a few waves of fear and anger pass through. Dwelling on them now could get her killed, but she couldn't completely stop them from forming.

The title belonged to somebody who'd tried to control her once long ago. Although the organization she thought of as the Shadow Council shared roots with the official CIA, they were distinct entities that occasionally pulled from the same resources. The training program that made her was one such resource.

Hawk recruited for the official team. Back then, he'd been brash, bold, and reckless. He'd accidentally killed her friend during a vain attempt to add Cassandra to his private hit squad.

"Keep Lia close to you," Cassandra said. "And give me a rundown on the latest updates. I think the building's been partially emptied, but that advantage won't last long."

"Which updates did I send you?" asked Gatton. His voice sounded stronger now that the conversation turned to business.

She rattled off the list for him.

"Meltdown and Scrapper are almost the same thing, but Meltdown's supposed to be gentler in case someone's still wearing Eagle Eyes when it's initiated," said Gatton. "Night Owl will let you work while unconscious, and Hive Mind should connect you to another unit. The only code it could link to now is Agent Luchek's, but not if she's out of range."

His summaries sounded very similar to what she'd expect from Eagle Eyes itself, which made sense as the program was essentially an extension of the tech genius.

"In theory, Siren will draw other units to you, but it's in a very experimental stage," said Gatton. "In some of the test cases, it accidentally set off external alarms—fire in two cases, security in the third. Use with caution."

"Thanks for the warning," said Cassandra. "I assume you're going to watch and monitor the show."

"As long as Overlord works properly," Gatton answered. "Thoughts are transferred faster through the program. Switching over now."

Cassandra waited with eyes closed as Gatton hung up the cell phone and joined her Eagle Eyes unit.

Feels good to be back in business.

"Ground rules are the same as always," said Cassandra. "Try not to get me killed. Show me the nearest targets and their weaknesses."

Let's clear out some competition first.

"How?"

Enter God Mode. Do you want the flashy version or the non-flashy version?

"Non-flashy. We're short on time."

Can I at least use the voice? The building has a PA system. It'll be awesome.

"Fine." She didn't have the energy to argue with the man-child, and she figured anything he considered awesome would likely be suitably frightening.

Gatton gave her a short tutorial on activating God Mode before providing her with the encryption key.

Masking effect in place. You're live in 3, 2, 1. Go.

"This is your one and only warning. Leave or I will destroy you." A chill ran through Cassandra when she heard the harsh, strangely distorted words.

The colored dots marking people collectively froze.

Great. Every tagged target will receive a personalized version of that, but I think we can do better.

Cassandra placed a question mark in the text box that let him access her thoughts.

You have twenty seconds of God Mode left. Try this.

Several lines of text appeared. Deciding to trust the young man, Cassandra spoke again.

"The lights are mine."

Every light in the building flickered at her announcement.

"Your phones are mine."

A small screen opened in the bottom left corner of Cassandra's vision. It showed a security camera view of two men leaping about and throwing down their phones.

"Run or die."

A power outlet near the men on screen exploded, sending them dashing toward the stairs. Several other outlets sent out sparks of electricity at intervals timed to happen as a figure passed them.

Cassandra chuckled.

How are you doing that?

Schematics showed Kuiza Industries made the wires. They're notorious for flaming out when placed under electrical

stress. **I just messed with the electricity flow where needed.**

Gatton's little light show kicked a hornet's nest. Light and dark red figures swarmed in every direction. A few headed for the exits.

God Mode has ended.

"Can you kill all the lights?" asked Cassandra, waiting until certain the words wouldn't be broadcast to the PA system.

Not for long. There's a backup generator not connected to the lines I control currently. Why?

"Darkness is psychologically difficult to deal with," said Cassandra. "It's also easier to move about unseen."

You got it. Lights out in 3, 2, 1.

The entire building plunged into darkness right on cue.

Emergency lighting kicked into place a few seconds later, but by then, Cassandra had escaped the supply closet and made it to the nearest stairwell. Taking out a small expandable baton, Cassandra flicked it out. Taking the stairs two at a time, she soon encountered a pair of security men. A combination of thermal view and the combat analysis program gave her a distinct advantage.

The first man was unconscious before the second began to turn toward her. The move left his right side open. She slammed the baton into his side. The close quarters didn't give her a lot of room to maneuver, but the blow knocked the man back into the railing. He grunted and pulled something out of a pocket. In the dim light, Cassandra couldn't tell what it was, but she didn't take any chances. Two flicks of her wrist brought her weapon down across the man's arm and then back across his jaw, eliciting two cries.

He started to fall down the stairs.

Grabbing hold of his collar, Cassandra used the man's downward momentum to drive him forward into the wall. He collapsed with a groan.

Weariness crashed down on Cassandra from the top of her head to her toes, but she drove it off with a surge of determination. According to the dots still in the building, she had at least two more pairs lurking around stairwells before she could move toward the interior.

Feeling around near the stairs, Cassandra recovered the thing the man had dropped. It was a stun gun.

A search of the other man yielded another one.

Tucking one stun gun away, Cassandra held the baton in one hand and the remaining stun gun in the other. Hopefully, the next pair of guards would require a tad less brute force.

A taser would be nicer, but this will do.

Chapter 12:
Immunity Card

The van driver dropped them off near the elevators, but a guard stopped them before they could enter the main building. Megan thought something might be off about the lights, but that concerned her less than getting inside the warm building.

"Hold up. You can't enter right now," said the guard standing in front of the elevator bank. He held out a hand in a stopping motion.

"Why not?" asked Tim.

The guard shrugged.

"Some psycho knocked out the power."

Megan's ears perked up at the guard's announcement. A small smile formed.

"The generator kicked in, but I wouldn't trust it," the guard continued.

Randy grabbed Megan's arm and flung her against the nearest wall. Before she could do much more than blink in surprise, he pinned her in place with his right forearm.

"You know something," he accused.

"I'm not helping you," Megan declared. A surge of internal heat temporarily drove off the cold. She suspected Gatton might have been responsible for the power problems.

Activating Eagle Eyes, Megan asked the program to confirm. It flooded her with images and updates, so she shut off the displays, letting it stay active in the background.

"You will help, whether you want to or not," Randy said darkly.

"How about a warning?" asked Megan, fixing Randy with a hard stare. "I keep several friends who fall on the wrong side of crazy. You do not want to mess with them."

"Let's try the stairs," suggested Tim, interrupting the staring contest between Megan and Randy.

Pulling a plastic zip tie out of a pocket, Randy tossed it to Tim.

"Tie her hands." Randy gave Megan a sharp warning look then backed up a step.

"Hold out your hands," said Tim, stepping into the space directly in front of her.

Pushing down the instinct to fight, Megan followed the instruction. She longed to slam an elbow into Randy's irksome face, but the knowledge that retribution could fall to Tara kept her from doing so. She didn't know how much more abuse her wrists could take.

Once the binding slid into place, Randy pushed her toward the stairs.

"Move," he said.

Tim stepped around her and led the way, jogging up the stairs.

Megan had to focus on each step to keep the pace and not take a painful tumble in the process. The stairwell wasn't much warmer than the garage had been.

A pair of bodies blocked the way to the third-floor landing.

Tim whistled. Randy cursed.

Megan wanted to check on them, but Tim and Randy only increased the pace up the next two flights of stairs. When they entered the fifth floor, the wave of warmth made Megan's hands tingle.

"Get her to the holding cell," said Randy. "I'm going to see what's going on."

"Do I cut the ties?" asked Tim.

"No. Gary's probably going to want to see her," said Randy. "Wait with them. I'll be right back."

Impatient to check on her sister, Megan ran past the other cells, fumbled with the gate, and stepped inside.

Tara lay curled onto her right side, fast asleep.

Guessing her knees wouldn't keep her upright for long anyway, Megan carefully knelt by the bed. A lock of blond hair had fallen across her sister's face. Absently, Megan reached to move the hair. As her fingers brushed the wayward lock, Tara's right hand snapped up and caught hold of her left wrist.

"Megan, you're freezing," said Tara, eyes widened with alarm and concern. She sat up quickly, then stood, pulling Megan up with her.

"Where's your jacket?"

"Serving as a blanket," Megan mumbled. She relaxed as Tara sat her down on the bed and wrapped her in a protective hug. The warmth and temporary safety made Megan drowsy, but she didn't want to miss anything.

The grunting noise Tara made simultaneously conveyed frustration, exasperation, and love.

"Why are you even back? I told you to leave." The hissed question came out strong, but the statement ended on a weary note.

"Should have known that was a lost cause," Megan said, amused despite their circumstances. "When was the last time I listened to you?"

"Well, maybe you should start," Tara retorted, poking Megan in a ticklish spot on her right side.

Megan instinctively jerked away, but Tara clasped her hands and held on tighter.

"Oh, relax. Not everything has to be a fight," said Tara. She sighed. "You'd be in less life-threatening situations if you took more sage advice."

"Like what?" Megan asked, humoring her.

"Become a banker. Listen to your sister. Rest so you can punch a bad guy. I don't know. Take your pick."

"We're going to get out of this," Megan promised, patting Tara's arm. "But I like your reason to rest."

"Go to sleep," Tara ordered. "I'll wake you if a punching candidate arrives. Continue to fight me on this and I'll start singing."

"I yield," said Megan, chuckling.

Her sister's many talents did not include singing well.

Instead of sleeping, Megan checked Eagle Eyes. The program brought her up to speed on the many updates, told her of Cassandra's presence and mission, and asked for instructions.

Find Cassandra. If Hive Mind is ready, connect me to her.

"The requested extension is only 67.21% downloaded. Would you like to be notified when it finishes?"

Yes. Is there an escape plan?

"Unknown. Radio chatter indicates that the hostiles are moving prisoners up to floor number seven. It is likely they are baiting a trap for Cassandra."

How is she doing?

"The number of inert figures indicates that she has successfully completed four encounters wherein—"

"Warning. Hostiles approaching."

Megan tensed but tried not to react.

Tim and Randy barged in.

Gently breaking free of Tara's hold, Megan stood.

The thugs attended to pre-determined tasks. Randy hustled Megan out the door while Tim bound Tara's hands.

Megan drew comfort from knowing they intended to keep Tara close, even as she fervently wished they'd leave her sister behind.

The hectic trip up to the seventh floor passed in a blur.

Once again, Megan's party arrived dead last. This time, the hostages were bunched together at the room's center. Brett Ringo, the EMT, sat on a stool near them. His eyes fixed on a blank portion of the gray carpet, and his face lacked expression. White bandages engulfed the upper portion of his left arm. Blood soaked through in one spot, staining the bandages. Only tear-stained cheeks indicated that Brett knew something bad was coming.

Tim added Tara to the cluster of hostages huddled in front of Brett. Randy led Megan over to the side where Shanice Nevins and Jacob Chantry stood.

"Bring her here," said Gary impatiently. Snapping his fingers, he pointed to a location about a foot to his left.

The air of righteous anger coming off him didn't bode well.

Switching directions, Randy moved Megan to the indicated spot.

A young man holding a video camera hovered nearby.

Megan silently instructed Eagle Eyes to interfere with the signal. She couldn't predict what would happen, but she doubted having a permanent record of it would be good.

Gary forced a wide smile.

"We've had quite a game so far," he said.

"With some technical difficulties," Megan said mildly. She turned her head in a slow, deliberate arc, indicating the soft emergency lights glowing around them.

Gary's expression immediately clouded.

"So it seems," he admitted, "but my men will deal with the intruder shortly."

"How do you know there's only one?" asked Megan. "Maybe there's a whole team at work."

"We'll know soon," Gary said. "That drama can wait. I want to focus on the first quest's drama. We had everything from escape attempts to cheating to timely heroics." He waved in the appropriate directions as he summarized. "Fortunately for everybody, the viewers loved it."

"You have your money. Let us go," said Jacob.

"Unfortunately for everybody, justice demands we address the wrongs done tonight," said Gary, completely ignoring the firefighter. He took a brief tour of the room, stopping near each of the hero candidates.

"Make your point, Gary," said Megan when he reached her.

"I don't like you," said Gary.

"Is that supposed to make me feel bad?" asked Megan, truly puzzled. She spoke slowly, trying not to provoke the crazy dude.

"But the audience does," Gary added. "Congratulations. You won the Audience Vote. This is for you." He held a small card out to her.

The side facing up was blank.

Accepting the card, Megan flipped it over and saw the word *IMMUNITY* printed in glossy, gold capital letters.

"We're about to play a game of chance," Gary explained. "Winner goes free, losers face the Tribunal."

"What does that mean?" Megan pressed.

"They die with as much entertainment value as we can muster," said Gary. "That card grants immunity to one person for three rounds. Unless they're incredibly unlucky, it should guarantee this person survives the game. Shall I give it to your sister?"

Megan sensed a trick.

Map the room. Mark the hostiles.

She had no idea what she'd do with the information, but she wasn't going to wait around for Gary and company to run their twisted little game.

Agent, stall them. Hive Mind should be ready in two minutes.

The voice sailing through her head carried Cassandra's voiceprint.

"Wait," Megan called as Gary reached for the card. "You haven't explained the game yet."

"It's a simple game of knockout," said Gary. "Each player will be assigned three numbers. We'll roll a pair of dice. If a person's number comes up, Al or Ty will hit them. If they get knocked out, they lose."

"That's a stupid game." Megan didn't have to work at inserting contempt. "I'm surprised your viewers want to see something that boring."

"Would you like to play?" asked Gary.

A nod from him prompted two men to step up beside Megan. One started deliberately rolling up his sleeves while the other placed his large hands on her upper arms, holding her in place.

Tara gave her a nervous look that simultaneously asked for more information and begged her to shut up.

"I think your viewers want to see more action than innocent people getting beaten," Megan said evenly.

"What do you think they want to see?" Gary inquired.

"Cut these ties and give them a real fight to watch," said Megan.

Agent, this works much better if you stay conscious. One minute and twenty seconds left. Try not to get yourself knocked out.

Megan wasn't sure how Cassandra monitored the exchange, but she couldn't dwell on the point.

"Maybe we should give the viewers a preview of—"

"I still haven't made my choice," said Megan, cutting Gary off. "Aren't you curious?"

"You're going to choose your sister," said Gary. "That much is obvious."

"No." Megan milked the shock of the denial for every second.

Gary studied her suspiciously.

"Who are you granting immunity to?" he asked.

Megan put off answering by meeting the gazes of the other candidates and hostages. Tara's stunned expression hurt, but Megan shoved the discomfort aside.

Sorry, Liv. Buying time here.

"Andre," said Megan, moving her attention to Shanice.

The soldier sagged in relief.

"He's the youngest. He should get the protection," said Megan. She tried to speak slowly to consume the remaining download time, but the explanation flew out of her at breakneck speed.

"Interesting choice," said Gary. He smiled. "Normally, we'd divide the numbers by four instead of three, but I think it'll be easier if we give Tara the boy's numbers."

Megan tried to step forward, but the goon holding her arms increased his grip.

"Give the numbers to me," she demanded. "I'll take Andre's place."

"Noble, but that's not how the game works. Besides, I'd like you intact for the second quest." Gary suddenly tilted his head to the side. "I guess we could take a poll on it." He snapped his fingers twice at the young man fiddling with the camera. "You, get on that."

Abandoning the camera, the young man hurried over to a laptop and started typing furiously.

"While we wait, let's deal with another matter," Gary said cheerfully. Drawing a gun from a shoulder holster, he pointed it at Brett. "The fallen hero."

Chapter 13:
Meltdown

Diversion. Now!

"Commencing Chaos Call." The computer program sounded both smug and gleeful.

Everybody's cell phone rang at once.

Most men drew their phones and tried to silence them. One man muttered something about the job being cursed, earning a glare from Gary.

"Bet it's the new tech," said the man who'd rolled up his sleeves. "Knew we couldn't trust it."

Agent, I need you to activate Siren. We're not quite connected yet, so I can't do it for you.

Lacking the time to question Cassandra's request, Megan conveyed the instruction to Eagle Eyes.

"Commencing Siren."

Eagle Eyes showed her a picture of a blinking purple dot with concentric lines radiating out of it, then moved it to the bottom left corner of her vision.

Although nothing else happened, Megan remained tense with anticipation.

"Should I check it out?" asked the man holding Megan's arms.

His grip loosened enough for her to shrug free.

"No, I don't—"

A radio tucked under one of the spotlights erupted with incoherent shouts, cutting Gary off. Seconds later, both stairwell doors banged open violently. Two sets of men sprinted in. One man held his head with both hands. Another staggered forward, bleeding from the

178

nose. A third could barely stand, so his companion helped him limp along. A fifth man stormed in and ran in Megan's direction.

She recognized him.

Instinct caused Megan to shrink away from Curtis D'Angelo since his expression was downright murderous. The move inadvertently brought her closer to Gary, but at least his irritation was currently directed at the general situation, not her specifically.

The first two sprinters halted when they got within ten feet of Megan. They stood trembling and breathing hard, watching Megan warily.

The towering goon with Megan made himself useful by stopping D'Angelo's mad rush forward.

"Make it stop!" D'Angelo sidestepped so he could deliver the command with direct eye contact.

Observing the results, Megan was inclined to agree with D'Angelo. By this time, even the slow pair had reached the ten-foot safe zone around her. They collectively formed a loose circle around Megan, Gary, the hostages, and Brett Ringo.

Shut down Siren.

"As you wish. Shutting down Siren."

"Why does everything revolve around you?" Gary's voice reached out to Megan with deadly calm.

His gun pressed hard into her back.

Agent, tell Gary to answer his phone.

"Answer your phone and find out," Megan said. She stood straighter to gain as much distance from the gun as possible.

Gary's phone rang, causing him to release a primal roar of frustration.

Megan braced, but she couldn't stop the blow as Gary's gun slammed into her back between the shoulder blades, knocking her into the thug who'd recently kept D'Angelo at bay.

"Kneel, so I know you won't go anywhere," said Gary as his phone rang again. He backed up the order with the gun.

Megan turned around and obeyed the order slowly, desperately hoping for a chance to fight.

The phone rang a third time.

"What do you want?" Gary demanded.

He must have hit the speaker button because Megan heard the answer loud and clear.

"You have stolen what's mine," spoke a chilling, mechanical

voice, before Gary could even utter a greeting. "You are unworthy. Remove my property from your people and return them to my servants or suffer the consequences."

One man—the one with a nosebleed—whipped his hands up to his right eye, removed something, and threw it to the ground. He repeated the process with something from his left eye before backing up a few steps. The others exchanged uneasy glances.

Irritation flashed through Megan. Someday she'd have to have a serious conversation with Gatton about their working relationship. This was not the first time he'd called her a servant.

"Hive Mind download complete. Initiating Meltdown and Scrapper protocols."

"I think I'll shoot your servant and see—" Gary's threat ended in a hideous scream.

Yelps, shouts, and curses flew out of the strange circle of men surrounding them. They knocked into one another and brushed frantically at their eyes. Then, suddenly, they went still.

"That was a sample of what's in store," said Gatton, still using the creepy deity voice. "You have three seconds to obey."

Megan finally began to understand as she watched D'Angelo rip the Eagle Eyes contacts out and toss them away. The others followed the two examples as quickly as possible. A contact landed in front of Megan. It sparked and made a faint popping noise as it burned a hole in the carpet.

Should I be worried?

"Negative. This unit is exempt from Meltdown and Scrapper."

"No!" screeched Gary. "I'm keeping it!"

Megan glanced back as the circle immediately widened around her. She wondered what had caused the change until she saw Gary's bloodshot eyes. He stood near the hostages swinging his gun back and forth.

A black-clad figure slipped out of the circle and whacked Gary hard across the shoulders, sending his gun flying. Another crack knocked him to the ground. He lay on his side moaning.

Most of the men stood dumbfounded, but a few drew handguns and pointed them at the figure.

"We have about ten seconds to save his eyes from burning out," said Cassandra, rolling Gary over onto his back. "I guarantee that sight will not be pleasant. Help or leave while you can. Somebody needs to hold him still."

Most of the guards fled.

"He was going to shoot me," murmured Brett.

Jacob Chantry grabbed a gun from one of the distracted guards and held it on him.

"I'm leaving. Robbie, let's go."

The guard backed away slowly.

"I'm out," declared one of the other remaining guards.

The second mad rush to exit the room included the last of the guards and the Chantry brothers.

Five seconds, Agent.

Uttering a noise that embodied her frustration and annoyance, Megan shuffled over on her knees and brought her bound hands down hard on Gary's stomach.

His breath gushed out.

"Keep still," she said. Since the move left her off balance, Megan landed stretched out across Gary's chest.

Cassandra's arms blocked most of Megan's view, but soon, a faint crunch reached her ears.

"It's done," said Cassandra. "All six units have been destroyed."

Excellent. I hate to rush you ladies, but the police are on the way. They're going to have a lot of uncomfortable questions.

"Looks like we cleared the room," Cassandra commented, helping Megan off Gary.

Alice and Brett Ringo had also slipped away. Only Shanice, Andre, and Tara remained.

"My father will kill you," Gary promised.

Cassandra gave him a brief look, then reached down and applied pressure to a spot on his neck.

"You should be grateful we saved your eyes," Cassandra noted.

His response was a hateful glare.

When Gary fell unconscious, she returned her attention to Megan and used a pocketknife to cut the zip tie.

"I'm going to leave this with you," said Cassandra, holding the knife out to Megan. "This isn't over yet, but there's nothing you can do now anyway. Free the others, deal with the police, and take your sister home."

"Don't I get an introduction?" asked Tara.

"Maybe someday," said Cassandra with a subtle nod toward the others. "Right now, I'm just a friend passing through."

Collecting the weapon she'd smacked Gary with, Cassandra turned to go.

"Wait. Thanks," called Megan. "Does this mean I owe you another one?"

"I was in the area," said Cassandra, folding the baton and sliding it into a pocket. "I'll see you around, agent."

Likewise, assassin.

She watched Cassandra stride toward the elevators and stairs.

"What should we do with him?" asked Tara.

"I guess we wait for the cops," said Megan, kneeling beside Shanice and Andre. "Hold still. This knife's pretty sharp."

Shanice followed the directive while Megan cut through the plastic binding her wrists together. Then she held her son still while Megan dealt with his bonds. The soldier whispered heartfelt thanks and clung to her son.

Finally, Megan cut through the ties holding her sister. She barely had time to move the knife away before Tara wrapped her in a tight hug.

Contacts incoming.

Megan tensed at Gatton's tone.

Good contacts or bad contacts?

"What's wrong?" asked Tara. Sensing the shift, she pulled out to arm's length and studied Megan's troubled expression.

South stairs are filled with hostiles. Get them to the north stairs and out of that building right now.

"We need to leave," said Megan.

Eagle Eyes provided a yellow arrow that pointed the way to the north stairwell. It also highlighted Gary's gun which had been abandoned where it fell. Scooping up the weapon, Megan released the magazine to check that it was loaded. Finding it full, she put the pieces back together and quelled the urge to shoot Gary. After everything he'd put them through, he deserved it, but that didn't change the fact that he was currently completely helpless.

Can't I wake him up and then shoot him?

Escaping is more important. Gatton reminded her.

How did you even hear that thought? She shoved the question into the box where Gatton could see it.

I didn't need to read a thought. Your stress levels are shouting. You also stared at Gary for 2.53 seconds with narrowed eyes. Wasn't hard to guess your thoughts would be murder-y.

Less psychoanalyzing. More leading the way out.

Shaking her head, Megan ushered her charges along the escape route Gatton highlighted.

Shanice initially let the boy run along beside her, but his tiny feet hit the stairs like jackhammers. She picked him up, sacrificing speed for semi-stealth. Thankfully, the nerve-wracking descent didn't last long.

Cops are three blocks over and moving fast. Send the hostages to the east corner of the building. It should be clear of bad guys. Then meet Cassandra. I'll send you the address when you need it.

Megan relayed the message.

Setting Andre down, Shanice gripped his hand, nodded thanks, and started jogging in the right direction.

Tara didn't budge.

"Go with them," said Megan. "The police will take you home."

"Where are you going?" Tara demanded.

"I have a meeting to discuss how to end this," said Megan.

We can reschedule the meeting.

Megan wasn't sure how she felt about sharing headspace with Cassandra. She'd forgotten about the Hive Mind connection.

I can teach you how to use Hive Mind later, Gatton promised. **Choose a path quickly. The hostiles found Gary and are descending. I don't like what they're saying. ETA two minutes.**

"Oh, never mind," Megan said, exasperated. Taking Tara's arm, she headed for the exit.

"You still don't have a jacket," Tara pointed out, stumbling along in her wake.

"That is the least of my worries right now," Megan said, quickening the pace.

"And you can't just run around a major city holding a handgun." Tara's voice slipped into lecture mode. "The police are as likely to shoot you as help you."

Your sister has a point.

She's right.

Cassandra and Gatton's contributions came through right on top of each other.

I will deal with both of you later, Megan silently vowed, making sure they saw the thought.

"I'm not putting this down until I can hand it—and you—over to a uniformed cop for safekeeping," said Megan. Nevertheless, she tucked the weapon into her shoulder holster.

They reached the edge of the parking garage and moved out into the city streets.

Travel went smoothly for two blocks. Then, the yellow arrow suddenly disappeared.

Megan stopped walking.

"Something wrong?" Tara inquired, also stopping.

"I don't know," Megan admitted.

Very wrong. Some of the cops you're headed toward are on the Club's payroll.

Great. Suggestions?

Find the nearest ritzy hotel. I'll book you a room under the name of Moira Jethro. You can rest and stash your sister while we sort through the madness.

I expect a very thorough debriefing later.

Reaching out, Megan gripped her sister's hand and smiled tightly.

"We're not going home yet," said Tara, correctly interpreting the gesture and expression.

"Not yet," Megan confirmed. "Let's get somewhere safe, and I'll explain what I can."

A new set of yellow arrows led her back the way they'd come. Megan stepped briskly, knowing that a hot shower and warm bed lay on the other end of this path. Once adequately rested, she could return her thoughts to ending the Cyber League's sadistic games.

Epilogue:
Loose Ends

"The FBI agent is still in the city," said Steel, handing his son a damp paper towel to hold over his eyes. "We'll find her."

"I want her dead," Gary declared. Pressing the cloth to his eyes squeezed some of the water out, giving the impression of tears running between his fingers. "She ruins everything."

"You have to admit she's profitable," Steel said, letting his gaze wander to the laptop displaying a summary of the Hero Contest.

Megan Luchek may not have won the only official quest, but her choices prompted an outpouring of Hero Worship. Gamblers from around the globe donated credits to purchase advantages for her. Had the game run to completion, she would have been worth a fortune. They could have auctioned her off on the black market or gone with the first plan and let the gamblers decide her manner of death.

We could still do both.

O's thought made Steel pause. He didn't usually agree with the second personality, but this thought intrigued him.

Capture her, fake her death, and sell her. Don't tell Gary about the last part.

"I don't care. I'll kill her myself," Gary muttered.

"You'll call your men and launch the next competition," said Steel.

"But we haven't even chosen all the tasks for the Criminal Contest," Gary argued. "It's slated to have the largest menu. The website's not even done yet."

"Doesn't matter. You only need the first task right now." Steel placed a hand on his son's shoulder to make sure he paid attention. "The agent's still in the city. We can't sweep all of Philadelphia, so use what you have. Work on the site while others do the hunting."

"What do you want the bounty set at?" Gary asked, looking unhappy with the plan.

"Free entry to the competition and another $10,000," said Steel, letting his hand drop from Gary's shoulder. "Be certain they understand accidentally killing her has severe consequences. She's worth a lot to us."

"I want to kill somebody," said Gary. "I *need* to kill somebody." His expression changed suddenly, brightening as a thought struck him. "What about the sister? Can I kill her?"

Steel considered the proposal. They might need to keep the judge alive to control the agent, but Gary's need for revenge seemed genuine.

"Put the same conditions and bounty out on the sister," instructed Steel.

Why not all of them? Mask the real target and give Gary a toy to play with.

Steel saw no reason to argue with O's logic.

"In fact, do the same for each hero and hostage from the Hero Contest, but make the bounty $2,500," said Steel. "They'll likely head for a police station, but they can't stay there forever. No one will suspect a second kidnapping."

Gary shrugged like he didn't care, but Steel could tell he was upset.

Let him kill the cousin.

O's suggestion had merit, but Steel needed Gary to build the website. They had others who could work on it, but this contest was mostly Gary's brainchild. The Popularity Contest had basically gone bust. The Hero Contest made money, but not as much as it could have if it ran smoothly. They needed the new competition to be spectacular to keep the investors happy. Thus, they needed Gary to be happy as well.

The cousin is in a hospital in Fairfax. It's not that far. Vinny also has Club debts.

Steel weighed the idea again. If they killed Vinny, his debts would go unpaid. On the other hand, getting revenge on the FBI agent through her cousin could be exactly what Gary needed to get his head back in the game.

The boy needs a win.

Steel thought O was pushing too hard, but he conceded the point.

"How about a little side trip?" Steel asked.

"What kind of side trip?" Gary asked skeptically.

"The kind where you get to murder somebody the agent values," said Steel.

A spark of interest entered Gary's eyes.

"Who?" asked Gary.

"Vinny," Steel answered.

Gary smiled and patted his jacket where his gun should be holstered. Finding nothing, he scowled.

"She stole my gun."

"I'll get you a new one," Steel promised. "For now, borrow one from Al or Ty."

"They ran off like cowards." Gary's lips curled in contempt.

"Not true. They called me," said Steel, stretching the truth a little. He'd been coming to check on Gary's progress anyway. His men had run into Al and Ty as they fled the building. "I sent them and some others to keep tabs on the escapees. As soon as you make the announcement, I'll have my people give you the updates to pass on to those wishing to enter the contest."

Hopping off the stool, Gary took three steps and froze.

"How will I get to the hospital keeping Vinny?" he wondered. "How will I get in? How will I kill him?"

Under other circumstances, Steel would find the stream of questions amusing.

"I think there's a retrieval expert hanging around," said Steel. "Take him with you."

Gary headed for the stairs with a new spring in his steps.

Curtis D'Angelo's help might come with a higher price tag than most, but Steel had it on good authority that the man's last job had collapsed in part due to Megan Luchek's interference. Maybe they'd get lucky and D'Angelo would give them a discount on his services for the chance at payback. Even if they weren't that fortunate, several million had been earmarked for the purchase of the Eagle Eyes units. D'Angelo's full fees would only amount to a fraction of that sum.

The agent knows something about Eagle Eyes.

O's reminder slammed into Steel.

Ever since the Club started chasing rumors of Eagle Eyes, the agent had shown up. Steel had people looking into Gatton Technologies and its mysterious founder and CEO, but once they had the agent again, perhaps she'd be willing to shed new light on the elusive technology.

Cyber League Crimes Book 3: The Criminal Contest

By Julie C. Gilbert

Table of Contents:

Prologue:
Shifts in Power

"Your side trip has been canceled. D'Angelo can handle it on his own." Lou Sands—a.k.a. Steel—concentrated to keep his voice strong, but the phone trembled in his hands. "Get up here."

The boy needs to do this. O's reminder failed to put Steel at ease. *Besides, we need Vinny cooperative, not dead.*

Frustrated, Steel cut the connection to his son, Gary.

"I didn't want this," Steel murmured, gazing down at the unconscious woman.

We must clear the Club of everything weak and inferior. Lillian tried to run. She betrayed us.

Normally, Steel agreed with his other personality, but lately, O's advice held mostly deadly intent. Resisting the urge to smooth Lillian Marquez's hair, Steel turned away.

Don't you want to watch?

"No," Steel said firmly. "I don't want it done at all. If she wants out, let her go. What's the harm?"

She knows about me.

"Nobody would believe her," Steel argued. "Besides, she knows when to keep her mouth shut."

A pleasant ding announced the elevator's arrival. Gary Sheffield stormed out, marching like an angry child.

"You promised I could kill Vinny," Gary complained. Opening his mouth to unleash a tirade, Gary raised a hand and stopped abruptly, ending with a sharply drawn breath. His expression flipped through half a dozen emotions, including surprise, confusion, understanding, and pure delight.

"We changed our mind," said O.

Surprise dominated Gary's expression when he heard O's voice, which always sounded harsher than Steel's voice. A smile slowly spread across Gary's face.

"Welcome back, O," he greeted.

"Get it over with before Steel's bleeding heart takes over again," O said, holding a handgun out to Gary.

"Here? Now?" Gary asked, suddenly wary. Despite the automatic questions, he eagerly accepted the weapon. "But—"

"Don't worry about the mess. We're leaving this building anyway," O said, cutting off Gary's protest before he could voice it.

He shuddered and gripped his head like he had a massive headache. His breaths turned labored as Steel fought O for control of their body.

"Don't … do it, Gary," said Steel, struggling to get the words out. "Give me the gun. You're not a killer."

Gary stiffened, and his expression darkened.

"I can do it," he declared.

"Now!" hissed O. *"You won't get this chance again. He'll stop you."*

"He won't get that chance," said Gary calmly. He checked the gun to make sure it was loaded. *"Thanks for everything, Dad."*

Turning the gun on his father, Gary pulled the trigger.

***

Gary felt nothing as he watched his father stagger back. The sound of the shot made Gary's ears ring.

Sudden pain tore through his gut.

His legs stopped holding him.

A wave of weariness crashed upon Gary as the ringing in his ears intensified.

A muffled crack sounded, and a new ache engulfed his chest.

***

Dropping the gun, Steel moved to Gary's side and pulled him partly onto his lap, weeping. His chest ached from where the bulletproof vest had caught the shot meant to kill him.

Traitors die! Traitors die! O's thought echoed through his head a few dozen times.

For a time, Steel could only endure under the mantra, hold his son, and feel waves of hatred move through him.

"He was my son!" Steel cried hoarsely. "Our son! Why?"

"He tried to kill us," O argued. *"He was unstable."*

"He was still our son. We could have helped him."

A strange, cold sense of calm deadened the pain.

Pull yourself together. We lost him a long time ago. Kill Lillian quickly. We have a lot of work to do.

Spotting the gun, Steel leaned over and grabbed it.

"You're not killing her," Steel declared. He pressed the gun barrel under his chin. "We're not losing both of them in one day. Back off."

You will regret this.

Steel felt a lightening in his soul as O retreated. Dropping the gun, he hugged his son one last time.

O had been right about one thing. They had a lot to do. Even though he couldn't forgive O for killing their son, Steel understood why he did it. If Gary had been any other hired hand, Steel would have fully backed the move.

Gently maneuvering out from under Gary, Steel arranged the body in a more peaceful pose and drew the eyelids down so he appeared to be sleeping.

The cleanup's not done yet.

O rattled off a long list of people who needed to die.

Steel thought maybe he should resist, but he was tired of fighting. Battling O always gave him a headache. O had never steered him wrong. Everything would be fine if he trusted O more.

Pulling out his phone, Steel started on the list of kill orders. Most would go on the list for the Criminal Contest contestants, but a few had to be handled with more care.

***

Jeffrey Gatton unconsciously paused before accessing IRA's latest summary. The Incident Report Analysis program had done its job well, but he didn't know what to expect now that he'd added some spyware and prediction modules to the mix. Normally, IRA would only comb through official police reports, but since the upgrade, she also stayed tuned in to certain cell phone logs and website traffic.

"What's wrong?" asked Lia.

Jeff flinched even though the woman had been his shadow for several hours now.

How does she do that?

As far as Jeff knew, the woman hadn't left her post by the door. She couldn't read his expression because he had his back to her. At least she had been good to her word about staying out of the way.

"Nothing," he said.

"If it's something that could blow up in our faces, I need to know about it," said Lia.

"Just a feeling," Jeff said, trying to sound reassuring. Entering the correct commands, he pulled up the reports. In another few seconds, he had the ancient projector fired up and displaying the contents on the wall.

Can she be trusted?

That disturbing thought fired through his brain as the projector finished waking up. Shrugging, Jeff started skimming the summary and highlights. The last bullet point in the highlights list consisted of a series of people still in danger. Most names made sense, including Megan Luchek, but several others required some digging. James Turner and Carlos Marquez meant nothing to Jeff, so he opened a separate window in Eagle Eyes and conducted some quick searches. IRA had included snippets of text message conversations to authenticate certain points. Jeff speed read those as well.

"What are we looking at?" asked Lia.

"The program analyzes police reports and other information sources to make connections between incidents and predict who might be in danger," Jeff explained.

"Are you sure it's working right?" Lia wondered. Reaching back, she massaged her neck with her left hand, winced a little, and dropped her hand to her side. "It's saying some guy in a nursing home might be targeted soon."

"That's not just 'some guy in a nursing home,'" said Jeff, absorbing information as fast as Eagle Eyes could flood his mind. "He was never convicted, but there's a very high chance he helped found the Club."

"That explains a little," Lia admitted, "but your machine also said this Carlos guy has spent the last decade in a nursing home. He probably made a few enemies along the way, but why would anybody care enough to kill him now?"

"Not sure," Jeff said, "IRA's getting good at what and how, but she's always a bit vague when it comes to why."

"I see Cassandra's FBI friend is still on the danger list," Lia commented. "Should we warn them?"

"It's late here. It'll be later there," said Jeff. "I'll conference with them in the morning. We should get some sleep. Uh, I mean separately.

Most of the guest rooms should be ready ... for guests. Luciana usually handles those details."

"Relax, Mr. Gatton. Until we're sure this CIA thing is over, you're stuck with me," said Lia. "I'll be fine with a chair and a blanket."

"Call me Jeff," he said, turning the chair around to face her.

"Fine by me. Got a lead on a blanket, Jeff?" asked Lia.

"My bed is more comfortable than a chair," said Jeff. Waves of internal heat shot up from his neck, making his cheeks flush. "It's a king-size bed. And the sheets are new. Luciana made sure of that. It doesn't even have dog hair on it since she took Mr. Pudges with her on vacation because she doesn't trust me to care for him without her. Anyway, you're welcome to it. I have a cot. I can sleep here." He consciously stopped talking and pointed to the cot.

"Wherever you sleep, I sleep," said Lia. "I mean—oh, you know what I mean. I was told to protect you, so I will. You're not leaving my sight."

Her awkwardness charmed Jeff, putting him at ease.

"You're welcome to sleep on the free side of my bed," said Jeff. "I sleep like the dead and don't move much."

"Thanks, but a chair will let me draw a gun faster if necessary."

Lia's statement reminded Jeff of the danger they'd already faced and could still face any moment. As his mind reviewed the day's events, including the unpleasantness of being held captive in his own home, the weariness compounded. Jeff ceased caring about who slept where and what the tabloids would say if they knew. He just needed to sleep.

Chapter 1:
Offense or Defense

"Rise and shine, Maggie Bear."

Though normally a heavy sleeper and a reluctant riser, Megan Luchek snapped to full consciousness, fueled by equal parts adrenaline and irritation. She hadn't heard that nickname since middle school. Her eyes fixed on her sister, Tara, who stood out of arm's reach holding a steaming cup.

"You look ... chipper," Megan commented, pushing herself to a sitting position. Her tone held mild reproof. "Where'd you get the clothes?"

"The magic closest," Tara answered with a shrug. She wore a silky, flower-print blouse and black dress pants. Stepping forward, she set the teacup on the end table. "Drink this. Then, get a shower."

"What is it?" Megan asked, eyeing the orange-yellow liquid suspiciously.

"A citrus tea with extra lemon and honey," said Tara. "I know you'd rather have coffee, so I ordered that too. It'll be here with breakfast, but you don't get either until the tea's gone and you're fully dressed. Your suit's ready with a brand-new jacket. I put it in the bathroom for your convenience. I think they even shined your boots."

"Where's Cassandra?" Megan asked, picking up the hot tea.

"Don't know," said Tara. "She said she had some 'errands' and stepped out. I'm under strict orders to rouse you and not leave the suite. Welcome to the fancy prison."

Despite the cheerful front, Megan sensed her sister's worry and unease with the situation.

Setting down the tea, which needed to cool anyway, Megan held out a hand to her sister.

"We're going to end this today," Megan promised. "Then, we'll get you home to Jason and the folks."

Tara took Megan's hand and squeezed hard.

"I'll hold you to that," said Tara hoarsely. Unshed tears glittered in her eyes. Squeezing Megan's hand again, Tara shook her head. "I take it back. I want you to stay safe and tangling with these people sounds like the opposite of safe."

"They're not the worst I've dealt with," Megan said, reclaiming her hand and disentangling from the sheets.

"That's not as comforting as you think," Tara noted, stepping back to let her get out of bed.

"Sorry. I'll be more coherent post-shower," said Megan. "Don't let anyone in until I'm back out here ready to greet them with a gun."

"Tea," Tara reminded Megan.

Sighing, Megan returned to the tea, drew a bracing breath, tested the temperature with a finger, and gulped down the hot liquid. Next, she showed her sister the empty cup for inspection.

"I see your manners are still sadly lacking," said Tara, "but at least you didn't fight me too hard on the tea. You may proceed to the shower."

Slipping around her, Megan headed for the bathroom.

"Don't forget to brush your teeth," Tara called. "There are three kinds of toothbrushes to choose from under the counter."

Twenty minutes later, Megan emerged from the bathroom feeling like a new woman. She hadn't taken that long in the shower, but even the rush job on her hair took some time. Finding a generous supply of bobby pins and hair ties next to the numerous toothbrush options, Megan had elected to go with a full twist updo. It was a style suited to warring with evil corporations and offshoots of the mob.

She found Tara chatting with Cassandra Mirren. Both had serious expressions.

"Agent," Cassandra said with a friendly nod.

"Do I want to know how you got in, assassin?" asked Megan, fairly certain Tara wouldn't have opened the door for her.

"Eat first," Tara advised. She gestured to the rolling cart holding a wide variety of breakfast foods.

"Why?" Megan wasn't trying to be stubborn, but she also didn't like delaying bad news. She'd much rather face it head-on.

"Because we have two problems," Gatton announced, "and as soon as you hear them, you're going to want to rush off with guns blazing." His voice came from the end of the king-sized bed where someone had tossed a cell phone.

"Am I going to need one cup of coffee or two?" asked Megan, only half-joking.

"Try a whole pot," said Gatton.

"Then, start talking," said Megan, perching on the bed. "I can eat and listen at the same time." She picked up a piece of buttered toast and took a large bite to demonstrate her point.

Nobody spoke.

Tara kept her hands busy by prepping a cup of coffee for Megan.

Cassandra went to the far side of the bed and started pulling items from a black duffle bag. She tossed a Glock 23, three ammunition magazines, a roll of money, and two cell phones in one pile. Another pile consisted of three cell phones and more money. A third pile formed with a phone, money, and another two Glock 23's.

"Keep eating," Cassandra said, not bothering to look up from the loot arrangements.

Rolling her eyes, Megan took another noisy bite of toast, causing a shower of crumbs to cascade down the nice new suit jacket.

"I'll eat faster if somebody starts explaining," said Mcgan, absently brushing at the crumbs. Setting down the toast, she picked up the plate of scrambled eggs and sausage. It smelled wonderful. She paused to inhale the tangy sausage-scented steam.

"I even had them put cream cheese in the eggs," said Tara, setting the coffee mug in front of Megan. "Eat them before they're cold."

Megan needed no more encouragement. Finding a fork on the tray, she scooped up a bunch of eggs and shoveled them into her mouth.

Tara made a face at her lack of manners but held in a comment.

Having successfully annoyed her sister, Megan continued eating with a slightly higher level of decorum.

"Thanks for ordering breakfast," Megan said to Tara. "Now, does somebody want to explain these problems to me?"

"We can't stay here much longer," said Cassandra. Picking up one of the handguns, she inspected it from several sides. "And we need to split up."

The lack of surprise on Tara's part told Megan she already knew that part. Before she could inquire, her sister explained.

"I'm going to one of Cassandra's safehouses."

"Why do you look like you're gearing up for a fight?" Megan asked cautiously. "I think a safehouse is a good idea."

"She volunteered to help."

Gatton's announcement startled Megan. She had forgotten he was still listening through the phone connection. Flicking her gaze from the phone to Tara to Cassandra, Megan decided the assassin would probably give her the most information, so she directed her next question across the bed.

"Help with what?" Megan prompted.

Tossing a handgun back onto its pile, Cassandra straightened and met Megan's gaze.

"Ending the Club and its part in the Cyber League," said Cassandra.

"I thought that was my job," Megan commented.

"It is," said Gatton, "but you're still a target. Staying alive is going to require keeping a low profile."

"Why do I get the feeling I'm not headed to the safehouse with Tara?" asked Megan.

"Because I need your help taking out one of the Club's safehouses," said Cassandra.

"One of their major hubs was that office building, but they're pulling out," said Gatton. "They have two other, smaller places in Philadelphia."

"Why aren't they leaving the city altogether?" Megan wondered. "If their major push is cybercrimes, they could be based anywhere with a solid internet connection."

"True, but you're here," said Cassandra.

"When I said, you're *a target*, I really meant to say, you're their *main* target," Gatton explained. "The Hero Contest didn't exactly go to plan, but the audience of gamblers loved you. Recovering you will not only save the organizers some serious payouts, but they also stand to make a lot of money by running several auctions centered around you."

"I'm guessing the auctions aren't about spa vacations for me," Megan commented. She finished the last of the eggs, stabbed a sausage link, and twirled the fork.

"My preliminary research says one would be for ways to kill you and another would be for selling you to the highest bidder," said Gatton.

Tara flinched.

Cassandra shrugged.

"Wouldn't it be a little hard to sell me after killing me?" Megan took a small bite of the sausage and washed it down with some coffee.

"Please don't joke about this," said Tara.

"You're assuming the criminals intend to be honest about killing you," said Cassandra.

"They can easily fake your death," Gatton assured Megan.

"Wonderful," Megan said. "Okay, 'lay low' check, but how does storming into one of the Club's safehouses qualify as laying low?"

"I never said it did," said Cassandra. "This is the part where you choose a plan, offense or defense. My plan is more direct—and aggressive—than Gatton's plan. It's also more dangerous. If something goes wrong, we'll basically be doing the Club's job for them by delivering you to their doorstep."

"What's your plan, Gatton?" asked Megan. She stared at the phone like that would give the question more weight.

"Buy you a car so you can get the heck out of that city," replied the billionaire. "If you're up for a long drive, you can come here or head to one of my other places in Texas or Kansas. I have a few options in both states that might qualify as good lay-low holes."

"Why can't she come to the safehouse with me?" asked Tara.

Megan fielded that question.

"Because if Gatton's right about the Club's interest in me—"

"Which he is," Gatton interjected.

"It means staying away from you is the best thing I can do to keep you safe," Megan finished. "What did you agree to do for the cause anyway? And why can't you take out the Club place yourself? I've seen your work." Megan directed the first question to her sister and the second one to Cassandra.

"Legality and practicality," answered Gatton. "You're right. Cassandra could bust one of the Club's safehouses, do some damage, set them back a few months, but that's it. If we want them to stay down, at least part of this must be through legal channels. That's where you and Tara come in."

"My focus is family law, but I have a lot of friends in criminal law, both lawyers and judges," said Tara, "and I have a vested interest in making sure the Club and the Cyber League stay legally dead and buried."

"I'll get Tara plugged in officially as a consultant for the task force," said Gatton. "She'll work on the legal side. You get the evidence and credible witnesses."

"That's all you," said Cassandra to Megan. "My job is to keep you alive through the first raid. Then, I have a separate issue to deal with."

"Aren't you going to ask for her help?" asked Gatton.

"No," said Cassandra. "She has enough problems."

"Which is why one more doesn't matter," said Megan. "If you don't tell me, I'm going to nag Gatton. He'll spill the beans eventually."

"The less you know, the less you can be compelled to testify about later," said Cassandra.

"Our CIA problem got worse," said Gatton.

"Gatton." Cassandra filled his name with a warning.

"It's my problem too, and I think she can help," he said quietly.

Cassandra didn't look happy, but she only shook her head and frowned as Gatton explained.

"My rogue CIA handler was recently dealt with, but multiple sources indicate that he answered to somebody else, somebody much higher up the food chain and much shorter on morals."

"Who?" asked Megan.

"Somebody called Hawk," answered Cassandra. "This person—or at least the codename—has been around for thirty years. He or she has a lot of contacts."

"They also have something personal against Cassandra," Gatton added.

"What'd you do to deserve that kind of attention?" Megan asked.

"Once upon a time, I refused to be recruited, but I can't think of anything within the last decade that should have landed me on Hawk's radar," said Cassandra.

"How do you know it's personal?" asked Tara.

"Several of my encrypted email accounts received the same message," said Cassandra.

"More like ultimatum," Gatton muttered.

"The message included a time, a date, an order to surrender, and a threat to reveal the Work History File for me and several others," said Cassandra. Her expression turned stony.

"That might not sound scary, but it's as good as a thousand kill orders," said Gatton. Before Megan could ask for a more detailed explanation, he continued, "It's a list of every identity a spy's ever taken on, what jobs they did, where and when those jobs took place, and a projected list of identities they could currently be operating under."

"But you're not a spy," Megan protested.

"Fixers work by almost the same rules as spies," said Cassandra.

"It could be an empty threat, but even the Shadow Council had some bureaucratic strings. If somebody behind the scenes took enough notes, a lot of people could die if I miss that meeting."

"And you could die if you make that meeting." The frustration in Gatton's voice said they'd likely had this argument before. "How many ways do they have to spell out the word 'trap' before you believe it?"

"We can only handle one problem at a time," said Cassandra. "We still have two days to the deadline. Let's deal with the Club first."

Megan had so many questions, but Cassandra looked set on not discussing her problem further right now.

I'll accept your help, assassin, but if you think you're getting rid of me after that, you are 130% wrong.

Chapter 2:
Simple Task

"Wake up, Vinny. We need to talk," said a friendly male voice.

Someone shook Vincent Carbonelli's good shoulder. He blinked up at the stranger before moving his head left to look at the empty chair that used to hold his mother.

"Your mother needed a break. I think she went to meet her sister for breakfast," said the stranger. "They'll be back shortly, as will the nurse, so let's make this quick. You can call me Curtis. I usually go by Bob, but since we're going to be good friends, I figured you deserve the truth."

"My mother has nothing to do with this," said Vinny. "I'll get the money."

"Believe it or not, I come bearing good news for you," said Curtis. "In fact, I'm here to tell you how you can square that pesky gambling debt immediately, but before we get to that, I wanted to start with some ground rules and things to say if anybody comes by."

"You're an old friend stopping by for a short visit," said Vinny.

"You catch on quick," Curtis said. "I like that. Make sure you're convincing. If this goes poorly, something terrible could befall you or your mother."

Vinny sat up straighter.

"Leave my mother—"

"Watch your temper there, old buddy." The man put a hand on Vinny's shoulder and applied enough pressure to get his attention. "We wouldn't want people to think you're having a heart attack."

"Tell me what you want, then get out," said Vinny, jerking his shoulder forward to shake off the man's hand. The move hurt but had the desired effect.

"My employer would like you to grab some personal photos of your cousins and put together a heartfelt plea to circulate on social media."

The implication filled Vinny with pride.

"They escaped," he said with a smile.

"They did, and you're going to help me re-acquire them," said Curtis pleasantly. "Just so we understand each other, this is the simple task that squares your debts. The alternative is I kill you, I kill your mother, and I kidnap your aunt and use her as bait for your cousins."

Vinny stared at the man, trying to measure the threat. The dead expression on the man's face convinced him to trust the threat even more than the words.

"I need a computer," Vinny said.

"You're in luck." The stranger bent down and pulled up a laptop case. "I came prepared." Unzipping the case, Curtis retrieved the computer and turned it on. "I know you're wounded, so I'll give you a half-hour to get it done. If I like your work, you never have to see me again. Remember, Vinny, you want me to like your work. Do me a favor and make a few versions. Be inventive. You don't win until my employer has what they want and that's Megan. Both would be nice, but if you have to choose one, make the plea for information about Megan."

Taking out his phone, the man deliberately set a timer for thirty minutes and let Vinny watch as he hit the start button.

"I'm going to the cafeteria to grab a cup of coffee and protect your mother and aunt for a few minutes," said Curtis. "Maybe I'll have a chat with them. If you're not here when I return, many bad things are going to happen."

Even one-handed, Vinny accomplished his initial task within ten minutes. He set a timer to keep himself on track. Despite the situation, he kind of enjoyed the work and decided to make a few more. Once the man left, he could take the messages down or post a rebuttal easily enough.

They'll be fine. Besides, you don't have a choice.

In one plea, he chose a picture of Megan as a teenager, described her as mentally unstable and suicidal, and claimed to be her estranged brother begging for leads on finding her. He wove in the few details they'd left him with: she might be in Philadelphia, she might be armed, and she may be traveling with another woman.

Vinny's second effort consisted of a more modern picture of

Megan and Tara with a similar story. This time, Vinny told a tale of a messy divorce and a father seeking to reunite with his beloved daughters.

The third fictional story featured only Megan and claimed to have urgent news for her. This time, he painted her as an army veteran with post-traumatic stress disorder. As he described the situation, Vinny unconsciously stuck in little bits of truth, like the fact that Megan's family desperately needed to find her.

He had to stop around minute eighteen to let the nurse check some readings and deliver a pill for lingering arm pain from the gunshot wound Gary gave him yesterday.

Twenty-six minutes into the allotted thirty, Curtis returned, escorting Aunt Susanne and Vinny's mother.

"Vincent, who is this man?" asked Aunt Susanne.

Vinny didn't need to look to see her suspicion.

"A friend," Vinny replied.

His mother sighed.

"Che terribile bugiardo," she mumbled in Italian.

Such a terrible liar.

"I'm afraid I'm going to have to insist you stick to English, ma'am," said Curtis. "Never had much of an ear for languages."

"What are you doing for the man?" Aunt Susanne patted Mama's hand reassuringly.

"Nothing to concern yourself with," said Curtis. He spoke slowly, but his hard gaze held a warning that drew Aunt Susanne and Mama closer together.

Stepping forward, Aunt Susanne reached for the computer.

In one smooth motion, the man slipped between her and the bed and brought a small switchblade to rest at Vinny's throat.

"Everybody stay calm," Curtis ordered.

Surprise and horror came over Vinny's mother and aunt, but the shock kept them relatively quiet.

"I asked Vinny to complete a simple task, which I'm hoping he's done with." A look from Curtis repeated the statement as a question.

"Done," Vinny said, swallowing hard.

"Great. Send me the work as attachments," Curtis instructed, tucking the blade back in his pocket. "It's all ready to go if you pull up the Gmail tab."

Vinny tried to comply, but the computer had trouble accessing the internet.

"It's not working," he reported. "The Wi-Fi around here gets spotty sometimes."

"Make it work." Curtis's tone was distinctly darker this time.

After a few tense minutes of trying every trick he knew from the computer itself, Vinny had Curtis open a hotspot from his phone and connected to that long enough to send the files through. Once Curtis confirmed receipt of the email on his phone, he tucked the device away, packed up the computer, and left, leaving Vinny to face his mother and aunt.

Knowing they wouldn't let him rest until he told them, Vinny explained the task.

The news sent Aunt Susanne tearing out of the room after the man.

Vinny sincerely hoped she would never catch him.

***

"Agent Luchek, you're out of time. You need to leave right now."

Picking up on the tension in Gatton's voice, Megan exchanged a concerned look with Cassandra.

"What happened, Gatton?" Megan demanded.

"Turn on Eagle Eyes. I'll show you," he said wearily.

Tara crossed her arms and looked at Megan expectantly.

Gesturing for patience, Megan followed Gatton's instruction.

Immediately, a series of six internet tabs opened in cascade fashion and arranged themselves so Megan could see each simultaneously. Soon, she realized each one featured a different social media platform but held a similar story.

"Where did they even find that picture?" Megan wondered, pulling up one post at random and skimming the fiction scrawled underneath a pensive photo of herself.

"It's been altered," Gatton reported.

"What picture?" asked Tara.

"Cup your hands together, look at them, and enter display mode," instructed Gatton. "I'll show her what we're talking about.

Megan did as bid. The picture appeared in her cupped hands. Not comfortable with the experience, she shut off display mode and shook her hands.

"It's a post asking for information on me," Megan explained for Tara's benefit.

"It's going to be trouble," said Cassandra. "I'd hoped to leave one by one, but this changes things."

"How?" asked Tara.

"Anybody who saw you check in could see that post," Gatton explained. "There's a reward attached and it's displaying as a sponsored ad, not just a viral post."

A sense of cold dread dropped into Megan's stomach.

"The whole city will be looking for you," Cassandra said, voicing the conclusion blazing in every mind.

"Surely people aren't that money-hungry," said Tara, moving instinctively closer to Megan. "They wouldn't just sell you out."

"They wouldn't know any better," Megan explained. "They'll think they're helping a traumatized army vet reunite with her family."

"Give me a phone with internet access, and I'll set the story straight." Anger pushed confusion out of Tara's expression.

"I already took the initial ads down, but it's being spread organically," said Gatton. "I can delete a few, but more are popping up from other sources. I'll keep tabs on some Club phones, but I can't guarantee I'll be able to give you more of a warning than this."

"You did fine. Thanks, Gatton. I'll call you when I can," said Megan. She turned off most Eagle Eyes displays, disconnected the call with Gatton, and hugged her sister. "Thought we'd have more time, but I guess this is it. Follow whatever instructions Cassandra gave you and be careful."

When she tried to pull away, Tara seized both arms, held tight, and shook her head.

"I don't know if I can do this." Rapid breaths indicated her rising panic.

"You can," Megan assured her. "We have a plan, and it's going to work. You're going to get to the safehouse, make some phone calls, then sit tight."

"Megan, promise—"

Megan cut off Tara's plea with a shushing noise and a shake of her head.

"None of that. I'll see you later. That's my promise." Not sure what to do, Megan cast a desperate look Cassandra's way.

"I can take her to the safehouse," Cassandra offered.

"No." Tara pushed away from Megan and stared hard at the assassin. "Stay with Megan."

Cassandra nodded briefly, loaded a small purse with several cell phones and a roll of money, and tossed Tara the package.

"Key's already inside," said Cassandra. "There's also a can of pepper spray. Skip the first two stops we covered and go straight for the destination. We need to get you there before they actively start looking for you."

Dashing away some tears, Tara nodded to acknowledge Cassandra's instructions before giving Megan one more worried look.

"My goody bag comes with a gun. I'll be fine," Megan said, forcing levity into her voice.

Clutching the bag close, Tara whirled and hustled to the door.

Megan held her breath until the door clicked shut behind her sister.

"All right, assassin. Tell me about this aggressive plan you had in mind."

Chapter 3:
Carrot and Stick

Curtis D'Angelo clenched his fist around his phone and concentrated on not smashing it to the ground. Twisting the kid's arm to get him to do a quick task was one thing, but the job didn't pay nearly enough to warrant turning this into a long-term babysitting gig.

A lengthy text message appeared from an unknown number. He paused beside his car to read it.

The volume of typos and odd word choices told him whoever sent the text had likely dictated the message. Still, if he understood the text correctly, the job had become a lot more lucrative. Needing to hear the offer aloud, he called the number.

"Good morning, Mr. D'Angelo," said a confident male voice. *"You may call me O. I understand you've done some contract work for my organization. I am prepared to offer you a new contract with a generous compensation package."*

The slight raspy quality to the voice made Curtis concentrate to absorb the words.

"So, you're the head of the Club," Curtis commented, mostly guessing. He climbed into his car to gain a bit of privacy, not that he had much to fear in the hospital's parking garage.

"Let's just say, I can gain the ear of those in power," replied the man.

"What can I do for you?" Curtis asked, not eager to play verbal games. "And what can you do for me?" He thought about the huge hits the Club had taken recently but refrained from dredging them up.

"I'm in need of a computer expert, and I understand you're in a position to help me acquire one," said O. *"I'm prepared to cancel his debts and make him a very wealthy man, but if threatening a loved one will work, do it. You can use the*

carrot or the stick approach. I don't care about methodology. Find out what it'll take to gain his full cooperation."

"And what do I get for my trouble?" Curtis asked. "I'm not sure I understand the terms provided in the text message."

"You'll receive your usual fee for each of the three targets acquired," answered O. *"I know I'm asking a lot. Deliver Silvia Carbonelli and Susanne Luchek to the Cornet Motel. I'll send a pair of men to take them off your hands and give you half your fee. Then, escort Vincent Carbonelli to me. My men will have the address when you meet them. When Vincent completes his assignments, you'll be given a bonus equal to two percent of the profits received from the Criminal Contest."*

"Four percent," Curtis countered.

"Two percent is more than generous," said O. *"The way we've arranged the betting structure, we'll make money regardless of the outcome as long as the contest runs to completion. That is ultimately what I'm hiring you to do. See that the contest has a smooth run."*

"How does Megan Luchek fit in?" Curtis wondered, thinking of the previous task he'd had Vinny complete.

"Acquiring her will boost the profit margin significantly," said O.

"How?" Curtis couldn't keep the skepticism out of his voice.

A knock on his window startled Curtis.

Susanne Luchek stood outside his door, trembling. Her expression made him think of a grizzly bear about to flip the car.

"I've got to go. My first customer arrived." Ending the call, Curtis calmly motioned for the woman to back up a step. When that failed to get her to budge, he eased the car door open.

The move released a torrent of Italian from the woman.

Exiting the car, Curtis glanced about for witnesses.

Closing the gap between them, the woman gripped his shirt and continued her verbal assault.

Seeing no witnesses, Curtis sidestepped, gripped the woman's right shoulder, and shoved her into his driver's door. Next, he turned her around, drew his switchblade, and pressed it into her side.

She went still.

"Lady, I don't speak Italian," said Curtis. "If you want to see your girls again, get in the car."

The woman stared at Curtis blankly. Her eyes fluttered, warning him she would probably pass out. Tucking the switchblade away, he caught her by the right arm and twisted it up behind her back so the pain would wake her up.

"I'm going to tie you up and put you in the car while I go get your sister and nephew. If you give me any trouble, I will hurt them. Do we understand each other?"

He waited for her brief nod. Slowly, he released the woman's arm and opened the back door for her.

Giving him one more deadly glare, the woman reluctantly climbed into the back seat.

Retrieving some duct tape from the trunk, Curtis bound the woman before she could recover her senses. Straightening, he admired his handiwork. The strip of tape across her mouth circled her head three times. He checked to make sure she could still breathe, then slipped the seat belt around her.

Guess this means I'll take the job.

***

"You must be out of your mind," Vinny declared.

"Sit there and shut up until we're out of the garage," said Curtis, regretting the decision to let the kid ride up front.

Thus far, the exit from the hospital had gone smoothly. The pitch to Vinny had taken three minutes, and the paperwork to secure his release took another twenty. The walk down to the parking garage had been tense, but they'd made it. Curtis hadn't even needed to back the threats up with his knife this time. Loading the car had proceeded without a hitch until it came time to truss the kid's mother. Then, he started whining. He hadn't stopped whining since. The GPS said the motel would be a twenty-four-minute drive.

It's gonna be a long ride.

He should have put the kid in the back and kept the mother up front or stuffed the lot of them back there. The decision to let Vinny ride shotgun had been a momentary lapse of judgment caused by pity. The Mazda 3's backseat hadn't been designed with hauling three adult prisoners in mind. At least he'd had the foresight to duct tape both women's mouths shut.

After paying the ridiculous garage fee, Curtis heeded the GPS lady's instructions and made a left.

"My cousin's going to kill you for threatening her mother," said Vinny.

"I'm not afraid of Megan," Curtis replied.

"I wasn't referring to Megan," Vinny said evenly. "She's the impulsive one. Tara's ... the emotional one with a lot of powerful friends."

"Thanks for the warning," said Curtis. "I'll just have to kill her before she can sic those friends on me."

The announcement caused a buzzing noise from the back as both women tried to voice protests through the duct tape.

"Take me," Vinny pleaded. "Drop my mother and aunt off somewhere safe."

"That's the plan," said Curtis.

The statement shocked the kid into a few seconds of silence.

"Where are we going?" asked Vinny when he recovered his powers of speech. He reached for the GPS on the dashboard to get a better look.

Whipping his right arm out, Curtis gripped Vinny's wounded arm and squeezed, eliciting a pathetic cry.

"Don't touch," said Curtis, releasing his hold.

The move earned a few minutes of blessed peace while the kid blinked back tears and sulked.

As they pulled into the motel parking lot, Curtis decided one more lecture was in order.

"I have to complete the delivery to get paid," he explained. "I'm going to leave you here to do that. I expect you to sit tight and not touch anything in my car or attempt to escape. The point of holding your mother hostage is to guarantee your good behavior. Now, fold your hands and hold them out for me."

"Why?" Vinny couldn't mask the fear that soaked the question.

Curtis didn't bother explaining. He silently counted the seconds until the kid obeyed the command. Grabbing a zip tie from the glove compartment, Curtis looped it around the kid's wrists and pulled tight. Given enough time, the kid could probably slip the bonds and escape, but Curtis didn't expect his delivery to take that long. The delaying tactic should ensure the kid remained tethered to the car while Curtis handled his business.

Exiting his car, Curtis pondered the best way to proceed. He'd probably have to cut the duct tape to walk the women to the correct room. The parking lot only held a handful of cars, but he didn't feel like carrying the captives. Besides, easy access to the highway meant anybody could drive by and see him. He didn't like the exposure.

The thoughts consumed enough of his attention that Curtis didn't immediately notice two men approaching. He considered diving back into his car to reach the center console where he had a gun stashed. He'd stowed the weapon there because he didn't want to smuggle it into the hospital when a switchblade would suffice.

Instead of going for the gun, Curtis spent the approach time measuring the newcomers. Both wore generic blue uniforms. The pants held a lot of pockets. The taller one stepped forward holding a heavy-looking black bag. The shorter man hung back, cradling something metallic in his hands. It took Curtis a few seconds to recognize the metal object as medical scissors. He reconsidered the uniforms, guessing the pair wanted to pass as Emergency Medical Technicians.

"O said you'd stop by soon," said the taller man. "Do you have them?"

"Do you have my money?" Curtis asked.

"Right here." The man hefted the bag. "It's inside the medical kit."

"Show me," Curtis ordered.

Setting the bag on the ground, the man dug out a soft red case and unzipped it. Peeling back the top, the man tipped the case forward so Curtis could see a neat stack of $100 bills.

"Fan it out," said Curtis.

The man looked annoyed but did so.

Sensing movement behind him, Curtis drew his switchblade and spun to face the second man.

Uttering a curse, the man leapt back and stepped behind the trunk.

"Whoa. Steady there," said the first man. "We're all friends here."

"Leave my money, take them, and back off," said Curtis, still clutching the switchblade tightly. He could take both guys if he had to, but he doubted his employer would appreciate the nuances of such a misunderstanding.

"That's what I was trying to do," complained the guy still hovering near the trunk. He straightened with as much dignity as possible and held up the medical scissors in a gesture of innocence.

Stooping, Curtis plucked the red case out of the black bag and tucked it under his arm. Next, he opened the back door for the man and waved him forward impatiently.

"I have another delivery to make," said Curtis.

The grunt holding the medical scissors did his job, carefully cutting away the duct tape from the woman's hands, feet, and face.

"You might want to threaten her before—"

A cry from the thug cut Curtis off. The man backed into the door, knocking it into Curtis.

Recovering the step, Curtis dropped the red case and shoved the man aside in time to see the woman clutching the medical scissors. Reaching in with his free hand, Curtis grabbed her wrist and squeezed until she dropped the weapon. While he admired her fighting spirit, he didn't have time to waste. The money at his feet was only a fraction of what he stood to make when this job completed.

He could release the seat belt, haul the lady out, and leave her in the hands of the semi-competent mob boys, but Curtis felt compelled to help. Leaning close, he met the woman's defiant gaze.

"It's in your best interest—and that of your daughters—to cooperate," Curtis explained. "Being a hostage is a simple job with a basic risk-and-rewards structure. Cooperation earns perks like comfortable accommodations and food. Defiance leads to varying amounts of pain. When I see Megan later today, I want to be able to give her a good report on your health. Can you do that for me?"

"Don't do this. Please, don't do this." The woman's mantra-like response told Curtis he'd wasted some finely crafted threats.

Shrugging, he backed up to allow the grunt to take over the extraction duties again.

Chapter 4:
Wild West

Jeffrey Gatton scowled at his screen. He wasn't used to being dismissed, and he didn't much like the feeling. No amount of words would get Megan Luchek to make a sensible move, but he would have appreciated the chance to adequately present his case for the run-and-hide plan.

"What's wrong now?" asked Lia. "You seem tenser than last night."

"That woman is going to get herself killed," Jeff declared.

"Which one?" Lia asked. "You were talking to three women."

"Agent Luchek," Jeff clarified. "Her sister should be safe enough if she stays away from them."

"The agent has your tech, and she has Cassandra with her," said Lia. "I'd say those facts improve her odds significantly. Are you worried about the tech falling into the wrong hands?"

"Not really," Jeff answered. "During the last patch, I included a permissions clause along with the advertised updates."

"Meaning …" Lia prompted.

"Meaning, that if anybody but Megan tries to use her Eagle Eyes unit without my permission, it'll self-destruct," Jeff finished.

Before Lia could comment, a yellow exclamation point appeared in the bottom right-hand corner of Jeff's screen. He stared at it, hesitating to check the notifications. The message could be about anything from the weather to an appointment reminder, but instinct told him that reading the alerts would ruin his day.

"Are you going to check that out?" Lia wondered.

Squaring his shoulders, Jeff moved the cursor into position and clicked on the urgent icon. Four windows cascaded open. The first message alerted him to the fact that cyberleaguesports.com had issued an update. The second textbox told him to call his mother, and the third said he should call Luciana to check on how Mr. Pudges was adjusting to vacation with the housekeeper. Jeff rolled his eyes. The spoiled pug already thought he owned the entire estate. His wrinkled little head did not need more inflating. The fourth notification declared that IRA had an unusually large number of incidents to analyze this morning.

Assuming the incidents had to do with the Cyber League's website update, Jeff swiftly worked his way into the Dark Web and zipped over to the correct address. A few commands duplicated his screen on the wall for Lia.

"What am I looking at?" she asked, moving closer to the wall.

"The Cyber League's latest bid to make crime profitable," Jeff answered. "They're the driving force behind several Dark Web sites. The various websites cater to everybody from criminal hobbyists with questions to networking terrorists and serial killers looking for special containment equipment. This one centers on gambling."

"If you know about this and other sites, why don't you shut them down?" Lia's naïve question told Jeff she didn't understand much about the Dark Web.

"Jurisdiction over any cybercrime is a mess, let alone ones buried in here," Jeff replied. "It's the Wild West in a place few people can get to and fewer still can understand. The task force I'm starting should begin to address the jurisdiction issue, but for now, we can only monitor and react."

"Can't you trace back to the source and shut them down … unofficially?" asked Lia.

Jeff cast a sideways glance at the woman. Up to this point today, she hadn't said anything terrifying. The question reminded him that despite her blond hair and college kid looks, Lia was a trained killer. Given the craziness that went down yesterday, he needed scary people on his side, but that didn't make hearing the way they thought any less disconcerting.

"The signal source gets bounced around too many times for most conventional means of tracking," Jeff explained. "I have some tricks that can get some results, but for it to be able to take down the whole network, I'd need to get code into one of their physical machines. That's the task Cassandra and Megan signed up for."

The homepage declared that the Criminal Contest had officially launched and offered a link to the rules page. Following the link, Jeff skimmed the welcome letter which went through the usual thanks for joining us, get-excited pep talk before providing yet another link to more details. Continuing his cyber journey, Jeff clicked on the details link and started reading. The juvenile font choice bothered him, so he ran a filter on his screen to switch the font over to something more legible.

The gambling opportunities can be found on the forums. This page is for contest participants.

Why should you enter this contest?
Money. Infamy. Thrill. You tell us. Join the discussion on the forums. What's in it for you?

Who can enter this contest?
Anybody. We don't discriminate. If you can do the crimes, you're in. **Disclaimer:** By entering, you agree to absolve the Cyber League of all culpability for your crimes. We do not force anybody to do something unwillingly.

What are the entry requirements?
Commit crimes that net you $5000 in the first 24 hours of the contest's launch. We've provided a list of common crimes and their value as determined by our generous private investors. Specifics are available on the forums.

Bonus: First 10 successful contestants get to keep their entry fee.

Criminal Contest Opening Tasks:
- East Coast Bounty – **Value:** $10,000. **Details:** Capture the star of the Hero Contest: FBI Special Agent Megan Luchek. Last known location: Philadelphia, Pennsylvania. **Caution:** Professionals only, please. Target is considered armed and dangerous. Tracking skills required. **Note:** Killing her carries severe penalties.

- Red Ribbon Murder – **Value:** $5,000. **Details:** Commit murder. Tie a red ribbon around the victim. Upload the picture to the appropriate forum.
- Kidnapping Priority Targets – **Value:** $2,500 **Details:** Priority targets are those previously featured on our website. Contestants for the Popularity Contest can be found here, and contestants for the Hero Contest can be found here.
- Kidnap Catch and Release – **Value:** $1,000 per victim up to 5 victims. **Details:** kidnap people from one state and move them to a different state. **Note:** You must hold them for a minimum of 12 hours. Proper documentation required.
- Assault and Bat Battery – **Value:** $500-$1,000 per victim up to 10 victims. **Details:** You must use a bat. The goal is to knock the victim out with one blow. If you require two or more strikes, you only get $500 credited to your account.
- Cashing In – **Value:** $5-$5,000. **Details:** Steel cash from anybody. **Note:** Proper documentation of the robbery is required. You cannot simply pay the entry fee.

"The contest is not going to work out the way they think it will," said Lia. "It's too sloppy. More than half their 'contestants' are going to wind up dead or in jail in the next 48 hours."

"I think that might be the point," said Jeff, skimming the rest of the crime options. The list went on for quite a while. His fingers itched to correct the horrific spelling of the word *steal*. To remove the temptation, he clicked away from the page over to the forums to gather some information. He had a program that attempted to unscramble usernames and trace back to the computers accessing the Dark Web.

Even facing away from Lia, Jeff could feel her attention shift his way.

"You think it's some kind of diversion?" Her question split the line between query and statement.

"I don't know how deeply the Club is involved with the Cyber

League, but it's convenient that this madness picks up when their businesses are under a lot of pressure," said Jeff. With a sinking feeling, he switched over to the normal web and brought up IRA's report. "Let's see how much damage has been done so far."

The Incident Report Analysis program hadn't been distributed to every police station and sheriff's office in the country, but Gatton Technologies had decent compliance from most major municipalities. The uptick in violent crime wasn't as high as he'd been imagining, but Jeff's cynical side admitted that it was relatively early.

Since Philadelphia appeared to be the physical arena the Club wanted to run the contest from, Jeff decided he owed Special Agent in Charge Louis Hatcher a courtesy call. Their relationship hadn't reached favor status yet, but keeping Luchek and the assassin alive today would require help from anybody willing to send it.

"I have to make a confidential phone call," said Jeff, glancing awkwardly at Lia.

"Guess I'll go make some coffee and rummage through the kitchen," said Lia. She massaged her temples with her fingers. "Want anything? And where do you keep headache meds?"

"Luciana makes sure every bathroom has at least a travel-sized container of each name brand and generic cold and headache remedy," said Jeff. "As for food, there should be some breakfast sandwiches in the freezer. Would you mind heating two up for me?"

Lia's parting look did not hide her disdain for his breakfast choice, but she nodded.

When the call to Hatcher's official line got sucked into the grand bureaucratic shuffle, Jeff sent a text message through to his personal cell phone before calling that line. When that failed too, he looked up the phone number for the agent Hatcher had recommended for the task force. Skipping right to personal cell phone, Jeff called Special Agent Samuel Kerman.

While waiting for someone to engage the line, Jeff grabbed one of his clean laptops and accessed the FBI's personnel files to find Kerman. He'd read the file already, but he needed the familiar exercise of hacking to calm down. Talking to new people always made him nervous. Kerman hadn't been available to speak when Jeff had met with the SAC to pitch the Cybercrimes Task Force.

The first call eventually went to voicemail.

Ending that attempt, Jeff sent a text message asking him to pick up and called again. Although mildly frustrating, Jeff understood that his unlisted number would show up as blocked and therefore be screened by most people.

"You've reached Special Agent Sam Kerman, FBI. How can I help you?" asked a deep voice.

"Agent Kerman, my name is Jeffrey Gatton. I run Gatton Technologies. SAC Hatcher forwarded your name for a special task force I'm forming to deal with cybercrimes. Did he speak to you about that yet?" Jeff spoke quickly, knowing he didn't have much time to explain himself.

"Only in passing," answered the agent. "I'm honored, but I need—"

"I'm not calling about that," Jeff said, cutting the man off. "I need your help saving another agent." A frustrated breath rushed out, ending in a grunt. He was explaining this poorly.

I need to prove myself.

"Call 911 if there's an emergency," said Kerman. "I don't have time to—"

"A lot of crimes are happening around the city," Jeff blurted. "I bet a memo went out early this morning and certain agents have been reassigned to help the Philadelphia PD today. You might even be one of those agents."

"How would you know that?" Suspicion laced Agent Kerman's question.

"It's a very complicated story I can't tell you in full right now, but the other agent I mentioned is going to need some serious backup today," said Jeff.

"You have my attention," Kerman said cautiously.

"I need you to convince your SAC to give me use of several agents and tech support people today," Jeff explained. "Specifically, I need people who can get into the Dark Web."

"Keep talking," ordered Kerman. "I'll speak to my boss, but he's going to want a lot more information than that before giving you anything."

As he began bringing Agent Kerman up to speed, Jeff returned to the Cyber League Sports website to continue poking around. If Kerman could get him some proper help, there might be a chance of crippling the site.

A number appeared in the upper righthand corner of Jeff's screen, telling him he had a new private message. Hovering over the icon showed him the subject was titled: *Good News.* With a sinking feeling, Jeff clicked on the message and read it quickly. He concluded it must have been sent to assure the high rollers their investments were safe. The link contained in the message derailed Jeff's current line of thought. He stopped speaking.

Silence fell for two seconds before Kerman broke it.

"Hello? Gatton? You still there?"

"I've got to go," said Jeff, speaking even faster. "I have to make a phone call. I'll send you a link, but you're going to need a first-rate hacker to access it. Get people on tracking the origin."

"What's the rush?"

Jeff hung up on the Philadelphia agent. He didn't have time to explain what he'd seen. He had to call Megan.

Chapter 5:
Videos

Ladies, I hope you're sitting down.

Gatton, nothing good begins with those words.

Megan placed the thought in the Eagle Eyes message box so Gatton could read it. She assumed Hive Mind would carry the sentiment over to Cassandra as well.

I need to show you something.

"We're just leaving the hotel room now," Cassandra reported, speaking softly even though they currently had the hallway to themselves. She kept one hand on the door to prop it open. "Can it wait?"

No.

Cassandra's expression didn't change much, but she nodded once, pushed open the door, and waved for Megan to re-enter the hotel suite ahead of her.

Baffled, Megan crossed over to the bed and perched on the edge near the end table.

"Show us," Cassandra said, leaning back against the closed door.

Close your eyes. I'm going to duplicate my screen for you.

Dread filled Megan as she complied with Gatton's instruction.

What am I looking at?

Nobody answered her, and nobody needed to answer her.

The video spoke for itself.

The camera panned from left to right and back again, showing first Megan's mother and then Aunt Silvia before remaining on her mother. Both women had been bound to metal folding chairs. Duct tape covered their mouths. The fear and desperation in their expressions stabbed Megan hard enough to make her quit breathing.

"That's enough," said Cassandra.

That's the end of that video anyway. There are more.

The video cut off, leaving Megan to weather the emotional storm it released in her.

"Give us a moment, Gatton," said Cassandra. "You can tell us about the *more* later."

Megan heard the words, but not much about them registered with her. Anger and helplessness made her tremble, sending flashes of heat coursing throughout her body. Adrenaline made her stomach queasy. Chills zipped painfully through her blood as shock sank in. Finally, a tidal wave of weariness slammed into her, sweeping all traces of emotion away.

As she started falling back on the bed, Cassandra caught her and tucked her into a comforting embrace.

"Let yourself cry," she said.

Megan shook her head weakly but couldn't muster enough strength to push away.

Cassandra's grip tightened.

"Megan, you have to level your emotions." Cassandra's words were low and urgent. "If you bottle this, it will cripple you. If that happens, you'll be useless to them. Let it out; then we'll form a new plan. I promise."

At first, no tears would come. Megan recognized the emotional void as a defense mechanism she'd developed during her short, hellish relationship with Derrick Belmont. The three months of bad decisions had left her with both psychological and physical scars.

Closing her eyes brought the memory of the video blazing to life. Fear provided a similar image, only this time her mother and aunt were dead. The thought set off another series of mental pictures. This time, Cousin Vinny, Tara, and Father gathered around two open caskets. Imagining what losing her mother would do to her father and sister finally broke through the barriers.

A tear slipped out and started the journey down her face. Megan swallowed hard, trying to keep a sob locked inside her chest. It burned her throat. The effort made her cough. The fit ended in a choking sob that flowed naturally into real sobs. Those brought a flood of tears and made her nose run. By the time the body-wracking, hysterical phase finally passed, Megan had a killer headache. Sniffling, she pulled out of

Cassandra's hug and gave her an apologetic smile.

"Sorry about the jacket," she mumbled, swiping at some straggling tears.

"It's seen worse," Cassandra replied. "Go wash your face with cold water. You'll feel better."

The task of rising and trudging over to the bathroom took a lot of effort, but the assassin's words proved true. The cold water dulled Megan's headache and cleansed away the evidence of grief. Her mind still raced with a hundred worries, but the blind panic had passed.

Upon returning to the main room, Megan's Eagle Eyes displays came on again. She hadn't even realized Cassandra turned them off when she cut the communication with Gatton.

Are you okay?

"I won't be okay until this is over," Megan said, striving hard to cling to her newfound calm. A nervous, buzzing energy coursed through her.

"Let's figure out how to get there," said Cassandra. "Gatton, where are we on the target to hit?"

The two we discussed before are still viable, but they're probably both traps.

"How far along is your solution?" asked Cassandra.

I'm getting some help from the local feds. We should be ready in a few hours.

"What are you two talking about?" asked Megan, feeling very left out.

The Club owns two apartments in Philadelphia. I think they're running some of their Cyber League business out of these locations.

A map of the city appeared in Megan's mind as Gatton pulled one up and highlighted two spots. They didn't mean much to her since she didn't know Philadelphia very well. Cassandra's thoughtful expression told her she was weighing pros and cons.

"Which is the priority?" Cassandra asked.

Both. There's no way to tell which will have the main equipment hub.

Gatton's answer prompted Cassandra to cast a concerned look Megan's way.

Realization slowly dawned on Megan.

"We need to hit them separately," she concluded.

And at the same time. I need to run a test before slipping

the code in, or it won't work.

"What are we trying to do?" Megan wondered, still not following Gatton's geek talk.

I'm creating a package that should flow through the Cyber League's system, but if we tip them off, they'll just reroute information through another hub.

"The parameters have changed enough that my original plan won't work," said Cassandra.

"What was the original plan, and what's different now?" Megan asked.

"If we only had one location to hit, we could storm in, subdue resistance, and hold the location long enough for Gatton's team to do their part," Cassandra explained. "Two hubs changes everything."

Two hubs means the operation could be much larger than we thought. The program would let us trace back to any computer that's ever prepared a webpage for the Cyber League.

"This can't be legal," Megan muttered.

It's not, but it'll give me enough information to send appropriate *anonymous tips* when the time comes.

"We also have a time limit," said Cassandra. "You don't need to see the other videos, but one has a countdown."

"A countdown to what?" Megan asked. Her tone hardened as she braced for the answer.

It doesn't say on the site, but the phone chatter from Club members says that's the time allotted to find you.

"Show me," Megan ordered.

That's not a good idea.

Megan repeated the demand.

"Show her the countdown, Gatton," said Cassandra. "She's going to fixate on it whether she sees it or not."

Megan thought seeing the video with the countdown would return the helpless feeling of dread, but instead, it just confused her. After watching four seconds tick down, she had Gatton shut off the video.

"What's my target?" asked Megan.

Are you—

"Look, the faster we destroy this operation, the sooner I get to bust Gary's nose and get my mother back."

Gary's dead. At least according to the Club chatter.

The news caught Megan off guard. She had never liked the Club guy, but she also didn't relish hearing about his death.

"Why is he dead?" she asked.

Not sure. The text message chatter says a higher up killed him.

"We can ponder his death later," said Cassandra. "Right now, we need to get into position. Gatton, can you find Megan's mother and aunt?"

Should be easy enough. I have the video size and the time of release to look for when backtracking the data trail. The last known sighting of your mother and aunt was security footage at a hospital in Virginia. The time between that footage and the video upload limits the distance they could have traveled.

Normally, Megan wouldn't care about the details, but Gatton's confidence comforted her.

"Message us when you locate them," said Cassandra. "Give the agent the Elmwood address. I'll take Strawberry Mansion."

"What am I supposed to do when I get there?" asked Megan.

You need to get within fifteen feet of the computer equipment and stay there long enough for my program to do its analysis and upload the tracers.

"Fifteen feet? I'd have to be in the room with them." Megan didn't bother hiding her frustration.

"Go through the apartment above or below," said Cassandra. "There will be less resistance."

"I'm not involving other people," Megan declared.

Cassandra shrugged. Her expression said she'd predicted Megan would take that stance.

"How do we even know there will be a bunch of computer equipment to find?" Megan wondered. "Couldn't one lone crackpot with a laptop be generating the webpages?"

They would need several screens or computers to monitor the gambling pages, control the moving pieces, upload new content, and rig the game as they wish. There are many reasons people have multiple computers running, but I narrowed down to these locations by tracking the phones Cassandra tagged yesterday.

"Any chance you or Tara can get me a warrant?" Megan wondered.

Not without more evidence. That's what we're digging for.

Megan drew a deep breath and let it rush out.

"Don't have much of a choice," she mused. "I'll go stir-crazy if I sit here anyway."

"You could head toward Virginia," said Cassandra. "I can make both data deliveries. Gatton will have that location for you soon."

No, he won't. He's busy writing a code to take down the Club. Even through the computer, the tech genius sounded annoyed. **A code that needs to be delivered simultaneously to work best.**

"Gatton, you said you had FBI help," said Megan. "Is there anybody you trust enough to send after my family?" She wanted that job, but if they didn't hit the Club now, the rats would do this to somebody else.

I'll ask around.

"Do that, but keep it quiet," said Cassandra. "We don't want them to panic."

We might be able to get an extension on that countdown. Gatton's tone was reluctant.

"How?" Megan demanded. She felt a catch coming.

A message went out to all high rollers explaining the countdown. It includes an email address to contact.

"It's a countdown until they kill my mother and aunt," Megan said softly. Gatton had studiously avoided stating that, but she didn't have time to dance around the issue. "What do they want for the extension?"

They want the answer to a series of questions only you or your sister would know.

"What are the questions?" Megan didn't like getting sucked into a stupid game, but if she could help her family in any way, she'd do it.

"He can't tell you," Cassandra said, trying to break the news gently.

It's an electronic trap. Answering on your behalf will compromise the identity. If that happens, I'll have to start from scratch on the tracers.

Megan's emotions warred with her logic centers. She understood Gatton's dilemma, but the chance to do something helpful gnawed at her.

"Will six hours be enough?" Megan's question was barely audible.

"Yes."

Cassandra's confident answer soothed Megan slightly.

Gatton echoed the answer a split-second later.

"Then, give me the address." Megan closed her eyes to let Eagle Eyes do its thing.

A blue line moved out from her, and a green line moved out from Cassandra.

Megan turned to head toward the door, but Cassandra caught her shoulder.

"Be careful, agent. I don't think we know everything that's happening, and you're still an integral part of their game."

A dozen answers sprang to mind, but a burning sensation in her throat prevented Megan from voicing any of them. Casting Cassandra what she hoped was a grateful look, Megan nodded once and resumed her march toward the door.

Chapter 6:
Proposals and Summons

Curtis D'Angelo's phone rang. Normally, he would answer a blocked number and mess with the person, but he didn't have the patience for it right now. The sooner he could offload the whiny computer kid, the better.

His phone rang again.

He blocked the call again.

"Maybe you should answer it," said Vinny.

When the phone rang a third time, Curtis stabbed his finger into the accept button and snatched up the phone. He didn't want the call to go through the car's speakers.

"Speak," he ordered.

"I understand you're in the middle of a delivery, Mr. D'Angelo," said a polished male voice with a British accent.

"Who are you?" Curtis gripped his phone harder as the reflex question flew out.

"I'm not important. Call me Smith if you like," said the man. "I have a job for you."

"Not interested," said Curtis. "As you said, I'm in the middle of a job."

"Please, finish your current delivery," Smith said cordially. "It should take you precisely where I need you to go."

"What are the terms?" Curtis asked, intrigued.

"$5000 in good faith and up to $50,000 more, depending on the outcome," Smith explained. "I will send you a contract with further details shortly, along with confirmation of the wire transfer. Do we have a deal?"

Curtis's heart beat faster. He had no reason to turn the mysterious man down, but he also didn't like such rapid shifts. In his line of work, those could be deadly.

It's an easy 5K to look at the contract. What's the harm in that?

***

Forty minutes after leaving the hotel, Cassandra Mirren stepped into position and paused to search her feelings. Instinct born of many difficult missions wouldn't let her relax.

Too easy.

She mentally reviewed everything that had gone right so far. The hired car had arrived within two minutes of her order. The apartment building in Strawberry Mansion seemed abandoned. The lock on the front door had been broken, which could be explained by the general run-down state of the neighborhood. However, she hadn't met one person. Since the building boasted several dozen units, that seemed an unlikely twist of good fortune. The apartment below her target was empty, but it looked lived in. The occupant might be at work, but Cassandra had learned long ago, that if everything went to plan, something was terribly wrong.

Hyper-alert, Cassandra glanced around the small apartment. The main room featured both the kitchen area and a living room. A pizza box had been thrown near the garbage. Soda cans and beer bottles had been piled up in the recycling bin. A framed degree on the wall told her the apartment most likely belonged to Xavier M. Lewis. Pictures on the refrigerator showed a mid-twenties, smiling young man with light brown skin. Several images also featured a young woman, but Cassandra was getting conflicting clues as to the apartment's occupancy.

It's too clean.

A faint scent of lemon hung in the air. The couch cushions looked like somebody had carefully placed them. Convinced something was wrong, Cassandra cautiously stepped toward the bedroom.

A shadow moved in the darkened doorway.

Cassandra stepped left as a loud pop boomed through the air. Twin taser prongs sailed past her right arm. She ducked low and charged forward as another pop announced a second set of taser prongs. These sailed over her as she slammed into someone's midsection. The impact knocked the man back, resulting in two startled cries. Pushing off the first man, Cassandra landed in a crouch. The man she'd hit landed on his backside. His companion leapt back and froze.

The shades had been drawn across both windows. Only a faint outline of light penetrated the darkness.

Switching over to thermal view, Cassandra quickly assessed the situation. She had about half a second before the first man recovered and less time before the second man attacked, since she stood between him and the only exit. Both figures showed up as blazing orange blobs. Dimming the effects, Cassandra drew the expandable baton from her jacket pocket and brought it down hard on the first guy's stomach.

He howled and curled into a ball. The move brought his face up in time for her to slam the heel of her palm into his chin as she regained her feet. Grunting, he flopped back against the bed.

The other man roared but didn't get to move because Cassandra hopped over the first guy, dropped low again, and swung the baton hard at the second man's left knee. His resulting scream was sharp and short as she put him down with a swift, slightly softer, blow to the head. He fell forward, landing partly across the first guy's legs.

Cassandra waited a second to make sure her foes would stay down before switching off the thermal view and turning on the lights. She met the first guy's terrified eyes. He had one hand over his jaw. The second attacker was out cold.

A body lay on the twin bed behind the first assailant. The three bullet holes in the sheet told her the guy was far beyond help, but Cassandra picked her way over the figures littering the floor to check for a pulse. The man's skin was cool enough to tell her he'd been dead several hours.

Returning her attention to the likely murderers, Cassandra re-crossed the sea of limbs and crouched near the conscious guy. She stayed close enough to react but just out of the man's reach. Splitting her attention between the man propped up against the bed and the one still lying flat on his face, Cassandra studied the man she needed to interrogate. He appeared mid-twenties and had decent muscle tone, but the fact that she'd caught him flatfooted told her he probably lacked formal combat training.

"I work by simple rules," Cassandra said, once certain the man had passed the blind-panic phase. "If you answer my questions completely and honestly, you and your companion get to live. Let's start with your name." She looked at him expectantly.

He stared back defiantly, testing her resolve.

She sighed and idly tapped the baton against her open palm.

"For the record, that qualifies as a question," said Cassandra. "If you're too stupid to figure that out, I'll take my chances with your companion. State your name, purpose, and employer before I lose patience."

"It wasn't a question," mumbled her prisoner.

Without warning, Cassandra whipped the baton out and rapped the young man across the knuckles.

He yelped and clutched his hand tight to his chest.

"Next blow knocks you senseless," said Cassandra. "Believe it or not, I'm trying very hard not to hurt you. Who are you and why are you here?"

"They're nobody," said a familiar voice from the doorway. His cold, dismissive tone lacked emotion.

Rising, Cassandra stepped away from the random criminal and turned to face the new threat. She maintained a good grip on the baton but lowered it to her side. Fortifying her emotions did little to cushion the gut-wrenching pain of seeing Owen Ramsey standing in the doorway pointing a gun at her.

After a split-second of utter shock, Cassandra really looked at her friend. Something was wrong. His position—centered in the doorway—was tactically useless. If she had a throwing dagger and the inclination to end him, he'd be dead already. He also looked ill. Sweat made his forehead shiny.

"Step aside, Cassie," said Owen. "Hawk doesn't want witnesses."

Cassandra glanced down at the young man leaning against the bed. The terror had returned to his eyes. A small step right placed her squarely between Owen and her former attacker. She hoped the guy had the sense to keep quiet and not attack her.

Gatton, tell Megan to go to ground.

After using Eagle Eyes to send the thought to the tech genius, Cassandra analyzed Owen's vital signs. His body language spoke of high stress as did an elevated blood pressure reading. The information comforted her. Owen wasn't doing this by choice.

"I wasn't aware you worked for Hawk," said Cassandra, striving hard for a conversational tone.

"You'd be surprised who works for me." The new male voice came from somewhere on Owen's right shoulder. While mostly matter of fact, the voice also contained a hint of smugness and arrogance. "Consider this your formal summons. We need to talk."

Since Owen wore all black, it took Cassandra a second to spot the tiny camera and speaker embedded into the fabric of his shirt.

Flicking her gaze over to her friend's face, Cassandra gauged his reaction. His expression still looked strained and weary.

What hold does he have on you?

As far as Cassandra knew, Owen had no immediate family to threaten.

"You seem to have no trouble talking now," Cassandra noted. "What do you want? Shall I call you Hawk?"

"Let Owen do his job," said the voice. "Then, you can come meet me in person, and yes, Hawk will do fine."

"How are you threatening him?" Cassandra asked.

Owen's expression had gone blank.

"All your answers await with me," said Hawk. "Now move."

"No." Cassandra let the word hang for a second before elaborating. "If you want my cooperation, you explain some things to me. If I find your reasons compelling enough, I'll follow Owen. You don't get to kill the nobodies."

A long, painful silence fell while the voice behind the camera pondered her offer.

"Fair, but I think they've heard enough," said Hawk. "Deal with them and meet Owen in the living room. You have thirty seconds to complete this task."

Lowering the gun, Owen backed out of the doorway.

Tucking the baton away, Cassandra knelt beside her prisoner.

"I'm going to knock you out, but if it wears off before we're gone, stay put and stay quiet."

The young man's glazed expression told Cassandra there was a good chance he heard nothing, including the warning, but she didn't have time to repeat it. Reaching for a pressure point on his neck, she pressed down hard and counted silently. Next, she checked on the other guy. Either the head knock was harder than anticipated or the man was a good faker. Pressing gently on the wound elicited a groan, so she gave him a shorter version of the pressure point treatment. Finally, she exited the bedroom.

A past version of her might have gone out one of the windows and taken her chances, but she couldn't abandon Owen and the random criminals. She also needed answers.

"What are you doing to Owen?" asked Cassandra, rewording an earlier query.

Her friend stood in the center of the living room. The military rest position contrasted with the strain etched throughout his taut facial features.

"He's upsetting himself," said Hawk. "Apparently, he doesn't like his orders."

"What orders?" Cassandra prompted.

"Bringing you to me." Hawk blew out an annoyed breath. "We should have this tedious conversation in person, but perhaps a brief demonstration will speed things along."

Suddenly, Owen's head jerked back, causing him to cry out and drop to his knees.

Reacting against her better judgment, Cassandra swept forward and steadied Owen's shoulders, aware of the danger. Once certain her friend wouldn't fall on his face, Cassandra retreated a step. He stared up at her miserably.

"Do you find my demonstration compelling enough?" asked Hawk.

Holding Owen's gaze, Cassandra nodded slowly.

"I can't hear a nod," said Hawk in a sing-song tone.

"Yes," Cassandra whispered, struggling to hold back tears. "It's enough."

Gatton, where are you?

Cassandra spared a thought to wonder why the tech genius hadn't gotten back to her yet. He might occasionally miss a message for a time, but his silences never lasted long.

"That's wonderful news," Hawk cheered. "Please uphold your end of the bargain and go with Owen, or my next demonstration won't be so brief."

"If you hurt him, I can escape," Cassandra said, struggling to understand the situation. "How would that help you?"

"True to a point," Hawk said, "but if his pain doesn't move you, perhaps Lia's will."

"You're bluffing." The words were more hope than statement.

Hawk laughed.

"Call her and find out." His dare came out light and playful. His next statement contained pure malice. "You can listen to her scream through the phone."

Although not convinced Hawk could hurt Lia, Cassandra wasn't eager to experience another demonstration.

"All right, Hawk. Where would you like to meet?"

"Stand still, please," Hawk instructed. "Our mutual friend will take some safety precautions before escorting you to me."

"No." The choking protest came from Owen. He leapt to his feet and stumbled back. "I can't. Please." He gripped his head hard with both hands. His face grew red. Tears flew out as he shook his head violently.

The sight sent shooting pain through Cassandra's heart. Closing the distance between them, she reached up and grabbed Owen's hands, which still gripped the sides of his head.

"Owen, stop," Cassandra pleaded. She tugged gently until his hands dropped away from his head. "Look at me." She waited until his eyes focused on her. "Don't fight him on this. I know it's not you."

Pushing her away, Owen stepped further back.

"Interesting," said Hawk. "He has a strong aversion to hurting you."

Owen's head dipped, and he closed his eyes. He nodded several times. When his eyes opened again, they appeared clear and in control yet still sad.

"We've reached a compromise," said Hawk. "Hold out your hands. He's going to bind them. Then, you're going to make a phone call."

Not having a choice, Cassandra followed the instruction.

***

"Agent Kerman?" Jeffrey Gatton knew he had the right number, but he was a little surprised when the FBI agent answered his blocked number for the second time.

"What can I do for you, Mr. Gatton?" asked the agent, keeping his voice neutral.

"How quickly can you coordinate a raid?" Jeff inquired.

"Are we speaking officially or unofficially?" Agent Kerman fired back.

"Unofficially," Jeff admitted. "You can tell your boss so you don't get fired, but the media can't know until it's over. At least two lives are at stake."

"I'm listening."

Chapter 7:
Phone a Friend

As the cab pulled away, Megan Luchek slipped into the alley across the street and used Eagle Eyes to check the building's various profiles. She searched for people, metal, and electronics through several filters. The thermal view showed her that the apartment below her target was empty, and the rest of the building had very few occupants.

Suspicious or convenient?

A faint noise behind her caused her to spin around, drawing the borrowed handgun in the process.

A cat hissed at her and darted away.

I'm not exactly here by choice.

She tucked the gun away but made sure the shoulder holster remained highly accessible.

The thought got Megan thinking of the many events that led her to the moment. The last few hours, she'd relied heavily upon Jeffrey Gatton's invention and advice. She had mixed feelings about the tech genius, but the recent events highlighted how vulnerable he could be. She didn't blame him for that, but it brought up the sobering point that at its heart, Eagle Eyes was still just a glorified computer program.

What would I do without Eagle Eyes?

The honest question required serious consideration. Shutting off every display, Megan studied the building with her eyes. Every front shade had been closed. The fact could have a very reasonable explanation, but a glance at nearby buildings revealed at least some variation in the visible windows.

Doesn't feel like a trap yet, but it sure looks like one from this angle.

Cassandra's care package came with some cash and two burner phones. Megan needed to keep one for an emergency, but that left her with one to use as she wished.

If I'm stepping into a trap, I might as well tell Dan about it first.

Cell phones had spoiled her, but Megan's mother had drilled the importance of memorizing significant phone numbers in case technology failed her. The lesson had saved her massive headaches on multiple occasions.

Gatton had insisted timing mattered, but Megan had compared her travel time to Cassandra's from the start and knew she had a few minutes to spare.

Stepping further into the alley, Megan leaned back against the graffiti-covered wall and dialed Daniel Cooper's personal cell phone.

"Cooper speaking." His greeting sounded tense.

"Is everything okay, Dan?" asked Megan.

"Megan!" Surprise, relief, and joy rang through his voice. "Where are ya? The world's gone mad today."

"Safe for the moment," Megan replied. "What makes you think the world's gone mad? You're supposed to be the optimist."

"Have you turned on the news at all today?" Dan demanded.

"No, I avoided it," said Megan. She'd muted the cab TV in favor of some thinking time.

"Didn't ya notice there's a cop on every corner of the city?" Dan asked.

"I did," Megan admitted, "but I'd assumed it had to do with the kidnappings yesterday." The rest of his phrasing sank in. "Wait. What city are you talking about?"

"Philadelphia," said Dan. "I'm under orders from Maddox and Beth to throw ya in the nearest safehouse and sit on ya 'til the danger passes."

Megan's spirits lifted, but she kept her voice even as she responded.

"I can't come in yet. There's too much to do."

Dan groaned.

"I knew you'd say that," he complained. "Just once, I wish you'd choose the easy way."

"They went after my mother," Megan said flatly. The reminder made her neck and face heat up with internal rage.

"I know," said Dan wearily. "Gatton told us."

"Then you should understand why I can't come in," Megan said.

"One way or another, I have to see this through."

"No, I don't see," Dan snapped. "Megan, the entire Philadelphia Field Office is working to locate yer ma. We will find her. As long as you stay free, they have to keep her alive."

He didn't continue the logic, but Megan completed the thought on her own.

If they catch me, they won't need my mother.

"They're not going to stop looking," Megan noted. She tried to force levity into her tone. "Apparently, I'm worth a lot of money."

"I do not like where this is going," Dan declared.

"You can track the phone," Megan said, thinking aloud.

"And they can destroy it," Dan countered.

"Gatton can track Eagle Eyes," she continued.

"We're having a hard time reaching the man," Dan argued. "I know your crazy plans have worked in the past, but this is different. The Club didn't know ya the first time, but they are fully aware of ya now."

"I can't hide, and running's only going to get people hurt," Megan reasoned. She stared across the street at the building with perfectly drawn blinds. "If the worst happens, there's a good chance I can cut a deal for my family."

"Throwing yer life away isn't going to save yer ma."

Dan's gentle words hit Megan like a sucker punch.

"Listen. I'm just calling to let you know I'm alive for now," said Megan, pushing past the pain of helplessness. "Whichever way this works out, I—"

"Megan, let me help ya," Dan begged. "If ya give me street names, I'll be there with the full might of the FBI and the Philadelphia PD. You need friends now, and we can help ya."

The offer made Megan step out of the alley and glance left at the nearest street sign. Blinking, she turned away from the name.

"I know," Megan replied, "and I'll take you up on that as soon as I can. I need to run an errand first."

A cop car turned onto the street several blocks up from Megan's position. Instinctively, she ducked back into the alley and stood in the shadows.

"If you want to help, find my mother and get her to safety," said Megan. She ended the call before Dan could respond.

Sorry, Dan, but if I can keep you clear of this mess, I will. Beth and the girls need you.

The cop car rolled to a stop outside the main door to the

apartment complex Megan was supposed to enter soon. Two officers stepped out of the vehicle and looked around.

A young man appeared in the doorway, said something to the cops, and pointed across the street at the alley currently holding Megan.

Not good!

Megan retreated further into the alley, looking around frantically for a side door to duck into. About the only thing to hide behind was a dumpster and even that wouldn't conceal her long if somebody physically walked into the alley. Drawing even with the dumpster, she crouched to be less visible. The instinct to surrender to the officers warred with natural caution and Gatton's warning that the Club owned several of Philadelphia's finest.

Drawing weapons, the police officers spread out and rushed to either side of the alley.

"Police! Throw down any weapons and come out with your hands up!" The announcement and order came from the taller officer.

Both men turned on powerful flashlights and trained them on the shadows.

Megan had less than a second to choose a path.

Fight, hide, or talk.

Standing, Megan held her hands out in a non-threatening manner and waited for the beams to find her. When they did, she spoke.

"I'm an FBI agent," Megan declared. She spoke slowly and clearly to avoid any unfortunate misunderstandings. "I am armed, but I'm not a threat to you."

"Good to know," said the same officer who'd spoken before.

Megan had enough time to think that a strange response before a loud pop signaled trouble. Pain registered in two spots along her left leg. A sizzling electrical noise underscored a pain-filled cry as Megan's entire body lit up with agony. Her legs quit, throwing her first into the side of the dumpster and then to the ground. She landed on her back.

When the pain disappeared, Megan tried to sit up.

"Lie still, or I light you up again," said the shorter policeman. He waved the weapon he held so she could see the yellow patches that declared it a taser.

"Go get the probes and help her up," said the slightly taller cop. He shot his partner an annoyed look and snatched the taser away. "We need to get her into the cruiser quickly."

"This is a mistake," said Megan. "You don't—"

"It's not a mistake," said the shorter cop. His badge read K.

Bentley. Kneeling beside her, Bentley broke the wires connecting the probes to the taser that had flattened Megan. She hardly felt a thing as he tugged the probes out of her left leg and tossed them into the dumpster. He then plucked the gun out of her shoulder holster, patted her down for other weapons, confiscated her cell phones, rolled her over, handcuffed her, and rolled her face up again.

"We know who you are, Agent Luchek," said the first officer. He too drew near enough for her to read his badge. It said P. Thorne.

"And what you're worth," added Officer Bentley.

Together, the policemen hauled Megan to her feet. Thorne took the time to smash both cell phones, leaving the sad remains on the street next to the dumpster.

Megan's legs felt shaky, but they held her weight as the officers hustled her to their cruiser and shoved her into the back. Frustrated, she tried one more time to reason with the pair.

"No amount of money is worth the risks you're taking," she warned.

As the cruiser started moving, Megan silently bid Eagle Eyes to begin tracking her movements.

"Don't worry about us," said Officer Thorne.

"We're only sticking around long enough to collect our money," added Bentley.

"Are you even real cops?" asked Megan.

"Of course, we are." Bentley's statement was defensive.

"Doesn't matter," said Thorne. He threw a warning look at his partner.

"Then you should know this isn't going to go smoothly," said Megan.

"Shut up," ordered Thorne.

"What do you mean?" wondered Bentley.

"She doesn't know anything," Thorne assured the other man.

"I know that criminals lie, cheat, and cut whatever deals best suit them," said Megan. "Do you really think people like that are going to honor payment promises?"

"Stop talking," Thorne ordered. He tossed the live taser to Bentley. "If she speaks again, shoot her with that."

Not eager to have her brain scrambled again, Megan took the hint and tried to find a comfortable position. It wasn't easy with the handcuffs holding her wrists behind her back.

Gatton. Cassandra. I hope you're doing better than I am today.

Chapter 8:
Breakfast Surprise

"I'm going to check for threats," Lia announced. "But here are your breakfast sandwiches."

Jeffrey Gatton waved to the small table tucked into the corner, indicating that Lia should drop them off there. He'd get to the food when he could. Maybe after the next few hundred lines of code. To his surprise, Lia stepped up behind his chair.

"You need to eat." Her tone elevated the task to one of vital importance. At the same time, Lia twisted Jeff's chair around and shoved the paper plate into his hands. "Now."

Jeff's experience with women was nearly nonexistent, let alone assertive women, so Lia's tone and behavior outright baffled him. Instinctively, he froze and watched as the woman whirled and strode out. When the shock passed enough to let him move again, Jeff absently picked up a sausage and cheese sandwich and took a large bite.

His teeth crunched down on a piece of paper.

Startled, Jeff spit out the food, dropped the sandwich onto the paper plate, and flipped off the bottom croissant piece. A greasy, mangled Post-It note had a message scrawled in atrocious handwriting.

HELP. I AM COMPROMISED.

He stared at the note for a solid five-second span and re-read the message about a dozen times. The individual letters were well-formed, but a few overlapped and the heights differed greatly. His mind went eerily blank, then filled with so many questions he struggled to keep them straight. As a headache threatened to start, Jeff plucked the most important questions out and pondered them.

Is this real? What does it mean? Compromised how?

Craving more information, Jeff eagerly checked his other sandwich. Unfortunately, it held no secret messages. Since the first note had left a weird taste in his mouth, Jeff chucked the first sandwich into the garbage and ate the second one. He made a mental note to dump the garbage next break to avoid having the air quality permanently marred by cold, stale grease. Luciana would not be pleased, and he'd learned long ago that keeping the housekeeper happy made life easier. Some billionaires could get away with a revolving door of staff, but Luciana had been with him since he'd made his first million.

Once he finished his sandwich, Jeff wiped his hands on his shirt and leaned back in his chair to think. Thirst nagged at him, so he scanned his desk for a drink. Finding a bottle of water with about an inch of liquid left, he picked it up and cautiously unscrewed the cap as he eyed the contents critically. Concluding it was probably less than a week old, he drained the bottle's contents in one large gulp, crumpled the flimsy plastic thing, and tossed it into the garbage after the sandwich. He could put it into the recycling bin later.

Lia didn't strike Jeff as the sort to joke about danger.

Threat's probably real.

She also gave off very strong self-sufficiency vibes, so asking for help likely didn't come easily to her.

Why turn to me?

They'd only met recently, but Jeff suspected Lia had read a very thorough file about him before accepting the job to become his temporary guardian. The reason might be no more complicated than that Jeff was literally the only other human for a twenty-mile radius, but he suspected she had deeper reasons.

How is she compromised?

Jeff checked the note again. He studied the bizarre ups and downs of the letters. On a hunch, he rooted around his desk until he came up with a piece of scrap paper and a pen. He scribbled the words from Lia's message onto the paper, using all capital letters as she did. Next, he closed his eyes and tried writing the words again without looking. He'd consciously tried to keep the letters flowing evenly, but they veered up and overlapped a few times.

Why wasn't she looking at the message as she made it?

The question kicked Jeff's brain into gear. He'd read some Dark Web articles on tech that could control people. As the creator of Eagle Eyes, he knew better than most people that such a thing could happen.

He frowned.

Lia wouldn't watch the message being written if she thought somebody else could see it.

Eagle Eyes could do something like that, but the program worked with the users, not against them. People could—and often did—shut Eagle Eyes displays down at will. Jeff guessed that wasn't an option if Lia's conclusion involved the word *compromised*.

Despite not being much of a movie buff, Jeff recalled several films that involved computer chips enhancing humans. Tech running amok and people seeking to control others through technology were popular genre tropes.

Is mind control possible?

Jeff immediately dismissed the question. Obviously not, since Lia figured out a low-tech way to get him a message. The idea of somebody using something like Eagle Eyes to control others incensed Jeff. At the same time, he drew comfort from the knowledge that some form of gadget must be involved.

As he concluded Lia's problem could be conquered, the lady returned from her walkabout. Sitting up straighter, Jeff froze the feeds to the projector and activated some of his Eagle Eyes displays. He chose basic scan, a metal filter, a bio-electrical analyzer, and a recorder. Nodding a friendly welcome, he also activated a few webcams set up around the room to find a feed that would let him continue the analysis without staring at Lia creepily.

"House is clear," Lia reported.

Jeff mumbled thanks, not sure how to respond to the news. Turning his chair to face the main computer, he saved his work, then continued to tap away at the code he was writing. He'd need to delete every addition later because he couldn't divide his attention well enough to handle both modifying the code and reading the scans of Lia.

The basic scans came back with normal ranges for blood pressure, heartbeats, body temperature, and breaths per minute. Of the readings, Jeff trusted body temperature the least, but he noted it was on the high side, despite falling in an *acceptable* range for a woman of Lia's height and weight estimates.

He'd need to run a deeper scan since the metallic reading came back as inconclusive, but the cameras were positioned wrong. The slight delay due to having to transfer the data was altering the readings.

I need to look at her.

A calculation of the time needed for the deep scan told Jeff he would need to stare at Lia for six seconds.

Long enough to be creepy.

A deep, frustrated breath filled Jeff's nose with the scent of greasy sausage. Inspiration struck.

Spinning toward the garbage, Jeff gathered up the little plastic bag and quickly tied it off.

"Better take this out before the scent becomes permanent," he explained, lifting his eyes to watch Lia.

She gave him a quizzical look but acknowledged the statement with a brief head-bob.

Walking as slowly as possible allowed Jeff to see Lia for 1.5 seconds.

Not enough!

"Could you put in a new bag for me?" asked Jeff. The question gave him an adequate excuse for another two-second look. "There should be some at the bottom of the container."

Shrugging, Lia attended the mundane task.

That let Jeff steal another 1-second look.

After dealing with his quick errand, Jeff obtained another two seconds of observation time upon the return trip. A contiguous 6-second observation period would have been best, but Jeff was grateful for what he got.

Just before settling down in his chair, it occurred to him that finding the source of Lia's problem was only one part of the solution. He would also need to deal with whatever he found.

Luciana to the rescue again.

Executing an about-face, Jeff rushed out of the room.

"Where are you going?" Lia asked, sidestepping to avoid a collision.

"Just gotta grab something," Jeff called, not bothering to look back. He'd let the program continue its Lia-analysis while he picked up a few items. "Stay here. I'll be back in a minute."

The first stop Jeff made was in the bathroom. A combination of too many mystery novels and a wild imagination made Luciana slightly paranoid. Since Jeff had given her full reign over stocking each room, every bathroom with a closet had a full self-defense kit to go with the first-aid supplies and common ailment remedies.

Ripping open the closet, Jeff found the stash of goods and pondered his options. Luciana had insisted on stocking pepper spray, a stun gun, and a baton. Reluctantly, Jeff tucked the pepper spray canister into his pocket, vowing to only use it if necessary. He didn't want to hurt Lia. To give himself more thinking time, he availed himself of the facilities and took his time washing his hands. Chances were very good that using the stun gun or baton would result in him getting hurt. A few seconds of thought made Jeff mentally discard the baton. Even if he hit Lia with a strong stream of pepper spray, she'd probably gain control of the weapon and beat him.

"Analysis complete."

Hearing his own voice from Eagle Eyes had ceased to disturb Jeff long ago, but the suddenness of the announcement startled him anyway. Muting the sound, he read the deep scan report. Lia had only one piece of metal inside her body and none on her.

Pulling up a miniature body outline, Jeff bid the program to highlight the affected part of the figure. A tiny red dot appeared on the digital dummy. At first, the dot covered the entirety of the figure's neck. Enlarging the dummy allowed the Eagle Eyes program to narrow the location down to the space at the back of the figure's neck.

An inquiry into the metal piece's chemical makeup said it contained mostly silicon, titanium, aluminum, copper, gold, and a few other elements that didn't surprise Jeff. He guessed the inner workings consisted of standard computer stuff while the outer casing dealt more with waterproofing and protecting the rest of the chip.

The size estimate said the chip was approximately 200 square nanometers. In terms of modern chips, it was a behemoth, but Jeff assumed much of that could be attributed to the protective shell.

Can I short the chip with enough electricity?

Since the thing was likely embedded in the delicate nerves near Lia's spinal cord, Jeff didn't like the idea of zapping her with a few million volts of electricity.

She asked for my help.

He was almost certain the stun gun would have enough electricity to deal with the chip temporarily, but what would he do then?

How am I going to remove the chip from her neck?

Chapter 9:
Rough Ride

Things can't get much worse.

Megan Luchek regretted the thought immediately. She tried to take it back, but then, a glance out the window drove coherent thoughts out of her head. A stream of people flowed from the nearest building.

"Um, we have—"

A loud curse from Thorne cut Megan off, assuring her that the driver had noticed the problem. Throwing the police cruiser into reverse, Thorne twisted around and braced his right hand on the passenger seat.

Fear and adrenaline put Megan on edge as the cruiser careened down the street backwards.

Thorne executed a wild K turn that tossed Megan from one side of the back seat to the other. She'd just about righted herself when Thorne braked suddenly, slamming Megan into the metal cage guarding the front passenger seat. She grunted as her body absorbed the new pain in her head and shoulders.

"Run them over!" cried Bentley.

"I can't!" snapped Thorne. "Dash cam's running." He leaned on the horn.

The noise made the crowd surrounding the vehicle flinch and back up a step, but they quickly recovered the ground and pressed close, putting hands on the car.

"Out! Out! Out!" chanted the crowd.

Megan couldn't tell if it was a general cry against police or something more specific, but she didn't think the mob looked ready to explain much.

"Call for backup!" shouted Bentley.

"And tell them what?" demanded Thorne. "We're miles away from our zone. I was going to fix the data later, but an impact report or a backup call will ruin everything." He inched the car forward, forcing the people near the front to back up. Activating the exterior loudspeaker, he said, "Move away from the vehicle!"

Suddenly, the crowd stepped back and parted enough to let a young man pass. He wielded a baseball bat and had a troublesome smirk.

"There's no impact sensors in the back," Bentley said urgently. "Remember? They're broken. I filed the paperwork to get them fixed last week."

The crooked cops exchanged elated looks.

"Wait!" cried Megan. "There has to be another way."

Thorne's grim, determined expression chilled Megan. Putting the car in reverse yet again, he mashed the gas pedal to the floor.

The vehicle lurched backwards, causing a chorus of shouts to ring out. Most were merely surprised, but a pair of thumps preceded a few pain-filled cries as well.

Bentley gripped the balance bar hard and whooped with delight as the car broke free of the crowd.

The insane driver performed another harrowing K turn before speeding away from the crowd.

Pounding the dash with his fist, Bentley whooped again.

"Payday, here we come!" he yelled.

"Keep it down," said Thorne. "We still need to deliver her. Call it in."

"But I thought—"

"The hotline," Thorne clarified. His voice contained significant weariness and strained patience. "Call the hotline and tell them to get our money ready. We're taking the cash option."

"Aw, but it's so much less," Bentley whined.

"It's also less traceable," Thorne explained.

Before Bentley could respond, something struck the back of the vehicle.

For the second time in about as many minutes, Megan crashed into the cage separating her from Bentley's seat.

"Make that call right now," Thorne ordered. He pressed harder on the gas pedal, coaxing a bit more speed out of the cruiser.

Bentley scrambled to find his phone, but Megan was too distracted to track if he followed through with the call.

Craning her neck around, she watched a large white van loom in the back window.

Faster. Faster. Faster.

Her mind spat the encouragement at lightning speed. Megan could scarcely believe she was cheering on her kidnappers, but the notion of being sold for a finder's fee appealed more than being crushed.

Horrified, she watched the van close the distance between the vehicles.

Megan tensed.

Her left foot slipped on the plastic floor mat, giving her an idea. As quickly as her bound arms would let her, Megan wedged her body into the foot space, bracing her feet on the bump separating the left and right halves of the car. Instinctively, she hunched forward to protect her head. The next impact tossed her into Bentley's seat, but the lack of space meant her body didn't get to pick up as much momentum this time.

A third crunch from the back slammed Megan's poor head into the plastic part of Bentley's seat, making the headache return with a vengeance. Before she could complain, a fourth crunch preceded the sickening scrape of metal across metal.

The cruiser shuddered to a halt.

Dazed but desperate for information, Megan awkwardly maneuvered to a kneeling position in preparation of rising.

Several shouts came from outside the car. Closing her eyes afforded Megan enough concentration to decipher the shouts as orders to get out. She couldn't obey that command if she wanted to, and regardless, she wasn't certain she wanted to obey. With effort, Megan turned and flopped back onto the hard plastic seat, sweating from the exertion. The new position let her witness the drama unfolding around her.

Both cops had their service weapons in hand and trained on different assailants. Bentley focused on a man standing directly in front of the cop car while Thorne aimed at a figure standing outside his window. Megan didn't have the correct angle to see the figure's face, but the voice was male.

"Unlock the door," said the man.

"Maybe we should do it," Bentley said reluctantly.

"No way," said Thorne. "They can't fire without the risk of killing her."

The figures outside the vehicle shuffled to new positions,

presumably to get better angles with which to fire on the cops without killing Megan.

She hardly dared to breathe.

"Bentley, forget the guys out front. Turn around and aim for the agent," said Thorne.

Unbuckling his seat belt, Bentley turned and followed the directive.

Thorne's order made a weird kind of sense, but that didn't make it any easier to stare down the serious end of Bentley's gun.

The figure outside bellowed in frustration and slammed something against Thorne's window. The noise made Bentley flinch, but thankfully, he refrained from pulling the trigger.

"Back off," Thorne barked. He cracked open his window and repeated the order.

"Hand her over," argued the man standing by Thorne's door. "I've more men and more weapons. That means I win."

"And I've got a gun to her head," Thorne retorted in a cold, even tone. "You fire, and we all lose."

The reality wasn't quite true because Bentley kept shifting positions to optimize his firing angle.

Megan's mind raced. If she dove into the foot space again, Officer Bentley would have a hard time tracking her with his gun. That would give the assailants a chance to shoot the crooked cops with relatively little chance of killing her.

She stayed put.

These cops weren't her favorite people, but she wasn't ready to throw them in front of a wall of bullets, especially not when she'd be inches from that wall of bullets.

Two very long seconds of tense silence fell.

Pulsing pain zipped through Megan's head. The urge to lay her head back and take a nap gripped her strongly, but self-preservation kept her focused. Forcing her aching throat to surrender words took a lot of effort.

"Negotiate with them," she said quietly.

"I'm not losing this much money," said Thorne.

"You can't spend it if you're dead anyway," Megan argued. Irritation drove off some of the discomfort, lending strength to her voice.

"She has a point," said Bentley.

"What are you suggesting?" asked the speaker hovering near

Thorne.

"Does the car still work?" asked Megan, ignoring the man momentarily.

"Probably," Thorne said tightly.

"Tell them to get back in their van and follow us," said Megan. "When we get to wherever we're going, you can split the money with them."

I'm inviting more bad guys to tag along. What is wrong with me?

Another long silence ensued.

Megan felt like a mouse being fought for.

Finally, Thorne's shoulders relaxed fractionally.

"Will you agree to that?" inquired Thorne.

Megan missed the man's response, if he bothered giving one, but she noticed the man in front of the car retreat.

"Nice work. Guess we all get to live a while longer," said Bentley. Heaving a sigh of relief, he lowered his weapon and resumed his seat.

Megan didn't bother replying. She remained acutely aware that the closer they got to their destination, the nearer they'd get to the psychopaths who wanted her dead enough to pay for the privilege of making it happen.

That takes dedication and some powerful motivation.

While she had a moment of forced downtime, Megan let her mind puzzle through the problem. She wanted to spend the time conjuring escape plans, but her brain fixated on the *why me* question. Instinct told her the answer would be important.

The surface reason of being worth something to the Cyber League seemed straightforward enough, but Megan wanted to know how she'd gotten on their radar in the first place. Despite her uncanny ability to attract unhinged men, she genuinely doubted she had made enemies on this level during her FBI career. The next leap of logic took her to the notion that she was a means to get to somebody else.

If they're not after me, who do I know worth threatening?

Megan ruled out her family since the masterminds seemed to be after them to gain a hold on her. They were involved too much. Dan Cooper wasn't involved enough. Besides, the bulk of his bigger cases had been handled with Megan. Detective Kailani Lang caught some strange cases. Megan had even unofficially consulted on a few, but once again, the connections were too weak to have any significant meaning.

That left Jeffrey Gatton and Cassandra Mirren as the logical choices for primary target. Between the pair, Megan honestly couldn't say who had collected more powerful, crazy, and ultra-rich enemies over the years. The assassin had more years over the tech genius, but both ran in the right circles to brew this brand of wacko. The focus of Gatton's company and his billionaire status gave him the edge when it came to the likelihood of attracting tech-savvy enemies, but Cassandra's career as a Shadow Council Fixer would have brought her into contact with countless rich, powerful, and unscrupulous types.

Before Megan could draw a conclusion, the cop car rolled to a stop. A swift visual sweep told her little because they had arrived in a parking garage.

Seconds later, Bentley pulled open the back door and ordered her out.

Disembarking took some effort thanks to the handcuffs, but Megan felt better once she got to stand and stretch her back. The relief vanished with the sound of multiple doors slamming. She'd forgotten about their armed uninvited guests.

The presence of so many people surprised the receiving team, but eventually, the parties got paid and Megan was officially handed over to Timothy Lyra and Randall Fuller. She wasn't sure whether to be comforted by or disturbed by the presence of familiar guards.

Bentley reclaimed his handcuffs before leaving, but Randy had a fresh pair waiting to replace them. His smile made Megan want to rearrange his teeth, but she confined her reaction to a glare as he slipped the linked metal bracelets into place. Tim held an expandable baton and projected an air of impatience. Megan decided not to test them just yet. As much as she dreaded what would come, part of her longed for the answers that awaited a few floors up.

"Handcuffs won't be necessary," announced a new male voice. "I have something better."

Megan's head whipped toward the newcomer.

"Heard you were dead," she commented, recognizing the face but not the voice.

"Officially, Gary Sheffield is dead," replied the man. He held something large, bulky, and off-white in color behind his back. "You can call me Hawk." Taking his cumbersome burden from behind his back, Hawk tossed it to the ground before Megan and her two captors. It hit the ground with a thump. "Hurry up and put that on her. I've got a show to run."

Megan stared down at the bundle of canvas and buckles.

Straitjacket. That's an odd choice.

Chapter 10:
Spike

After debating a hundred different ways to approach Lia, Jeffrey Gatton finally chose the direct route. He expected to find her leaning against his office doorway like normal, but she wasn't there.

"Lia?" he called.

"In here," she answered.

Try as he might, Jeff couldn't gather any context clues from her tone. Nevertheless, innate caution bid him to slow his steps as he neared his office. Crossing the threshold, Jeff absorbed the odd sight.

The young assassin sat in Jeff's chair. She had raided his cord and cable supply box and bound herself to the chair. One ethernet cable secured her feet together while another looped several times around the chair and her waist. Her wrists were zip tied to the cable encircling her waist. She kept her eyes closed.

Jeff froze. His fear and instinct to protect collided. If he proceeded with his plan, he'd hurt Lia, but if he did nothing, somebody else would hurt her worse.

"Hurry," Lia said. "He's not monitoring me right now, but that's not going to last."

Clinging to his rapidly escaping courage, Jeff stumbled into the room, pressed the stun gun to Lia's left shoulder, and activated the device. Bracing did little to protect his nerves as a violent crackling noise filled the air a second before Lia's pained cry. The self-defense instructor had been quite explicit about keeping the stun gun activated for a minimum of three seconds to fully incapacitate a person. Tears blurred his vision as he counted out the longest three seconds of his life.

The resulting pain caused Lia's entire body to stiffen, twitch, then collapse with exhaustion.

Jeff dropped the stun gun and caught Lia's shoulders.

"Did it work?" he asked anxiously.

The mixture of fear, resignation, and frustration in her expression answered long before she voiced a reply.

"It's not enough," said Lia. "It worked for a few seconds, but the system reset already."

"Do you want me to try again?" Jeff wondered tentatively. He didn't bother hiding the dread he felt at that prospect.

The fear on Lia's face flipped to fierce determination.

"Go get me a kitchen knife," Lia ordered.

Her words—and clear intention—made Jeff flinch.

"No way! That's crazy," he argued.

Unshed tears made Lia's eyes shiny as she pleaded with Jeff.

"Please. I won't have control for much longer," Lia explained. "What choice do I have? If the program asserts full control over my nervous system, Hawk can force me to do anything. He'll make me kill you, then use me against Cassandra."

"Give me another option," Jeff commanded, refusing to believe Lia's fatalistic predictions.

"There is no—" Lia cut herself off and sucked in a sharp breath. She considered something carefully for a few seconds before letting the breath out again. "I guess you could cut it out."

"How?" Jeff demanded. "It's microscopic. I wouldn't even be able to see it!"

Hope lit up Lia's entire spirit.

"The carrier," she answered. Her eyes darted around the room as she built up the baby plan.

Jeff wanted to demand further explanation, but he didn't want to interrupt Lia's thought process. At least they'd moved beyond suicide being her only option. He shivered at the memory of her expression.

"I'm going to need your help again," said Lia. This time, she appeared sympathetic.

It was not an improvement.

Jeff groaned, then sighed.

"Let's hear it."

***

The brief phone call Hawk insisted Cassandra make had been to Lia. It only confirmed she was still with Gatton and somehow being manipulated from afar, much like Owen Ramsey. Cassandra longed to see her friend, even though it hurt to know he too was a captive of some sort. She almost wished the chains binding Owen were visible. Then, at least, she'd have a concrete problem to puzzle over.

Given Hawk's eagerness to meet, Cassandra had expected to immediately be rushed into his presence, but instead, Owen had left her in the custody of two Club men. The mid-level thugs had escorted her to a makeshift prison cell and left her alone. She tried a few lines of conversation as she examined the cell for weak points. The men refused to speak with her, but Cassandra didn't care. She had already drawn her conclusions. Escape would be a relatively simple matter of faking an injury and waiting for the guards to panic. Nobody had bothered removing the handcuffs Owen had applied, so she even had a ready weapon at hand if the right opportunity arose.

Under normal circumstances, Cassandra would already have made a move, but the apartment scene haunted her. She hadn't come this far to abandon Owen to Hawk's tender mercies. Freeing him would require a lot more information.

When pacing the small cell failed to deal with Cassandra's restless energy, she sat down in the exact center, closed her eyes, and reviewed some memories of past fights, concentrating on the ones where she'd faced multiple opponents. During her apprenticeship to Smith, he'd taught her the value of learning from every experience. The odds of escaping with Owen and without a physical fight were negative something.

The mental exercise occupied her until the guards interrupted by bringing her food. The greasy chicken sandwich wouldn't have been Cassandra's first choice, but she knew it might be the only thing offered for the day. She hesitated a second before sipping from the plastic cup of water offered. Slipping a drug into a liquid took less effort than poisoning food, but she guessed Hawk would want her fully alert until he had a chance to gloat. As she finished the simple meal, she noticed the guards straighten. Crumpling up the wrapper, she placed it on the ground and stood to greet her captor.

A subtle hand gesture sent the Club men away. Four men flanked Hawk, two to either side. They each pointed a handgun at her, but since they were merely a gesture of power, she ignored them.

"Cassandra Mirren," said the youthful male voice she had spoken with in the apartment. "I'm disappointed. I thought you'd be harder to catch. You used to change identities every few months in your prime."

"Been a little busy," Cassandra replied. "I assume you have a reason for walking around with a projection of Gary Sheffield's face. Care to explain?"

"This old thing?" said Hawk with feigned surprise. "Sometimes, I forget I'm wearing it." Reaching into his pocket, he took out his phone and typed something in. His facial features flickered, then changed, revealing a similar yet very different countenance beneath. "Better?"

Cassandra studied the young man. He had neat brown hair with subtle waves in it. His skin tone was darkened by an even tan. Faint scruff outlined his chin. He had warm brown eyes that currently held genuine amusement, but everything else about him was forgettable. She'd seen him before, but it took her several seconds to piece together the correct place.

"You checked Megan into the hotel last night," she said. "How did you know we'd be there?"

"You're good." Hawk's tone implied: *I'm better.* He ignored her question. "What other grand deductions have you made?"

"You're not the original Hawk, and you haven't had the title long," said Cassandra. She pointedly swept her eyes up and down the young man. "If I had to guess, I'd say three weeks, maybe four."

"Close enough," Hawk confirmed with mock applause. "What gave it away?"

"You were probably in grade school when your predecessor tried to recruit me the first time," Cassandra explained. "I based the rest of the timing off when my life got more exciting a few weeks back. Your handiwork, I'm sure. What I'm not clear on is the motive."

"I intend to succeed where my mentor failed," Hawk declared. "You're going to work for me." He waited a few beats for her to react. When she said nothing, he gave her an exaggerated frown. "Don't you want to know how I'm going to accomplish this feat?"

"I'm sure you'll tell me soon," said Cassandra.

Taking a small white box out of his pants pocket, Hawk opened the gate and tossed the box to her.

She caught the box.

"Open it," he said eagerly.

Flipping the lid up, Cassandra checked the box's contents. Mostly, it held a black cushion with a thin piece of plastic strapped to the center.

"That is going to let me control you," Hawk said smugly.

***

It's so ... simple.

Jeff studied the small object he'd worked so hard to obtain.

Lia still lay on the cot, unconscious.

He'd have to wake her soon, but he wanted to give her as many pain-free moments as possible. The last fifteen minutes had been very unpleasant. Lia had walked him through the process of securing her hands and feet effectively so she wouldn't kill him while he helped her. Next, she'd described what he was looking for and where on her neck to start searching. Her final instruction had been on how to knock her unconscious through a pressure point in her neck.

The impromptu surgery would have gone worlds smoother if Jeff had a proper medical instrument like a sharp scalpel, but the best he could conjure on short notice was a pocketknife and a needle from a sewing kit he stole from Luciana's room. He'd almost quit outright when opening a shallow cut on the back of Lia's neck resulted in a few droplets of blood. After dabbing away the blood with a tissue, Jeff had forged onward, gently probing with the knife and needle until he found the hard, plastic spike embedded in her neck. Finding the blasted thing had been only a quarter of the battle. The rest consisted of getting a good enough grip with slippery tweezers and slowly extricating the object.

When the traumatic experience was over, Jeff cleaned his hands with several cleaning wipes. He wanted to wash up properly, but Lia's neck still needed to be patched up properly. Tossing aside the third wipe, Jeff riffled through the First Aid Kit until he found gauze and medical tape. The task was complicated by stray hairs that escaped the quick bun Lia had established before dictating how Jeff could free her from the evil tech somebody had shoved into her neck. Eventually, Jeff managed to get a strip of gauze onto the open wound and fasten it down with generous swatches of medical tape.

Once certain he'd done everything he could for Lia, Jeff reached to wake her up. Upon spotting the wreckage left by his clumsy efforts, he hesitated. After using the cleaning wipes to clear blood from the knife and needle, Jeff tossed the wipes into the garbage and hastily righted the First Aid Kit. Finally, he used the pocketknife scissors to deal with the zip ties around Lia's ankles and wrists.

When his hand landed on her shoulder to shake her awake, Lia rolled over onto her left side, looking tired but alert.

"How long have you been awake?" Jeff asked.

"A few minutes," Lia replied. "Help me up."

"You should rest," said Jeff.

Lia started shaking her head, winced, and stopped moving.

"There's still work to do," Lia said. "If things go the way I think they will, Cassandra and her FBI friend are going to need similar surgeries today." She stopped speaking while Jeff helped her to a sitting position. After gingerly touching the bandage on her neck, Lia let her gaze linger on Jeff. "Thank you. I know that wasn't easy."

"Are you all right?" Jeff mentally kicked himself for the stupid question. "How did they get that thing into you? When did it happen? What do we do with it?" He consciously cut off the flow of questions and looked at the spike so he wouldn't have to meet Lia's eyes. He felt the attention anyway and flushed accordingly.

She answered with a question.

"How fast can you type?"

The question piqued Jeff's interest.

"Pretty fast," he said modestly. "What'd you have in mind?"

"The chip in that spike links directly to Hawk's network," Lia explained. "That's how he delivers orders directly to a person's nervous system to encourage obedience. He's been after Cassandra for a while, and I think this time he's working with the Cyber League."

"Who's Hawk? And how are you making that connection?" Jeff wondered.

"Nobody knows Hawk's identity," said Lia, "but he claimed to be in charge of the men who ambushed me in your mother's apartment. It's probably a title used by several spies. I'm not positive there is a connection to the Cyber League, but I know they're after Agent Luchek and she's the best lead Hawk has to my mentor."

Jeff's mind latched onto the implications immediately.

"If the spike can receive information packets, I can probably modify it to send them as well." Jeff had to concentrate to keep from shouting as excitement lit him up from the inside. "And if they're working together, there's probably some electronic connections!"

He understood that such contacts wouldn't guarantee he could exploit the situation, but the idea gave him a surge of hope. It'd been a while since a true challenge lay before him. The recent events terrified him, but they also might have given him the key to deal a death blow to the Cyber League's latest scheme.

Chapter 11:
Terms

Megan started questioning Hawk's sanity when he changed his mind midway through the process of having her stuffed into the straitjacket.

"Wait. Go back to the handcuffs and take her up to Cell 2," said Hawk. "I have a few phone calls to make."

The relief at returning to normal handcuffs was offset by Hawk's excitement. He must have received good news via text, for he stood staring down at his phone, practically bouncing. Anything that thrilling to him couldn't be great for her or some other poor innocent soul.

Tim seemed annoyed, but Randy merely shrugged and started tugging the straitjacket off Megan.

"Come on, guys. Can't we skip the cuffs?" Megan asked, once Hawk slipped back into the stairwell. "It's not like I'm ready to bust out of here." She internally cringed at how much truth that last statement held. The rough delivery had rattled her in multiple ways.

If I live long enough, I'm going to feel that ride for days.

Neither man bothered answering verbally.

Randy merely snapped the handcuffs firmly into place and gripped her right arm.

She'd known that would be the answer, but irrational disappointment filled her anyway. Pushing the feeling aside, Megan focused on the surroundings. Unfortunately, there wasn't much to see as they walked up several flights of bare metal stairs and then traveled a few blank office corridors. A look around with Eagle Eyes only revealed a depressing number of armed men, several metal cages, and a few prisoners.

A sense of déjà vu smacked Megan as Randy pushed her into a makeshift holding cell. This one lacked furniture, making Megan miss the cot from the last prison cell she'd been tossed in.

Was that yesterday? Seems longer.

Her arms ached from the awkward position.

"Can we lose the cuffs now?" she asked.

Randy hesitated, looked to Tim for a judgment call, received another shrug, and made a decision.

"If you try—"

"I'm not going to ruin the chance to get feeling back into my arms," Megan said impatiently.

Randy entered the cell, released her, and scampered back out. In other circumstances, his furtive movements would be amusing.

Once she rubbed some feeling back into her tingling arms, Megan sat down and wrapped her arms around her knees. She hated waiting, but she also didn't want to miss anything. As time ticked by, she decided to hold her vigil from the prone position. Tucking her hands behind her head, Megan laid down, closed her eyes, and conducted several more scans with Eagle Eyes. She debated calling Dan, but the option wasn't available.

Why can't I make a phone call?

"There is an active signal jammer." Eagle Eyes answered, using Gatton's voice as usual.

How are you still working if there's a jammer in place?

"I can do anything that does not require fresh data from the satellite," the program explained.

After instructing the program to place a call for help as soon as possible, Megan reviewed everything she knew. The Club had kidnapped her sister for a bizarre live online gambling scheme. She'd found and freed her sister only to get sucked into a separate yet similar sadistic game. They'd escaped again, but the Club's obsession with her hadn't ended.

Why didn't it end? This is about more than money. It's personal, but how?

When she tossed the facts at Eagle Eyes and asked for an analysis, the program said she probably wasn't the true target, but it couldn't get more specific with the number of variables present.

After chasing the thoughts in several circles, Megan dozed, hoping to pass the time. She'd almost forgotten how mind-numbingly boring captivity could be.

"Would you like music played?"

Sure.

Without asking what she'd like to hear, Eagle Eyes played a soft piano medley. The music lulled her into full sleep within minutes.

A few hours later, the ever-present duo woke her for a bathroom break and a midday meal which consisted of a slightly burnt burger and a bottle of water. Megan paced the cell a while after eating, expecting a summons at any moment.

When nothing happened for twenty minutes, Megan sat on the floor and rolled the half-empty water bottle back and forth a few dozen times. As she concluded a second nap might be in order, Hawk appeared with another man.

"You two can go to the main event," said Hawk with a dismissive wave.

Randy and Tim left.

Megan sat up slowly. The new angle let her see the man standing behind Hawk. To her surprise, she recognized him as the man who'd shown up at her Great Aunt Celia's place with Cassandra. The association resulted in a jolt that brought Megan to her feet.

"Is she here?" Megan addressed the quiet question to Cassandra's friend. Her heart quickened with anticipation, dread, and several other conflicting emotions. Having the former assassin present would improve her odds of survival, but Megan didn't feel right wishing such a fate on her friend.

The man's expression spelled out the answer long before his tight nod confirmed it. He kept a tight rein on his emotions, but Megan got the distinct impression of simmering anger and resentment from his stiff body language.

Hawk beamed.

"Megan Luchek. Allow me to introduce Owen Ramsey," said Hawk. "I believe you two have a mutual acquaintance. You'll get to see her shortly."

Hawk's smug attitude irritated Megan.

"How are you controlling him?" she wondered.

"Who says I'm controlling him?" Hawk asked.

"Your face does," Megan answered, growing weary of the verbal duel. She rubbed a sore spot on her forehead. She must have hit it in the police cruiser.

And his. She kept that part to herself, though Hawk probably already knew his help was disgruntled.

"Don't worry. You'll find out soon enough," Hawk promised.

"In fact, I'm planning on demonstrating with your friend in a few minutes. Stand still while Mr. Ramsey applies the handcuffs."

"They're not necessary," said Megan. "Can't I just promise to cooperate? You know I want to see Cassandra."

"They help me make my point," said Hawk. He gestured for Owen to get on with it.

"What point?" Megan asked.

"I could tell you," said Hawk, "but that would be less fun."

Owen entered the cell to fulfill the order. Megan fought her instinct to fight as he stepped up beside her and reached for her arms. The closeness gave her a better appreciation for his height.

How did Hawk overpower him?

Cassandra's friend stood almost a foot taller than the scrawny weasel still using Gary's face. Megan idly wondered about that too while waiting for the familiar clicks of the handcuffs settling into place. Megan flexed her shoulders, trying to get her arms into a more comfortable position.

Hawk led the way. Megan followed with Owen at her side. The fast pace made her trip twice, but thankfully, Owen's grip on her arm prevented complete wipeouts. Hawk swept through one last door and gallantly held it open for her.

Megan entered the room and stopped walking.

Owen pushed her forward another few stumbling steps toward the crowd in the center. Megan's feet numbly carried her forward until Owen pulled her to a halt.

Cassandra stood flanked by at least a dozen men. She didn't wear restraints, but several men held clubs, tasers, or stun guns at the ready.

"Are you ready to join the cause?" asked Hawk.

"Not quite," Cassandra answered carefully. "Letting you hand the agent over to the Club to be killed hardly qualifies as improving her situation. If you can't come through on that part, there's no deal to be made."

Agent, stall them. Help is coming.

Cassandra's brief message almost made Megan cry. She had about a hundred questions for the assassin, but now wasn't the best time to catch up.

I thought there was a jammer in place.

Megan didn't realize Eagle Eyes could follow the thought until she received an answer.

"At this range, there is a direct, line-of-sight option for me

to connect to other EE units."

"How about now?" asked Hawk.

The cold touch of Hawk's handgun against her head refocused Megan. She twitched her head right to gain some distance from the weapon.

Half the men in the room started protesting loudly.

"She's worth a lot to us," said a middle-aged man, "but only if she's alive."

Megan had mixed feelings about that. While completely in favor of not being shot now, she doubted the Club guys had her best interests in mind.

"You'll get paid either way," Hawk assured the man.

"Stop using my son's face," grumbled the man. "Everybody knows who you are."

The last statement wasn't quite accurate, but Hawk shrugged and tapped something into his phone. His face ceased looking like Gary Sheffield and changed into another young man. The hair and eyes stayed the same, but his forehead appeared broader, his nose looked blunter, and his lips appeared thicker.

Two of the Club men crossed themselves. Another cursed. Most stared with a mixture of shock, horror, and morbid fascination.

"Why are you bothering with these games?" asked the older man. "We have both women. You take the one you want and leave us the other. I'll even lend you some men to keep that one in line." He stabbed a finger in Cassandra's direction.

"The control chip is vulnerable for a few minutes after insertion." Hawk's entire face lit up with passion as he explained. "Besides, it'll be most effective if she works with the program instead of resisting the commands."

"I gave you my terms," Cassandra said. "Megan and Owen walk away."

"Now, let me give you *my* terms," Hawk countered. The joyful expression melted away behind an air of contempt. "And let me clarify something. This isn't about their freedom. It's about how unpleasant the next few minutes of their lives will be. You already saw what I can do to Owen. My agreement with the Club gentlemen says I deliver the agent alive. You're bargaining for *how* alive."

"This isn't necessary," argued the older man. "Throw her in a straitjacket until you can control her."

Agent, you're going to have to do all the fighting for us. Let

Owen help you.

Hawk glared at the older man for a second, but soon, his expression turned thoughtful.

"That's not a bad idea," he admitted. He waved for the older man to fulfill the wish.

The first two Club thugs who approached Cassandra got bloody noses for their trouble. The third got hit with taser prongs aimed at Cassandra.

Before Megan could cheer, something hard struck her back, throwing her forward. Thanks to the handcuffs, the best she could do was turn left so the ground met her shoulder first instead of her face.

Owen loomed above her. He held an expandable baton in his right hand.

"Hold still," he whispered, reaching down to help her up.

She felt the handcuffs loosen then fall off her right wrist, but she kept her hands behind her back. He pressed the key into her right palm and hauled her up to her knees, pausing a second to let her free the other wrist. Megan's heart leapt with hope. The good feeling vanished in the next instant as she caught sight of the other side of the room.

The Club men had wrestled Cassandra into the straitjacket. She knelt between two men, looking like a mummy they were about to bury. Hawk hovered near the assassin, fiddling with a small black object.

Do you trust me?

Megan hated when Cassandra asked things like that but didn't have the energy to tell her properly.

What do you need? Despite her irritation and confusion, Megan tossed the question into the box to let Eagle Eyes—and hopefully Cassandra—read the thought.

Activate Hive Mind and go for Hawk first.

"Hang onto this tight," Owen said softly. "I'll toss you in the right direction."

As Megan tried to wrap her mind around that statement, her hand closed around the baton. She dropped the handcuff key. Next instant, a strong shove sent her flying toward Hawk.

Chapter 12:
Retirement Plan

"Hive mind activated."

Having never fought with a baton before, Megan raised it high to put momentum behind her swing, but midway through her charge, something shifted in her. She automatically adjusted her grip and brought the weapon in close to her chest.

Several men moved to block her.

As the first man raised his arm back to swing at Megan with a baton, she darted in close and slammed her weapon into his left ribs. The blow didn't have much force because Megan reversed the strike to knock a taser out of another man's hands. Another baton-wielder stepped in front of her. He grinned and aimed a devastating blow at her side.

Blocking would probably shatter something in her arm, so she dodged.

The swing's momentum carried the man past Megan.

Spinning, she tagged his back to keep him moving away from her.

Somebody grabbed her left arm.

Whipping the baton down into the man's left leg resulted in a sickening crunch and a bloodcurdling scream.

Sweat threatened her grip on the weapon. Megan scanned for threats. With the path to Hawk temporarily clear, she sprinted forward.

He tapped furiously at his phone.

A desperate shout rang out behind her, but Megan couldn't investigate. She barely had time to wonder how she'd heard the cry amidst the chaos of yelling, fighting men. Her sprint brought her directly into Hawk, knocking the man back into two of the men still struggling with Cassandra. The man's phone went flying past Megan's head as she desperately tried to keep her balance.

Somebody tackled her.

Desperate, Megan rammed the baton's handle up into her attacker's face. The blow caught him in the chin with enough stunning force to let her roll away.

He scrambled over and threw his weight into pinning her down.

A gunshot smashed through the general battle noise, making everybody freeze for a split-second.

Megan got a good look at her attacker.

Vinny!

Shock and anger sucked the strength from her arm. The baton dropped from her nerveless hand. The click of handcuffs brought her back to her senses.

"Hive Mind deactivated."

"What are you doing?" Megan hissed the question to her cousin.

"Saving your life," Vinny said, pulling her to a sitting position with his good arm.

The other handcuff half had been secured around his right wrist.

Remembering the gunshot, Megan leapt to her feet. The move pulled her cousin up as well. The desire to interrogate Vinny vanished when Megan saw another familiar figure.

Curtis D'Angelo stood over Hawk's body, squaring off against the Club men. His gun wasn't quite pointed at the other men, but he certainly had it ready for action.

"Take your men and go, Steel," said Curtis.

"Give me the agent, and we'll do that," Steel countered. "I've still got a contest to run."

Megan recognized him as the middle-aged Club man who had been arguing with Hawk.

"Hawk's not going to be able to help you with that anymore," Curtis commented, gesturing to the body at his feet. "As to the agent's fate, that depends on my negotiations. I'll send her along if things go your way."

"Not good enough," Steel said, pulling a handgun from a shoulder holster.

Curtis aimed at Steel's chest.

"Unless you're eager to experience Hawk's fate, leave. Now," said the assassin.

Megan forgot to breathe while Curtis and Steel held a staring contest.

Curtis won.

Growling, Steel lowered his gun and motioned for his men to stand down.

Most of the men filed out after the Club leader.

Curtis tracked Steel's exit with his gun, then let the weapon drop to his side before returning his attention to Cassandra.

Megan started breathing again, but she knew trouble still brewed. Pulling her cousin along via the handcuff link, Megan moved toward the main event. They made it four steps before Vinny halted the forward progress.

Still sporting the straitjacket, Cassandra stood flanked by Tim and Randy.

Megan tried to interpret her friend's reaction to Curtis D'Angelo's presence. If she was surprised, Cassandra hid it well. A slight dip in her shoulders spoke of weariness, but her expression betrayed nothing.

"State the terms, Curt," said Cassandra. "What do they want?"

"Three jobs," Curtis announced. He gently tapped his handgun against his leg.

"What do I get?" asked Cassandra.

"Freedom for the agent and her family, Ramsey's life, and a retirement plan," replied Curtis.

"What does that mean?" Megan demanded. Fear for her friend made her tense. *Retirement plan* sounded like a euphemistic term for a bullet to the back of the head.

Cassandra met Megan's eyes and smiled gently.

"It's the government's version of a step-down program," Cassandra explained.

"They're not going to kill you?" Megan's inflection turned it into a question that carried her deep-seated skepticism.

"Not yet," said Cassandra.

"What's your answer?" Curtis asked.

Letting her eyes fall shut, Cassandra bowed her head and nodded slowly. Her face moved through several expressions, including pain and resignation, before clearing as she opened her eyes and lifted her head.

"Don't do it if you don't want to," Megan whispered.

"She doesn't have a choice," said Curtis.

"Of course, she has a choice," Megan argued.

"Shut up. Shut up," Vinny chanted, tugging on Megan's arm. "This is how we save them!"

Holstering his gun, Curtis took out a switchblade and strode over to Megan and Vinny.

"Back off, Curt," called Cassandra. "I'll take the deal."

"Good," said Curtis, keeping his eyes on Megan, "but she still needs to understand what's at stake."

A groan drew Megan's attention to a body several feet behind Curtis and to his right.

"You're lucky her skills give her some bargaining power," said Curtis, bringing the point of his switchblade up under Megan's chin. "And I'm lucky she's willing to cut a deal because the alternative's a heck of a lot more work."

"I get it," Megan muttered, trying to minimize movement.

"You don't," said Curtis with an exaggerated sigh. "I'd have to shoot Ramsey, hand you over to the Club guys, and track down the rest of your family." Retracting the blade, he tucked the weapon back into his pocket. "It's so much easier this way."

"Let her go," said Cassandra.

Curtis shook his head.

"My contract says to get her to safety," he explained. "Releasing her now would get her killed. Your benefactor would be disappointed— and pay much less—if I let her death endanger the deal."

Much as Megan wished to argue, the man had sound logic.

"Who is my benefactor?" asked Cassandra.

"A man named Smith delivered the contract," said Curtis. "You'll have to ask him."

"I'll do that," Cassandra said absently. She turned to glance at Randy. "Are you my escorts?"

"For now," said Tim.

"Good. Get this thing off me," Cassandra ordered. "We need to do two things before we leave."

Tim and Randy looked to Curtis for instructions.

"What two things?" Curtis inquired.

"Save Owen and destroy the Club's contest," said Cassandra. She addressed her answer to Curtis through eye contact. "As long as that contest stays active, Megan will be a target, and if Owen dies, you'll have one less hold on me."

"Correct," Curtis agreed. He gestured to give Tim and Randy

permission to release Cassandra. "How do you plan to kill the contest?"

I believe I can help with that.

"We'll manage," said Megan, not wanting to explain Eagle Eyes to Curtis.

"As soon as I find a computer, I'll show you," Cassandra promised.

Tim and Randy began the arduous process of releasing Cassandra from the straitjacket.

Turning to her cousin, Megan pierced him with a pointed look. "Give me the key."

"I have the key, but why should I release you?" Curtis held up a small key as proof. "You'll just—"

"I'm not running from this thing," Megan declared.

And how are we destroying the contest? She silently sent the question directly to Gatton through Eagle Eyes.

Hawk left Lia with a computer chip connected to his network. Quick version: it's sharing cyberspace with the Club. I can bust a back door into their system if you stay there long enough, but it'd be easier if you can access their website editor.

Curtis studied Megan for a long moment before slowly approaching with the handcuff key.

"I've been hired to protect you, but if you give me trouble, I won't hesitate to lock you in a trunk until this is over. Do we have an understanding?"

Pushing down the impulse to take a swing at Curtis, Megan faked a smile.

"Curt, I'm not exactly in a position to turn down help, even from you. As long as you're invested in keeping me alive, we have an understanding."

He handed her the key which she promptly used.

By this time, Cassandra was also free from her restraints.

"I need to borrow your switchblade," Cassandra said.

"For what?" Suspicion filled Curtis's question.

"Owen has a computer chip in him," Cassandra explained. She touched the back of her own neck to demonstrate. "I need to remove it from his neck."

Reluctantly, Curtis handed Cassandra his switchblade.

Nodding thanks, she moved toward the fallen form Megan had forgotten about, pausing to scoop up a taser.

"What do you need that for?" Curtis wondered, voicing the

question blazing in Megan's head as well. His hand crept closer to his gun.

"The chip's defenses need to be lowered before I can remove it." Cassandra aimed at Owen's left leg and fired the taser.

Megan winced as Owen's body jerked with the stream of electricity.

The man moaned.

"Megan, can you help me hold him down?" The tension and grief in Cassandra's voice touched Megan. "This is going to be difficult."

"Absolutely," Megan declared, handing the handcuff key over to her cousin. "Come on, you're helping too."

Tim, Randy, and Curtis moved closer to watch but didn't offer to help. In a strange way, Megan felt privileged that Cassandra had asked for her help.

As Cassandra reached for Owen's neck, he caught her hand and spoke in fits and spurts.

"Cassie. Sorry." The man's chest heaved as he struggled for each breath. Sweat beaded on his forehead and strange red streaks marked his neck. "Might … die. Poison."

"Shhh. Save your strength," said Cassandra. "I'm going to get that out of you."

"Love you," said Owen.

Shifting her grip, Cassandra clasped his hand.

"I'm going to wait until you're less delirious to take your word on that. Now go to sleep."

A faint smile and Cassandra's tender tone told Megan her friend returned the sentiment.

Chapter 13:
Little Bird's Ascension

Following Gatton's instructions through Eagle Eyes, Cassandra Mirren successfully dug the computer spike out of Owen's neck. She sent Randy to fetch a medical kit, a few bottles of water, and some paper towels to deal with the aftermath of amateur surgery. Under normal circumstances, she would call 911 anonymously and let them handle things, but her friend didn't have that kind of time.

Tim and Curtis hovered silently. Megan and her cousin knelt beside Owen, quietly awaiting further instructions. Cassandra considered her plan one last time. She had nine issues to deal with: Curtis D'Angelo, the Club, Lia, Owen, the agent, the agent's family, Gatton, his family, and her personal freedom. The plan solved most of her problems in one fell swoop, but everything hinged on Gatton's ability to code quickly and accurately. She'd never liked leaving her fate in another person's hands.

Is this the only way? Cassandra carefully kept that question far away from the Eagle Eyes box that would allow Gatton to read it. No matter which angle she considered the problems, she kept drawing the same conclusion.

Should we tell the agent? Gatton inquired, breaking into Cassandra's thoughts.

Randy dropped the supplies next to her.

After murmuring thanks, Cassandra cleaned her hands and patched Owen's open wound before silently replying to Gatton's question.

Not until we know this will work. Do you have the program ready?

She's ready. The mods you asked for were pretty easy to do,

but are you sure this is what you want?

I'm sure.

Initiating now. Getting the contact number was much harder, but I think he'll respond as predicted. Stall for a few more minutes.

Cassandra cleaned the switchblade, sanitized her hands again, dried them, and reassembled the First Aid Kit before returning the weapon to Curtis.

"We should hurry," said Curtis, pocketing the blade. "The Club guys probably have every exit blocked off. If I'm going to have to fight them, I'd rather get it over with."

"Give Megan your cell phone." Cassandra directed the instruction to Curtis.

Megan and Curtis eyed each other warily before turning their skeptical looks on her.

"The FBI and police can keep the Club busy while we finish the work," Cassandra explained.

Curtis frowned deeply but reluctantly followed the suggestion.

The agent accepted the phone and stepped off to the side to kick the backup into gear.

"Do you know if they have a computer room in the building?" asked Cassandra.

She received three negative headshakes from Tim, Randy, and Curtis.

I can lead you to a computer but getting there's going to be tricky. There are about two dozen thugs waiting for you to leave that room. Might be easier to have somebody fetch a laptop.

"Could you find me a laptop?" Cassandra aimed the question at the lot of them.

"I have one," said Curtis, "but explain what you need it for first."

"Hitting the Club hard." Cassandra didn't have to work hard to conjure irritation, and she certainly wasn't going to tell him what else she needed the computer for.

He'd try to kill her if he knew, and she didn't need that on top of everything else.

After a short debate, Curtis sent Tim to fetch the laptop. Cassandra couldn't pin down Tim and Randy's true loyalties. The way they'd taken orders from Hawk hinted at government ties. They didn't come across as stereotypical spooks, but they were neutral enough to be able to pass the Club people in peace.

"There are units on the way, but ETA for enough SWAT teams is an hour," Megan reported, tossing Curtis's phone back to him. "Not sure the Club has that much patience in them."

"This shouldn't take long," Cassandra assured the agent.

"I can help." Vinny's statement drew every eye to him.

"I thought you had your own Club troubles," said Curtis.

"I do, but this might make those go away." Vinny's tone didn't quite manage to hit hopeful notes.

"Get me into the contest's website editor, and I'll take care of the rest," said Cassandra. She didn't trust the young man enough to let him help beyond that.

Almost there. The bar says 89%.

Tim arrived with the laptop. After firing it up, Curtis logged on and turned the machine over to Vinny, who navigated to the correct website and accessed the editor. Finally, Cassandra followed Gatton's instructions for connecting the laptop to her Eagle Eyes unit. She accomplished the important work within the first five minutes, but she followed yet more instructions from Gatton to ensure that the Cyber League would have perpetual money problems on the site. When she ran short of ways to stall, Cassandra closed the laptop but made no move to rise from her seat beside Owen.

"All done?" asked Curtis.

"Can we leave now?" asked Vinny at the same moment.

"We're waiting for a phone call," said Cassandra.

"No. We're leaving now." Curtis backed up the declaration by drawing his gun, but he didn't point it at anyone.

"Backup's still a few minutes away," said Megan. The agent's words drew Curtis's attention.

"The Club guys still value your life; we're going to use that fact to get out."

Curtis's gun now pointed at the agent, but she looked to Casandra for a decision.

Where's that phone call?

It's ringing. The program's still applying the finishing touches to the encryption algorithm. They may not realize there's a problem yet.

"I think you'll want to wait for this phone call," Cassandra said, keeping all traces of urgency out of her voice. Curtis would not like the changes to come, but hopefully, he'd abide by them.

"What did you do?" The assassin's question held considerable frustration and suspicion.

Show time.

Hawk's phone rang from the floor halfway across the room.

Cassandra started to rise to go get it but stopped when Curtis's gun swung her way.

"Get me that phone." Curtis barked the order to Tim and Randy.

The pair looked annoyed, but Randy trudged across the room to retrieve the phone. He accepted the call and handed it over to Curtis.

"I better like what you have to say," said Curtis into the phone.

Cassandra watched Curt's expression carefully as he listened. The impatience quickly flipped to surprise before settling on wariness. He hit the speaker button, adjusted the volume, and placed the phone on the floor. He'd ceased pointing his gun at the agent, but he still had it in hand.

A swift mental calculation told Cassandra she could safely disarm him, but that would still leave Randy and Tim. She was better off seeing what good could come of this phone call.

"As I hold your contract, do have a care with your words, Mr. D'Angelo," said Smith. His British accent made the statement more formal than it would be otherwise.

The familiar sound washed over Cassandra, giving her mixed feelings. She'd always suspected her mentor stayed in the game long after his official retirement, but she didn't like the notion of being at odds with him. First, because he was a very dangerous enemy to have, and second, because she genuinely respected the man.

The mild rebuke made Curtis stiffen.

"Are you there, Little Bird?" asked Smith.

"Yes, sir." The automatic response made Cassandra feel like a child, but she pushed the feeling away.

"Good. Explain what I'm seeing," said Smith.

Cassandra stood and considered her words carefully. The vague order was designed to lead the other person into revealing more than they wished. Smith had taught her the trick very early during her training. She'd employed the tactic many times. Being on the receiving end of it was not a position she relished. On the other hand, the many curious gazes directed her way said she had to explain anyway.

"If you're looking at anything connected to Hawk's private network, you're probably seeing many lines of random symbols," said Cassandra. "I am prepared to deliver the encryption key once we come to an understanding."

"Are you and Mr. Gatton aware that this is cyberterrorism and punishable by lengthy prison terms?" asked Smith. "Your actions could get hundreds of American and British agents killed."

"Are *you* aware of the events from the past few days?" Cassandra held her anger in check, but some of it bled into her tone anyway. "If so, you don't get to pull the morality card."

"I am not judging your actions," Smith clarified. "Though they are bolder than your usual strategies." He paused for a two-count. "Regardless, Falcon has authorized me to negotiate. What would you like?" His casual question offset the seriousness of the moment.

Recognizing the new tactic didn't help Cassandra adjust, but she forged onward anyway.

"You know every demand I'll make," she said.

"Humor me," said Smith. "My superior will want a thorough report."

Do I really want this? Cassandra couldn't stop her brain from dredging up that question one more time.

"One, the chips for Hawk's program come from Gatton Technologies, so we know there's no poison built into them." Cassandra's anger skyrocketed when she looked down at Owen's still form. Even with the chip gone, enough poison remained in his system to keep him very near death's door. "Two, Gatton and I receive regular reports from the program. Three—"

"You want to oversee the program?" Surprise carried through the question.

"I want the agents to be safe." Cassandra let that statement stand for a solid second before continuing her list. "Demand number three: Owen receives the antidote for whatever Hawk gave him. Four, Lia and Owen get the choice to stay or go. Five, after this mission, D'Angelo stays far away from me."

"Is that all?" Genuine mirth lightened Smith's tone.

Curtis too looked amused by point five.

"I'm getting to the main points." Cassandra glared at the phone as if it could carry her displeasure through the speaker. "Six, Gatton, his family, the agent, and her family are off limits permanently. The Shadow Council, the Club, the Cyber League, if any of these are connected to you, you put a tight leash on them, and you keep them there. Seven, I reserve the right to refuse any job for any reason. None of these points are negotiable."

"You don't have to bargain for me," commented the agent.

Confusion clouded her expression.

I do. Especially since I may not be available to protect you.

Cassandra tried to convey the rebuttal to the agent with a look but needed to concentrate on the delicate negotiations underway.

"What do we get in return?" Smith wondered. "And if you planned on running the program, why cripple it?"

"Besides the ethical shifts, I plan to keep Hawk's legacy running smoothly," Cassandra answered. "I assume this was the desired result."

"Are you sure you're not overestimating your worth, Little Bird?" asked Smith.

"Ask Falcon, and tell me what he says," Cassandra replied evenly.

To her surprise, Smith laughed. The joyful sound held real warmth and affection.

"I don't have to ask him. I know precisely what he'll say, and you are correct," said Smith. "Welcome aboard. I'll work out the details with the young fellow and give you a ring in a few days."

"Before you hang up, I'm going to need you to confirm the appointment," said Cassandra. "This won't take long."

Chapter 14:
Balance of Power

Don't react. Just listen. It may not seem like it, but we have a plan. Let the assassin work.

Show me what you're doing.

That's not—

If you want me to stand by and watch, give me something to watch.

Gatton finally relented and activated some of Megan Luchek's Eagle Eyes displays. One showed a blue bar slowly filling. The label above it read: *Improved Chances of Living*. Another showed her a small map of the building complete with red dots for hostiles. A third display presented a tiny map with little blue, gray, and red car icons representing police vehicles. The fourth window held several timers next to brief descriptions. The timer indicating *First Cop ETA* hit zero, changed to say *Second Cop ETA*, and reset to two minutes and thirty-four seconds. The timer that disturbed Megan the most read: *Steel's Patience*. She had no clue how Gatton's program was measuring the Club leader's patience, but the gathering number of red dots outside the various entrances to this room did not bode well.

Wrapped up in absorbing the information overload, Megan missed much of Cassandra's conversation with the mysterious caller. When the assassin set her safety as one of the conditions, Megan tried to tell her it was unnecessary. The protest earned a distracted smile, but Cassandra didn't break stride in her negotiations. Megan tuned in fully as the assassin told the caller she wanted him to stay on the line.

Stick close to Cassandra.

Before Megan could question Gatton's advice, the display

window holding the timers flashed several times. The *Steel's Patience* counter went from thirty-five seconds to zero instantly. All six doors banged open and belched out several well-armed Club thugs. Once again, their primary weapons consisted of expandable batons, stun guns, and tasers.

They're persistent. I'll give them that.

Tim, Randy, and Curtis each drew guns and tracked a different group of men.

Megan flinched and looked about frantically for a weapon. Finding nothing close enough, she clenched her fists, beat back the impulse to run, and edged closer to Cassandra, who stood near Owen.

Cousin Vinny hadn't moved from Owen Ramsey's side. Megan motioned for him to keep his head down, and he dutifully hunched lower.

"Far enough," Curtis barked, centering his weapon on Steel's chest.

"I'm done playing games, kid," Steel declared. His face turned deep red and his breaths sounded ragged. He too had a gun, which he pointed at Curtis's face. "Hand her over."

"The game has changed," said Cassandra. "There's no longer a bounty on capturing Agent Luchek. Police officers are arriving as we speak. Your window for leaving is closing quickly."

"Nice try," Steel complimented, "but a bad lie isn't going to save any of you. My men—"

"Are each going to lose their life's savings if they help you," Cassandra interrupted smoothly. She let a heavy gaze rest on the group of Club men in front of her.

Can you do that?

Watch the magic. Gatton sounded smug.

Slowly, one thug took out his phone and accessed his bank account. Megan's Eagle Eyes unit focused on the phone, copied the password data remotely, and shot the information through cyberspace to Gatton.

"They're bluffing," said the man.

Wait for it. There.

The man stiffened and cried out like he'd been shot. Three companions crowded around him and looked at his phone.

Eagle Eyes kindly provided Megan with a view of the screen. One by one, the balances in each account dropped to zero.

How are you doing that?

I'm not doing anything. It's a masking program that should last about a half-hour but keep that to yourself.

"Any man who leaves right now will have his accounts restored," Cassandra offered.

The first man to check bolted from the room. The two men nearest him followed close behind.

Several more men checked their phones, fell for the masking program, and retreated.

Eight less. Not bad.

The remaining men inched closer.

Someone grabbed Megan's right arm.

She spun to wrench her arm free and found three men standing entirely too close. The one who'd touched her arm held a baton. The others held tasers. Nobody could miss at that range.

Stepping toward the man holding a baton would protect her from the tasers, but that would still leave her in a precarious position.

Megan slowly held her hands in front of her body to ward off the baton. It didn't improve anything, but it made her feel slightly safer.

"Get them to back off, Steel," Curtis ordered.

Do we have any more moves, Gatton?

Just one. But you need to get them to listen to Cassandra.

How am I supposed to do that?

Several men shouting conflicting orders complicated matters.

I don't know. Do something unexpected.

Turning and adjusting her position so Steel had an unobstructed view, Megan knelt and clasped her hands behind her head.

Most of the Club guys stopped shouting.

"Finally, one of you shows sense," Steel muttered.

"Your move, Cassandra," said Megan.

It'd better be a stellar one.

"Hawk's dead," Cassandra began, stepping up beside Megan. "And I have a message for those who worked for him." She held the dead man's phone up for the thugs to see.

When her arms started burning, Megan slowly lowered them, but she stayed kneeling to keep from drawing attention away from Cassandra.

A scan of the men in front of her revealed little, but most listened raptly.

"Falcon has chosen me to succeed Hawk," Cassandra announced. "You work for me."

"Where's your proof?" asked one of the men.

"Appointment confirmed," said the mysterious British caller. "Authorization code: T51 Z34 H02. This is the new program director. It's in your best interests to obey her."

Megan caught the spark of recognition in at least two pairs of eyes.

"What does that mean?" demanded Steel.

"It means the balance of power has shifted," said Cassandra, ending the phone call and tucking the phone into a pocket. "You and your men have one last chance to leave before I have my people kill you. I suggest you run."

"I have over two dozen men!" said Steel.

"At least four of them aren't yours," Curtis corrected the Club leader. "I second the lady's advice. Get out while you can."

The standoff lasted another thirty seconds before two more Club guys broke ranks to flee. That started a stampede as the common criminals decided their lives mattered more than their Club paychecks.

A strangled cry from Steel warned Megan the man was about to do something stupid.

His gun slid her way.

Megan had no time to move, but Cassandra was already moving.

Stepping forward, the assassin pickpocketed the switchblade from Curtis D'Angelo, brought out the blade, whirled, and sent the weapon straight at the Club leader. It struck Steel high on the left shoulder and lodged there.

Screaming, he dropped the gun.

Tim and Randy leapt into action, grabbing Steel's shoulders and forcing him to his knees.

The move broke the will of the remaining Club men.

Soon, only three men stood their ground.

"What should we do with him, ma'am?" asked Tim, maintaining his grip on Steel.

"Leave him for the police," said Cassandra. She held out a hand to help Megan stand. "They came a long way. We should give them something."

Accepting the help, Megan wearily rose.

"Can't. We're supposed to stay with you," said Randy, looking uncomfortable.

"I'll take care of it," said Curtis. He retrieved his blade from Steel's shoulder, wiped it off on the man's shirt, and tucked it away. "I have another delivery to make anyway." He nodded in Megan's direction. "Anybody have handcuffs?"

Spotting the handcuffs she'd worn into the room ages ago, Megan retrieved them and brought them to Curtis.

"You deserve to do the honors," said Curtis.

Tim and Randy lifted Steel to his feet and held his arms in position until Megan could slap the cuffs into place. The delicate clicks did wonders for Megan's soul.

Steel gave her a vicious look as she returned to her original position beside Cassandra.

"We should go, Director," said Tim.

Ignoring him, the assassin offered Megan a sad smile.

"Didn't peg those two for spies," Megan commented, trying to fill the sudden silence.

"Then they did their jobs well," said Cassandra. She held out a hand. "I'll see you around, agent."

Brushing the hand aside, Megan drew the taller woman into a hug.

"I'm Italian. We're huggers," Megan explained, maintaining her grip for a few seconds. "Be careful, assassin."

Hate to rush you, ladies, but the police are on their way up.

"Technically, it's spymaster now," Cassandra said when Megan finally pulled back. "When things settle, I'll give you a call. Go save your family."

They're fine. Agent Cooper and Agent Kerman rescued them a few hours ago. You're the one headed to jail if you don't move it!

Gatton's voice boomed in Megan's head even though she knew he was addressing Cassandra.

"You should mute him," Megan suggested.

"Wish I could, but he's right," said Cassandra, surveying the scene.

The men stared at her expectantly.

"You three take Owen," Cassandra instructed. "Get to the nearest safehouse. I'll bring the antidote by once I retrieve it. Curtis—"

"Still on Luchek guard duty," he said. "I got it."

In less than a minute, Megan, Vinny, Curtis, and Steel were the only ones left in the large room.

Epilogue:
Normal Human Stuff

Brushing condensation from her iced chai tea latte, Megan Luchek observed the flow of people popping in and out of various stores in the Ala Moana Center. She frowned at the mint tea sitting primly in front of an empty seat.

Did I get the time or place wrong?

She doubted it. Cassandra's message had been as plain and pointed as ever. 10:00 A.M. Ala Moana Starbucks.

Having nothing better to do while she waited, Megan considered the past week. Against nearly everybody's advice, she had joined the building sweep when the Philadelphia police and FBI teams arrived. They'd made several interesting discoveries, including Gary Sheffield's body and a thoroughly drugged Lillian Marquez.

I wonder how she's doing.

Despite their turbulent relationship, Megan couldn't bring herself to hate the Club woman, especially after learning that Steel had Lillian's father murdered in his nursing home bed. Gatton had alerted them to the possibility and some phone calls had confirmed everything. Thanks to a few additional tips from the nosy billionaire, the thugs responsible were caught within a few days, but the justice seemed hollow compared to the personal loss experienced by Lillian.

Pushing the depressing thoughts aside, Megan recalled the chaotic reunion with her mother, sister, and aunt at the police station. Her mother hadn't let the detectives get a word in edgewise until she'd confirmed several times over that Megan was in good health and injury-free. Even so, it had taken the combined efforts of Tara, Dan Cooper, and Aunt Silvia to distract Susanne Luchek long enough for the detectives to slip Megan into one of the interrogation suites. Things had gotten even more interesting when Thorne and Bentley strolled in like they owned the place. Originally, it had been their word against Megan's, but the dashcam had confirmed enough details to support Megan's version of events.

After answering about a million questions and filling in several written statements for the police, Megan got to spend the rest of the day repeating the paperwork nightmare for the FBI's Philadelphia Field Office. The one bright spot in that mess had been meeting Special Agent Samuel Kerman, the man who had spearheaded the rescue effort that saved her mother and aunt. Finally, Dan Cooper drove everybody back to Tara's apartment, where Megan faced a third inquisition courtesy of her family. Thankfully, Vinny had borne some of the brunt of that. Afterwards, as Megan prepared to battle the Lincoln Airport's customer service people, her father had surprised her by presenting her freshly returned purse and gun.

Happy endings ... I think.

As Megan boarded the plane for the long flight back to Hawaii, her mother had dropped a bombshell. The memory of the announcement stirred up mixed feelings.

Tara knew.

Her older sister rarely let her be blindsided by their mother, but this time, she must have been sworn to secrecy. Given the horrors they'd shared, Megan couldn't stay mad at her sister. She wanted to at least smack her, but even that was unfair with Tara being pregnant.

This is Cassandra's fault too. It's a conspiracy.

The scrape of a chair yanked Megan out of her thoughts.

"Want to help me bury some bodies?" she asked as her guest sat down.

"Depends on the bodies," said Cassandra. "If it's my new tenants, I'll have to decline. We just settled both sets of contracts."

"You set me up," Megan complained.

"I saved you a lot of money on airfare," Cassandra countered, picking up the hot tea.

Megan considered the statement and reluctantly admitted it held some truth.

"Your mother needs to see you to heal properly," Cassandra added quietly. "Your father too, though you might have gotten away with regular phone contact with him."

"I suppose I ought to thank you for putting Tara and Jason in the Honolulu apartment and letting the folks rent the Waipahu one instead," Megan said. "But did you have to make things that easy for them?"

After cautiously sipping the tea, Cassandra responded with a question.

"Tell me, agent, where would your mother go if she had trouble securing an apartment in Oahu?"

The answer struck Megan instantly.

"My apartment." Heaving a sigh, she said, "Fine. You read the situation better than I did. Let's move on to more interesting topics. How's Owen?"

"Fully recovered," Cassandra reported. "Each of Hawk's men had a dose of the antidote on them, so getting some into him was simple. He'll be around. We're laying some groundwork for future operations."

"Don't you want to be on the mainland?" asked Megan.

"We're setting up there too," said Cassandra. "Truth is, we need a lot of new safe places to test the chip enhancements and train the agents."

"You sound like you've been doing this forever," Megan noted.

Cassandra shrugged.

"It's been a long time coming."

"So, who's Falcon?" asked Megan, lacking a more graceful way to transition to the personal question.

"My father," Cassandra answered. "If you couldn't guess, I didn't have a traditional upbringing."

Several questions formed a traffic jam in Megan's head.

"What's he like?" she inquired, selecting one of the less awkward questions.

"I've never met him," said Cassandra. "I know him by reputation only, though I'm sure a meeting's in the works."

"You're not worried about it?" Megan tried to rein in the shock but didn't quite manage the feat.

"All families are complicated," Cassandra pointed out. "I consciously stopped resenting my father years ago. Choosing the Fixer path as a teenager was my act of rebellion. It carried me away from him for more than a decade."

"Why did he want you to join him?" Megan wondered. "When did you know he was behind Hawk's actions? Was it connected to the Cyber League's contests?"

"I've always known my father was a spy," Cassandra said. "I didn't figure out Hawk's connection to him until we were waiting for the Club guys to bring you in. Hawk wanted me to join him to impress Falcon."

"And the Cyber League?" Megan prompted, hoping to gain the last few missing pieces in her mental puzzle of the whole affair.

"I believe they dreamed up the contests on their own," said Cassandra. "Hawk. Falcon. They merely exploited the situation to get what they wanted."

"You," Megan finished.

"Lucky me," Cassandra said, raising her tea in a toast before drinking some of the hot liquid. "Are they letting you return to work soon?"

"Maybe next Monday if I can get a shrink to sign off on it," said Megan. "Administrative leave is going to be the death of me."

"Enjoy the rest," said Cassandra. Getting up, the spymaster reached into her back pocket and pulled out a sealed envelope. "I couldn't get the report you asked for on the drug dealer's murder, but I got a letter from the case agent stating his killer died soon after him. You should deliver it to Gavriel's family today. Give them some peace."

"Maybe I will," Megan murmured, accepting the letter. "I've got nothing better to do."

"Relax, Megan. The bad guys will be there when you're ready to chase them again."

The use of her name forced Megan to look at her friend, but before she could respond, the spymaster melted into the crowd.

Take care, Cassandra. I'm going to make it my mission to force you to do normal human stuff more often.

THE END

Thank You for Reading:

I hope you've enjoyed Megan's latest adventures. She's already had some cool cases in Hawaii, Pennsylvania, Las Vegas, Reno, and Dallas. If you need to catch up and fill in some gaps, check out the Shadow Council series and the Eagle Eyes trilogy.

If you'd like to try a different flavor of mystery or another genre, check out my website (juliecgilbert.com). Many stories can be experienced in ebook, paperback, or audiobook. I highly recommend the audiobooks, as I've worked very hard to hire talented people to bring these stories to life.

Hop on the newsletter (https://www.subscribepage.com/n7e8l8) if you want to keep up with life and new release news. Plus, subscribers get the first crack at exclusive giveaways.

Please consider leaving a review at your favorite retailer. Your opinion matters, and it will help other readers find this series.

Sincerely,

Julie C. Gilbert